Boom

SABRINA STARK

CHAPTER 1

Arden

I was lathered in the shower when I heard it – a loud thud from somewhere outside the bathroom. With a gasp, I whirled toward the sound.

My hair was foaming with shampoo, and the shower was still running. From behind the shower's frosted glass, I stared at the hazy image of the locked bathroom door.

When nothing happened, I tried to laugh. Obviously, I was only hearing things, which made total sense considering that the events of today would've driven *anyone* insane.

See, I wasn't in any danger. *I was merely losing my mind.*

It was such a cheery thought – not that I had time to enjoy it. Way too soon, I heard the sound again. A split second later, the bathroom door flew open and banged into the nearby wall, where for some stupid reason it stuck like a magnet to metal.

Well, that was weird.

But that was hardly the worst of it.

In the now-open doorway stood the shadowed silhouette of a man. He was tall with broad shoulders and narrow hips. He wore faded jeans and a plain white T-shirt.

The jeans were tattered, and the shirt was soaking wet – so wet that it clung to him like a second skin, accenting muscles so fine, I might've marveled at their perfection, if only I didn't feel like screaming.

But I *didn't* scream. *And why?*

It was because this wasn't my bathroom. *Not officially.* And there was the *tiniest* chance that I might be trespassing.

Still, my heart hammered as I crossed my arms over my naked breasts and blurted out, "Who are *you?*"

Sounding a lot calmer than I might've expected, he replied, "I might ask the same."

And yet, he didn't ask – not directly, anyway. Instead, he strode to the bathroom sink and stopped when he reached it. Turning once again to face me, he leaned his ass against the ancient countertop and crossed his muscular arms, all casual-like, as if he *hadn't* just busted through the bathroom door.

I should've been terrified. And part of me was. But I'd been on edge for so many hours now that I'd grown nearly numb to its effects. "The house…" I stammered. "I thought it was empty."

In a voice tinged with amusement, he replied, "Obviously."

I stiffened. *Well, at least someone was jolly.*

I sure as heck wasn't.

And yet, I had *one* thing to be thankful for. My thin, white towel was draped at hip level over the dented towel bar that spanned the narrow shower door. This meant that my pelvis was hidden from his prying eyes – assuming they *were* prying.

I couldn't be certain either way. Between the steam and the frosted glass, I was having a hard time making out the guy's face.

Sure, I saw a mess of thick dark hair, a strong jaw, and all the standard features where they belonged. But as far as the specifics, it was impossible to say.

On the upside, this meant that he couldn't see *me* clearly either.

Still, he could surely tell that I was naked – not that he needed eyes for *that.* It was, after all, customary to remove one's clothes before stepping into the shower.

Clothes?

My stomach sank. *Oh, no.*

My fresh clothes. I'd laid them out near the sink with my undergarments on top – black panties and a lacy black bra. And my *other* clothes – the ones I'd just taken off – were lying scattered across the faded wooden floor.

I scanned the familiar worn surface, and felt myself frown. Unless I was mistaken, that bit of pink fabric near the guy's left boot was the bra I'd removed just ten minutes ago.

Well, this was just terrific.

If I wasn't already so traumatized by the rest of it, I might've had the luxury of embarrassment over the fact that my unmentionables were on clear display – and in imminent danger of being stomped.

But now? Well, let's just say, trampled undies were the least of my worries.

The truth was, I had no idea what to do.

It was the middle of the night, and by now, I was pretty sure I didn't belong here. If *he* belonged here, I might be arrested. *And if he didn't belong here?* Well, that was infinitely worse, wasn't it?

Just then, shampoo slid into my eyes, making them sting like a mother-you-know-what. With a stifled curse, I plunged my head back under the steaming water and tried to rinse the suds first from my face and then from my long, dark hair – all without using my hands, because the way I saw it, keeping my goodies covered was infinitely more important.

Stinging or not, I kept my eyes partially open, keeping a watch on my new bathroom buddy.

He *wasn't* leaving.

But he wasn't moving toward me either. *That was good, right?*

Still, as I squinted at his silhouette, I couldn't help but wonder just how much trouble I was in.

A lot?

Probably.

The whole thing was beyond maddening, and not only because I was naked with a stranger. Once upon a time, this property –

bathroom included – had belonged to *my* family – and to me too, in a roundabout way.

Not anymore.

Or at least, not according to the "sold" sign I'd spotted earlier in the front yard.

If that sign meant what I thought it meant, I was definitely trespassing. But in my own defense, that hadn't been part of the plan.

I wasn't the trespassing type. When it came to laws and what-not, I was a real stickler. Cripes, I didn't even jaywalk or drive above the speed limit.

And why? It was because every time I did, it came back to bite me on the butt. Like *when*, you ask? Well, like now, actually.

As far as the house itself, it was old, massive, and depressingly vacant – a Victorian beauty that had seen better days.

Early this morning, I'd arrived as planned, only to find the house mostly empty, much like my bank account, thanks to Jason, my no-good, deadbeat cousin.

But forget Jason.

In the bathroom, the stranger still hadn't budged.

By now, I was officially clean and rinsed. And yet, for some inexplicable reason, I dreaded the thought of turning off the water, just like I dreaded the thought of facing him, whoever he was.

His voice, cool and conversational, carried over the sounds of the running water. "So, do you come here often?"

It was either a joke or the lamest pickup line ever. Either way, I wasn't in the mood. "I don't know," I muttered. "Do you?"

"I will *now*," he said.

I gave a soggy blink. "What?"

"I didn't realize it would be so interesting."

Interesting? Well, that was one way to put it.

When I made no reply, the guy spoke again. "Three minutes."

"What?"

"It's a thirty-gallon tank. And old as dirt."

Obviously, he meant the hot water tank. But he was wrong on both counts. The tank was *fifty* gallons, not thirty. And it was nearly brand new, installed just last month according to my cousin.

I frowned. *Yes. That* cousin.

The deadbeat who'd stood me up.

My frown deepened. *Cripes, maybe he'd been lying about the hot water tank, too.*

The stranger continued, "So do the math."

I didn't get it. "What math?"

"I'm just saying, you've got three minutes, maybe less, 'til the water runs cold."

I liked math, with one exception – story problems. I hated them. I always had. Or maybe I just hated the stranger, whether he deserved it or not.

Not only had he scared the crap out of me, he sounded way too cocky in his calculations, which was especially annoying considering that he didn't look like any math wizard *I'd* ever seen. Math and muscles – they *weren't* known for going hand-in-hand.

I repeated, "So?"

"So, you can stall if you want," he said. "But if you stall too long, you're gonna freeze your ass off."

As if he cared. Stubbornly, I said it again. "So?"

"So you *want* a cold shower?"

"No. Do you?" As soon as the words left my lips, I wanted to take them back.

I was naked.

He wasn't.

And I'd be smart to keep him that way. Quickly, I added, "And just so you know, that *wasn't* an invitation."

He gave something like a laugh. "Good thing."

I shook my head. "What?"

"That shower – it's narrow as hell."

He didn't need to tell *me*. I was the one inside it, after all. "So?" I said for the umpteenth time.

"So I'd need a crowbar to squeeze myself in."

I gave his imposing silhouette a good, long look. *He was right.* He would need a crowbar – unless his stupidly hot body was slippery with soap, in which case…. *Oh, for God's sake. What on Earth was wrong with me, anyway?*

And now the idiot was laughing – not loud, but loud enough for me to hear it, even over the sounds of the running water. His laughter was warm and almost contagious, which made everything ten times worse, because the sound of it was lulling me into a false sense of security.

I wasn't secure.

Far from it.

And the fact that I'd almost let down my guard showed a shocking lack of common sense. *Seriously Arden, get a grip, will ya?*

I told him, "And stop laughing. This *isn't* funny."

Sounding more amused than ever, he said, "Two minutes."

My teeth were grinding now. "Will you *please* stop that?"

He practically snorted. "Why?"

"Because it's making me nervous." At this, I almost winced. *What an asinine thing to say.* My nerves should've shattered the moment he'd busted through the door. And maybe they would've, if only I hadn't become numb to nasty surprises.

Today had been way too full of them.

"Good," the guy said.

So he was happy that I was nervous? What kind of sicko was he, anyway? With a sound of annoyance, I said, "And why is that good?"

"Because," he said, "you're in *my* house. And you're gonna tell me why."

CHAPTER 2

Arden

His words hit like a hammer. *His* house?

My stomach twisted with new despair. So the house *had* been sold out from under me? *To him?*

In spite of the evidence, I didn't want to believe it. Over the sounds of the shower, I called out, "Says you."

"Yeah," he scoffed. "Me and the deed."

Crap.

I didn't know the guy, but he didn't sound like he was lying. Plus, his bold claim meshed all too well with everything else I'd seen ever since rolling into town – on a Greyhound bus, no less.

When I considered everything I'd gone through to get here, my fingers tightened into fists. *Jason – that lying rat-fink bastard.*

I was gonna kill him. Already I could think of several ways to do it, *slowly.*

The guy said, "What, you wanna see it?"

The deed?

Hell no.

What I *wanted* was to light the stupid thing on fire and watch it burn. But that sort of thing was hardly productive – as I'd learned the hard way back in high school.

"No," I snapped. "What I want is for you to get out."

He shifted his stance, making his muscles pop enticingly under the wet fabric of his shirt. "Did you miss the part where you're in *my* house?"

"I don't care," I told him. "You need to step outside, like *now.*"

With a laugh, he said, "Forget it."

"What?" I sputtered.

"It's raining buckets out there."

Well, that explained the wet shirt. Through gritted teeth, I clarified, "I *meant* out of the bathroom."

No response.

No movement either.

With blatant sarcasm, I asked, "Unless it's raining in the hallway?"

"Hey, you never know."

It was then that I realized something. "Wait a minute. You knew exactly what I meant, didn't you?"

"Maybe."

"So…you're just giving me a hard time?"

"Trust me," he said, his tone growing a shade darker. "You could be dealing with a lot worse than me."

He was right. I could. In fact, it was a small miracle that all he'd done was give me a hard time. If this truly was his house, he'd have plenty of ways to make me miserable beyond simple teasing.

But if he thought I was going to show him anything he hadn't seen already, he had another thing coming. "I don't care," I insisted. "Just give me some privacy, alright?"

He still didn't budge.

I sighed. "Please?"

"First, tell me your name."

"Why?" I felt myself swallow. "So you can call the police?"

"Your name," he repeated. "First *and* last."

Arden Weathers. That was my name. Still, I refused to say it because the last thing I needed now was more trouble. I tried to think. *What if I gave him a fake name? Would that do the trick?*

Probably not. But hey, it was worth a shot, right?

"Fine," I said. "It's Clara Cooper."

His posture stiffened. "What?"

I felt my eyebrows furrow. Obviously, something had changed, and not for the better. *Did he know that I was lying?*

Maybe. I bit my lip. *But maybe not.*

Pushing my luck, I said the name again, this time with more bravado. "Clara Cooper."

His only reply was a single world, spoken almost too low to make out. "Fuck."

Now it was *my* turn to stiffen. It wasn't just the profanity. It was something in his voice, something new and ominous.

Either he knew that I was lying, or some girl named Clara Cooper had really done a number on him. Either way, this *wasn't* good.

I held my breath and waited.

Finally, the guy turned – but not toward the open doorway. Instead, he reached toward the sink behind him. While I watched in new confusion, he gave the faucet a hard twist.

As water gushed into the sink, I asked, "Why'd you do *that?*"

A moment later, I had my answer in the form of icy water shooting from the shower head and pelting my naked skin. With a little yelp, I hollered out, "Hey! What the hell?"

When the guy spoke again, his voice was so cold, it made the water feel warm in comparison. "See you in the hall, '*Clara.*'"

All modesty forgotten, I jerked back and fumbled for the shower handle. Desperately, I twisted until the icy water stopped running.

I looked outward just in time to see the stranger leaving through the open bathroom doorway. He didn't even bother to shut the door behind him.

Well, that was nice.

Shivering now, I stared after him, wondering what on Earth had just happened. Already, the image of his departure was burned into my brain, and *not* because he had the tightest ass I'd ever seen.

It was the other thing I'd noticed– the blurry handle of what could only be a gun, poking out from the rear waistband of his jeans.

When I shivered again, this time it *wasn't* because of the cold.

Still, I tried to look on the bright side. At least he hadn't shot me. *Not yet, anyway.*

CHAPTER 3

Brody

Clara Cooper, my ass.

I'd just realized who she was, and her name *wasn't* Clara. It was Arden Weathers, my least favorite psycho.

I hadn't seen her in years – six to be exact. But if I had a shit-list from high school, her name would be right at the top.

From inside the bathroom, she was muttering, "Oh, and thanks a million for closing the door."

Was she talking to me?

Not likely. Yeah, I *was* the only one here, and yeah, it was me who'd left the door open. But judging from her tone, she was talking to herself, as if I couldn't hear what she was saying.

It was vintage Arden. She'd done that in high school too, back when I'd had the sorry luck to be partnered with her in chemistry.

We weren't friends. And that wasn't going to change any time soon.

I was standing just a few feet away from the bathroom doorway, leaning sideways against the wall. From here, I couldn't see into the bathroom, but I'd be sure to catch her if she tried to run off without explaining what she was doing here.

I called back, "Hey, you're welcome."

Silence.

I scoffed, "What, you thought I couldn't hear you?"

More silence.

That was fine by me. I was busy, anyway. On my way out of the bathroom, I'd snagged her cell phone off the counter near the sink.

And why?

It was because I wasn't a dumb-ass, that's why.

The last thing I needed now was for her to start making phone calls, serving up stories to the police – or hell, even to the media – about how I'd accosted her in the shower.

My shower.

My house.

My rules.

It was my hot water, too, and I wasn't sorry for cheating Arden out of the last of it.

Inside the bathroom, the sink's faucet was still running. I couldn't see it, but I could hear it loud and clear, even out here in the hall.

Just to be a dick, I called out, "Oh hey, turn off the sink, will ya?"

I heard a sigh, but nothing else. Probably, she was still hiding out in the shower, as if she *wouldn't* need to come out eventually.

But hey, I had all night. And the delay wasn't all bad. It gave me more time with her phone. With one hand, I started scrolling through her texts. I started at the top, where she'd left dozens of messages for someone named Jason.

Her boyfriend?

Maybe.

If so, they were definitely on the outs. Her texts fell into one of three basic categories.

Where are you?

Why aren't you calling me back?

Will you please text me or something?

Some of the messages, the later ones in particular, included a good bit of profanity. All of them reeked of desperation.

The cursing surprised me. In high school, Arden hadn't been the type. Instead, she'd been all prim and proper – well, except for that one time, when she'd cursed up a storm.

And me? I'd been on the receiving end.

As far as her desperation, that surprised me too. I didn't like Arden. Hell, I might even hate her. But I wasn't blind to what I'd seen back in high school *and* just now in the shower.

A girl like Arden – she wouldn't need to beg.

At the memory of her silhouette, naked and slippery with suds from her hair, I felt my jeans tighten only a fraction before I remembered who she was.

Arden Fucking Weathers.

No way I'd be tapping *that*, even if she *did* beg – which, truth be told, happened to me more than you'd think.

From inside the bathroom, she called out, "Will you *please* shut the door?"

I didn't move. "Why?"

"Why else? For privacy."

"From me?" I said. "Don't worry, I'm not interested."

"I don't care," she called back. "You were the one who opened it. You should shut it."

My guess? She still hadn't budged from the shower. *Little Miss Modesty.* She'd been like that in high school, too. Her clothes were never tight. Her shirts were never too low in the front or too high on her midriff. And her skirts – on the rare occasions she wore them – were never short enough to be interesting.

She'd been a good girl all the way through – *until she wasn't.*

When I made no reply, she said, "Alright fine. But promise me you won't look."

I was still scrolling through her phone. "Don't worry. I couldn't if I wanted to."

"Why not?"

"Because I'd have to move," I told her. "And trust me, you're not worth it."

Was I being an asshole?

Hell yeah.

But this was Arden Weathers, and the way I saw it, she was just lucky I hadn't tossed her naked out into the rain.

She said nothing in reply, but soon, I heard the soft creak of the floorboards, followed by quick footsteps and the sudden slamming of the bathroom door.

I didn't look up *or* flinch. *Hell, I'd been expecting it.*

A moment later, Arden groaned, "Oh, my God. Did you see this hole?"

Now *that* was a dangerous question. If I were twelve, I might've snickered. The shit-lord in me had to ask, "Which one? Front or back?"

She was silent for a long moment before saying, "If you mean what I think you mean, I don't appreciate it."

I smiled, but made no reply.

A few seconds later, she spoke again. "And just so you know, I meant the hole in the wall."

"Yeah," I laughed. "Front or back?"

"What?"

My gaze strayed to the nearby hole in the plaster – the one I'd made just fifteen minutes ago while trying to figure out who was in my bathroom. The hole was big on my side, and very small on hers.

Probably, she hadn't even noticed it.

From the other side of the door, she muttered, "You know what? Forget it."

"Done."

She sighed. "I'm just saying, there's no need to trash the place."

Right. My place. Not hers. I replied, "Nice of you to care."

"Yeah, well maybe *you* should care, too," she said. "They don't build them like this anymore, you know."

I knew. In fact, I knew a lot more about construction than Arden Weathers – or any other person who wasn't in the trade. I was damn good at what I did, and I'd gotten filthy rich doing it too, along with my older brothers.

If Arden were a person worth telling, I might've assured her that she didn't need to worry about the house. It was in very good hands. *Mine.* And when I was done with it, there'd be no holes anywhere they didn't belong.

And there'd be no Arden Weathers. That was for damned sure.

CHAPTER 4

Arden

As I hurriedly dried myself off, I kept glancing at the perfectly round dent in the plaster. Yes, I'd called it a hole, but the jackass in the hallway might disagree, considering that the hole didn't go all the way through.

Still, it *was* ugly.

The dent was the exact size and shape of a doorknob. *No coincidence there.* The doorknob was, after all, what had made the dent in the first place – thanks to the maniac who'd busted in.

As I surveyed the damage, I felt myself frown. In addition to the hole, there were new cracks in the door itself. And don't get me started on the casing *around* the door. To my amateur eyes, it looked utterly ruined.

The whole thing was incredibly depressing. My grandparents had loved this place. Sure, maybe the upkeep had gotten harder as they'd gotten older, but unlike the maniac, *they*'d done the best they could.

And *I* would've, too, if only I'd had the chance.

But this was a problem for another time. *Now* what I needed was some quick inspiration, a way to talk myself out of whatever trouble I'd gotten myself into.

Unfortunately, I was seriously short of ideas. Even that stupid name I'd given, Clara Cooper, had come straight from a high school English project – a junior assignment where I'd had to write a short story starring a character like myself.

At the memory, a bitter laugh escaped my lips. High school – now *that* had ended with a bang, or more accurately a boom – a *flaming* boom, to be exact, even if that hadn't been my intention.

But forget high school. Now, I had to face the music with whoever was waiting in the hallway.

After I finished getting dressed, I scooped up the *other* clothes, the ones I'd taken off before getting into the shower. Hoping to hide them from prying eyes, I wadded them up into the smallest ball possible and tucked them under my arm.

And then, I reached for my cell phone, only to receive yet another nasty surprise. *My phone – it was gone.*

Frantically, I scanned the bathroom, but it was no use. I'd placed it right there on the far side of the sink. And now, it quite simply wasn't there.

Terrific. Obviously, the stranger had swiped it when I hadn't been looking.

Through the bathroom door, I called out, "Hey! Where's my phone?"

The stranger replied, "You've gotta ask?"

"So you *do* have it?"

"Hell yeah."

"Why?" I demanded.

"Why do you think?"

Because you're a jerk, that's why. Through gritted teeth, I said, "Do you seriously want me to answer that?"

He paused, as if thinking. "No."

"Why not?"

"Because I don't care," he said. "Are you dressed?"

"Maybe."

"Good," he said. "Now open the door."

For a whole host of reasons, I didn't want to. The thought of actually facing him was more than a little scary – and not only because of the gun.

When I made no reply, the guy spoke again. "You know you've got to come out eventually, right?"

"Why?" I scoffed. "So you can shoot me?"

"If I wanted to shoot you," he said, "I would've done it already."

Well, that was comforting. *Sort of.*

I called back, "And why do you have a gun in the first place?"

"Listen," he said, "gun or no gun, we both know I could come in any time I want. So cut the crap and open up already."

Damn it. He was right. The bathroom had no windows, and it's not like I could call anyone to rescue me. And even if I could, who would come?

In the end, I decided I might as well get it over with. Bracing myself, I sucked in a deep breath, reached for the knob, and yanked open the door.

And there he was – looking even better, now that we were standing face-to-face.

His dark hair was a damp, tousled mess, and his T-shirt was still wet. The thin white cotton clung to his chest and abs, showing off muscular pecs and a perfect six-pack just above his tattered jeans.

As for his face, it was pure perfection, with nice cheekbones, a rugged jaw, and dark, brooding eyes.

At the sight of him, my pulse jumped, and my spine grew twitchy. I could hardly breathe, but *not* because he was so stupidly gorgeous.

It was because – *son-of-a bitch* – I knew him.

Now, it was *my* turn to say it, even if only in my own head. *Fuck.*

CHAPTER 5

Arden

To my infinite horror, I was staring into the hard gaze of Broderick Blastoviak – aka Brody Blast, a guy I'd known back in high school.

We had a history, and it wasn't terrific.

In school, he'd been a total trouble-maker through-and-through. *Cocky. Obnoxiously brilliant. And too dangerous by half.*

Unlike me, he never, ever followed the rules – and yet, he never seemed to pay for it.

That dickweed had cost me a full-ride scholarship. *He* was the reason I'd been working two jobs to pay for college, even while taking on far too many student loans.

In a roundabout way, this *also* meant that he was the reason I hadn't been able to purchase this house on my own, back when I'd had the chance three years ago.

I freaking hated him.

And boy, did he hate me, too.

Even if I hadn't known this already, the look in his eyes would've been proof enough.

I sputtered, "What are you doing here?"

He gave me a look. "You mean in my house?"

"Oh come on!" I said. "It can't be your house. There's no furniture. And besides, why would you want to live *here*? Don't you have houses all over the place already?"

This wasn't as far-fetched as you'd think. Brilliant or not, Brody hadn't gone to college. Instead, he'd founded a tool-and-die company with his two older brothers and then proceeded to take the market by storm.

These days, Blast Tools – that was the name of their company – was famously successful, just like the company's three founders.

And I meant "famous" quite literally.

A few years ago, by some miracle, the brothers had gotten themselves a weekly cable show on the Home Network, where they used their own tools to remodel older homes or sometimes build new ones.

And just for the record, they looked *very* good doing it.

By now, they were total celebrities, not just here in Michigan, but all over the world. Of course, it didn't hurt that all three of them were obnoxiously hot.

Damn it.

I was still pondering the unfairness of it all when Brody said, "Yeah? So what if I do?"

It took me a moment to realize that he was responding to my question – the one about him having plenty of homes already.

As usual, he was missing the point.

I tried again. "I'm just saying, if you have houses all over the place, why do you need another?"

My heart clenched. *And why, oh why, do you need this one?*

His only reply was a tight shrug, which – adding to my frustration – made his wet T-shirt slide enticingly over his abs.

But forget the abs.

With growing concern, I asked, "Are you actually going to live here?" The thought was literally painful – a hard ache deep in my stomach. While I'd been growing up, this house had been filled with love and laughter.

And now, it would be filled with *him.* Oh sure, Brody liked a good laugh as much as anyone. I recalled *that* well enough from high school. And as far as love, he would never be short of offers.

But he was still my enemy. And besides, the kind of love *he'd* bring into the house was temporary at best.

He was a total horn-dog.

I almost shuddered at the thought of him screwing some bimbo in my grandparent's bed. Okay, yes, the actual bed was no longer there, but you get the point.

In reply to my question, he said, "That's *my* business, not yours."

I stiffened. "But—"

"And I've got questions of my own."

Oh.

Yeah. I guess he *might* have a question or two.

When I made no reply, he said, "So what are you doing here?" He smirked like he knew something I didn't. "Looking for Jason?"

And just like that, so many pieces slid into place. Obviously, my rat-fink of a cousin had sold the house out from under me – *and* to my arch-enemy no less. *Was it any wonder that Jason wasn't returning my messages?*

Under my breath, I said, "Un-freaking-believable."

"You're telling *me*."

Back in high school, Brody had vowed to get revenge on me, one way or another – because, well, the thing is, I'd *sort of* torched his pickup.

I hadn't meant to. Still, some might say I had every reason in the world to get all torchy – and not only because he'd cost me a scholarship.

In high school, he'd torched my eyebrows. *And* my bangs. Sure, they weren't *completely* torched, but they *were* a whole lot shorter after that stupid incident with the chemistry lab.

His fault, not mine.

The jackass.

And now here we were, six years later. He was rich and famous. I was broke and desperate.

Score one for Brody, huh?

The way it looked, he'd finally gotten his revenge, served nice and cold, too. The jerk had bought my legacy – the family homestead – right out from under me.

At the realization, I felt like screaming. Or crying. I still couldn't decide which.

The whole thing was so incredibly unfair. Brody could've bought a million homes. But me, I only wanted one.

This one.

I wanted to build a life here, and if I met a nice guy, maybe even a family. Who knows, I might've filled the house with kids of my own someday.

I shoved a hand through my wet hair and tried to think. *Maybe there was still hope. Maybe he'd only bought the house to fix it up. Maybe he planned to sell it afterward.*

At the thought, my pulse quickened. *Maybe I could buy it.*

Sure, I had no money, but I *had* graduated from college – just last week, in fact. I had a decent degree, too – in business administration.

All I needed now was a job. Unfortunately, jobs hadn't been so easy to find, especially since I'd been hoping to find one here in my hometown.

I'd been hoping for a lot of things. But all I'd found was trouble, and plenty of it.

In front of me, Brody said, "You can start explaining any time now."

"Oh yeah?" My chin lifted. "Well, maybe I don't owe you an explanation."

At this, he looked almost ready to laugh. He eyed me up and down, taking in my wet hair and disheveled appearance. "You sure about that?"

Heat flooded my face. "Alright, fine. I *guess* you have a point, assuming you're not lying about the house thing."

"Which I'm not."

To my ever-growing despair, I actually believed him. Back in high school, Brody had been a lot of things, but never a liar.

I sighed. "Alright, fine. I'll tell you. But first tell me one thing, okay?" I bit my lip. "Assuming you truly *did* buy the house, are you planning to live here? Or sell it? I mean, after you fix it up or whatever."

With cool deliberation, Brody took a long look around, as if seeing the place for the first time. As he did, I tried to see it through his eyes.

Counting the attic, the house was three stories. At the moment, Brody and I were standing on the second floor near the open staircase. The staircase was original to the house, but rickety here and there, just like everything else.

Around us, the plaster was in need of patching, and that dark spot in the ceiling could only mean a roof leak.

Still, the bones of the house were good. *Very good.* And the location – right here on the Saginaw Bay – was another huge bonus.

It was beachfront property, which was, sadly, one of the reasons I hadn't been able to buy it on my own. In spite of its less-than-pristine condition, the property's value was shockingly high, just like the taxes.

I knew, because I'd been paying them for the last three years. Or at least, I *thought* I'd been paying them. I'd been giving the money to Jason, who'd been hitting me up far too often for home-related expenses.

This latest round had cost me my car. *But hey, cars were replaceable, right?*

As for Brody, he was still looking around.

The fact that he hadn't yet answered was making me a little nervous. *Was he deciding right now?*

I held my breath and waited.

Finally, he said something that sent my heart straight into my throat. "Hard to say." He shrugged. "This place? Might not be worth saving."

CHAPTER 6

Brody

In front of me, Arden sucked in a breath. "What?"

I stared down at her. *Oh man, the look on her face was priceless.* It was probably the same look *I'd* had back in high school, when she'd torched my pickup.

I smiled. "Is there a problem?"

Her hair was long, dark, and dripping wet. In high school, thick bangs had covered her forehead. Not anymore – or at least not the way it was combed now. She was wearing black jeans, a little red T-shirt, and red sneakers – the old-fashioned kind. She wore no makeup.

Still, she looked too damned appealing whether she knew it or not. Her cheeks were flushed, and her lips were parted. If she were anyone else, I might've called her sexy. But she *wasn't* anyone else. And crazy hot girls weren't my thing.

Hot, yes.

Crazy, no.

And Arden Weathers was the worst kind of crazy, the kind that snuck up on you when you weren't expecting it – like a pack of hornets nesting in the ceiling. One minute you're pulling down drywall, and next minute, you're wondering what the hell happened.

Been there, done that.

Arden Weathers – no way she'd be stinging *me*.

In front of me, she gave a hard swallow. "You're not serious?" She blinked a few times before continuing. "I mean, you wouldn't *demolish* the house or anything, would you?"

I made another show of looking around. "Like I said, it's hard to say."

Her voice rose. "Hard to say if you're serious?"

I pointed to the ceiling, where a dark stain marred the smooth, white surface. "See that? The roof – it's shot to hell."

She glanced up. "What?"

"It needs replacing. And there's another floor above us, which means..." I paused for emphasis. "...the leak's gone straight through. Stuff like that, it doesn't happen overnight."

The more I talked, the less happy Arden looked. "Yeah, so?"

"So we're looking at floor damage, too. Maybe structural."

"Yeah, but—"

"And the wiring – no way it's up to code."

"You mean the electrical wiring?"

"Unless you know another kind."

She hesitated. "But the electricity...it still works."

I gave her an ominous look. "For *now*."

"Yeah, but the house....it could always be rewired, right?"

"Why?" I scoffed. "It's missing bathrooms."

Her eyebrows furrowed. "Missing how?"

"A place this size – two bathrooms doesn't cut it."

"But wait," she said. "I thought you were talking about the wiring."

"I was," I told her. "But I've moved on. Try to keep up, will ya?"

Her mouth tightened. "Fine. Whatever. But about the bathrooms, you can just put in more, right? I mean, you've done it before. I've seen you."

Now *that* made me pause. "Oh yeah?" I almost laughed. "Where?"

I knew where. Our show was killing it in the ratings. But I was curious to see if she'd admit it.

Her face, already flushed, grew a shade redder as she said, "Well, I *do* flip through the channels once in a while."

From the look on her face, she wasn't a fan. That was fine by me. I had millions already.

I smiled. "If you want my autograph, just lemme know."

She looked at me like I was the biggest piece of shit on the planet. "I don't want your *autograph*," she said. "I want to know what you're planning to do with the house."

"You mean *my* house?"

"I don't care if it's yours," she said. "You *can't* just demolish it."

I could if I wanted to. But the truth was, that wasn't part of the plan — not that *she* needed the details.

I almost laughed in her face. "Why not?"

"Because it's a waste and you know it." She was glaring now. "Just be honest. Are you doing this to get back at me?"

I paused. At *her?*

What the hell was she talking about? Tomorrow, I'd be sure to find out. But for now, I only shrugged.

She made a sound of disgust. "So you *are?*" Under her breath, she muttered, "I knew it."

She was wrong. *No surprise there.* In high school, she'd been wrong about a lot of things.

Even now, it pissed me off. "I never said that. And you're forgetting something."

"What?"

"You owe *me* answers, not the other way around."

"But—"

"Forget it," I said. "I'm not telling you jack — not 'til you tell me what you were doing in my shower."

"What do you think I was doing?" she said. "I was showering. What else do people do in there?"

Boy, if that wasn't a loaded question. My lips twitched. "Well, one time, there was this blonde in Milwaukee—"

"Oh shut up," she said. "That was a rhetorical question, and you know it."

"Do I?"

She sighed. "Alright, fine. You want the truth? I was going to crash here for the night. And before I did, I figured I'd just, you know, get cleaned up a little."

I frowned. *So she was staying here?*

If so, this was a new development. Just yesterday, after we'd closed the deal, I'd been through every inch of this place. And there'd been no Arden Weathers – or anyone else who didn't belong.

I'd dealt with squatters before – vagrants mostly. None of them had showered – *or* looked half as good as the girl in front of me.

I shook my head. "So you were squatting."

"I wasn't 'squatting,'" she said. "I was supposed to meet Jason here. And the truth is..." She glanced away. "... well, he didn't show."

I'd seen the texts. "No kidding."

Her gaze narrowed. "And I guess we both know why, huh?"

I didn't know why, but hell if I'd admit it.

Still, I had a decent guess. The way it sounded, this Jason guy had planned some sort of hookup, maybe a mid-week fling or whatever. And he'd picked this place as the location.

Short-term, it made sense.

The house was big, empty, and right on the beach. Summer was still a few weeks off, but a beach was a beach. And this one was nicer than most.

Still, what a sorry bastard. When *I* hooked up with someone, we didn't do it on the floor of some abandoned house, well, unless she was into that sort of thing.

But Arden – what the hell?

I didn't like her. But for some messed-up reason, I didn't like the idea of her hooking up with losers in vacant properties either. Call me sentimental, but the thought of my old chemistry partner rolling around in a dilapidated house, well, it was damned disappointing.

At the realization, I frowned. *Shit.* What did *that* mean?

CHAPTER 7

Arden

The longer we talked, the more I felt like throttling him.

When I considered everything Brody had cost me, this latest development was just icing on the cake.

I mean, who does that, anyway?

Who buys a house purely out of spite?

Brody Blastoviak, that's who.

And yet, the thought of him buying *this* place, only to destroy it, well, it was impossible to fathom. Something inside me twisted, and I couldn't stop myself from telling him exactly what I thought. "You're vile. You know that?"

If the insult bothered him, he didn't show it. With an obnoxious smirk, he said, "Hey, don't blame *me* if your hookup went South."

I shook my head. "Hookup? What hookup?" And then, it hit me. "Wait a minute. You think I was here to, what, have some sort of rendezvous?"

He shrugged. "That's a fancy way of saying it."

"What, compared to the way *you* talk?" I rolled my eyes. "That's rich."

"Yeah, I am," he said. "Deal with it."

I stiffened. *God, what a total asshat.*

Okay, so he was loaded. *Big freaking deal.* Obviously, the money hadn't bought him any maturity whatsoever.

"Well, that's nice," I said. "So now you're rubbing your money in my face?" I forced a laugh. "What, you wanna toss some cash onto the floor so we can roll around in it?"

At the image, I almost cringed. *Good Lord. What was I saying?*

His eyebrows lifted. "Is that a request?"

I drew back. "No."

"Good," he said. "Because I'm not interested."

So I'd heard. I made a sound of annoyance. "Do you realize that's the second time you've told me that? What is it? You think everyone in the world wants to sleep with you? That's a little arrogant, don't you think?"

"Not if it's true."

I started to object, but then thought better of it. Probably it *was* true. I mean, just look at him. The money aside, he was hot as sin, with the face to match. Probably he had a line of girls a mile long, just waiting to get a piece of him.

Good.

They could have him for all I cared.

"For your information," I told him, "I'm not interested in *you* either."

"Good," he said. "Because I'm not into crazy chicks."

My jaw dropped.

Crazy?

Chicks?

At this, I think I might've growled. "If I'm crazy – and that's a huuuuuge 'if' – it's only because of you. You ever think of that?"

He paused as if thinking. "No. I can't say that I have."

"Right," I shot back. "Because you never think about anything. *Nooooo.* Not you. You just waltz through life, and everything turns out all peachy-keen."

I lowered my voice an octave and continued. "Oh, look at me. I'm Brody Blast, and I'm a billionaire. And I'm hot, too. And everyone wants to sleep with me, even though I smash historic houses for no good reason."

He stared down at me.

I stared up at him.

We were still staring when a sudden gush of water poured down between us. With a yelp of surprise, I jumped back. *What the heck?*

But then, I slowly looked up. As I did, my stomach sank. *Oh, no.* That dark spot in the ceiling was now officially a hole. *Not a dent. Not a ding. But a real undisputed hole about the size of a dinner plate.*

And through that hole, a steady stream of water was pouring down between us, splashing onto the faded wooden floor of the hallway. As my gaze bounced from the ceiling to the floor and back again, I literally groaned.

Brody said, "Told ya."

Asshole.

I wanted to lunge for him. But I didn't. Because I was too horrified to move. The wet floor between us was littered not *only* with bits of busted plaster, but also with scattered clothes – *my* clothes, the ones I'd tucked under my arm on my way out of the bathroom.

They weren't tucked anymore.

No. They were lying there, all spread out, like someone had gotten naked in a hurry. I saw rumpled jeans, a ratty sweater, plain white panties, *and* the pink bra that Brody had nearly stomped on earlier.

How totally humiliating.

Especially the panties.

They were old, ugly, and decidedly unsexy – even more so *now* that they were nestled in clumps of soggy plaster.

Brody said, "If you're waiting for me to pick those up, forget it."

"Oh, for God's sake," I snapped. "I wouldn't let you near my panties."

He laughed. "I meant your keys."

"What?"

He pointed. "Your keys."

I looked to where he was pointing. Sure enough, my small ring of keys was lying near my left foot. *Crap.* They must've fallen out of my pocket – maybe even out of the pocket of my discarded jeans.

As far as the specifics, I didn't know, and I didn't care.

With a muttered curse, I squatted down and gathered up the keys *and* the clothes. I shoved the keys into my front pocket and then wadded up the now wet and grubby clothing.

I tucked the clothing back under my arm and stood to give Brody a long, withering look, which only made him smile like he knew something I didn't.

Fine. Whatever.

I returned my attention to the ceiling.

From somewhere above us, rainwater was still coming down – now more a trickle than a gush.

Still, with ever-growing concern, I looked once again to the floor. Already, water was pooling at my feet and seeping into my cheap red sneakers.

I didn't care about the shoes. But I *did* care about the house.

A lot.

It was in that awful moment that I realized something. Even if I could've purchased the house on my own, I still would've been totally screwed, because the place was obviously falling apart.

To repair it would cost a fortune – a huge fortune, at least by *my* standards. Nobody *I* knew had that kind of money – nobody except, well, the guy standing in front of me.

The realization hit so hard, I nearly staggered under the weight of it. Brody – he was good at repairing things. *Really good.* And he *already* owned the place.

Sure, the thought of him living here was a little hard to stomach – okay, *really* hard to stomach – but it was a lot better than the alternative.

Some might say this was just a house. And maybe it was. But my parents had divorced when I'd been just a toddler. Over the years, I'd moved way too often. *Different cities. Different houses. Different schools.* Different boyfriends and girlfriends, too – not mine, my parents'.

They'd shared custody – probably because neither one of them had wanted to be a full-time parent. But through it all, one thing had remained constant – *this* place, where my grandparents had lived.

Thanks to them, it always felt like I had a home, a *real* home.

In high school, I'd actually lived here for four blissful years when both of my parents had decided that even *part-time* parenting was more trouble than it was worth. Turns out, it was blessing in disguise, because in the end, those were some of the happiest years of my life.

As far as the house itself, I knew for a fact that my grandparents had always planned for it to stay in the family. *They'd told me so personally.*

But now, I had to face facts. Obviously, that wasn't going to happen.

I'd failed.

Not keeping it in the family was bad enough. But to think of the house not being here at all, of it being razed to the ground to build some McMansion in its place – it made me want to cry.

But I refused to cry, especially in front of *him* – the guy who'd been ruining my plans for years

I was still looking down to the floor. By now, my shoes were utterly soaked, and the rain was seeping into my socks. Softly, I heard myself say, "You could save it, you know."

When Brody said nothing in reply, I looked up.

He wasn't smiling anymore. His eyes were dark and intense, like a storm of his own was brewing somewhere beneath the surface.

In a tone that wasn't encouraging, he said, "Save what?"

"The house." I gave him a pleading look. "*This* house, I mean."

His mouth tightened. "Why?"

"Because it's the smart thing to do. You know it is."

He crossed his arms, making his muscles pop in a way that might've distracted the heck out of me, if only I weren't distracted enough already. With a low scoff, he said, "You're gonna have to do better than that."

"What do you mean?"

"I mean your presentation needs work."

I didn't get it. "Okay, so what do you want?" I forced a laugh. "For me to beg you or something?"

He cocked his head as if thinking. As he did, a terrible silence stretched out between us. Finally, he said, "That's one approach. But not my *first* choice."

At this, I grew very still. "So… what are you suggesting instead? Because if you're suggesting something, um, physical—"

"I'm not." His voice hardened. "I already told you, I'm not interested." And now he looked pissed-off.

Yeah, well, that made two of us. I wasn't even sure who I was angrier at – him for being so rude about it, or me for jumping to such an asinine conclusion.

Of course he wasn't interested.

I wasn't interested in *him*, either. But more than that, I wasn't the prostituting type. *And Brody?* He could get plenty of action for free. *I mean, just look at the guy.*

Still, the whole thing was beyond humiliating. "So what *do* you want?" I said. "Are we back to begging?"

He eyed me with obvious contempt. "Sure, why not?"

My mouth opened, and I made a sound. I'd *meant* it to be a laugh. But it wasn't. It was something else, something raw and jagged. "So you're telling me I need to beg?" I swallowed. "Seriously?"

With a shrug, he said, "Hey, it can't hurt."

He was wrong. It could hurt. And it *would* hurt. It would hurt a lot – but only my pride. And the truth was, I'd sacrifice just about anything to keep the house standing.

When I spoke again, my voice was barely a whisper. "Alright."

He looked unimpressed. "Alright, *what?*"

I took a deep breath and just said it. "I'm begging you."

His gaze flicked to the floor. "You're not on your knees."

Again, I tried to laugh. "Oh come on. You don't really expect—"

"Don't I?"

My stomach clenched, and I looked down to my feet. Even now, the puddle in the hallway was spreading. If it spread much further, it would soon be dripping down the stairway like some sort of perverse, slow-motion waterfall.

I didn't understand. Three years ago, when my grandpa had died of a sudden heart attack, my cousin Jason had ended up with the house. *Long story there.* But, after some serious persuading on my part, Jason had agreed to share ownership with me – *and* to let me buy *his* share after I graduated from college.

In the meantime, he'd been *supposedly* living here – enjoying the house and keeping an eye on things.

It had been a win-win, or so I'd thought.

But now Jason was nowhere to be found. And already, I'd come to the sad conclusion that even though I'd been sending him money for repairs, he hadn't been making them at all.

I blinked away unshed tears. *My own cousin had totally screwed me over.*

Now, in hindsight, I realized just how stupid I'd been all along. Worst of all, there was nothing I could do about it.

I had nothing in writing, which meant that I had no claim on the house, not officially.

God, I'd been such an idiot.

As I stared down in stupefied silence, the first drops of rainwater began easing down the stairway. *Oh yeah. I'd been an idiot, alright.*

When I finally looked back to Brody, he appeared angrier than ever – not at the damage. *At me.*

Under the weight of it all, I felt like sinking to the ground. In fact, I *was* sinking to the ground. Almost before I knew what was happening, I was already on my knees – whether with raw despair, or as some sort of desperate response to Brody's demand.

Either way, he was getting exactly what he wanted. *As usual.*

As water seeped into the denim of my fresh jeans, I tried not to dwell on it. I tried not to dwell on a lot of things.

During my twenty-four years on this Earth, I'd never sunk so low – literally *or* figuratively. Buy hey, I was already down here, just like he'd asked.

I might as well finish it, right?

I stared up at him and refused to flinch or look away, even when his expression darkened with an emotion that I couldn't quite decipher. As tears slid from my eyes, I choked out, "Fine. I'm begging you. There. You happy?"

CHAPTER 8

Arden

On the other end of the phone, Cami sputtered, "I'm gonna kill him."

I huddled deeper under the covers and tried to smile. Cami was my very best friend. Until just last week, she'd been my college roommate, too.

She was loyal to a fault, and her righteous anger was a soothing balm to my battered soul.

Even though I was alone in the small, unfamiliar bedroom, I kept my voice low, just above a whisper. "You can't," I told her. "Well, not until he finishes the house, anyway."

It was just past nine o'clock in the morning, and I was giving her an update on everything that had happened between me and Brody. I'd just reached the part where I'd begged him to save the house.

Cami said, "Can I least maim him or something? I mean, seriously, what a lunk-blaster."

As a general rule, Cami didn't swear. Or at least, she didn't use traditional swearwords, which meant that she sometimes had to get creative when she got all worked up, like now for example.

On the phone, she was still raving. "He seriously made you get on your knees?"

At the memory of last night, heat flooded my face. Technically, he hadn't *made* me do anything, but yes, that *had* been Brody's price for his promise to save the house.

And he got it, alright – my total humiliation.

I sighed. "Yeah, well, I guess it could've been worse."

"How?" she demanded.

"Well…" My face burned at the memory of me begging in the hallway, with my knees in the puddle and my face at his pelvis. "He could've expected, you know, 'services' while I was down there."

"Oh, please," she scoffed. "How do you know he *wasn't* expecting that?"

"Because," I said, "I wasn't down there long enough to do anything. Cripes, you should've seen him. He practically yanked me to my feet, like he was worried I'd try to convince him *orally* if you know what I mean."

From start to finish, the whole thing had been beyond mortifying. Still, I'd gotten what I'd needed, so it was worth it, right?

Cami muttered, "He's still a lunk-blaster."

I didn't even know what that meant. Looking to move on, I said, "But you haven't heard the rest of it."

Sounding decidedly disgruntled, she asked, "Does it get better or worse?"

"Better." I hesitated. "Mostly."

As Cami listened, I went on to tell her that Brody had agreed not only to spare the house, but to fix it up, too.

Sure, he hadn't looked too happy about it, but he *had* agreed.

I finished by telling her, "And when you think about it, fixing it up is almost as important as not tearing it down."

"How so?" she asked.

"Well, let's say he *only* agreed to not demolish it. Yeah, that's good for *now*. But what happens if he sells it? If it's not even livable, the next person might demolish it anyway."

"But I don't get it," Cami said. "If the house needs so much work, why would anyone want to buy it in the first place?"

"For the land," I said. "It's right there on the beach and *really* valuable, by local standards anyway."

Property values were relative, after all. If my grandparent's house had been located almost anywhere else, like in California for example, the land alone would've cost millions.

But here in Michigan, it wasn't like that. Between the smaller economy and harsh winters, beachfront properties weren't *completely* out of reach for an average person – providing they had a great job or lots of savings, preferably both.

Unfortunately, I had neither.

On the phone Cami was saying, "But the way you always talked, I thought your grandparents didn't have a lot of money."

"They didn't," I said. "But the house has been in our family for a long time, over a hundred years now."

It almost hurt to say it. Thanks to my own personal failure, the line of custody had ended with Jason rather than continuing on with me.

Still, I had to focus on the positive. "But now I don't need to worry, because it's going to be fixed up. See?"

"Oh sure," Cami said. "By your arch enemy. I mean, come on. You seriously believe he'll do it?'

Yes. I did. In spite of his *many* other flaws, Brody was the kind of guy who never went back on his word.

I recalled *that* from high school, too.

I replied, "Yeah. I do believe him, actually."

She gave a snort of derision. "Like you believed Jason?"

Her words found their mark, and my stomach twisted with new worry. Or maybe it was just hunger. For all kinds of reasons, I hadn't eaten a single thing yesterday.

And now I was starving. In fact, I was so hungry, I was beginning to smell things – bacony things.

I *loved* bacon. I swear, even now, I could smell it wafting through the walls. I poked my head out from under the covers and took a tentative sniff. Maybe that *was* bacon.

On the phone, Cami said, "Well?"

By now, I was so distracted, I could hardly think. "Well what?"

"You were about to tell me what happened next."

"Oh, right. So anyway, once he gave me back my phone—"

"Wait, what? He took your phone?"

"Uh, yeah. Didn't I tell you?"

"No."

"Oh. I guess that slipped through the cracks. Anyway, when I was in the shower, he swiped my cell phone."

Her voice rose. "And you *let* him?"

"I didn't *know* he swiped it until it turned up missing," I said. "And even if I *had* seen him take him take it, what was I supposed to do? Tackle him naked?"

At the thought, something fluttered in my stomach. It wasn't hunger. Or at least, it wasn't hunger for food.

The truth was, even though Brody was the last person I'd ever sleep with, I wasn't blind to his appeal. And, when it came to sex, let's just say it had been a while.

For me.

Not him.

Obviously.

On the phone, Cami said, "You could've yelled at him or something."

"Right," I muttered. "As if *that* would stop him. But forget the phone. I haven't told you the rest. After he agrees to fix up the house, he tells me that he *also* owns the place across the street."

"You mean across from your grandparent's place?"

"Right," I said. "And he invites me – no *orders* me, actually – to stay the night over there, I mean, over *here*, in the guest bedroom, so we can work out the details in the morning, meaning today."

Sounding more horrified than ever, she said, "And you agreed?"

"What else was I gonna do?" I said. "You already know that Jason stood me up, which meant that I had no place to stay. And you remember what happened with my car."

Just last month, I'd sold it to send Jason more money – payment for some sort of plumbing issue, something that according to Jason couldn't wait.

Now, I wanted to kick myself. *God, what a total waste.*

Thanks to my own stupidity, I had no house, no car, and maybe fifty bucks total in my purse.

When Cami's only reply was a string of non-curses, I continued, "So really, whether he realized it or not, Brody was actually doing me a favor by making me stay here."

"Oh yeah?" she shot back. "And what about *him*? Is *he* staying there, too?"

"You mean Brody? Actually, I don't know. Maybe he is. Or maybe he went back to his condo."

"Wait," Cami said. "He owns a condo, too?"

"Supposedly. I mean, that's what he said." I sighed. "And I'm sure it's true. Cripes, he probably owns half the town."

With obvious concern, Cami said, "So you don't even know if he's staying with you?"

"No, I don't," I replied. "Last night, all I wanted was to be alone. What Brody was doing, I had no idea. And I sure as heck wasn't gonna ask him."

The reason for this was obvious. By then, I'd had more than enough humiliation for one night.

If I'd asked Brody *anything* about where he planned to sleep, he surely would've assumed that I was hitting on him or something – because yes, he was that arrogant.

Cami said, "But you at least locked the door, right?"

"To the bedroom?" I flopped over on the bed and gave the door a quick glance. *Oh yeah, I'd locked it, alright.* But probably, that was a waste, too. As I'd seen firsthand, a locked door would hardly keep Brody out.

Still, I assured Cami that I was being careful and finished by promising her another update after Brody and I talked.

After we ended the call, I got up, trudged into the small private bathroom, and prepared to face him.

Using toiletries from my own duffle bag, I brushed my teeth and washed my face. I threw on fresh clothes and even a little makeup – not because I wanted to impress him, but rather because it's what I normally did before venturing out.

Turns out, it was all for nothing.

Other than myself, the house was empty.

Standing in the modest kitchen, I took a quick look around.

Thanks to the home's location – directly across the street from my grandparent's place – I'd seen this house plenty of times from the outside. It was a tidy ranch-style home with three bedrooms, maybe four.

As far as the exact number, I wasn't sure. I mean, it's not like I started opening doors or anything.

Still, I remained fairly certain that the house was empty. It *felt* empty, even if it *did* smell like bacon. My mouth watered at the mere thought, and I couldn't stop myself from opening the fridge, just to check.

No bacon.

In fact, the fridge was completely empty, except for maybe a dozen bottles of water.

Well, that was disappointing.

With a sigh, I closed the fridge and turned away. As I did, I spotted a note taped to the oven. The note was written in big, bold handwriting. It said, *"For Clara."*

I frowned. *Clara? As in Clara Cooper, my fake name?*

Slowly, I walked to the oven and opened the door just a crack. The oven was slightly warm and smelled so bacony that my breath caught.

On the oven's top rack, there was a silver takeout tray covered in foil. With primal longing, I stared at the thing. *It could only be for me, right?*

Still, I didn't want to assume anything, especially when it came to Brody. Reluctantly, I closed the oven door and took another look at the note. At the very bottom, in the same hand-writing – only *much* smaller – there was a very tiny P.S.

It said, *"Yeah, I mean you. Don't overthink it."*

It was vintage Brody, and I fought a sudden, stupid urge to smile. Even when he did something nice, he managed to make me just a little bit crazy.

But hey, I wasn't complaining. *Bacon was bacon.*

With unseemly haste, I yanked open the oven and reached inside. The container was warm, but not hot. When I tore off the lid, I saw bacon, scrambled eggs, and even buttered toast.

Oh, man.

Without bothering to sit down *or* search for silverware, I devoured the breakfast in two minutes flat.

When I finished, I felt a million times better. With renewed optimism, I wandered to the front window and opened the blinds.

What I saw outside made my stomach sink, even in spite of the breakfast. *My grandparent's house – it looked absolutely terrible.*

The blue paint was peeling and faded. The front porch was missing spindles. The grass was nearly knee-high. Even the shrubbery was a total overgrown mess, like it hadn't been trimmed in years.

Sure, I'd noticed all of this when the ride-share had dropped me off just yesterday. But now, looking at the place with new, critical eyes, I realized just how neglected it had been.

Still, I tried to look on the bright side. The situation wasn't *all* bad. Neglected or not, at least the house wasn't slated for destruction, not anymore.

As relief coursed through me, I felt a surge of something that felt a lot like gratitude – to Brody Blastoviak of all people. *He was going to save it.* He hadn't wanted to. That much was obvious. But he'd agreed anyway – even though he *had* made me beg.

Yes, it had totally sucked, but it could've been so much worse. He could've said no, whether I was on my knees or not.

At the thought, I stifled a mortified shudder. How awful would've *that* been?

But I refused to dwell on it. Instead, I squared my shoulders and focused on the positive. Begging wasn't *all* I could do. *I could help.* For starters, I could trim the hedges, and maybe even mow the lawn.

In spite of last night's rain, the morning had dawned sunny and bright. The day was windy, too, judging from the rustling of the trees and the windswept motions of the overgrown grass.

If the sun and wind cooperated, the grass – even as tall as it was – would almost surely be dry by this afternoon, which meant that I could get a decent start on the mowing.

With growing excitement, I dashed back to the bedroom, made the bed, and then ventured into the attached garage in search of the things I'd need – a lawn mower, hedge trimmers, and maybe a rake or shovel.

I found everything I needed in no time flat, including a gas-powered push-mower and a spare can of gas.

It was a sign. It *had* to be.

With a renewed sense of purpose, I hauled everything across the street and got to work. The work was hard, messy, and filled with all kinds of challenges I hadn't anticipated.

By noon, I was a sweaty, bedraggled mess, but I hardly cared. I kept on working, fueled only by bottled water and raw determination.

By late afternoon, the property was looking a whole lot better – or so I thought, until I was rudely informed otherwise.

CHAPTER 9

Arden

I was in the final stages of mowing the front yard when a big, white SUV pulled into my grandparent's driveway.

At the sight of it, I stopped mowing, but didn't cut the mower's engine.

Bright sunlight reflected off the vehicle's windows, making it impossible for me to see who was driving.

Was it Brody?

It *had* to be. After all, I hadn't seen him all day, in spite of his claim – or should I say *threat* – that we'd be talking.

For a long moment, nothing happened. But then, the passenger's side door flew open, and a sleek blonde in a tailored cream-colored business suit slammed out of the vehicle and began stalking toward me, in high heels no less.

She looked like she wanted to kill someone – me in particular.

With growing unease, I turned off the mower.

I waited in confused silence as she stalked ever closer – using the front walkway and avoiding the grass entirely. I knew why, too. It was because of her cream-colored shoes. I was no fashion expert, but they looked *very* pricey, just like the rest of her.

Without breaking stride, she hollered out, "Just what the hell are you doing?"

I glanced around. The way she was acting, you'd almost think she'd caught me crapping on the front steps.

I replied, "I'm, um, mowing actually."

She stopped on the edge of the walkway, leaving a good fifteen feet between us. Through gritted teeth, she said, "I *know* you're mowing. What *I* want to know is why."

I had no idea who she was or why she was flipping out. Still, I could tell by her clothing that she *wasn't* from around here. She looked too polished, too slick, and way too expensive for Bayside, Michigan.

I couldn't resist saying, "If you knew what I was doing, why'd you ask?"

Ignoring my question, she extended her arm and pointed an elegant finger vaguely toward the mower. "And where did you get *that?*"

She said "that" like it was a picture of her mother, naked with a goat.

I wanted to tell her that it was none of her business. But the sad truth was, this wasn't my family's home, not anymore. And for all I knew, she was Brody's girlfriend or something.

Normally, I wouldn't care *who* she was. But Brody was doing me a favor, a big one, too. And in spite of our longstanding grudges, I wasn't going to take his help for granted.

So I sucked it up and tried to smile as I said, "If you mean the lawn mower, I found it in the garage across the street."

She looked at me like I'd just confessed to grand-theft-mower. Her lipstick was very red, and her mouth twisted as she gritted out, "In the crew house?"

I shook my head. "Crew house? What do you mean?"

Again, she didn't answer. Instead, she looked toward my grandparent's front porch and literally gasped. "Oh, my God. The shrubs – what happened to them?"

I turned to look. *Wasn't it obvious?* This morning, I'd spent nearly two hours trimming them. And hey, I wasn't a professional landscaper or anything, but even *I* knew that they looked a whole lot nicer than they had just yesterday.

"I trimmed them," I explained. "And you've got to admit, they *do* look better." Or at least, *I* thought they looked better. *What on Earth was I missing?*

She whirled to face me. Her nostrils, narrow as they were, literally flared as she said, "I *know* they look better." Her voice rose to a new crescendo. "What the *hell* were you thinking?"

Huh?

Now, I didn't know what to say. After a long moment, I managed to stammer out, "Well, I was thinking that better is good, right?"

"Un-fucking-believable." She turned and hollered out toward the SUV. "Roy, get your ass out here!"

Turns out, Roy was the SUV's driver. He was a big burly guy with wavy red hair and a matching red beard. Unlike the blonde, he was dressed in jeans and an oversized plaid shirt.

When he lumbered over, she said to him, "*You* speak yokel. Explain to this… " Her hands gave a little flutter. "…*whatever* she is, that she fucked up."

I was still gripping the mower, and my fingers tightened around the handle. "Hey!" I said. "Just what's your problem, anyway?"

She turned to sneer in my direction. "At the moment, *you're* my problem." She turned back to Roy and said, "The grass – can we put it back?"

Roy frowned. "Uh…sorry. Come again?"

She gave a loud sigh. "Can we rebuild it or something?"

Roy looked at me. I looked at him. In unison, we both looked at the blonde.

Finally, I said what needed saying. "Are you freaking nuts?'

Her eyes narrowed to slits. "Of course I'm nuts," she practically spat. "You ruined everything!" She turned once again to Roy. "So we *can't* put it back? Is that what you're telling me?"

Technically, Roy hadn't told her anything.

I spoke up. "But why would you *want* to put it back?"

"Because," she said, "we need the 'before' footage. And for *that*, worse is better."

When I gave Roy a questioning look, he explained, "We're fixing the place up. Filming starts tomorrow."

Filming?

This could only mean one thing. Apparently, the house was going to be featured on Brody's TV show, the one he starred in with his two brothers.

Probably I should've seen this coming, but for some reason, I hadn't. I mean, I was still grateful and all. It's just that I never envisioned Brody moving so quickly to turn a favor into an opportunity.

I heard myself say, "Wow, that was fast."

The blonde hissed, "And stop talking. I'm trying to think."

And *I* was trying to keep from slapping her. But you didn't see *me* complaining, did you?

When I looked once again to Roy, he gave me an apologetic smile.

I could barely smile back. Maybe *he* was used to the blonde's rudeness, but *I* wasn't.

It was all I could do to keep my mouth shut as she paced back and forth on the front walkway, looking from me to the house and back again – as if of both of us had personally wronged her.

Finally, she reached into her designer purse and pulled out her cell phone. She tapped angrily at the screen and put the phone to her ear. Without so much as a goodbye, she turned and began stalking back toward the SUV.

As she moved, I caught bits and pieces of her conversation. I heard lots of profanity, peppered with words of impending doom. The phrase "total fucking disaster" was said more than once.

As I watched, she yanked open the passenger's side door, climbed into the SUV, and slammed the door behind her.

I turned to Roy and said, "Does this mean you're leaving?"

Looking surprisingly calm, he asked, "Why do you say that?"

"Well, because she got back into the vehicle."

"Eh, she does that all the time," he said. "Trust me. When she wants me, she'll holler." He gave the SUV a wary glance. "Until then, I'd be smart to stay away."

Now *this*, I believed. Even now, I could still hear the muffled sounds of her rage as she talked to whoever on the phone.

By now, I had no idea what to think. I sidled closer to Roy and said, "I'm really sorry. I honestly thought I was helping." I bit my lip. "I mean, Brody never said anything about not touching the house."

In fact, he hadn't said a lot of things.

And it suddenly struck me that only half a day had passed since Brody had surprised me in the shower. *Was that even enough time to plan whatever was going on?*

I didn't think so. And this meant, what exactly?

Let's say he *had* planned to fix up the house all along. *Had I begged merely for Brody's entertainment?*

I frowned. *Was it not a favor at all?*

With growing unease, I looked once again to Roy. "Hey, can I ask you something? This project – restoring the house, I mean – how long have you known about it?"

"This one?" Roy gave a rueful laugh. "Not long at all." He glanced toward the SUV. "That's part of the reason she's so tense. Rush jobs – they make her a little crazy."

"Oh." Relief coursed through me, along with more than a little shame. There I was again, all too willing to assume the worst of Brody. *What was wrong with me, anyway?*

With an embarrassed laugh, I said, "Oh yeah? So you just found out today, huh?"

"Today?" Roy gave me an odd look. "Nah. It's not *that* big of a rush. A project this size? It takes some planning, you know?"

"Oh?" My stomach clenched. "So…how long have you known about it?"

"Let's see…" He paused as if thinking. "Two, maybe three weeks."

My jaw dropped. *Brody — that total bastard.*
Boy, was he gonna get it.

CHAPTER 10
Brody

I stared, dumbstruck, at my oldest brother. "You're not serious."

From behind his desk, Mason said, "Is there a problem?"

Mason was five years my senior, and ten times the prick.

Normally, I'd call that a compliment. *Not today.*

I was standing in his office, which was situated on the top floor of our largest factory. By design, the factory was located right here in Bayside, where we'd all grown up.

Mason's office was cold and impersonal – with one lone exception. On his desk was a framed crayon drawing of a scribbled figure who could only be Mason, complete with a smile and a red necktie.

The tie was familiar. The smile wasn't.

On the bottom of the picture, the same childlike handwriting had scrawled out, *"World's Best Daddy."*

Yes. He was.

Mason might be a dick to me and everyone else, but he was good to Willow. I had to give him credit for *that*, even on days like today when I felt like lunging over his desk beating him senseless.

As for my own desk, it was located just down the hall in a private office of my own, not that I spent much time there. Unlike both of my brothers, I liked to work with my hands, not cool my ass in climate-controlled comfort.

But now, I was anything but cool. "Come on," I said. "You're just messing with me, right?"

"No." Mason glanced at his watch. "So just spit it out. What's the problem?"

It was nearly five o'clock in the afternoon, and my problems were piling up – building supplies delivered to the wrong property, a busted machine on the factory floor, and a landscaping emergency at some unspecified address.

Yeah. "A landscaping emergency." That's what Waverly had called it.

The way *I* saw it, there was no such thing. Unless the bushes had come alive and were eating neighborhood children, I figured that was a problem for the back burner.

And yet, it wouldn't go away.

Waverly – the new producer of our TV show – had been texting me for over an hour now. She'd been short on details, but long on drama, along with a few sexual innuendos that I was choosing to ignore.

Tomorrow, she'd be arriving here in Bayside to begin filming at the house on Lakeview – which meant that I had only one day to square things away with Arden.

Arden might be a pain in the ass, but she was smart. Once the film crew arrived, it wouldn't take her long to put two and two together and realize that the house had been safe all along.

I frowned as I recalled last night's scene in the hallway. The situation had gotten way out of hand.

Her fault.

And mine.

She'd been crazy. And I'd been an asshole. But now, come to find out, I'd been missing a big piece of the puzzle – the piece I'd just gotten from my brother.

Turns out, my latest acquisition – the house on Lakeview Drive – had been in Arden's family for generations. And the latest family member to own it – some guy named Jason Smithers – hadn't been so eager to give it up.

That name – *Jason* – rang a familiar bell, and I wasn't happy to hear it. My frown deepened as I recalled all of those text messages on Arden's cell phone.

Jason – he was no boyfriend. *And no hookup either.*

Apparently, the guy was Arden's cousin – a low-level administrator at the nearby community college. He'd owned the house for three years now. And in spite of his early reluctance to sell, he'd come around soon enough, thanks to some creative pressure applied where it counted.

I'd learned all of this just today, courtesy of Mason, who handled the business side of things.

I considered his question. *"What's the problem?"*

Shit. Where to begin?

I said, "So you *knew* that her family owned it?"

"Sure, I knew," he said. "Why do you think I bought the place?"

I gave him a look. "*I* bought it, not you."

"Yeah. And *I* did the deal." He gave me a tight smile. "So you're welcome."

I'd already thanked him once, and I wasn't about to do it again. He'd *wanted* to handle it. *And me?* I'd wanted it handled while I kept the construction side of things running on schedule.

He did his thing. And I did mine. Until now, it hadn't been a problem. But this? It was a problem – one I hadn't seen coming.

A few weeks ago, I'd spotted the house while scouting a different property on a neighboring street. *That* property had been a dud.

But the house on Lakeview had it all – good bones, a killer location, and plenty of room for improvement. It would be great for the show, and even better for the city. And the neighbors? Hell, they'd be sending us thank-you cards by the time it was done.

The place was a mess, inside and out. As bad as it was, it was a miracle it hadn't been condemned.

As far as purchasing it, the deal had been in the works for weeks. During this time, no one – including my prick of a brother – had said a single word about Arden Weathers.

I gave Mason another hard look. "Why didn't you tell me who owned it?"

"Because it wasn't worth mentioning."

It was a lie, and we both knew it. Mason held a grudge for longer than anyone I knew, me included. *And that was saying something.*

Sure, Arden and I had a history. And that history was on the explosive side. But Mason should've known better.

My discussion with him ended the way it always did, with stoic silence on his part and a good deal of profanity on mine. By the time I stalked out his office, neither one of us was happy.

But hey, what else was new?

And now I was running late. I'd meant to check in with Arden at noon. But noon had come and gone hours ago. The day had been a shit-show already and showed no sign of improving – not after last night.

In my mind's eye, I could still see her – gazing up at me with those big, tearful eyes. She'd been on her knees, and not in a good way.

It had surprised the piss out of me.

I hadn't expected her to do it.

After all, it was just a house, even if she *did* have a habit of poking her nose where it didn't belong.

Last night, I'd been plenty ticked-off – and with good reason, too. She'd busted into my house, and then insulted the hell out of me.

She'd called me vile.

Arrogant, too.

I felt my jaw clench. *What else had she called me?* By now, I could hardly remember.

But I *did* recall her begging me for a project that was already in the works.

I'd been pissed. And I'd taken it too far. But hey, I didn't deserve all of the blame.

On top of the other bullshit, she'd acted like I'd force her to have sex with me as some sort of payment.

What the ever-loving fuck?

It was the worst kind of insult. *I didn't pay for it.* And even if I *were* heading down that sorry road, I'd never want anyone who wasn't willing and eager.

Arden Weathers? She wasn't willing, eager, *or* my type. We weren't friends, and I didn't like her, but I *did* owe her an explanation, and maybe an apology, too.

Like all unpleasant things, I figured I might as well get it done and call it good.

It was a decent plan, or so I thought until I spotted a certain white SUV in the driveway on Lakeview.

Shit. From the looks of things, trouble had come early.

CHAPTER 11

Arden

With murder in her eye, the blonde hissed, "I *said*, 'Put it back.'"

I glanced around. *Yes.* She *had* said that, just a moment ago. But I still wasn't quite sure what she meant.

A full hour had passed since her surprise arrival, and she'd spent most of that time hunkered down in the SUV, talking to whoever while I made uneasy chit-chat with Roy.

I was trying to be a good sport. *Really, I was.* But between the blonde's rudeness and the realization that Brody had made me beg merely for the fun of it, I was feeling more than a little cranky.

I gave the blonde an annoyed look. "Put what back? The mower?" If that's what she wanted, I'd be all too happy to return it to the garage across the street, if only to escape all the drama.

I probably would've left long ago, if not for the fact that I'd been hungry for more information. And Roy, for his part, had fed me plenty.

Turns out, my grandparent's place was one of several properties they were featuring during the show's upcoming season. Apparently, Brody had picked this one personally and had even mentioned the possibility of living here after the house was fully restored.

The jerk.

The way Roy talked, this had been Brody's plan all along – not that Brody had bothered to enlighten me himself.

I knew why, too.

It was because he was a total vindictive bastard. That's why.

And now the blonde was saying, "I don't mean the lawn-*mower*. I mean the lawn."

Huh?

When I gave Roy a perplexed look, he appeared to be just as confused as I was. I turned back to the blonde and asked, "What do you mean? I can't exactly regrow it, you know."

With a derisive snort, she replied, "No shit, Sherlock."

I felt my eyebrows furrow. "So…?"

"So grab the clippings already." She gave a frantic wave of her arms. "Scatter them around, like an animal got into them or something."

I was staring now. "An animal?"

"Yeah. Like a goat." She sighed. "I mean, they eat grass all the time, right?"

"I, uh…" I shook my head. "Not around here, they don't."

"I don't care," she said. "Landon Tarrington will be here any minute, and I need this place to look like shit."

I stared with growing confusion. "What?"

"Yeah." Her mouth tightened. "The shittier the better."

I frowned. Gee, maybe I *should've* crapped on the front porch.

I gave Roy another questioning look. "Landon Tarrington?" I said. "Who's that?"

"The executive producer." Roy flicked his head toward the blonde. "Her boss."

The blonde gave a loud huff. "He's not my boss. He's my *boss's* boss." She turned back to me. "Now get your ass in gear. Or else."

I felt my gaze narrow. "You're not *my* boss. Or my boss's boss for that matter." With a brittle smile, I informed her, "For your information, I have no boss."

Her lips twisted. "So you're unemployed? I can't say I'm surprised."

And *I* couldn't say that I wouldn't smack her with a shovel. But that was a fantasy for another time.

In the end, I told her to shove it. If she wanted the grass clippings scattered or whatever, she could damn well do it herself.

And boy, was she delighted to hear *that*.

She was just in the process expressing this delight when a big black pickup pulled into the driveway.

At the sight of it, we all turned to look. The sun had shifted during the last hour, and the driveway was now shaded by the thick branches of my grandparent's favorite oak tree.

With no glare on the truck windows, I had no trouble seeing exactly who was behind the wheel.

It was Brody Blastoviak – the asshat himself.

CHAPTER 12
Brody

I frowned as I cut the truck's engine. *Shit.* What was *she* doing here?

This time, I didn't mean Arden – although I wasn't happy to see *her* either.

Hell, I wasn't happy to see any of it.

Waverly was standing on the front walkway while Roy – the head of the traveling film crew – stood beside Arden on the property's front lawn.

The lawn. I shook my head. *Huh.*

Someone had cut it. Or at least they'd cut most of it.

It was easy to guess who that someone was.

It was Arden. Her red sneakers were stained green, and there was a streak of dirt along the side of the face. Her hair was tied in a loose ponytail, and her yellow T-shirt clung to her curves in a way that might've caught my attention if I weren't so distracted by the rest of it.

The house – it looked different. I glanced toward the front porch and did a double-take.

Someone had trimmed the hedges. They'd done a decent job of it, too.

Arden?

It had to be.

This explained Waverly's scowl. *Oh yeah. She was ticked.*

Still, she wiped the scowl from her face and flashed me a smile as she turned and began striding toward my truck.

As she moved closer, I looked to Arden.

She wasn't smiling.

And neither was I.

Memories of last night came flooding back, making me shift uneasily in my seat. Judging from the scene in front of me, I'd lost any chance to explain before Arden figured things out on her own.

I was too late.

My fault. Not hers.

But then again, I hadn't been expecting company, not until tomorrow.

By the time I climbed out of the driver's seat, Waverly was standing beside my truck. When I shut the truck door behind me, she leaned closer and breathed, "Oh, my God. I'm *so* glad you're here."

Yeah, well, that made one of us.

Again, I looked to Arden. *She* wasn't glad. And I didn't blame her.

I wasn't glad either.

Last night had been a real shit-show. But there was plenty of blame to go around. And hell if I'd be taking all of it.

Waverly said, "So you received my messages?"

I gave her a look. "Yeah, all twelve of them."

Her chin lifted. "It wasn't twelve. It was ten at the most."

Ten, twelve – it didn't matter. When I said nothing in reply, she asked, "So why didn't you text me back?"

"Because I was busy."

Her mouth tightened, but she didn't push the issue. Instead, she pointed toward the front yard and said, "But you see the problem, right?"

Oh yeah. I saw.

Turns out the "landscaping emergency" was right here in Bayside. It was easy to see what had happened. Arden had ruined the establishing footage, the part where we showed just how bad the house looked before we got to work.

Silently, I took in the scene. The house still looked bad, but not *as* bad as when I'd bought it.

In fact, the place looked a lot better than just this morning.

The hedges looked nice and neat, and a bunch of weeds were missing from the area around the front porch. The yard still had a long way to go, but Arden had made a decent start of it, especially for someone working alone – and for less than a day.

If Arden were anyone else, I might've been impressed.

Next to me, Waverly was saying, "See? It's a total fucking disaster."

I shrugged. "Hey, it could be worse."

"How?" she demanded. "It's a catastrophe, and you know it."

No. A catastrophe was when your dad went out for beer and never came back. Or, when your mom decided she'd rather take up with some washed-up fighter and move to Miami, instead of raising her own kids.

Now *that* was a catastrophe – as I'd seen firsthand, even more so when they'd died in separate accidents not too long afterward.

I told Waverly, "Trust me. It's not that bad."

"Not that bad?" she sputtered. "You're kidding, right?"

I'd known Waverly for only a few weeks now. But it was long enough to know that she wasn't cut out for this sort of gig. In construction – hell, in everything – things went wrong all the time. The secret was to roll with the punches and get back up – not to whine like a…well, you know.

I told her, "Don't worry. We'll figure something out."

"Like what?" she said. "I *already* told the mower person that she should put it back."

At this, I almost smiled. "Oh yeah? How'd *that* go?"

"Terrible," Waverly said. "She got all snippy."

Recalling her words from a moment earlier, I frowned in confusion. "Wait a minute. Put what back?"

"The grass," Waverly said. "I'm thinking if we scatter it around, we can still get some decent footage."

From the sidelines, Arden called out, "And don't forget about the goat!"

Waverly whirled toward her and hollered back, "Hey! I wasn't talking to *you!*"

"Good!" Arden yelled. "Because *I've* got a lawn to mow."

Waverly gasped. "You wouldn't!"

Arden smiled. "Oh, wouldn't I?"

From the looks of things, Arden had done plenty of mowing already. But there was still a good chunk to go. In the front yard alone, maybe a quarter of the grass – the spot closest to the street – was still nearly knee-high.

As Arden fired up the mower, Waverly whirled to face me and said, "You've got to stop her!"

Shit.

She was right. I did – not because Waverly was flipping out, but because the last thing I needed now was more work. The house had been a last-minute addition to our season, and we were a month behind filming already.

As it was, we'd be busting ass to get the project done in time, which meant that another delay wasn't gonna cut it.

I told Waverly, "Wait here." And with that, I began striding toward Arden, even as she shoved the mower into the nearest patch of tall grass.

As I moved toward her, she yanked the mower back again, maybe a foot or two, before shoving it forward into the patch of overgrown lawn.

The process was ugly, but effective.

Grass that high – it couldn't be cut in a single pass – which made me marvel all over again that Arden had finished as much as she had.

From the sidelines, Roy was watching with a goofy grin, like Arden was the sweetest thing he'd seen all year.

Obviously, the guy didn't get it. *Arden wasn't sweet.*

Sure, she *looked* sweet, with those big brown eyes and tight curves.

But she was something else – trouble – the kind that kept on giving, as I soon rediscovered for myself.

CHAPTER 13

Arden

I was just gearing up for another push into the tall grass when Brody appeared directly in my path.

His eyes were dark, and his jaw was set. He was wearing faded jeans and a black T-shirt. The jeans hugged his hips, accenting his narrow waist and muscular torso. Even his biceps looked annoyingly perfect, bulging in a way that was stupidly distracting.

From head to toe, he looked too good by half.

And he knew it, too.

After all, he wasn't stupid – even in spite of his reckless disregard for his own safety.

Whether he realized it or not, the guy was playing with fire. *I had a mower. He didn't.* And he was dangerously close to becoming human mulch.

My flingers flexed around the mower's handle. One good push, and well, you get the idea.

But mowing him down wasn't part of the plan, so I focused all of my energy on glaring.

Over the sounds of the mower's engine, Brody called out, "Turn it off."

I called back, "Forget it."

His jaw clenched. "Turn it off," he repeated. "Or I'll do it for you."

"Why?" I shot back. "Because you're sooooo helpful?"

"No, because if you mow any further, it'll be *my* ass on the line."

He had a nice ass. Oh sure, I couldn't see it now, but I'd caught glimpses here and there, especially last night, before everything had spiraled so far out of control.

I called back, "Has it ever occurred to you that I don't care about your ass?"

He crossed his arms, making his biceps pop to perfection as he said, "It'll be *your* ass, too."

I didn't get it. "What?"

"You want the place done, don't you?"

If he meant the house, yes, I did want it done.

If I didn't, I wouldn't be mowing the freaking lawn.

And, on a more embarrassing note, I wouldn't have begged for such a thing last night. At the memory, I felt a surge of heat flash across my face – and not because of his distracting biceps.

I told him, "You are *such* a bastard. You know that?"

I expected him to argue. But he didn't. Instead, he gave a tight shrug and replied, "Sure. But you've still got to turn off the mower."

So he was admitting that he was a bastard?

I felt my gaze narrow. It was a trick. It *had* to be.

And, as far as the mower, I didn't *want* to turn it off. For the last hour, I'd been treated like garbage for mowing the stupid lawn, so the way I saw it, I might as well finish the job and be done with it.

And yet I didn't *really* want to run him over, as delightful as that sounded. I mean, hey, my shoes were messy enough already.

I tried to think. *Maybe I could simply mow around him?*

No. I couldn't.

And why? It was because just then, the mower's engine sputtered out on its own.

I glared down at the thing. *Well, this was just terrific.*

Brody said, "You're out of gas."

Thank you, Captain Obvious.

And now, I felt doubly foolish.

This was exactly how it *always* turned out whenever I went toe-to-toe with Brody Blastoviak. He *always* won.

Damn it. Even the lawn mower was on his side.

When I looked up, Brody's lips were twitching at the corners. He wanted to laugh. I could tell.

I coldly informed him, "That doesn't count, you know."

"Doesn't count for what?" he asked.

"A win for you."

"No kidding," he said.

I wasn't even sure what that meant. And I had no time to figure it out, because just then, someone new appeared at Brody's side.

It was a man I'd never seen before. He was short and stocky, with wavy brown hair, greying at the temples. He wore an expensive-looking business suit and a very bright smile.

Confused, I glanced around the front yard. *Where on Earth had he come from?*

When my gaze landed on the driveway, the answer became obvious. Sometime within the past few minutes, while I'd been arguing with Brody, yet another vehicle had arrived on the scene. It was a long black limo with dark tinted windows.

Funny, I hadn't seen one of *those* since prom.

When I looked back to the stranger, he held out his hand. "Hi. I'm Landon. And you are…?"

Sweaty.

Without thinking, I'd already moved my hand halfway toward his. Now I pulled it back with an embarrassed laugh. "Actually," I said, wiping my hand on my jeans. "I'm not sure you want to shake this. I'm a little messy."

From somewhere to my left, I heard a delicate snort. I turned to see the blonde standing within slapping distance – this time on the lawn, *not* on the walkway.

I looked down at her shoes and almost smiled. The shoes were still *mostly* cream-colored, but now, the front half of each shoe had a slight greenish tinge.

Suddenly, my day felt just a little bit brighter.

She muttered, "Oh, shut up."

With mock innocence, I asked, "Did I *say* anything?"

"No. But you were thinking it."

The stranger's voice cut between us. "Waverly, is there a problem?"

The blonde straightened. "No sir. No problem here."

"Good," he said. "Let's keep it that way, shall we?"

When I turned back to the stranger, he gave me another friendly smile as he said, "You never told me your name."

Now, I was *really* confused. Obviously, this was Landon Tarrington, the blonde's boss – or her boss's boss, if I wanted to get all technical. *But why wasn't he angry with me?*

I mean, shouldn't he be yelling about the lawn or something?

I replied, "I'm Arden – Arden Weathers, actually."

During this whole exchange, Brody had been giving Landon a look that I couldn't quite decipher. Still, one thing was glaringly obvious. *Brody wasn't delighted to see him.*

Then again, Brody hadn't seemed delighted by much of anything today – well, except for the mower running out of gas.

Landon looked to Brody and said in a friendly sort of way, "So, you and Miss Weathers know each other?"

Brody frowned. "You might say that."

Landon gave a slow nod. "I figured as much." He turned back to me, and his gaze grew speculative. "So, you two have a history, huh?"

I wasn't quite sure what he was getting at. "Well..." I stammered. "...we knew each other in high school, if that's what you mean."

"So what were you?" he asked. "High school sweethearts?"

Me and Brody? I gave a bark of nervous laughter. "No. Definitely not."

From the sidelines, Brody said, "Is there a point to this?"

The guy smiled at both of us in turn. "I'm just seeing some chemistry here, and I'm wondering what's up."

Chemistry? At the very word, I almost groaned out loud.

I looked to Brody, and we shared a long, sullen look. In high school, we'd been chemistry partners – and not by choice.

Brody told Landon, "You thought wrong. No chemistry here."

"Yeah," I chimed in. "That goes double for me."

Undaunted, Landon gave me another long look. Something in his gaze made me feel just a little bit naked – not physically, but definitely mentally.

He reached up to stroke his chin before asking, "So what's your connection to the house?"

The blonde – Waverly – answered on my behalf. "There *is* no connection. And she was just leaving."

"Actually," I said, "my grandparents owned the place." I turned and gave Waverly a pointed look as I continued. "If you want the *truth*, it's been in my family for generations."

At this, Waverly gave me a smile that looked more like a grimace. "How nice."

When I looked back to Landon, he was nodding again. "Interesting." Slowly, he turned and surveyed the lawn before turning back to ask, "So that's why you were mowing? To fix up the ol' homestead?"

It was a simple question. But the answer was obscenely complicated. Yes, family nostalgia had played a role in it. But I'd also been mowing out of misguided gratitude – to Brody of all people.

I mumbled, "Something like that."

"Right," he said. "So, how'd you like to join the team? Maybe do some consulting?"

I froze. *Wait, what?*

CHAPTER 14

Arden

The question caught me off guard. After a long, perplexed pause, I asked, "What kind of consulting?"

Landon pointed toward my grandparent's place. "You know they're fixing that up as part of the show, right?"

Boy, did I ever – now, anyway.

When I gave a silent nod, he continued, "And I *know* you've seen the show."

Yeah, me and the rest of the world. Against all logic, *Blast* was the network's number-one show of all time. Aside from the monster ratings, it had spawned countless memes, a cult-like following, and plenty of unique offers for the brothers – movie roles, cameos, endorsement opportunities, and even marriage proposals from multiple fans.

The whole thing was beyond crazy.

And yet, the brothers declined everything, unless it directly involved either the TV show or their tool company.

As far as the show itself, I was pretty sure that I'd seen all of the episodes. *Multiple times.* It wasn't that I was a fan or anything. It was just that, well, I'd been curious, that's all.

Plus, I loved the whole remodeling thing. Seeing houses restored to their original beauty was oddly addicting, especially when I happened to know one of the stars.

I said, "I might've caught an episode or two."

"So tell me," Landon said. "Where are you working?"

"Sorry, what?"

"A job," he said. "You *do* have one, right?"

Oh, God. Talk about embarrassing. "No. Not really. I mean, I just graduated from college, so–."

"Perfect."

"What? Why is that perfect?"

"Because I'm thinking we can use a consultant, someone with a vested interest in seeing the place restored to its former glory and all that."

From my left, I swear I heard a gasp.

Apparently, Landon heard it too, because he looked to Waverly and said, "Is there something you want to say?"

But it wasn't Waverly who answered. *It was Brody.* In a deadly calm voice, he told Landon, "She's not interested."

I gave him an annoyed look. "I never said that."

Brody replied, "Yeah, but you will."

"Oh, so now you're a psychic."

With a low scoff, he said, "Better a psychic than a psycho."

I gave him the squinty-eye. "What's *that* supposed to mean?"

"Nothing that a lit match won't solve." His gaze hardened. "Isn't that right?"

"Oh, for God's sake," I said. "It wasn't a match. It was a lighter."

And the lighter wasn't even mine. It was Brody's. But that was an argument for another time – when I wasn't defending my own sanity.

I looked back to Landon and explained, "In high school, I *accidentally* set fire to Brody's truck."

"Accident, my ass," Brody said.

I whirled to face my high-school nemesis. "Oh yeah? And what about you? You practically blew us up."

Brody reached up to rub the back of his neck. "It wasn't *that* bad."

"Oh yeah?" My voice rose. "Tell that to my missing eyebrows."

He shrugged like this was no big deal. "Hey, they grew back."

"Not in time for graduation!"

It was true. In all of my senior pictures, there I was, with *painted* eyebrows, because my real eyebrows had gotten so singed, they were practically invisible.

On top of that, my perfect G.P.A. had been ruined by the fact that I'd not only failed my senior chemistry project, I'd been suspended for two whole weeks and wasn't allowed to make up all of my work.

One little boom – or more accurately one *ginormous* boom – and all of my plans went up in smoke.

Now, years later, I was still suffering the consequences.

As far as the boom itself, it was a huge miracle that no one had been seriously hurt. Against all odds, I hadn't been injured so much as made to look ridiculous. *And Brody?* He'd gotten away utterly unscathed. *As usual.*

We were still going back and forth when Waverly's voice cut through our bickering. "Enough already!"

In unison, Brody and I turned to look.

Sometime in the last minute or so, she'd sidled closer to Landon. Her lips thinned as she eyed me like I was something to be scraped off her pricy shoes – which, yes, were looking just a little greener than before.

Hah! Take that, City Slicker.

Still, I waited in polite silence, not because she'd asked for it, but because it suddenly occurred to me that I was arguing in front of a stranger – two strangers, actually. Or three, if I wanted to include Roy.

I glanced around, but saw no sign of him.

Well, that was weird.

And now, Waverly was saying to Landon, "This will never work." She gave a shaky laugh. "Seriously, just look at them. They'll be at each other's throats."

Landon smiled like this wasn't such a bad thing. "We'll see."

Brody looked to Landon and said, "You're forgetting something."

Looking only mildly curious, Landon replied, "Really? What's that?"

"Arden hasn't accepted. And trust me." Brody gave me a look filled with warning. "She won't."

His message was clear. If I knew what was good for me, I'd decline the unexpected offer. *But didn't Brody get it?* Thanks to him, I had nearly nothing to lose.

Obviously, the house would be fixed up regardless of anything *I* said or did. Plus, at the moment, I had no job and no place to live.

I'd be a fool to turn this down.

Then again, I wasn't quite sure what the offer was.

At something in my gaze, Landon said, "Don't worry. I'll make it worth your while. You got an email address?"

When I rattled off the address, he gave another nod. "Check it in an hour. You'll have my offer." He smiled. "I look forward to your acceptance." And then, looking strangely satisfied, he turned and strode off toward the limo.

Just before he reached it, a uniformed driver materialized out of the front seat and held open a rear door while Landon Tarrington climbed inside.

As the limo backed out of the driveway, Brody looked to me and said, "You're not taking it. You know that, right?"

I crossed my arms. "Oh yeah? Why not?"

"Because you'll be a distraction, and you damn well know it. You want the house done, right?"

"Oh, please," I said. "It's going to be done regardless. I'm not falling for *that* again."

To his credit, Brody didn't ask what I meant. Obviously, he *knew. We both did.*

Less than a day ago, he'd used my love of the house against me – to humiliate me, to make me beg, to drive me more than a little crazy.

But I wasn't crazy. I was smart – smarter than he knew. Already, a plan was forming in my mind. I'd just graduated from college, and I hadn't yet found a job. But today I *had* been offered one, as a consultant no less.

It was a nice title. It would look terrific on a resume, especially with the show's brand-name recognition. Plus, the job was temporary, which meant that it would offer me the perfect opportunity to look for something permanent while earning an actual income.

Brody's voice – sounding more irritated than ever – interrupted my thoughts. "It's gonna be a worksite. There's no glamor in it."

I made a show of looking down at my clothes. They were streaked with dirt and grass clippings. My hands were stained green, and I was a hot sweaty mess.

I knew exactly how I looked, and it *wasn't* glamorous.

But didn't he get it? Glamor meant nothing to me in the big scheme of things.

With a stiff smile, I informed him, "I'm taking the job."

His jaw clenched. "But you don't know what it is."

This was true. But it didn't matter. If it offered any sort of paycheck, I *would* be taking it. Sure, I'd be dealing with Brody, which would be no picnic. But hey, I had experience with that sort of thing.

In some ways, it would be a repeat of high school. Brody and I would be stuck with each other regardless of our mutual loathing.

But this time it would be different. I was older and wiser. Plus, this was my own decision, not some random teacher's.

And damn it, *this* time, I'd come out *a lot* better than I had the first time around.

CHAPTER 15

Arden – Six Years Earlier

He was late.

I wasn't surprised. But I *was* irritated. Somehow, by the worst luck ever, I'd been assigned Brody Blastoviak as a lab partner for my senior project in advanced chemistry.

I hated group projects. They were such a pain, especially for me, considering that I needed to maintain a perfect grade-point-average if I wanted to secure that scholarship – a full ride to Michigan State.

In reality, the scholarship was mine already – signed, sealed, and delivered, as long as I didn't blow it during my final semester.

If it weren't for group projects, I wouldn't even be worried.

But now, I was.

And why? It was because I knew exactly how this would go.

When it came to group projects, if anyone in my group *ever* slacked off, I had to make up the difference.

Normally, I didn't mind as much as you'd think. I mean, if I wanted a bigger reward, it was only natural that I'd need to put in a bigger effort, right?

But today I *wasn't* in the mood.

So I stubbornly waited, watching the minutes tick by on the big white clock hanging in the school's back hallway. Except for the janitors, I was utterly alone. No surprise there, considering it was Saturday.

Finally, seventeen full minutes after noon, Brody sauntered up looking like he had all the time in the world. He was wearing what he always wore – jeans, a plain T-shirt, and a faded jean jacket.

I was wearing pretty much the same thing, except that my jean jacket was white, and I didn't look half as good wearing it. But Brody Blastoviak – he *always* looked good, no matter what he wore.

I gave him a quick once-over and mentally checked off the list. *Killer body, killer face, killer hair, killer everything.*

No wonder everything came so easy for him.

And speaking of killing, I said, "Nice of you to show up."

With a casual shrug, he replied, "Hey, *I* thought so." He glanced toward the locked door of the chemistry lab. "I figured you'd start without me."

My jaw clenched. That's what they *always* figured. And they were usually right.

But today, I was too tired and cranky to be a good sport about it. Just yesterday, my mom had rolled into town unexpectedly, bringing with her the usual chaos.

She hadn't wasted any time either. Within hours of her arrival, she'd announced that she was engaged – to some guy named Eddie who'd I'd never met – had hit up my grandparents for money – as if they had any to spare – and had *almost* made off with my white jean jacket – as if it weren't also my only jacket, not counting my winter coat, which would look ridiculous in April.

And now Brody was frowning. His nose literally wrinkled when he said, "What's that smell?"

Heat flooded my face. The smell was me – or rather, the jean jacket I'd wrestled from my mom just this morning. To Brody, I muttered, "Oh, shut up."

With a crooked grin, he said, "Hey, I'm just asking."

"Well, don't."

Now he looked ready to laugh. "Rough night, huh?"

"What makes you say that?"

"Because you smell like it."

How nice.

He didn't say what "it" was, but I knew exactly what he meant. I smelled like a freaking bar fly. Silently, I added up the aromas – cheap perfume, even cheaper booze, and lots of smoke.

I'd be naïve to think it was only cigarettes.

Last night, within hours of her arrival, my mom had found her way to the nearest dive bar, where she'd apparently had a lovely time, until she'd been kicked out for fighting in the ladies room. *Again.*

I glanced down at my jacket and felt my own nose wrinkle in disgust. Last night, it had rained, and the jacket was still damp.

But at least she hadn't gotten any blood on it, so hey, it was an improvement over the *last* time, right?

When I made no reply, Brody said, "If you need a light, let me know."

I wasn't following. "What?"

He reached into the front pocket of his jeans and pulled out a green disposable lighter. He flicked it to life and held it out near my face.

I gave the flame an annoyed look. "In case you didn't notice, I don't actually *have* a cigarette." Under my breath, I added, "Or anything else, for that matter."

"So?"

"So I don't need a light."

"Eh, your loss," he said, flicking off the lighter and lowering it to his side.

With growing irritation, I said, "You *do* know, I had to get special permission to use the lab today."

This wasn't even a good thing.

All of our classmates had completed the experiment on Thursday. But not us. *And why?* It was because my so-called partner had decided to skip class, and Mr. Chesterfield had refused to let me do the experiment on my own.

"So?" Brody said again.

I sighed. "So let's just get it done already." I glanced toward the locked door of the lab. "And we need to be quick. I'm making cookies with my grandma at two-thirty."

My grandma loved to bake, even in spite of her arthritis. And although I wasn't in the mood for cookies, I'd promised to bake them with her anyway – something to cheer her up after my mom had blown out of town just as quickly as she'd arrived.

I didn't need any cheering. The truth was, I'd been shamefully glad to see her go. But my grandparents – well, they were softies when it came to my mom, probably because she was their only surviving child – and the youngest, too.

In the school hallway, Brody's lips formed a sneer. "Sorry, I didn't know 'cookies' were on the line." He said "cookies" like it was a four-letter word.

I tried for a scoff. "Oh? So you've got something against cookies?"

"Me? Nah." He gave me a rude look. "Just people who make them."

My gaze narrowed. "I hope you're talking about me, because if you mean my grandma—"

Once again, the lighter appeared in my face. Without flicking it on, he asked, "You sure you don't need a light?"

I glared at the lighter and then at him. "Trust me. I'm sure."

With cold defiance, he flicked it on, anyway. The flame wasn't terribly close, not even within cigarette-lighting distance, but it *was* annoying. No doubt, it was meant to be.

He was trying to goad me. That much was obvious.

This shouldn't have been a surprise.

When the list of lab partners had been posted three weeks ago, Brody hadn't been any happier than *I* was.

I knew why, too. Unlike me, he never took any of it seriously. Oh sure, he took all of the advanced classes, but his grades were lackluster at best.

Between cutting class and missing half of his homework, he surely would've flunked out entirely, if only he didn't have this annoying habit of acing all of his tests.

But me? I had to study. *Hard.*

I gave a silent scoff. *But that was Brody for you.* I'd known him for nearly four years now, ever since I'd moved in with my grandparents just before my freshman year.

Turns out, it was the best thing that ever happened to me. Unlike my parents, my grandparents actually liked having me around. And I liked *being* around. Plus, this gave me the stability to try for a scholarship.

And my parents? Well, they got their freedom, I guess.

Let's just say, parenting wasn't their thing.

When I considered how lucky I felt just to be standing in this particular school, it made Brody's casual attitude all the more maddening.

He nudged the flame a tad closer, as if preparing to light my face on fire.

I told him, "You know that's not allowed, right?"

Talk about a massive understatement.

With a laugh, he finally flicked off the lighter and lowered it once again to his side. Normally, I liked his laugh, even if I'd never admit it. But today, it sounded all wrong, laced with cruelty rather than humor.

His mouth twisted as he said, "Relax. I'm not gonna burn your cookies."

For some reason, his words sounded vaguely suggestive and just a little bit insulting.

I stared up at him. "I don't get it," I said. "If you were just gonna be a jackass, why'd you bother to show up at all?"

With no trace of laughter, he replied, "Because I told you I would."

"So?"

"So I always do what I say."

"Oh, really?" I scoffed. "Do you always do it seventeen minutes late?"

His mouth tightened. "Better late than never."

It was *so* easy for him to say. Unlike me, he got away with everything. Still, I couldn't resist saying, "Has it ever occurred to you that if you just applied yourself, you'd be getting all A's?"

"Has it ever occurred to *you* that it's none of your business?"

Yes. It had, actually.

Still, I had to ask, "But what about college?"

"What about it?"

"Aren't you worried you won't get in?"

With another scoff, he replied, "Hell no."

His attitude grated. *Gee, it must be nice to be so confident.*

But probably he was right. No doubt, he'd ace some assessment test and get into whatever college he wanted without even trying. With as brilliant as he was, he'd probably get a scholarship, too.

Thinking of my own scholarship, I pulled out the lab key – the one I'd wheedled out of Mister Chesterfield after school on Friday. As I inserted the key into the lock, I couldn't resist muttering, "Just try not to blow anything up, alright?"

I'd opened the door barely a crack when that stupid lighter flared again. This was followed by something infinitely worse – a gigantic flash of light, loud and scorching hot.

With one giant boom, the lab practically exploded, sending me and Brody reeling backward as the door flew off its hinges. Brody tackled me to the ground, as if he were trying to smother me with his own body.

Around us, I smelled smoke and chemicals and burnt hair. My mind reeled, and my body shuddered. I gave Brody a frantic push. "Get off me!"

His voice was low in my ear. "Not yet."

With a string of curses, I eventually pushed him aside, only to realize that the burnt hair was my own. *My face. Oh, my God.* I reached up to touch it, half expecting to find it melted or something.

But it was fine.

Or maybe not – because when I looked to Brody, he stared at me like I'd just turned into some sort of goblin. I was almost crying when I asked, "How bad is it?"

He hesitated way too long before saying, "Not too bad. You're okay."

Was I?

I *felt* okay. Once again, I reached up to touch my face. That's when I realized something. My eyebrows – they weren't quite there. I looked up to my bangs and frowned in momentary confusion.

My bangs were still there, except they were a whole lot shorter and singed on the ends.

But it wasn't until I looked at the smoldering ruins of the lab itself that I realized how close *both* of us had come to losing a lot more than eyebrows.

Later on, investigators would determine that the explosion had been caused by a leak in the gas line that fed the Bunsen burners. After being closed for hours, the small lab had filled with flammable gas.

All it needed was a spark.

But it could've been so much worse. If we'd been inside the lab when the flame had caught, probably neither one of us would've lived to tell about it.

So I tried to be thankful – even as Brody and I were *both* suspended for two full weeks, which was a lot better than the school's initial threat to kick us out entirely. There'd even been some talk of us being sued for damages, in spite of the fact that the gas leak itself was hardly our fault.

But then, suddenly, out of the blue, all of that talk went away – much like my college scholarship as my grades tanked due to my sudden suspension.

When all was said and done, nearly four years of perfect work were destroyed by one single boom.

Oh sure, I'd still gone to college, and I *had* gotten a few minor scholarships here and there. Still, it was hardly the full ride I'd been counting on, and it meant that I'd had to begin my college career not at a four-year university, but rather at the local community college, where I could rack up some credits on the cheap side.

But it wasn't *this* that broke my heart. It was everything else. My grandma died of a sudden illness only a week after my high school graduation, and then, my grandpa had died of a heart attack only three years after that, during my first year at Michigan State.

Together, the loss of them had left a hole so big, I might've tumbled into it forever, if only I weren't so determined to keep their traditions alive. This included saving the house and keeping it in the family, just like they'd always wanted.

But in order to save it, I needed money. And to get *that* kind of money, I had to finish my college degree.

It was a total catch-22, and in the end, I split the difference – continuing on with college while sending my cousin Jason enough money to keep the place from getting repossessed or falling into ruin.

In the end, it was all for nothing. The house had fallen into ruin anyway, and Jason *still* wasn't returning my calls.

This left me with only one option – working with the guy who'd torched all of my plans in the first place.

Brody.

Still, I had to give him credit for one thing. He'd definitely lived up to his nickname.

Brody Blast.

CHAPTER 16

Brody – Present Day

Waverly was still griping. "You *know* this is a mistake, don't you?"

With a noncommittal shrug, I leaned sideways against the door of my truck. "Hey, it's not *my* mistake."

"Oh, I know," she assured me. "I just mean, the whole situation. It's a total disaster."

Disaster – it was her favorite word, and she'd been using it nonstop for the last fifteen minutes, ever since Arden had disappeared into the crew house across the street, where she'd slept last night.

I hadn't slept – not there or anywhere else.

Instead, I'd spent the bulk of last night dealing with the roof leak. I hadn't fixed it. That would've required scaffolding and a crew. But I *had* been able to minimize the damage by devising a crude funnel-and-hose system that diverted the rainwater into the nearby shower drain – and not down the main stairway.

Afterward, I'd used some rags from the basement to dry what I could while making arrangements to have the roof replaced.

The replacement would begin later this week – or sooner if rain showed in the forecast.

Hell, if this weren't part of the TV show, I'd have a crew here already to guarantee no further damage.

But the show was important – not because I gave two shits about the entertainment industry, but because the ratings generated millions in tool sales along with a few hundred local jobs.

Thanks to the show, the brain child of my brother Chase, Blast Tools had gained two decades of growth in three short years.

The show was free advertising on steroids, which meant that I was willing to deal with more than my share of bullshit to keep it going. Hell, I'd deal with a *hundred* Ardens if that's what it took.

And I wouldn't waste my time bitching about it either. Bitching was for pussies – and for pampered producers who wore high heels to job sites.

Next to me, Waverly said, "Maybe she won't take it. I mean, people turn down job offers all the time, right?"

I gave her a look. "Not this time."

"But we can't be sure," she said.

We. That was another word she used a lot – sometimes related to the show, and sometimes for sly innuendos like, *"We should test out that jacuzzi sometime."*

So far, I'd been playing dumb. I knew how these things ended – with more drama than I wanted or needed. If I was lucky, she'd get the hint soon enough. And if not – well, I'd deal with that later.

Thinking of Arden, I told Waverly, "Trust me. She'll take it."

Landon Tarrington had copied both of us on the email containing his offer. It had come across Waverly's cell phone just five minutes ago, and she'd made a point to wave the offer in my face – as if I couldn't read it on my own screen.

It didn't matter. One glance was enough for me to know that Arden wouldn't be turning it down.

With a sigh, Waverly said, "I still don't know what Landon saw in her."

I did. Arden was the classic girl next door – long brown hair, a perky nose, and dimples in both of her cheeks when she smiled.

She hadn't smiled much lately, especially at me. But she'd hit Landon with a smile or two.

The guy wasn't blind. And he was damn good at what he did, even if some of his decisions weren't to my liking.

When I made no reply, Waverly said, "I have a theory. Do you want to hear it?"

Nope.

Not me.

When I remained silent, Waverly announced, "I think she has a thing for you."

Now *that* got my attention. "What?"

"Oh come on," Waverly laughed. "When you were standing in front of the mower, she was practically drooling."

I frowned. *Arden? No.*

She hadn't been drooling. She'd been sweating. And she'd looked obscenely good doing it. Her cheeks had been flushed, and her yellow T-shirt had been clingy with perspiration. And her bra? Well, let's just say the lace wasn't nearly thick enough to hide the outlines of her damp nipples.

And now, my jeans were growing tight. *Again.*

Shit.

The hot-and-sweaty look shouldn't have been sexy. But on Arden, it was.

Good thing she didn't realize it, or I'd have *real* trouble on my hands – because if Arden ever turned on the charm, assuming she had any, I'd be more tempted than I wanted to admit.

I told Waverly, "Sorry, you're wrong."

"I sure hope so," she said, hitting me with a sultry smile of her own. "Because *we* don't need her."

We. There was that word again. The way she talked, it was just the two of us against the world. *But that's not how it was.*

For the last few years, it had been *three* of us against the world, and Waverly wasn't part of the team.

No. The trio consisted of me and my two brothers. *No parents. No aunts. No uncles. No doting grandparents either.*

It had been like this for a while now, beginning late in my senior year.

And this – in a roundabout way – was why Arden Weathers hated my guts. *And vice-versa.*

CHAPTER 17

Brody – Six Years Earlier

It was Saturday, and the last place I wanted to be was in school. But I'd promised Arden Weathers – my overachieving lab partner – that I'd be here.

So here I was.

Yeah, maybe I wasn't on time, but if Arden knew the grief I'd gone through to get here, she'd be kissing my ass, not scowling like someone had peed on her pancakes.

I spotted her before she spotted me.

She was wearing jeans and a gray T-shirt along with a little white jean jacket. Her long brown hair was tied in a tight ponytail, and her bangs fell loose over her eyes.

She was waiting outside the door to the chemistry lab, staring up at the clock on the opposite wall. She wasn't leaning either. *No. Not Arden Weathers.* She was standing straight-up, as if to make it obvious that she wasn't one to lounge around, waiting for anyone while there was schoolwork to be done.

At the sound of my footsteps, she turned to look. When she spotted me, her scowl deepened.

No surprise there.

She didn't like me. But hey, the feeling was mutual. Arden was too uptight, too worried about her grades, and too ready to raise her hand for extra credit.

She was the kind of girl who made guys like me look worse than I was. And considering how little I cared for school – or for kissing ass – *that* was saying something.

She was cute, even when she scowled, but that didn't mean I was interested.

I had bigger problems than school and no time for girls who were such a hassle. I made a point to slow my pace as I approached.

When I reached her, she said, "Nice of you to show up."

No kidding. This morning had been a shit-show at home, and the way things had looked when I left, I might not have a home to return to.

But I wasn't one to complain and saw no reason to start now. So with a shrug, I replied, "Hey, *I* thought so." I glanced toward the door of the lab. "I figured you'd start without me."

I wasn't kidding. The last time we'd met up, she'd gotten there early and was half-way done by the time I'd arrived.

Not today.

Today, she hadn't budged from the hallway. That wasn't the only thing that was different. Something in the hallway reeked like a party gone stale. I asked, "What's that smell?"

Her cheeks flushed. "Oh, shut up."

So the smell was coming from her?

No way.

She smelled of smoke, booze, and cheap perfume. I grinned in surprise. *Maybe there was more to my partner than I'd thought.* "Hey, I'm just asking."

"Well, don't."

I was still grinning. "Rough night, huh?"

She stiffened. "What makes you say that?"

"Because you smell like it."

Now she was scowling again – like she was embarrassed to be caught doing something other than studying.

I couldn't resist tweaking her. "If you need a light, let me know."

She blinked. "What?"

Obviously, she didn't get the joke. But hey, I had a prop to drive the point home. I reached into the pocket of my jeans and pulled my lighter. I flicked it to life and held out in front of her, old-school style, as if offering her a light.

She gave the flame an annoyed look. "In case you didn't notice, I don't actually *have* a cigarette." Under her breath, she added, "Or anything else, for that matter."

She looked so annoyed that I couldn't let it go. "So?"

"So I don't need a light."

"Eh, your loss." I flicked off the lighter and lowered it to my side.

Sounding less than amused, she said, "You *do* realize, I had to get special permission to use the lab today."

Yeah. Bummer for me.

If only the teacher had said no, I wouldn't be here at all.

Instead, I'd be dealing with the stuff at home, or maybe working at my side job, just like I had last Thursday, when everyone else had been sitting in school like good little boys and girls.

At the time, I'd figured it was no big deal. *I had a lab partner, right?* Arden never missed class, and she was a lot more vested in this than I was. But when Arden had informed me – not too nicely either – that she hadn't been allowed to do the experiment on her own, I'd felt almost guilty.

Now, thanks to her attitude, the guilt was fading fast. I said it again. "So?"

She sighed. "So let's just get it done already." She glanced toward the door of the lab. "And we need to be quick. I'm making cookies with my grandma at two-thirty."

Something inside me soured. *Cookies with grandma, huh?*

The image was way too sweet compared to the bitterness I'd left at home.

Arden and I – we ran in different circles – her with the smart kids and me with a crowd several times rougher. Still, we'd sat in plenty of the same classes during the last four years.

She never said much about her home life, but in that one statement, she told me more than I needed to know – more than I *wanted* to know.

Her life was soft, easy, and filled with sentimental bullshit. Cookies with grandma, home-baked casseroles, and a big, happy family – maybe a few aunts, some uncles, Christmas trees, Easter baskets, and other shit that I didn't know much about.

It was the kind of life I'd seen on TV, but never in person.

Still, it fit with Arden Weathers – with her prissy attitude and obsession with grades.

Now, I regretted coming in. "Sorry, I didn't know 'cookies' were on the line."

"Oh? So you've got something against cookies?"

"Me? Nah." At that moment, I almost hated her. She didn't know how good she had it. Probably she never would.

I replied, "Just people who make them."

"I hope you're talking about *me*," she bristled, "because if you mean my grandma—"

Cutting her off, I lifted the lighter to her face. Without bothering to flick it on, I asked, "You sure you don't need a light?"

She glared at the lighter and then at me. "Trust me. I'm sure."

Like a total dick, I flicked it on, anyway. The flame wasn't close, but she got the idea. I was tired of her bullshit, of her perfect life, and her talk of grandma's cookies.

Her mouth thinned as she eyed the small flame. With all the prissiness of a schoolmarm, she said, "You *know* that's not allowed, right?"

So what? I did a lot of things that weren't allowed. But hey, at least she'd stopped talking about the fucking cookies.

Forcing a laugh, I flicked off the lighter and lowered it to my side. My laugh sounded fake, just like it felt. "Relax," I scoffed, "I'm not gonna burn your cookies."

She stared at me like I'd just asked for a blow job in the hall. "I don't get it," she said. "If you were just gonna be a jackass, why'd you bother to show up?"

The answer to this was easy. "Because I told you I would." Hell, I might regret it, but I *had* promised. So here I was. *For all the good it was doing.*

She shook her head. "So?"

"So I always do what I say."

"Oh, really?" Her mouth tightened. "Do you always do it seventeen minutes late?"

"Better late than never."

She stared up at me, like I was puzzle she was trying to figure out. *I didn't like it.* And I especially didn't like it when she said, "Has it ever occurred to you that if you just applied yourself, you'd be getting all A's?"

Sure. I'd thought about it. But unlike Arden, with her life of Grandma's cookies and who-knows-what else, I had bigger problems. *And bigger plans, too.*

Those plans didn't include college.

But a girl like Arden Weathers – she'd never get it. So all I said was, "Has it ever occurred to *you* that it's none of your business?"

"But what about college?" she persisted.

"What about it?"

"Aren't you worried you won't get in?"

What a joke. "Hell no." *Me? Forget college.* At this rate, I'd be lucky to graduate from high school.

I was only taking the advanced courses at all because they offered more grade points than the others, which meant I could blow off more classwork and make it up on the tests.

I wasn't stupid. I just had other things on my mind – and no plans to spend money and time paying for a so-called education.

The only reason I remained in school at all was because my dick of an older brother promised to kick my ass if I flunked or dropped out.

He didn't scare me. By now, I was pretty sure I could take him. But there were no guarantees. And besides, graduation was only two months away.

I was almost done.

Arden sighed. "Fine." And with that, she pulled out the lab key and inserted it into the lock. As she did, she muttered, "Just try not to blow anything up, alright?"

She didn't get it. My whole life was a powder keg, just waiting for a spark. Looking to drive the point home, I gave the forbidden lighter a final flick.

As the flame lit, I caught a whiff of something new – a smell that sent the blood rushing from my face, even as a sickening flash of light exploded out of the room. I gave Arden a hard shove as the door flew off its hinges, sending both of us reeling backward.

I dove forward and tackled her to the floor.

Was she hurt?

Fuck. If she was, it was all my fault.

If anyone should be hurt it was me. At that moment, I would've welcomed death rather than hurting a girl who'd done nothing worse than annoy me.

Arden was good. Yeah, annoying as hell, but good at heart. She was nice, too. People would miss her. *But me? Not so much.*

As these thoughts slammed around in my head, Arden kicked underneath me, trying to buck me off.

I refused to budge.

I didn't know if she was on fire or just freaking out. The smell of burnt hair filled my nostrils, making my blood run cold as sweat – or hell, maybe blood – dripped down my back.

Arden gave me a wild push. "Get off me!"

I still didn't move. "Not yet."

With a string of curses, she shoved again. *And again. And again.* Everything was a hazy blur until a surprising truth hit home. *Holy shit, we were okay.*

Or, at least, I sure as hell hoped so. Finally I moved aside and watched as Arden slowly sat up. With a trembling hand, she reached up to touch her face. She let out a long unsteady breath and lifted her gaze to mine.

I was staring now.

I was so fucking relieved she was okay.

And, as far I could tell, I was okay, too. Still, the explosion – or whatever it was – had left its mark on the girl in front of me.

Her bangs were singed, and her eyebrows were mostly missing. Still, in that one terrible moment, her face was the most beautiful thing I'd ever seen, because by some miracle, I hadn't destroyed it.

Thank God.

Now, she was gasping like she was about to cry. *Hell, I wouldn't blame her.*

I wanted to gather her close and tell her that everything was okay, that she was alright, and that I'd never let anything hurt her again.

But I didn't. She wouldn't want it. And I'd done more than enough already.

She choked out, "How bad is it?"

I looked deep into her frantic eyes and told her the simple truth. "Not too bad. You're okay."

She frowned.

Once again, she reached up to touch her face. When her fingers brushed the spot where her eyebrows should've been, she gave a little gasp. Slowly, she peered up toward her hairline and froze.

She was seeing what I saw. Her bangs were a whole lot shorter and burnt on the ends.

She shook her head. And then, she looked to me. "You asshole!" Soon she was on me, like a cat on a mouse – except I was twice her size and several times stronger.

Still, I did nothing as she slapped, kicked, and cursed me up and down. By the time the janitors arrived to see what the hell had happened, I had a split lip and a bloody nose.

When they pulled her off me, I called out, "Don't!"

Still struggling in the janitor's arms, she demanded, "Don't what?"

I was lying on the ground where she'd tackled me. "I wasn't talking to you," I said. "I was talking to *him*." I meant the guy who was holding her back.

Ignoring him now, I looked up, meeting Arden's gaze. "If you want to kick me, go ahead."

By now, she was panting and crying. Through choked sobs, she said, "I don't want to *kick* you. I want to *kill* you."

I didn't blame her. Hell, I wanted to kill myself. And yet, I was surprised to discover I was happy to be alive.

Huh. How about that?

As far as Arden's words, I figured she was speaking metaphorically.

Turns out, I figured wrong.

CHAPTER 18

Arden – Present Day

On the phone, Cami gave a little squeal. "Oh, my God. You're kidding!"

Me, *I* wasn't squealing. I was *reeling*. In the privacy of the bedroom where I'd slept last night, I murmured, "No. I'm not, actually."

The offer for consulting services had arrived by email just ten minutes ago – barely twenty minutes after Landon Tarrington had disappeared into his limo.

Obviously, he had plenty of minions to do his paperwork, because nothing else could explain how he'd been able to send me a job offer in record time – and from the road, no less.

But that was something to ponder later. Now, I was too busy marveling at the offer itself.

According to the contract he'd sent for my electronic signature, I'd be paid seven thousand dollars a month for a period of four months, plus a twenty-thousand-dollar bonus at the end, after the project was fully completed.

It was the bonus that had sent me reeling.

Adding everything up, the total was an impressive sum. With a low whistle, I said the number out loud. "Forty-eight thousand dollars."

It was a lot more than I'd expected, especially for a gig that lasted only a few months. It even included room and board.

On the phone, Cami asked, "So why aren't you happy?"

"I *am* happy," I said. "I'm just surprised. That's all. I mean, there's got to be a catch, right?"

"Of course there is," she said. "There's *always* a catch. But with this, you already know what it is."

I frowned into the phone. "You mean Brody."

"Exactly!"

Oh yeah. She was right about *that*. But I was starting to think there was even more to this story. "You wanna know what I think?"

"What?"

I winced. "I think I'm the new Miss LaRue."

She laughed. "Oh stop it. You are not."

It was no joke. During the show's previous season, a new team member had appeared on the scene. Her name was Rebecca LaRue, and she was a high-end interior designer – mostly for rich and famous people, like movie stars and what-not.

Although the show featured several houses per season, Miss LaRue, as she preferred to be called, had helped with only one house – a vintage mansion in Beverly Hills, where her business was located.

Her taste had been decidedly upscale and even more impractical.

I almost smiled at the memory. The brothers had *not* been thrilled with any of her suggestions, and they hadn't bothered to hide it.

Still, it had made for some great television as "Miss LaRue" tried to convince all of them that kitchens without countertops were *"just the thing."*

Even now, I wasn't even sure what that meant. But this – along with a whole bunch of other insane ideas – had made for some great fireworks, with Brody in particular.

On the show's final episode of the season, Miss LaRue had quit in a huff, leaving a trail of bleeped-out profanity in her wake.

The episode had slaughtered the competition, ratings-wise, and had spawned a multitude of memes and parodies.

I heard myself say, "Landon – that producer guy – he thinks we're not gonna get along."

"Who? You and Miss LaRue?"

"No. Me and Brody. That's why Landon made the offer. He thinks we're gonna fight."

Cami snickered. "Either fight or donk."

Donk – I'd heard this word plenty of times over the last few years, and I knew exactly what it meant, to Cami, anyway.

"Trust me," I told her. "Brody and I are *not* going to donk." I didn't care that he had a hot body or that everyone else drooled over him. *I didn't like him.* And I didn't *want* him either.

Cami replied, "Yeah, but the producer doesn't know that. And really, when you think about it, he wins either way." She hesitated. "I mean the producer guy, not Brody."

At the mention of Brody's name, I bit my lip. As Cami went on to speculate on the producer's motives, I wandered to the nearby window and peeked out through the gaps in the blinds.

Brody was leaning against the door of his pickup, glowering as Waverly griped up a storm.

From here, I couldn't hear a single word, but the look on her face was clear enough. *She wasn't happy.*

It was easy to guess why. After Landon and his limo had disappeared down the street, she'd coldly informed me that if I took the job, *she'd* be my boss.

She'd said it like a threat – as if such a thing could scare me off. *Hah!*

I'd waitressed my way through college – in restaurants *and* in dive bars. It would take a lot more than a bad boss to scare me away.

It was a good thing, too, because just when I'd resigned myself to the idea of working under Waverly, Brody had coldly announced that *he'd* be my boss, *not* her.

As if that were an improvement.

The funny thing was, Waverly didn't even put up a fight. Instead, she'd simpered up at him like he was the juiciest morsel in her favorite steak house. And then, she'd apologized for the mistake. *To him. Not to me.*

But in the end, both of them were wrong.

According to my contract, assuming that I'd be signing it, I'd have no boss, not officially anyway. The contract had been *very* clear about that, along with its final clause. If I didn't make it to the end of the season, I'd receive no bonus whatsoever.

Oh, I'd make it, alright.

It wasn't just about the money. For years, I'd dreamed of fixing up the house. And I wanted it done right, not just the mechanics of it all, but the feel of the place, too.

And now, by some miracle, I'd been given a once-in-a-lifetime chance to help make that happen.

So, after I hung up with Cami, I did the only thing that made sense. I added my electronic signature to the contract and sent it on its merry way.

Brody or no Brody, there was no going back now.

CHAPTER 19

Arden

Barely two minutes after I accepted the offer, I heard the sounds of rummaging in the kitchen.

Funny, I hadn't heard anyone come in.

Still, I had a pretty good guess who it was. Deciding that I might as well face the music, I left the safety of the bedroom and padded in my socks toward the kitchen, where sure enough, I saw Brody reaching into the fridge.

Without turning to face me, he said in a tight voice, "Welcome aboard." The words said one thing, but his tone said something else entirely. As I watched, he grabbed a bottle of water and shut the fridge before turning around to face me.

When our gazes locked, I felt myself swallow. His eyes were dark, and his lips, normally so full, formed a thin, angry line.

Welcome?

Not hardly.

Still, I said what needed saying. "Um, thanks."

Without breaking eye-contact, he twisted the lid off the water and said, "I was joking."

Terrific. Now I felt stupid. "Yeah, well…" I stammered. "You're not laughing."

He lifted the bottle and took a long drink before saying with no trace of a smile, "I'm laughing on the inside."

"Yeah. Me, too."

At something in his eyes, I felt almost guilty for barging in where I wasn't wanted. But then I recalled the scene from last night, and any remorse went straight out the window.

I couldn't stop myself from saying, "And thanks for making me beg, by the way."

"You're welcome."

I did my best Brody impression. "I was joking."

"No shit."

"Why'd you do that, anyway?" At the memory of him making me kneel in the hallway, I felt like throttling him.

I'd *so* hated that. And now I hated it even more, because I'd come to realize something. *Brody would never do me a favor, even if I was begging.*

Cripes, probably I was just lucky he hadn't kicked me while I was down. And I meant that literally.

When his only reply was a tight shrug, I refused to let it go. "I'm just saying, you could've told me up front that you weren't planning to tear down the house."

"Yeah. But I didn't. So deal with it."

"Don't worry," I said. "I will."

His eyebrows lifted. "Do I look worried?"

Oh, please. He didn't look worried. He looked like every girl's fantasy. But that was hardly the point. I replied, "I don't know. *Are* you? Worried, I mean?"

"Me?" He made a sound that was almost a laugh. "Nah. This'll be fun."

The implication was obvious. *It would be fun for him. Not for me.*

Probably the script called for me to gather up my stuff and run for the hills. But that wasn't going to happen, no matter how unwelcome I felt.

I wasn't giving up. And besides, thanks to him, I had no place to go.

And even if I *did* have a home to return to, what would I do when I got there? *Obsess over the house, anyway? Watch on TV as Brody turned my grandparent's legacy into something godawful, purely out of spite? Or worse, cry later on when he pulled a major plot twist and demolished the house anyway?*

In my mind, I could almost see it.

Hello, Wrecking Ball.

Goodbye, any chance to reclaim the house.

But now, thanks to that surprising job offer, I wasn't without *some* degree of influence. Plus, the truth was, I needed the money more than I cared to admit.

So I stiffened my spine and told Brody flat-out, "If you think you can run me off, forget it."

"Me?" He offered up a cold smile. "I wouldn't dream of it."

God, I hated this – the tension, the anger, the pressure building between us. Desperate to release at least some of it, I tried for a joke. With a nervous laugh, I said, "You *do* realize, if I *happened* to 'slip' off the roof or something, you'd get some super-bad publicity."

His expression only darkened. "Let's get one thing straight," he said. "You're not getting anywhere near that roof."

Oh, for crying out loud. "I was joking."

"It's no joke," he said. "I don't need some amateur messing this up."

"Oh come on. I just meant—"

"I *know* what you meant." A new edge crept in to his voice. "And let me tell you something. Even though *I* wouldn't toss you off – since I'd be stuck cleaning up the mess – I can't say the same for my brothers."

At the implied threat, I felt the blood drain from my face. "What?"

"You heard me," he said. "Now, you want some advice?"

"From you? Not really."

"Stay out of their way," he said. "And mine, too, while you're at it."

I made a sound of frustration. "I already told you, I was joking."

But in front of me, Brody looked like he wouldn't know a joke if it hit him in the face with a hammer.

Still, I tried again. "And *you* were joking, too." I hesitated. "Right? I mean, your brothers wouldn't seriously toss me off the roof or anything." I felt myself swallow. "Would they?"

"Think what you want," he said. "We start tomorrow at eight." His gaze raked the length of me before he said, "And wear a jacket or something, will you?"

I frowned. "What?"

His gaze settled rudely on my chest. "Unless you *want* to put on a show."

I looked down and immediately saw what he meant. My pale-yellow T-shirt was still damp, and my bra wasn't nearly thick enough to hide the fact that my nipples were embarrassingly erect.

Well, this wasn't humiliating or anything.

But it wasn't my fault.

Earlier I'd been hot. Now I was cold. And, so were my nipples, apparently. Or maybe – and this was the worst part – they were responding to Brody on some primitive level.

The little traitors.

Now, my mortification was complete.

Still, whether Brody meant to or not, he'd done me a favor by reminding me that I'd need to be more careful in my attire – unless I *wanted* to flash my goodies to millions of strangers.

And to him.

The jackass.

But I hadn't meant to flash anyone, especially someone who was making it his personal mission to humiliate me. *Seriously, even when he was giving me a heads-up, did he have to be so rude about it?*

But this *was* Brody Blastoviak, so yes, apparently, he did.

And already, he was turning away.

I called out, "Wait!"

He turned back and eyed me with a distinct lack of enthusiasm. "For what?"

"A question." I cleared my throat. "The job offer – it included room and board. Do you know anything about that? Like where I'll be staying?"

He glanced down, taking in my stocking-clad feet. "Seems to me you already know."

My face flushed with renewed embarrassment. *Great.* Now like I felt like an oaf for removing my shoes. But I'd had a good reason. Stiffly, I informed him, "My shoes were messy."

"So?"

"So I didn't want to track grass through the house. It *is* your house, right?"

Without bothering to reply, he said, "Are we done?"

"No. You never answered my question."

"Which was…?"

"Where I'm staying. Is it here? In the crew house? That *is* what Waverly called it, right?"

"You could say that."

I wasn't even sure which part of my question he was replying to, but it was pretty obvious that my hunch was correct. "So…do you know who else is staying here?"

He looked at me for a long cold moment. And then, his lips formed a tight imitation of a smile. "Waverly."

My stomach sank. "What?"

I'd feared as much. Still, the confirmation felt like a kick to the gut. Even so, I reminded myself that it could always be worse. Sure, Waverly obviously hated me, but somehow, I'd make it work.

And besides, it wasn't like I'd be living with a whole group of people who hated me.

The thought had barely crossed my mind when a wicked gleam appeared in Brody's eyes. Almost as an afterthought, he added, "And me."

CHAPTER 20

Brody

Chase was laughing his ass off. "No fucking way. Have you told Waverly?"

It had been only ten minutes since I'd walked into my brother's condo. He'd spent nine of those minutes laughing – at *me*.

Hell, I might've laughed too, if only *I* weren't the one in the hot seat.

We were standing out on his main balcony overlooking the river. An hour had passed since I'd left Arden at the crew house, and I was still royally ticked – mostly at myself for letting Arden get under my skin.

In reply to Chase's question, I said, "Oh yeah. I told her." In fact, I'd called Waverly on my cell just as I'd pulled up to the place I called home – a waterfront development that contained a dozen upscale condos, including mine and Chase's.

This made us brothers *and* neighbors, which worked out better than you'd think.

Chase grinned. "I bet she loved *that*."

Waverly? She had, actually – but only after she'd learned that I'd be staying at the crew house, too. This begged a serious question. *What the hell had I gotten myself into?*

Under normal circumstances, Waverly and I would be staying in separate hotel suites while the camera crew stayed in a rental somewhere near the job site.

But this project was local, which meant that I'd been planning to stay at my own place, just a short walk away from where I was standing right now.

But instead, I'd be shacking up with Arden Weathers, and Waverly, too, while I was at it. *Obviously, I'd lost my fucking mind.*

And now Chase was laughing again. "So, what are you gonna do? Sleep in a big ol' pile?"

I gave him a look. "I already told you, it's got three bedrooms."

"You didn't need to tell *me*," he said. "I saw the place. Remember?"

Had he? Shit, the last few months had been so packed, I couldn't recall much of anything. When my only reply was a loose shrug, he suggested, "Or maybe you could take turns."

I wasn't following. "What?"

"You know," he said with a laugh. "Waverly one night, Arden the next."

Nope. Not a chance. There's this saying – *Never stick your dick in crazy.* It was a good rule. And unlike Chase, I followed it easy enough. Crazy chicks weren't my thing, which ruled out *both* of my new roommates.

I gave Chase a stiff smile. "If you want to trade places, let me know."

At this, he paused as if actually considering the idea.

I wasn't buying it.

We both knew that he wouldn't be going anywhere near the crew house, not unless we were filming. He had responsibilities of his own – duties that didn't involve supervising construction projects, here or anywhere else.

Chase was the face of our company.

He was the one who shook hands and smiled for the cameras. He wasn't a politician, but he was good at dealing with people – government officials, suppliers, and the public in general.

He dressed sharp, talked smart, and made people feel like they really knew him, whether it was true or not.

He had a real knack for marketing, too, which is how we'd gotten the show in the first place. Chase had made it happen. *And me?* I was making it work.

Unlike my brother, I was the one who got dirty, who inspected the houses and ran the crews. It was the way I liked it, and I didn't need Chase or anyone else honing in on my turf.

But I wasn't worried. Even though I'd offered to trade places, we both knew that Chase wouldn't consider trading any more than I would. He was juggling projects of his own, along with enough crazy chicks to fill an asylum.

With a laugh, he said, "You think I won't."

I made a show of eyeing his hands. *No callouses. No scars. No raw knuckles from the occasional mishap.* Still, I had to admit, the guy could swing a hammer with the best of them.

When I made no reply, he said, "Eh, forget it. I'm too pretty for construction."

Pretty? It's not how I would've put it. Like myself, the guy was six-foot two and packed with muscle. But I knew what he meant. If he ever decided to give up on the business, he could make a decent fortune modeling underwear.

I wasn't kidding. He'd been offered such a gig already. Then again, I had, too. We *all* had, even Mason, who had all the charm of a hitman heading to the gallows.

And speaking of gallows, I recalled my murderous new roommate. "Get this," I said. "Arden warned me that if I tossed her off the roof, the show would suffer." I made a scoffing sound. "Like I'd try to kill her."

Of everything she'd said, *this* was the thing that had set me off. *I didn't like her.* But she wasn't worth killing. And more to the point, I took my responsibilities seriously.

The film crew, the carpenters, the plumbers – everyone under me was as safe as I could make them. And whether I liked it or not, this now included Arden Weathers.

She wouldn't be getting hurt. *Not if I could help it.*

Chase said, "It might not be *too* bad."

I wasn't following. "What?"

"The roof thing." His tone grew speculative. "Let's say she 'fell off', but landed in a dumpster filled with insulation. The audience – man, they'd eat that shit up." He gave a half-shrug. "Assuming she survived."

From the look on his face, he wasn't kidding.

It was a good reminder that his easy persona was skin deep at best. I replied, "Well, there *is* that."

He reached up to stroke his chin. "And think of the cliffhanger," he continued. "She goes over, and we're like, 'Tune in next week to see if she makes it.'"

And here I thought I was cold.

I crossed my arms and waited for him to finish.

At something in my expression, he said, "Hey, don't give me that look. If I were Mason, I'd just toss her off and be done with it."

He wasn't joking.

And when I nodded in agreement, neither was I.

There was only one person who hated Arden Weathers more than I did, and that person was my oldest brother, who'd taken a strong personal interest in the torching of my truck.

I told Chase, "Forget it. She's not getting anywhere near the roof."

And if I played my cards right, she wouldn't be getting anywhere near the actual work either.

After last season's fiasco with that dumb-ass interior designer – "Miss LaRue" or whatever she wanted to be called – I'd had more than enough crap from people who didn't know what they were doing.

Chase said, "Don't look so glum. There's still time to back out."

"Of what?"

"The living situation," he said. "Tell Arden you were kidding or that you changed your mind. Or hell, don't tell her anything. Just stay the fuck away. She'll figure it out."

"And let Arden off the hook?" I said. "Forget it."

Maybe a smarter guy would've taken Chase's advice. But I wasn't feeling smart. And backing out now would be all too easy.

For her.

Not me.

And besides, I reminded myself, I was juggling several other projects across the country, which meant that I'd be doing my share of travel – without Arden Weathers.

Good thing, too.

Every time she opened that sweet mouth of hers, something sharp came out to sour my mood – like that thing about tossing her off the roof.

She might not know it, but I ran the safest job sites of anyone I knew. And yeah, maybe Chase or Mason might want to send her flying, but they wouldn't act on it, not while I was around.

And why?

It was because I didn't need the hassle. Or the mess.

And shit, like I'd let a rookie anywhere near the roof.

The way I saw it, Arden had one job – to look pretty for the cameras so Landon Tarrington got his money's worth.

But when the cameras *weren't* rolling, she could sit at the crew house and mind her own damn business.

It was a nice thought. But Arden, as usual, had ideas of her own.

CHAPTER 21

Arden

I woke long before dawn, wondering if I'd slept at all. Today would be my first day as a consultant, and I was stupidly nervous.

In spite of Brody's claim that he and Waverly would be staying at the crew house, I'd spent last night alone, with no sign of either one of them.

This should've been a good thing. And it was. But waiting for them to show up at any moment had done a real number on my nerves.

Even now, hours later, the pizza I'd had delivered for last night's dinner wasn't sitting so great. But I wasn't going to let *that* stop me, so I scrambled out of bed, showered, and dressed in clothes that were decidedly not sexy.

Soon, I was officially ready – and with nearly two hours to spare. *Now what?*

With sudden inspiration, I decided to take a detailed walk through the house – meaning the one we were fixing up – and gather my thoughts before Brody's arrival.

If I used the time wisely, I figured, I could be smart *and* prepared. And just maybe, I wouldn't make a giant fool of myself while the cameras were rolling.

There was only one problem. When I walked out the front door of the crew house, I spotted a familiar black pickup in the driveway across the street.

It was Brody's.

I felt my brow wrinkle in confusion. He'd told me that we started at eight, but it was barely six-thirty.

Crap.

But hey, if we were going to be working together, I couldn't avoid him forever, so I threw back my shoulders and marched across the street, anyway.

When I found the front door unlocked, I walked inside and called out, "Hello?"

No response.

But I *did* hear activity upstairs – the sounds of footsteps and a few thuds, like someone was moving supplies or equipment.

Following the noise, I headed up the front stairway. When I reached the top, I spotted Brody in the upstairs hall. His back was turned, and he was wearing his usual outfit – jeans and a T-shirt.

He was yanking at a green garden hose that snaked from the middle of the hallway and disappeared into the bathroom – the one where he'd caught me showering just a couple of nights ago.

Several feet to his left, I saw a bucket filled with rags and a large funnel lying on its side.

Forcing a smile, I tried again. "Good Morning."

Without turning to look, he said, "What are you doing here?"

Wasn't it obvious? "I work here. Today's my first day. Remember?"

Finally, he turned to face me. With a look that was anything but welcoming, he lifted his wrist and studied his watch – a big, black thing that looked like it could take a sledgehammer and keep on ticking.

Without returning my hello, he said, "You're early." He said it like it was a *bad* thing.

"I know." I lifted my chin. "I wanted to take a look around."

"And you didn't do that already?"

I stiffened. I knew exactly what he was getting at. "If you mean the other night, sure I looked around, but with not with an eye toward remodeling."

He gave me a dubious look. "Uh-huh."

"And," I continued, "after you listed all of those problems, I figured I should look again, and maybe see if I have any ideas."

He eyed me with zero enthusiasm. "About what?"

"You know, like what to do with the house."

His jaw clenched. "Right."

I sighed. "Look, if we're going to be working together, don't you think it would be better if we got along?"

"Not for me."

"What do you mean?" I asked.

"I mean, I don't care what you do," he said. "Just stay out of my way." And with that, he returned his attention to the nearest garden hose. He gave it a hard yank, and the hose's other end flew out of the bathroom.

Watching this, it suddenly dawned on me that the hoses and other stuff hadn't been here the other night, when rainwater had been pouring down into the hallway.

In fact, when Brody had hustled me away from the disaster zone, water had *still* been trickling down onto the wooden floor.

But sometime since then, he'd rigged up a system to minimize further water-damage.

I asked, "When did you do that?"

As he coiled up the hose, he replied, "Do what?"

"The hoses and everything. The other night, it was still raining in here when we left."

"So?"

"So..." I tried to think. "Did you come back? I mean, after you took me to the house across the street?"

He didn't pause in his work. "I might've."

I frowned. "But it was so late."

"So?" he said again.

My gaze drifted to the bucket of rags. "Did you wipe up the water, too?"

"Well, I wasn't gonna let it just sit there."

For a long awful moment, I surveyed the scene in front of me – the hoses, the rags, and the guy who'd been using them. *Just how long had all of this taken?*

Minutes?

Or hours?

Either way, I felt like some sort of slacker. "You should've had me help you. I mean, I was right here."

At this, he stopped working and gave me a hard look. "Yeah. And you weren't supposed to be."

As if I needed the reminder. "Well maybe I didn't know that."

"Sure you did."

"Not for certain," I said. "The last *I* knew, my cousin lived here. And I was supposed to meet him."

"Uh-huh."

Obviously, Brody still didn't believe me. But I continued anyway. "So like I already explained, it's not like I was squatting or anything."

With a sarcastic smile, he said, "Sure, I believe you."

"Yeah, well you should," I told him. "So who owns the house now?"

"Me. Like I said."

"You personally?"

In a tight voice, he replied, "As opposed to what?"

"Well…" I said, thinking out loud. "If the house is going to be featured on the show, I'm thinking that *maybe* the network owns it. Or your tool company. Or an investor."

"Yeah," he said. "And the investor's me."

I bit my lip. This *wasn't* what I wanted to hear. "You *personally?*"

"What, you wanna see the deed?"

It was the same thing he'd offered the other night. I didn't need the deed. What I needed was the truth. "I just want to know."

He crossed his arms, making his biceps bulge like they always did. "Why?"

"Well…" Again, I hesitated. "Maybe I'm wondering if I'll have the chance to buy it. You know, when it's done."

"Forget it," he laughed.

But I wasn't laughing. "Why?"

"Because you can't afford it."

My cheeks warmed at the bluntness of his statement, even more so because it was true. "Well, maybe I can't afford it *now*," I admitted. "But after the bonus—"

"It'll still be out of your range."

Damn it. Probably he was right. The house was huge, historic, and located directly on the beach. Plus, it was being fixed up as part of a famous TV show. The publicity *wouldn't* make it any cheaper.

Still, I refused to let it go. "But I'd have a down payment."

"Doesn't matter," he said. "The owner's not selling."

"You mean you?"

"That's what I said, isn't it?"

Just then, I heard the muffled sounds of car doors slamming in the driveway. This was quickly followed by the sounds of voices – male *and* female.

Brody cursed under his breath.

"What's wrong?" I asked.

"Do me a favor," he said. "Go stall 'em, will ya?"

"Why?"

"Just do it, alright?" Without waiting for my reply, he began coiling up the next hose. When I made no move, he said, "Or if you want, *I'll* stall them. And *you* hide this stuff."

Hide it? Seriously? "But wait. Why would anyone need to—"

"Just stall them," he said. "And I'll tell you later."

"You promise?"

"I'll tell you *one* thing," he said. "I won't tell you jack if they get in here before I'm done."

This was all the encouragement I needed. Without further protest, I turned and scrambled toward the stairway, giving Brody one final glance before my feet carried me out of sight. The last I saw of him, he had two hoses coiled over his shoulder and was reaching for the bucket of rags.

By the time I reached the front door, it was just swinging inward. I stopped it with my foot and practically leapt into the narrow opening.

On the front porch, the new arrivals drew back, as if startled by my sudden appearance. The group consisted of Waverly, along with Roy and two other guys who looked to be somewhere in their mid-thirties. Like Roy, the guys were dressed casually in jeans and work shirts. As for Waverly, she wore a sleek navy dress with matching high heels.

I poked my head further out of the doorway and plastered on a giant smile. "Oh, hi. So, how's it going?"

It was Waverly who answered, "Shitty. Now get out of my way."

Well that was pleasant.

Still, I put on my concerned face. "Oh, no. Is something wrong?"

It was Roy who answered. "Nothing *too* bad. They messed up her coffee order."

Waverly whirled to face him. "Not too bad? Seriously?" Through gritted teeth, she warned him, "You *don't* know what I'm like without coffee."

Looking surprisingly unterrified, Roy replied, "Actually, I'm pretty sure I do." Behind him, the other two guys nodded in solemn agreement.

I chimed in, "Wow, that sounds *really* awful." Hoping to keep the conversation going, I asked, "So, um, who messed it up?"

Waverly's eyes narrowed as she turned to face me. "Are you mocking me?" she said.

"Me? No." Shockingly, this was actually true, even if I *did* think her distress was totally mock-worthy. But then, a moment later, I heard myself say, "So, who did this atrocity?"

Okay, so maybe I was mocking her *now*, but how could I help it?

Waverly sighed. "The yokel who works there, that's who. Now where's Brody?"

I tried not to snicker. "Really? There was a yokel?" I lowered my voice. "Tell me, did you report him to the authorities?"

"I tried," she huffed. "Turns out he owns the place."

"Wow," I said. "How terrible."

"Yeah. Tell me about it." As she spoke, she took a single step forward, as if expecting me to throw open the door and step aside. And when I didn't, she stopped short and eyed me with open hostility. "You're *not* moving."

I gave a few stupid blinks. "I'm not? Are you sure?"

Her jaw clenched. "I can see you."

"That's funny," I said. "I can see you, too."

"Oh, for God's sake." Waverly turned to Roy and said, "Move her out of the way, will ya?"

Roy looked from Waverly to me and back again before telling her, "I'm pretty sure that's not in my contract."

"Fine," she snapped. "*I'll* do it."

But just as she started to move forward again, a familiar male voice from somewhere beyond the porch asked, "Is there a problem?"

In unison, we all turned to look. As we did, Brody sauntered into view, as if he had all the time in the world.

I smiled in relief. Obviously, he'd slipped out the back while I'd been guarding the front.

At the sight of him, Waverly said, "There you are!"

"Yeah," he said. "So what's the problem?"

Waverly jerked her thumb vaguely over her shoulder and said, "She won't let us in."

Brody gave a loose shrug. "Yeah, well. It's hard to find good help, you know?"

Hearing this, I didn't know whether to laugh or throttle him. And besides, by now I'd *already* pulled open the door nice and wide – not that Waverly seemed to notice.

And why? It was because she was giving Brody that look again, like he was the tallest, tastiest cup of coffee ever.

I spoke up. "If you wanted to come in, you should've said so."

At this, I swear Roy snickered, even if he *did* cover it up with a cough. As for Waverly, she ignored me completely as she turned away and hustled off the porch to join Brody on the front walkway.

With a flirty smile, she leaned toward him and asked, "So, where were you?"

"Here," he said. "Where were you?"

"I was *trying* to get inside." Her tone grew breathless as she said, "Did you know it rained the other night?"

"Yeah, so?"

Her smile widened. "I'm betting we've got *major* damage." She said this like it was a good thing.

But Brody wasn't smiling. "You think?"

"Sure," she said. "I heard it rained like *four* inches." Sounding nearly orgasmic, she breathed, "Just think of the 'before' footage. If the ceiling caved in, we're gold, baby."

Baby?

Good grief.

I spoke up. "If you were so excited about the rain, why didn't you look inside yesterday?"

It was a valid question. Yesterday, she'd shown up at this very house, only to spend all of her time griping about the lawn. To the best of my knowledge, she hadn't even bothered to open the front door.

With a sound of annoyance, she turned to face me. "Because I didn't *know* it rained until I saw last night's news coverage." Under her breath she added, "And besides, I didn't have a key."

I said, "But that didn't stop you today."

Her mouth tightened. "What do you mean?"

"I mean, just now, you opened the door without one."

"Right, because *today* it was unlocked." She threw up her hands. "And why am I explaining myself to *you*?" She turned to Brody. "Did you know it was unlocked?"

"Yeah," he said. "Because I unlocked it."

"Oh." She perked up. "So? Was there rain damage?"

He gave a half-shrug. "Some."

With obvious disappointment, she said, "Just some?"

"Well, it's not like the ceiling caved in," he said.

She was frowning now. "Oh."

Brody glanced toward the house. "But we've got major damage on the third floor."

At this, she brightened considerably. "Really?"

"Yeah. The way it looks, the damage has been there a while."

"Thank God," she breathed. Turning to Roy, she said, "Go ahead and start setting up. Remember, we've got only two days to get the 'before' footage."

I asked, "What happens in two days?"

"Isn't it obvious?" she said, turning once again to beam at Brody. "*We* get straight to work."

CHAPTER 22

Brody

We. There was that word again. I gave Waverly a long, penetrating look. "So, you're gonna help?"

The question made her pause. "Excuse me?"

"You said we'd get straight to work. You mean fixing the house?"

She smiled. "Right."

I didn't smile back. "So, what are *you* gonna do?"

"Me?" she said. "I was thinking I'd help supervise."

It was time to set her straight. "Nope."

Her smile faltered. "What?"

"That's not gonna happen."

With a shaky laugh, she said, "Well, I mean I know that you're in charge of the actual work, but it's all a team effort, right?"

Normally, I might see it that way. But I'd come across Waverly's type before. She was the kind of person who'd never get her hands dirty, but would gunk up the gears for everyone else.

I told her, "You deal with your crew. I'll deal with mine."

She frowned. "You mean the film crew?"

"That *is* your crew, isn't it?"

"But what about everyone else?" she said. "Like plumbers and…" She made a vague waving motion with her hand. "…other construction people?"

"They're part of *my* crew," I said. "And I'm telling you up front, they take orders from me. Not you. Got it?"

Her fade reddened, and she lowered her voice. "Surely, you don't think I'd cause trouble? I mean, you and I – we…" Her words trailed off, and she glanced toward the front porch, where the others stood watching us.

Waverly barked out, "Hey! What are *you* looking at?"

None of them answered.

But hey, *I* had something worth saying. "And *that's* why you're not in charge."

Waverly whirled to face me. "What do you mean?"

"I mean, I won't have you barking at my crews."

"What?" she sputtered. "Like a dog?"

A female dog, maybe. But I wasn't into name-calling, so all I said was, "Just stay in your own lane, and we'll be fine."

Her lips pursed. "We'll see about that." With a huff, she turned and stalked toward the familiar white SUV.

I watched with only mild interest as she yanked open the passenger's side door, pulled out her cell phone, and climbed into the passenger's seat, slamming the door shut behind her.

The sounds of muffled yelling quickly followed.

I didn't know who she was calling, but I wasn't worried. She was replaceable. I wasn't. And we were killing it in the ratings.

I was on firm ground, and the last thing I needed was an uptight rookie acting like she was in charge. It was the kind of thing that led to mistakes, or worse, accidents.

That *wasn't* going to happen. Not on my job.

And already I had more than enough trouble with Arden Weathers, who was proving to be more persistent than I'd expected.

Still, I had to give her credit. She'd done a decent job of stalling the film crew while I finished up with the hoses. And she'd kept her mouth shut, too.

I glanced toward the house. Sometime within the last minute, the film crew had disappeared inside. But Arden, she'd moved away from the front door, and was now standing alone on the edge of the porch.

Her jeans were loose, and her shirt was nothing special – a basic blue pullover, thick enough to be decent regardless of what she was doing.

Still, I could see the rising and falling of her chest and the tilt of her chin as she eyed me with a look that I'd never seen – or at least, not on Arden, and never directed at me.

As our eyes met, I had to ask myself, *"What was she thinking?"*

CHAPTER 23

Arden

He was magnificent. It was true that I didn't like him, but I had to respect the way he'd handled the situation with Waverly.

My grandpa had been a tin-knocker. In construction, those were the guys who ran the heating and cooling ducts from one end of the house to the other, with lots of places in-between.

Bending sheet metal – it wasn't an easy job, and his hands – even long after he'd retired – had retained plenty of scars to prove it.

And the stories he'd told – about bad bosses, unsafe conditions, and people who lost their cookies when things didn't go their way.

All of those twisted tales had been enough for me to know that Waverly would be the worst kind of person to have in charge of anything that involved power tools.

But Brody? He was turning out to be something different than I'd expected. When he turned to look in my direction, I should've looked away. But it felt cowardly to be caught staring and not own up to it.

So I gave him a little wave and an unsteady smile. His eyebrows furrowed for a long moment as we stared across the distance. But then, he did something that I never would've expected.

He actually smiled back.

It wasn't a big smile, but something about it sent my traitorous heart fluttering to dangerous new levels.

And now, I was embarrassed.

To cover my sudden discomfort, I mouthed, "You owe me." And then, fearful of making a fool of myself, I turned away and headed back into the house.

Supposedly, I started work at eight. A quick glance at my cell phone told me that it was just past seven, which meant that I still had nearly an hour of free time before I'd be needed for whatever.

I decided to spend that time as I'd originally planned – going through the house to see for myself just how bad everything truly was.

As I traveled from room to room, I occasionally crossed paths with the guys from the film crew, who were busy setting up big standalone lights powered by lots of extension cords.

In passing, I learned that the two new guys were named Mitch and Jerry. Mitch was a sound technician, and Jerry was a backup cameraman and general gopher – or at least, that's how he described himself. Unlike Waverly, they both seemed pretty nice.

As far as Waverly herself, I saw no sign of her – not that I was complaining.

Still, as I wandered through the house, I saw plenty of things to concern me – scuffed floors, cracks in the plaster, and water stains around several windows. As far as things that needed fixing, the more I looked, the more I saw.

But it wasn't until I ventured up to the third floor – a big converted attic – that I saw the worst of it.

It was bad. *Really bad.*

From floor to ceiling, it looked like a disaster zone, with gaping holes in the slanted ceiling and dark water-stains running down the walls.

My stomach sank. *Was this even fixable?*

As I stood on the top step of the secluded stairway, I silently surveyed the damage. It was then that I spotted Brody standing near the rear window – the one that overlooked the beach and endless waters beyond.

His back was turned, and his silhouette looked *very* fine, especially in contrast with the destruction all around him. His waist was narrow, and his shoulders were broad. His jeans fit to perfection, showing off long legs and a tight ass. Even his work boots made him look sexy.

How was that even possible?

With a pang, I decided that Brody was the only beautiful thing in the whole attic. Everything else literally hurt to look at. *But looking at Brody?* Well, it made me feel *something*, but it wasn't pain.

So was it any wonder that I couldn't stop staring?

I was still staring when he turned to face me. When he saw me standing on the top step, he frowned across the distance. "So you came to collect, huh?"

"On what?" And then it hit me. "Oh. You mean about the hoses." I cleared the top step and began moving toward him. "Now that you mention it, you *did* promise to tell me."

He held up a hand. "Don't."

I stopped in mid-step. "Don't what?"

"Don't come any closer."

Now, *I* was the one frowning. *What did he think? That I'd come to molest him or something?*

Talk about arrogant.

I mean, sure, he looked entirely molestable, but he wasn't my type, and his attitude grated.

I was just about to set him straight when he pointed to the vast expanse of floor between us. "Rotten floorboards."

"Oh." *Great. Now I felt stupid again.* With an awkward laugh, I said, "So that's all?"

But Brody wasn't laughing. "Hey, it's enough. Trust me, you don't want to fall through."

He was right about that. Still, I had to ask, "But aren't *you* worried?"

"Me? Nah. I know where to step." And then, as if to prove his point, he strode toward me, sidestepping several areas along his path.

When he finally reached me, he did the strangest thing. He held out his hand as if offering a handshake.

I glanced down. *What was this? A truce?*

To my surprise, I discovered that I was willing to go along if he was. So, with a decisive nod, I reached out and shook his hand with

enough gusto to prove that I wasn't afraid to set our differences aside –
at least for now, while we worked toward a common goal.

I was still shaking it when Brody laughed.

I paused in mid-shake. "What's so funny?"

"You." He glanced down at our hands, still joined. "I was gonna
guide you to the window."

"Oh." My face burned with new embarrassment. And yet, for
some reason, I was still holding onto his hand. And *he* was still holding
onto mine.

His hand felt big and warm, and so very strong, even if his touch
was surprisingly gentle. Suddenly, I was finding it just a little hard to
breathe.

Why *was* that?

Maybe it was the attic. I glanced around. *Probably we had a mold problem.*
Yeah. Spores – that had to be it.

When I looked back to Brody, his lips twitched as he said, "Unless
you want me to carry you?"

My breath caught. *Actually, I'd love to be carried by him.*
What?

No, I reminded myself. *Not him.* But someone *like* him. Or rather,
someone who *looked* like him, and maybe *acted* like him just a little, but
didn't have all the baggage between us.

And yet, to my infinite annoyance, I was still finding it hard to
breathe. I gave the attic another wary glance before asking, "Do you
think we have a mold problem?"

"Probably."

I breathed a sigh of relief. "Thank God."

Brody's hand flexed around mine. "What?"

"I just mean, it's good to know." Determined to break the spell, I
gave my hand a light tug, which proved to be totally useless. *Brody*
wasn't letting go.

I gave our joined hands another quick glance. "You don't have to hang on," I said. "I'll just um, follow you to the window, and walk where you walk."

He didn't budge. "Forget it."

"Why?"

"Because, if you misstep," he said, "you'll want someone hanging on."

"But aren't you worried *you'll* misstep?"

"Hasn't happened yet," he said, giving my hand a gentle tug toward the window, where he'd been standing, looking oh-so fine, earlier. "Now come on," he said. "There's something I want you to see."

His ass?

I gave a little gasp. *Shit.* Where had *that* thought come from?

Brody paused in mid-tug. "What's wrong?"

"Nothing." I cleared my throat. "Probably just the spores." I summoned up a little cough, followed by an awkward smile. "Anyway…" I said, putting some extra pep into my voice, *"Lead on, Macduff."*

It was an old joke.

In high school, Brody and I had taken advanced English together. This included a month of Shakespeare – primarily Macbeth. The line was *supposed* to be, *"Lay on, Macduff,"* as our English teacher had reminded us repeatedly while ranting about how often it was misquoted.

As far as the play itself, I'd hated it, mostly because nearly everyone died by the end. *But Brody? He'd loved it.* I could tell. He'd been sitting across from me, and I'd seen with my own eyes how the story had captured his imagination – well, on the days he actually attended class, that is.

Now, as he began leading me toward the window, he replied, "Sure thing, *Clara.*"

At the sound of that name on his lips, my steps faltered.

Brody's grip tightened, and he turned to look. "You okay?"

I was fine, just irritated, that's all.

In high school, he'd called me that name at least fifty times, and *not* in a good way. This would've been merely annoying if only he hadn't begun that whole "Clara" thing by trying to ruin my grade in English.

Now, years later, he was mocking me *again*, just like he had back in high school.

It was a good reminder that he'd never liked me, and probably never would. And if I were smart, I'd return the favor.

CHAPTER 24
Brody

Too late I recalled the full history of that name – *Clara Cooper.*

During our junior year of high school, Arden and I had the bad luck to be seated next to each other in advanced English.

The seats had been chosen by the teacher, not us, which is how Arden Weathers had found herself stuck in the back row, next to someone like me who preferred to fly under the radar.

But not Arden. No. She liked to sit up front, where the teachers could see when she raised her hand for brownie points or extra credit.

Now in the attic, her hand stiffened in mine as she gave me the same disgruntled look she'd given me back in high school after we'd graded each other's fiction-writing projects.

I said, "Aw come on. You're not still pissed about that, are you?"

From the look on her face, she clearly was. "You tried to flunk me."

"A D-minus?" I scoffed. "That's not flunking. Trust me, I know."

"Yeah, I'm sure you *do* know," she said, "because you never bothered to try."

"I didn't have to," I said. "You 'tried' enough for both of us."

"Well *someone* had to," she said. "And I didn't give *you* a D-minus."

She'd given me a C-plus, which, yeah, was probably more generous than I'd deserved.

The assignment had been to write a fictional story starring a character like ourselves. Me? I'd scribbled out two pages of bullshit, starring a space alien who devoured the world.

But Arden? She'd typed up ten, maybe fifteen pages of lollypops and gumdrops. *Not even kidding.* Her main character, Clara Cooper, had lived above a candy store, where all the neighborhood kids had come daily to get wise advice from Clara's doting parents.

The whole thing had made me sick.

I said, "Better a D than an F."

"A D-*minus*," she corrected.

With my free hand, I reached up to rub the back of my neck. At the time, I'd thought the minus was a nice touch. Now, I had to admit, it was a dick move. But hell if I'd admit it to *her* when she was hassling me over something that happened seven years ago.

And besides, the teacher had the final say, so it's not like the D-minus would've stuck, especially to a teacher's pet like Arden Weathers.

I told her, "Yeah, well, maybe your story had too many gumdrops."

She glared up at me. "It was relevant to the story. They *did* own a candy store. Remember?"

Hell yeah, I remembered. And I *also* remembered the story's mom baking homemade casseroles and the dad asking about homework while taking her out for ice cream – as if a fucking candy store weren't enough.

Like I said, sickening.

In the attic, Arden gave her hand a hard yank. When I refused to let go, she made a sound of annoyance. "That's how you knew it was me in the shower, wasn't it?"

At the thought of Arden in the shower, my brain went fuzzy. "What?"

"When you asked for my name," she said, "I gave you that stupid character name from my story."

"At least we agree on *that.*"

"On what?"

"The name Clara."

Through gritted teeth, she informed me, "That was my grandmother's name."

"Hey, don't blame *me*," I said. "You're the one who called it stupid."

"Yeah, well, I meant it differently."

"Good for you."

At this, she gave her hand the hardest yank yet. "Will you *please* let go."

"Yeah," I said. "When we reach the stairs." Still gripping her hand, I turned and made a move toward the stairway.

Arden didn't budge as she announced, "I can make it on my own."

I stopped and turned to look at her. "Maybe. Maybe not. But I'm not taking that chance."

"Why?" Her tone grew sarcastic. "Because you're such a nice guy?"

"No. Because if you fall through, it'll be my ass on the line."

"Oh, for crying out loud," she said. "Will you *please* stop talking about your ass."

Huh? I didn't recall mentioning my ass at all. "What?"

Now she was blushing. "Nothing."

"It was *something*," I said.

"Well…" she stammered. "I guess…speaking of your ass…" Her words trailed into silence, and she glanced around, as if looking for an escape.

"*I* wasn't speaking of it," I told her. "*You* were."

"Oh, shut up," she said. "I'm just saying that as long we're talking about stuff in your pants—" She froze. "Damn it. That's *not* what I meant either."

Her blush deepened, and I fought a sudden urge to smile. "So you've been thinking about my pants, huh?"

"No." Her chin jerked upward. "Definitely not. I mean, yes, but not the way *you* obviously think." She cleared her throat. "I'm just saying, I'm surprised you didn't shoot me the other night."

"With what?" I laughed. "The 'gun' in my pants?"

"Oh, stop it," she said. "You're making it sound all worse."

"Worse than a gun?"

"Forget the pants," she said. "So you admit it? You had a gun?"

"Hell yeah, I had gun," I said. "What? You think I'm gonna go looking for an intruder without one?"

"I wasn't an intruder," she said. "I was waiting for my cousin. And you broke down the door."

"Yeah. *My* door," I said. "So don't worry about it."

If Arden were anyone else, I might've taken the time to explain that it wasn't the door that broke, but rather the casing around it.

And, as far as the gun, it's not like I'd been waving it in her face. In fact, once I'd peered through that new hole in the wall and had seen the silhouette of a naked female in the shower, I'd actually tucked the gun into the back of my jeans to keep her from thinking that she was about to get murdered.

I'd been doing her a favor.

The way I saw it, she was lucky I'd taken the time to look first and shoot later – or rather, not shoot at all.

And *this* was the thanks I got.

It was vintage Arden.

From the look on her face, she wasn't done yet. Sure enough, she demanded, "And why'd you do that, anyway?"

"Do what?"

"Break down the door."

I gave her a look. "You're kidding, right?"

"Do I *look* like I'm kidding?"

I took a long moment to study her face. *No, she definitely wasn't kidding.* But she *was* beautiful. Her eyes were flashing, and her lips were full. And her chest – the perfect size, by the way – was rising and falling in time with her agitated breathing.

Memories of her little yellow T-shirt – and worse, her pretty pink nipples – came flooding back to me. *She'd looked good.*

She *still* looked good.

I gave a silent curse. If I kept up this line of thinking, I *would* be dealing with a problem in my pants, except this time, it wouldn't be a gun.

In reply to her question, I said, "Put yourself in my shoes. You go in to check on a house – a house that's supposed to be empty. And you find someone naked in the shower."

At the word "naked," her lips parted and then quickly shut again. The movement, as small as it was, sent my thoughts straight into the gutter.

And now I was pissed. *I didn't want this.* I didn't want *her.* And I didn't want to be thinking X-rated thoughts about someone who violated that all-important rule – the one about sticking your dick in crazy.

With a hard look, I told her, "So like I said, put yourself in my shoes. What do you *think* I'm gonna do? Knock and wait politely for you to grab a gun of your own and shoot me through the door?"

"Hah! I didn't even *have* a gun."

"Yeah. But I didn't know that, did I?"

She gave a hard scoff. "You didn't know a lot of things." And with that, she yanked her hand so hard that I forgot to hang on. Faster than I might've thought possible, she turned and tried to stomp off before I lunged for her wrist.

I grabbed it hard and held on tight. *Good thing, too.* Because already, her left foot had broken through the rotted floor.

She gave a little scream as I yanked her back. Her body collided into mine with enough force to leave us breathless. Or maybe it was just me, because she felt too damned good, with her sweet body pressed tight against my own.

Her arms closed around me. And mine closed around *her.*

But then, both of us froze.

Neither one of us said a word.

She made no move to pull away.

Neither did I.

As we stood there, my jeans grew uncomfortably tight, and I stifled a groan at the thought of finding a safe spot in the attic and screwing her silly.

I could practically see it. In mind, I could feel it too.

It was the final straw. "Damn it, Arden." By now, I was irritated to the bone. Even worse, I wasn't sure why.

Yeah, sure, I was pissed that she'd been so careless.

But I was even more pissed at myself – for letting her walk on the floor in the first place, *and* for the way my body was responding to hers.

I didn't even like her.

And she sure as hell didn't like me.

When she dropped her arms, I dropped mine, too. Now I was even *more* angry, because part of me wanted to yank her back and kiss her hard and heavy, until her knees buckled and she forgot about Clara Cooper and that stupid D-minus.

Instead, I reached once again for her wrist, intending to guide her back to the stairway. But when I looked in that direction, I found one more reason to curse.

Roy was standing on the top step, *with* his video camera.

And it was pointed straight at us.

CHAPTER 25

Arden

At something in Brody's expression, I froze.

When I turned to follow his gaze, I stifled a gasp. Roy was standing on the top step of the attic stairway, exactly where *I'd* been standing when I'd first spotted Brody looking out the rear window.

The fact that Roy had seen our little scuffle – or whatever it was – would've been humiliating enough on its own. But unless I was mistaken, he was filming us, too.

What the hell?

I called out, "What are you doing?"

In reply, he made a forwarding motion with his free hand, as if to indicate that I should ignore the camera and keep on with whatever he'd just interrupted.

I felt my jaw clench. *Didn't he get it?*

Whatever had just happened, it was done.

Now, if I had *my* way, I'd simply stomp off into the proverbial sunset – except I couldn't, because I'd just learned the folly of *that* idea.

Brody was still hanging onto my wrist. And this time, I *wasn't* pulling away.

With growing desperation, I looked back to him, intending to swallow my pride and ask him to guide me back to the stairway.

Turns out, I didn't need to. The request died on my lips when Brody gave my wrist a decisive tug and began leading me toward the stairs – and yes, toward that godawful camera.

I refused to look at it, even as Brody practically dragged me first past Roy and then, all the way down the stairs.

As soon as we reached the bottom, Brody slammed the stairway door shut behind us and gave me a hard look. "Let's get one thing straight," he said. "The attic – it's off limits. And if you can't remember that, I don't care who the hell hired you, you'll be out faster than you can say Clara's Fucking Candies."

Jerk.

Okay yes, I saw his point about the attic. And he had every right to be angry. But that crack about the candy store was yet another low blow.

I coldly informed him, "Don't worry. I'm not going anywhere near it."

Or you.

I didn't say that last part, because I refused to give him the satisfaction of knowing that I was thinking of him at all.

But the sad truth was, it had felt achingly good to be held in his arms, to feel his heartbeat against mine, and to feel the proof of his arousal pressing against my hip.

All of this posed a dangerous question. *What on Earth had happened up there?*

As Brody turned and silently stalked away, I made a point to look in the opposite direction. But when I did, I spotted Waverly eying me from the nearest bedroom doorway.

Her posture was stiff, and her eyes were hard. From the look on her face, I wasn't the only one wondering what had happened up there.

Terrific.

Technically, my work day hadn't yet begun. But already, I was more exhausted than I cared to consider. Between the lack of sleep and raw nerves, I felt like finding a nice closet to hide in.

No such luck.

The thought had barely crossed my mind when Roy emerged from the attic, looking perfectly at ease, as if he *hadn't* just violated our privacy twice over – once by watching us with his own eyes, and a second time by filming us, too.

At least now, he was holding the camera loose at his side, which told me that he *wasn't* filming at the moment.

Thank God.

And yet, for some stupid reason, I almost felt like crying.

Judging from Roy's cheerful smile, *he* didn't feel like crying. No. *Not him.* With no trace of awkwardness, he said, "So…you ready to mow?"

I blinked. "What?"

"The lawn," he said. "I've got an idea – a way to solve the 'before' problem."

The before problem? Oh, that's right. I'd ruined their "before" footage by working on the yard.

Waverly said, "You mean her screw-up?"

I turned to glare at her. "Hey! Maybe I wouldn't've 'screwed up' if someone had told me not to mow it."

With a nasty smirk, she shot back, "We shouldn't *have* to tell you. Let's get real here. It's not exactly natural to go around mowing lawns that aren't your own."

On this, she might've had a point. But I was in no mood to be reasonable. I plastered on a smirk of my own. "Yeah. And it's not exactly 'natural' to shove a mower up someone's ass. But hey, I'm game if you are."

She drew back. "What's wrong with you, anyway?"

It was a good question. *This wasn't me.* I mean, yeah, I didn't like Waverly, and she'd been on my case from the get-go. But who was I kidding? I'd never shove a mower up anyone's ass.

As if the stupid thing would fit anyway.

I was just debating an apology when I happened to look to Roy.

Son-of-a-bitch.

He was filming me.

Again.

Already, it was like a nightmare that wouldn't end.

And later on that night, after a full day in front of Roy's persistent camera, the "fun" only continued.

CHAPTER 26

Arden

At the crew house, Waverly was standing just inside the front door, surrounded by at least a dozen suitcases. She looked to me and demanded, "Where's Brody?"

I was still marveling at the number of cases. Were they *all* hers? They *must* be, because they'd arrived at the same time she had.

And yet, she hadn't lugged in a single one herself. Instead, she'd left that dubious honor to Jerry, who'd had to make five trips out from the SUV.

Turns out, Jerry hadn't been kidding about that whole "gopher" description.

Now, unlike Waverly, he was gone, along with the SUV, which made me wonder what exactly Waverly would be doing for transportation.

The same thing as myself?

After all, *I* didn't have a car either, and I *guess* I was doing alright. *For now, anyway.*

Waverly sidestepped the largest suitcase and moved deeper into the living room. She glanced around and grimaced, as if the place wasn't living up to her lofty expectations.

Personally, I didn't see it that way. The house was nice. It was clean and furnished, with a modern kitchen and at least two decent bathrooms. When it came to *bedrooms*, I still knew very little, because I hadn't explored beyond my own room and the general living area.

Still, everything I *had* seen would've made me delighted to be staying here, if only my future roommates weren't two of the most unpleasant people I'd ever met.

"Well?" Waverly said. "Where is he?"

I shrugged. "I have no idea."

It was true. I hadn't seen Brody all day, not since that incident in the attic. But of course, I'd been far too busy to see much of anything.

Under Roy's direction, I'd finished mowing the lawn while he'd filmed my activity from several different vantage points.

In the beginning, he'd startled me by literally lying out on the front sidewalk, shooting toward the house at an upward angle to disguise the fact that most of the lawn had been mowed already.

Whether I'd been startled or not, I had to admit, Roy definitely knew what he was doing when it came to getting good footage. And he'd been nice enough to show me some of it afterward.

But that didn't mean he was looking out for me.

I needed to remember that.

I'd even confronted him about that scene in the attic, where he'd filmed my encounter with Brody.

If I'd been expecting an apology, I would've been sorely disappointed – because all Roy said was that he'd only been doing his job, and that anything in or around the house was – in his words – "fair game."

And then, he'd offered me half of his second bacon sandwich, as if *that* would make it all better.

It hadn't, even if the sandwich had been pretty darn delicious.

Unfortunately, it was also the highlight of my day.

After I'd mowed the lawn, Roy had filmed me trimming the bushes – not that they'd really needed it. And then, he'd directed me to toward the rear of the house, where he'd filmed me weeding my grandmother's long-neglected flower beds.

I didn't mind the work. If I were on my own, I would've done it, anyway.

But now, hours later, I was utterly spent – not just from all the physical activity, but from being under the microscope for so many hours in a row.

When I'd signed up for this gig, I'd naively assumed that I'd be merely a side player, not a featured performer.

But of course, I reminded myself, this was only the first day. When the actual construction began, I'd surely fade deeper into the woodwork.

Or at least I sure hoped so.

At six o'clock that evening, I'd returned to the crew house, exhausted, but relieved to get some much-needed privacy.

The reprieve lasted only an hour – until the arrival of Waverly and her suitcases.

Until that particular moment, I'd been holding out a tiny bit of hope that Brody had been kidding about Waverly staying here.

No such luck.

And now, she was asking, "So, where's his bedroom?"

I blinked. "What?"

"Brody's bedroom," she said. "Which one is his?"

The question irritated me more than it should've. "How would I know?"

At this, she smiled. "So you don't?"

"No. Do you?"

Her smile grew sly. "Not yet."

Yet? What did *that* mean? Now, I was only *more* irritated. And on top of *that*, I was irritated for being irritated. After all, she and Brody totally deserved each other.

If they hooked up, it would be a *good* thing because it would keep both of them occupied and away from me. Or at least, that's what I kept telling myself, even as the thought of them together festered like an open wound.

Would they seriously hook up?

She obviously had a thing for him, even now, *after* he'd told her to butt out of the construction side of things. And, whether I liked Brody or not, I could totally see why she was interested. He was rich, famous, and dangerously hot.

Even in high school, before all the fame and fortune, Brody had dated more than his fair share of girls. I'd heard rumors, *mouth-watering* rumors that might've interested me if only I weren't still a virgin at the time.

Now, I watched in sullen silence as Waverly glided past me, heading toward the rear hallway, where the bedrooms were located.

I held my ground for like two whole seconds before it suddenly dawned on me that I'd be smart to follow, if only to preserve my own space.

As I strode after her, I called out, "The last room on the right is mine."

Without looking back, she said, "We'll see about that."

I kept on going. "No, *you'll* see, because I'm already settled in."

In the hallway, she stopped at the first door and opened it to peer inside. Curious in spite of myself, I joined her at the doorway to get a look of my own.

The unfamiliar bedroom was nice and roomy with a queen-sized bed, two tall dressers, and a big window overlooking the private back yard.

I remained stubbornly in the hall while Waverly entered the bedroom and pulled open a random dresser drawer. It was empty, just like the next one she opened. Without bothering to shut either drawer, she strode to the bedroom's opposite wall, making straight for a narrow wooden door that led to who-knows-what. She yanked it open to reveal an empty closet.

With a sound of disgust, she said, "There's no bathroom."

"Yeah, well, there's a really nice one at the end of the hall."

She turned and gave me a dubious look. "*How* nice?"

"Really nice," I said. "It has a bathtub *and* a shower." The distinction seemed important, because my own bathroom had only a shower, not that I was complaining.

She asked, "How's the lighting?"

"In the bathroom?" I said. "Good. I guess."

"How good?"

I jerked a finger toward the bathroom. "It's right down the hall. You *could* check it out for yourself, you know."

"Oh, believe me, I will." And with that, she left the first bedroom and brushed past me, heading deeper down the hall.

She stopped at the next door and opened it. Inside, there was king-sized bed, a wide dresser, and another interior door. Waverly marched into the bedroom, yanked open the mystery door, and looked inside.

It was another closet – empty, just like the first one. She looked to me and demanded, "Where's the bathroom?"

"How should *I* know?"

"Well, you told me about the *other* bathroom."

I crossed my arms. "Which you *still* could see for yourself."

"Oh, I intend to," she said, leaving the second bedroom and striding once again past me. When she reached the hallway bathroom, she opened the door to reveal everything the bathroom had to offer – a nice long countertop, two sinks, a small jacuzzi tub, and a separate shower.

She flicked on the lights and eyed the whole setup with obvious disappointment. "The lighting's awful."

The lighting looked fine to me. But then again, I wasn't nearly as put-together as Waverly. Her makeup was flawless, and her long blonde hair was twisted into an elaborate knot, making her look more like a movie star than a show producer.

Who knows, maybe she *needed* good lighting to achieve such a perfect appearance.

As for myself, I tended to favor a more natural look, which meant that I could probably get ready in near-darkness if I needed to.

With a huff, Waverly turned away from the bathroom and pushed past me yet again. She headed toward the third bedroom – the one where *I'd* been staying.

The door was shut, and with good reason.

I told her, "That one's mine."

She turned to face me. "Oh really? Do *you* own the house?"

Already, I didn't like where this was going. Grudgingly, I replied, "No."

"Then if I were you, I wouldn't be so picky."

My fingers clenched. *I* was picky?

She had no idea what she was talking about. I hadn't even picked the bedroom. Brody had picked it *for* me, on that very first night, when he'd insisted that I stay here.

I told her, "I didn't pick it. Brody did."

With a tilt of her chin, she said, "Yes, well, that was before *I* came along."

And with that, she turned and flung open my bedroom door.

As she looked inside, I looked, too – scanning the bedroom with fresh eyes. The room had a double bed, a decent size dresser, a medium-sized closet, and a small private bathroom.

All of this was clearly visible, since I'd left the closet and bathroom doors wide open. *Maybe that had been a mistake.*

Waverly pointed toward my duffle bag, resting atop the only dresser along with a small pile of receipts. "Whose stuff is that?"

Wasn't it obvious? "It's mine. You *did* hear me say this is my room, right?"

With a little laugh, she replied, "Not anymore."

My jaw dropped. "What?"

"It's mine now."

Talk about nerve. I gave her a stiff smile. "Are you sure? I mean, have you checked the bathroom lighting?"

"It doesn't matter," she said. "I'll have them put in new lighting tomorrow."

"Who?" I asked.

"The construction guys," she said, as if this should've been obvious. "Seriously, how long can it take?"

Not being an electrician, I had no idea. But this was the least of my concerns. As far as the bedroom, now I didn't know what to do. The truth was, she actually had a point about it not being my house.

If Waverly weren't being so heavy-handed about it, I might've volunteered to switch on my own. Sure, I liked having a private bathroom, but I'd shared bathrooms before. It really wasn't such a big deal.

And yet, the thought of sharing a bathroom with Brody – well, that made me feel just a little bit unsettled.

Thinking out loud, I said, "Maybe Brody should take this room. And you and I can take the others."

She frowned. "Why would we do that?"

"Because," I explained, "that way, Brody can have his own bathroom. And you and I can share."

She looked at me like I'd just suggested drinking out of the toilet. "You're kidding, right?"

"Um…no?"

"Well forget it." She turned and pointed once again toward my duffle bag. "Now grab your stuff and pick another room."

"Oh, come on," I protested. "You can't be serious."

With a scoff, she said, "Well, *I'm* not going to move it."

Obviously, she was missing the point. I tried again. "Yeah? Well maybe *I'm* not going to move it either."

"Sure you will," she said, looking *very* sure of herself.

"But—"

"And don't forget anything in the bathroom."

I bit my lip. I hated the thought of being driven out. *But could I truly refuse?*

She was a producer, and I was a temporary consultant. On top of that, I'd been a late addition to this whole setup.

My shoulders slumped. As much as I hated it, I felt compelled to do what she asked. "Fine," I said. "If it's so important to you."

Still, my face burned as I strode into the bedroom and grabbed my duffle bag off the dresser. With quick, jerky motions, I retrieved the few shirts I'd hung in the closet, and then reached for the pair of jeans that I'd left lying across the bed.

As I stuffed the loose clothing into the duffle bag, Waverly called out from the open doorway, "And you *are* planning to change the sheets, right?"

My teeth were grinding now. "No. But I can point you toward the washing machine."

"Why should *I* have to wash them?" she said. "I wasn't the one who slept all over them."

"And *I* wasn't the one who insisted on changing bedrooms."

"Now you just being a poor sport," she grumbled.

Whatever. Silently, I stalked into the bathroom and shut the door behind me – because the last thing I wanted now was an audience for this latest humiliation. With a string of muttered curses, I scooped up the few toiletries I had – a toothbrush, a small tube of toothpaste, and my tiny makeup case.

One by one, I tossed everything into the duffle bag.

And then, I took a deep, calming breath. *I could do this.*

Sure, it was embarrassing, but the worst was over, right?

Wrong.

Because when I emerged from the bathroom, there wasn't just *one* person watching from the hallway. There were *two*.

CHAPTER 27

Arden

Brody was standing behind Waverly as they both eyed the interior of my bedroom – except it *wasn't* my bedroom, not anymore.

It was *Waverly's* bedroom. And from the look on her face, she was loving every minute of my inglorious departure.

Behind her, Brody didn't look nearly as orgasmic. His eyebrows furrowed as he studied the duffle bag slung over my shoulder. In a low voice, he asked, "What's going on?"

Waverly gave a little jump and whirled to face him. "Oh, there you are!" she breathed. "I didn't hear you come in."

"Obviously." He looked back to me and said, "Going somewhere?"

My chin jerked upward. "Yes, actually. I just don't know where. That's all."

Now he was frowning.

Waverly spoke up. "What she *means* to say is that we're switching bedrooms."

Brody's mouth tightened. "Is that so?"

Just then, my cell phone rang in my pocket. From the ringtone, I knew exactly who it was – my cousin Jason.

My breath caught. *Finally.*

I blurted out, "I've got to take this." During the past couple of days, I'd been going crazy trying to reach him. I'd called. I'd sent text messages. I'd even sent him a few emails.

In return, I'd gotten nothing. *Until now.*

Frantically, I dug the phone out of my pocket, rushed back into the bathroom, and slammed the door shut behind me.

Waverly called out, "Hey! That's my bathroom."

"In a minute!" I called back, even as I tapped the screen to accept my cousin's call. "Jason?" My voice rose. "Where have you been?"

On the other end, I heard with nothing but silence.

I tried again. "Hello? Jason?"

"Uh, yeah," he finally said. "So, um, how's it going?"

I felt my jaw clench. Judging from the tone of his voice, he knew exactly how it was going.

"Terrible," I said. "What happened with the house?"

"Well, you see…it's kind of a long story."

"I'm sure it is," I snapped. "So what happened?"

More silence.

"Oh, for God's sake," I said. "Just spit it out, will you?"

"Alright. Jeez, calm down."

Calm down? Seriously? Through gritted teeth, I informed him, "I *am* calm."

"You don't sound calm to me."

He was right. I wasn't. But I had plenty of reasons to be agitated. He'd given me a promise. He'd taken my money, *repeatedly*. And then, in spite of everything, he'd sold the house anyway, with no warning whatsoever.

Adding insult to injury, he hadn't even bothered to tell me any of this himself. Instead, he'd let me find out on my own*, the hard way.* Cripes, even Brody discovering me naked in the shower was my cousin's fault in a roundabout way.

Still, I wanted answers, not a scene. So in the calmest voice I could muster I said, "On Tuesday, you were supposed to meet me. Remember?"

"Tuesday? Are you sure?"

"Oh, come on," I said. "You *know* you were. I waited for you all day. And half of the night, too. But you never showed."

He mumbled, "Sorry 'bout that."

"You should be," I said. "And then, I find out from someone else that you sold the house – the one we *supposedly* owned together. So tell me. What happened?"

He hesitated. "Who told you I sold it?"

"Well, for one thing, the sign."

"What sign?"

"The sold sign," I said. "You know, in the front yard."

"Well, *I* didn't put it there."

At this, a spark of wild hope kindled in my heart. "So, what are saying? You *didn't* sell the house?"

"Well...I didn't *want* to sell it," he said. "I just had to, that's all."

My heart sank. *So much for hope.*

Jason said, "So who told you it was sold?"

By now, my jaw was so tight, I could hardly speak. "You mean aside from the sign? *And* from the fact you stood me up?"

"Sure, whatever. How'd you find out?"

The question grated. "Does it matter?"

"It might."

"Fine," I said. "I heard it from the guy you sold it to."

At this, Jason swallowed so loud, I actually heard it through the phone. Sounding sick to his stomach, he said, "You did?"

"Well, I certainly didn't hear it from *you.*"

In a hushed voice, he said, "He's not with you now, is he?"

Brody? No. But he was still nearer than I would've liked. From somewhere just outside the bathroom, I could hear his voice, muffled, but unmistakable as he and Waverly discussed whatever.

When she gave a flirty laugh, it reminded me of fingernails on a chalkboard. Or maybe I was just irritated with everyone, especially my elusive cousin.

In reply to his question, I told him, "No one's with me. I'm in a room by myself."

"You mean in Lansing?"

Obviously, he meant East Lansing, where Michigan State was located. "No. I graduated. Just last week. Remember?"

"But you're not still here in Bayside, are you?" He hesitated. "I mean, you went back home to Lansing, right?"

Didn't he get it? East Lansing wasn't home. *This* was home. After graduation, I'd been planning to build a life here, to get a local job, to fix up the house and keep it in the family.

And if Jason thought I'd simply wander off into the sunset, it was time to inform him otherwise. "I'm not going anywhere until I get some answers."

"From who?"

"From you. Obviously."

"Oh. Right." Again, he hesitated. "So where are you staying?"

"At the house across the street."

"From where?" he asked.

"From Grandpa and Grandma's place." My fingers clenched around the phone. "You know, the house we *supposedly* owned together?"

"Shit."

With growing irritation, I said, "What now?"

"Nothing," he said. "Just do me a favor. Don't tell anyone I called, alright?"

Talk about nerve. "Why should I do *you* a favor? You totally screwed me over. You *do* realize that, right?"

"Hey, it wasn't my fault."

I considered all the money I'd sent him, and the all of the plans he'd ruined by selling the property out from under me. "Well it certainly wasn't *my* fault."

"I know," he said. "But don't worry. I'm gonna make it right."

"How?" I demanded.

"I just will," he said. "Trust me, okay?"

I gave a snort of derision. "Like I trusted you to keep the house?"

"Alright, maybe I deserved that," he said. "But when I explain, you'll get it. I promise."

Now, *this* I had to hear. "Alright, fine. Go ahead."

"Sorry, what?"

"Go ahead and explain. I'm waiting."

"Later," he said. "I've gotta go."

"But—"

I heard a click, and then dead silence.

Damn it.

When I tried to call him back, he didn't answer.

Lovely.

After a few choice words, I emerged from the bathroom more confused than ever, especially when I found myself alone.

I stopped in the bathroom doorway and looked around. Waverly and Brody were nowhere in sight. The bedroom door was now shut, and I heard no noises from the other side.

But I'd be a fool to get too comfortable. After all, it was only a matter of time before Waverly barged in and demanded the bedroom.

Looking to get it over with already, I did a final sweep, checking inside the closet and under the bed for anything of mine that might've fallen out of sight.

When I found nothing, I returned to the dresser and scooped up the pile of receipts and shoved them into the duffle bag, on top of the rest of the stuff.

I left the bedroom with my bag slung over my shoulder, only to find a new reason to be confused. *Except for myself, the house was empty.*

Well, that was weird.

Even weirder, there was a note taped to the fridge, written in bright purple ink. It said, *"Arden – I've decided I don't want that bedroom after all. So it's all yours. You're welcome. Waverly."*

More confused than ever, I glanced around. When my gaze landed on the living room, I did a double-take.

Waverly's suitcases were gone.

What did *that* mean?

I wandered to the front window and peered outside. I saw no sign of Brody's truck.

My pulse quickened. *Maybe they'd decided to stay at a hotel or something?*

I considered this possibility for nearly an hour until curiosity overcame my better instincts.

Silently, I padded down the bedroom hall and listened at each bedroom door for the sounds of activity.

I heard nothing.

Feeling like a total idiot, I called out, "Hello? Is anyone home?"

Silence.

Cautiously, I opened the nearest bedroom door and peered inside. On the floor near the bed was a single black duffle bag. *Brody's?*

Probably.

I padded to the second bedroom and rapped lightly on the door before calling out again. When I received no response, I pushed open the door and frowned at what I saw inside. There it was – all of Waverly's luggage lined up against the far wall.

Apparently, I still had roommates – and my bedroom.

By now, I had no idea what to think.

Had Brody stuck up for me?

It seemed incredibly unlikely. But no other theory made sense.

Already, I'd figured out that he wasn't the same person I recalled from high school. But what he'd become since then, I couldn't be sure.

And all of the mixed signals weren't helping.

Sometime around midnight, I was hiding out in my bedroom when Brody and Waverly returned from who-knows-where. *Maybe dinner? Or something else?*

As far as my own dinner, I'd eaten alone, consuming the rest of the pizza from the previous night.

After the return of my roommates, I remained firmly in my bedroom, preferring solitude over their dubious company.

Waverly, I could handle. *But Brody?* He made me nervous, because my feelings for him swung so wildly – from pure hatred to something a lot more unsettling.

Right then and there, I decided that I'd be smart to avoid him as much as possible.

And I would've, too, if only I weren't forced to spend some serious time with him the very next day.

CHAPTER 28

Arden

I gave Roy a puzzled look. "But what are we supposed to talk about?"

"That's up to you," Roy said, hoisting his video camera higher onto his shoulder. "It's visual only. No audio."

I was standing on my grandparent's front porch with Roy and Brody. It was just past seven-thirty in the morning, and Roy had greeted me at the front door with an unsettling announcement. Apparently, Brody and I would begin the day by walking along the beach while Roy filmed us.

I gave Brody a sideways glance. From the look on his face, he wasn't any happier about this than I was.

I asked Roy, "But what does that have to do with the house?"

"You're the consultant," Roy said, as if this explained everything. *It didn't.* "But—

Brody spoke up. "Let's just get it over with, alright?"

My jaw clenched. *Get it over with? Like it was some sort of punishment?* "Fine." I looked back to Roy. "Just point me where I need to go."

In reply, Roy flicked his head toward the rear of the house, the part that faced the beach. "Act like you're showing him the sights or something – you know, sunrise over the beach and all that."

I loved the beach at sunrise.

While living with my grandparents, I'd seen it so many times that maybe it should've gotten old and boring. But it never had. And, considering how much I loved it, it probably never would.

Under normal circumstances, I'd be thrilled to share it with just about anyone – well, anyone *except* Brody Blastoviak, especially with the way he was looking at me now.

Judging from his expression, he'd rather be anywhere but here – and with anyone but me. As he looked me over, I returned the favor, giving him the same level of scrutiny.

Today, he was wearing his usual getup – jeans and a T-shirt, along with heavy work boots. His jeans were slightly loose, hanging low on his hips and hinting at the amazing abs resting just above the button of his faded jeans.

Thanks to the loose cut of his shirt, I couldn't actually see his abs, but I'd caught enough glimpses over the past couple of days to imagine plenty, assuming that I cared to dwell on it, which I totally didn't.

When I refused to look away, Brody said, "Is there a problem?"

I stiffened at his tone. "Yes, actually."

I gave his boots a long, concerned look. During the whole time I'd lived at my grandparent's place, I'd never seen anyone strolling along the beach in work boots.

Since I was supposedly the consultant here, was this something I should point out?

Probably.

I looked to Roy and said, "If you want it to look authentic, shouldn't he be wearing tennis shoes or something?"

Brody's voice sliced out between us. "The boots are fine. It's a discussion, not a date."

I felt my eyes narrow. *Talk about arrogant.*

"Good," I said. "Because I wouldn't want to date you, anyway."

"Good," he shot back. "Because you're not my type."

"Yeah? Well you're not my type either."

He glowered at me. I glowered at him. And then, as if remembering that we had an audience, we both looked to Roy.

Son-of-a-bitch.

Roy was smiling like he'd just gotten lucky. *And* he was filming us.

Of course.

I gave Roy the squinty-eye. "You *did* say this was visual only, right?"

In reply, Roy made that now-familiar forwarding motion with his hand, as if to indicate that we should ignore him and keep on doing whatever.

Suddenly, I decided that Brody had the right idea. *Let's just get it over with.*

Without further commentary, I turned and stomped toward the rear of the house, with Brody at my side.

In spite of the work boots, his stride was long and easy, especially compared to my own. But as far as everything else, there was nothing easy about him. As we traveled ever closer to the beach, I studied him from the corner of my eye. His jaw was set, and his mouth was tight. From head to toe, he looked royally irritated.

Yeah, welcome to the club, buddy.

By the time we reached the actual beach, I'd already had more than enough of his attitude.

Still, a job was a job, so I turned to the right, ignoring the glorious ocean-like view as I stalked stubbornly along the water's edge without saying a single word to my equally silent companion.

When I snuck a quick glance over my shoulder, Roy was following along behind us, out of earshot, but filming nonetheless.

When he saw me looking, he called out, "You're supposed to be talking, remember?"

I looked forward and muttered, "As if he could tell."

Next to me, Brody gave a low scoff. "He can. Trust me. I know."

And that was the extent of our conversation.

From behind us, Roy called out again, "You're still not talking!"

Fine. Roy wanted us to talk? I had the perfect topic. I looked to Brody and said, "You never paid up, you know."

"For what?"

"Yesterday morning, with the hoses – you promised to tell me why it was such a big secret."

"It wasn't *that* big of a secret," he said. "*You* knew, didn't you?"

"Yeah, but I didn't know why you were hiding it from the others."

"Sure you did."

I had a theory. And it was good one, too. Still, his confidence grated. Grudgingly, I said, "Alright. If I *had* to guess, I'd say it was because you didn't want to get scolded for ruining the 'before' shot – you know, like a flooded hallway or water seeping down the stairs."

"I don't get 'scolded,'" he said. "I get grief. And I wasn't in the mood."

I knew the feeling. Not too long ago, I'd gotten plenty of grief for simply mowing the lawn. Still I had to point out the obvious. "Oh, come on. You'd never get the kind of grief *I* got."

"Got that right."

I almost laughed. "So you're not even bothering to deny it?"

"No. Why would I?"

"I don't know," I said. "But if you're not afraid of getting scolded, why keep it a secret?"

"Because," he said, "there'll be a hundred more battles before the project's done. Why fight one I don't have to?"

"But the whole thing's ridiculous," I said. "I mean, *anyone* could see that you did the smart thing in preventing further damage." The pronouncement had barely left my lips when I realized something totally dreadful.

I'd just complimented him.

Damn it.

I picked up the pace, even as I gave him a secret sideways glance. From the look on his face, he felt the compliment just as much I did – except he didn't look nearly as horrified.

Quickly, I added, "But you're still a coward for not owning up to it."

Abruptly, he stopped moving, and so did I.

As we faced off, he said, "That's what you think?"

No. It wasn't. Not really. With a loose shrug, I mumbled, "I don't know."

"Yes, you do."

He was right. *I knew Brody.* And for all of his *many* other flaws, he was no coward.

"Alright, fine," I said. "I take it back. But I still don't get it. Why not do whatever you want and tell Waverly to shove it if she gets mad?"

He gave me a look. "You mean on camera?"

"No. Like in private."

"Where? In the house we're fixing up?" His gaze dipped briefly to my lips, and his eyes softened. In a low voice, he said, "There *is* no private, as you damn well know."

Something in his look made my knees go embarrassingly wobbly. Or maybe I was just mortified at the memory of Roy and his camera catching us in the attic.

Either way, I felt distinctly unsettled, even as I said, "Yeah, well, maybe you and Waverly could've discussed it across the street, away from the cameras."

"Or maybe," he said, "I could just do what needed doing and skip all the bullshit."

I started to argue, but then thought better of it. After all, the same sort of logic had driven me to mow the lawn – except unlike Brody, *I'd* gotten caught.

As usual.

I studied his face. "So what are you saying? You didn't want to waste the energy arguing about it?"

"The energy *or* the time," he said. "I've got four months to finish the house. And yeah, the show's important. But that doesn't mean I'm gonna stand by and watch the property rack up more damage – not if I can help it."

On this, we were in total agreement, and I might've told him so, except Brody wasn't done talking.

"And," he continued, giving me a hard look, "I'm sure as hell not gonna waste my time arguing with someone who doesn't know what the hell she's doing."

"Hey!" I bristled. "I know more about the house than you think."

At this, he looked almost ready to smile. "I wasn't talking about *you.*"

"Oh." I cleared my throat. "So, I'm guessing you mean Waverly?"

Brody nodded. "She's no construction expert."

No kidding. "So why is she the producer?" I asked. "I mean, it seems an odd choice, doesn't it?"

"Not if you know who she is."

I wasn't following. "Sooooo...Who is she?"

"Landon's Tarrington's niece."

My jaw practically hit the sand. "Really?"

"Really."

"But the other day, they didn't *act* like they were related."

"Right. Because in Waverly's mind, she got the gig on her own."

"But she didn't?"

Brody's eyebrows lifted. "What do *you* think?"

The answer to this was so obvious, it didn't require an answer. "But if she's his niece, why did he hire *me?* I mean, even then, it was pretty obvious that Waverly didn't want me around."

"My guess?" Brody said. "He wants fireworks."

"Why?"

"Because it's good for the ratings."

Hearing this, I almost cringed. Apparently, just as I'd feared, I *was* the new Miss LaRue – someone who'd bring more drama than anything useful. With renewed concern, I asked, "What kind of fireworks?"

With Miss LaRue, the fireworks had ranged from mild disagreements to full-blown hissy-fits. I wasn't the hissy-fit type, but even *I* had to admit that my relationship with Brody promised enough friction to rub everyone raw.

Brody shrugged. "I guess that's up to you, isn't it?"

"So you're saying they *want* us to argue?" It made sense in a way, considering that we'd been arguing on the front lawn just before Landon had offered me the job.

Brody looked at me for a long, penetrating moment before saying, "Arguments. Or worse."

I frowned. "What could be worse than arguments?" But then, I froze. "Oh. *That.*"

Slowly, Brody looked around, as if taking in the beauty around us – the endless water, the blue sky streaked with the orange remnants of sunrise, the sand at our feet, and the waves lapping at the shore. With a humorless laugh, he said, "Why do you think we're out here?"

I saw what he meant. "So you think they're building a narrative or something?"

"A narrative. A story. Call it what you want. Maybe they're throwing us together to see what happens."

I could think of plenty of things that *could* happen. None of them were good, at least not long-term. I told him, "But nothing's going to happen."

Brody stiffened. "Right."

And yet, the thought of *one* certain something happening was far too appealing for my liking. And, in spite of all my good intentions, I couldn't help but wonder what would it be like to clash with Brody in the naked sense.

The mere thought of it sent a bolt of heat where it definitely didn't belong.

This wasn't good.

I gave myself a mental slap and focused on the issue at-hand. "So if Waverly is just a figurehead, who's really running the film crew?"

"Who do you think?"

Slowly, I turned to look. And there Roy was, standing out of earshot, with his camera pointed in our direction. When he saw me looking, he gave me a thumbs-up, followed by the usual forwarding gesture.

With a sigh, I turned and began walking again, even as Brody did the same.

In a hushed voice, I asked, "Are you sure that Roy can't hear us?"

"I'm sure," Brody said. "He would've mic'd us if he was getting audio."

Well, that was a relief.

As we walked farther along the beach, I said, "Hey, can I ask you something? How come you're the only one here? I mean, the show supposedly stars you and your brothers, but I haven't seen either one of them at the job site."

"No. But you will."

As I listened, Brody went on to explain that he and his brothers divided up responsibilities according to their personal interests. Although both of his brothers had plenty of skills, neither one of them had the same passion for using the tools their company produced. And more to the point, he added, neither one of them had any interest in dealing with construction crews – or film crews for that matter.

After taking all of this in, I said, "But you'd never guess it from watching the show. I mean, the way it looks, the three of you run things equally."

"We do," Brody said. "It's just that we handle different pieces of the larger pie. And the things *they* handle…" He gave a mock shudder. "Not my bag."

I laughed in spite of myself. "So you divide and conquer, huh?"

"Something like that." And then, Brody surprised me by revealing that he had a real thing for historic homes, fixing them up, restoring them to their original glory.

Listening, I was surprised not only by what he was saying, but that he was saying it at all.

I found myself nodding in agreement when he launched into a long tirade of how people were too quick to tear things down, rather than fix them up.

And just when I was beginning to conclude that he might not be *too* terrible, I recalled how all of this had started. "Hey, wait a minute," I said. "Does this mean you *never* considered tearing down the house?"

"Not for a minute," he said. "It would've been a crying shame."

Even though I agreed, I couldn't resist saying, "Yeah, but speaking of shame, don't you feel bad for telling me otherwise?"

"I didn't *tell* you anything," he said. "You assumed."

"Yeah, but you *let* me assume it."

"Well maybe I get funny when people break into my house."

My stomach sank. *His* house. Not mine. *As if I needed the reminder.*

Still, I protested, "I didn't break in. I had a key."

With a half shrug, he replied, "It's still my house."

For now? Or forever? Bracing myself, I asked, "So, are you planning to keep it?"

He was silent for a long moment. And when he finally spoke, his answer was entirely unsatisfying. "Don't ask."

CHAPTER 29

Brody

Next to me, her pace slowed. "Don't ask?" she said. "What does *that* mean?"

"It means what I said. Don't ask."

She gave me a subtle sideways glance. She did that a lot. She thought that I didn't notice. But I did, just like I'd noticed how her eyes had lit up when I'd mentioned fixing up old houses – and how those same eyes hadn't glazed over when I'd gone deeper into the details.

The crazy thing was, she'd looked genuinely interested – which probably explained why I'd told her more than I'd planned.

Funny, I hadn't planned to tell her anything at all.

But she had this way of getting under my skin, of making me say more than I wanted – and making me think things that were best unthought.

Like right now, I was thinking how sweet she looked with the morning breeze lifting the ends of her long hair and how the flush of her cheeks made me want to smile – although hell if I knew why.

"But about the house," she said, "you're either planning to keep it, or you're not."

"Yeah, so?"

"So why won't you tell me? Is it because you really don't know? Or because you don't want to say?"

I *had* been thinking of keeping the house – not as a rental, and not as a vacation spot either, but as my own personal residence.

I liked my condo well enough. It was big, luxurious, and right on the river. Even so, it had never felt like home.

Come to think of it, no place had felt like home – or at least not in a long while. But there was something about *this* place that made me think otherwise. Maybe it was the full package – the beach, the view, the architecture, and yeah, maybe Arden Weathers, too.

So, why was I being such a dick about it?

I didn't want to be. *Not now.*

"Listen," I said, "the truth is, I don't know, just like I said."

"But don't you already have a condo? I mean, right here in Bayside?"

"Yeah, on the river."

She frowned, but said nothing.

I asked, "Is that a problem?"

"No," she said. "It's just that, well, if you *already* have a place that you like, why would you want another? Especially another place on the water. And in the same town." Her voice picked up steam. "Because really, when you think about it, you *already* have it all."

She was wrong. Yeah, I had plenty of money. And dozens of houses – including the crew house across the street. I didn't live in them. Mostly I rented them out – only *after* fixing them up.

Arden might not realize it, but I juggled a lot more than the show and the business – and yeah, enough "dates" to make life interesting. But sometime in the past year or so, the game had lost its luster.

Or maybe I was just tired of life in the fast lane.

I stopped walking and took a long look around. The beach was quiet, except for the sounds of seagulls and the waves lapping at the shore. It was like something out of a children's book – the kind that decent parents read to their kids on Sunday afternoons.

That hadn't been *my* life. And yet, I'd seen enough of luckier kids to know how life *could* be.

As my thoughts churned, I scanned the horizon. This place – it would be a nice spot to raise a family, assuming I were into that sort of thing, which I wasn't.

Except now, it wasn't sounding so bad.

I stiffened. *What the hell?*

I looked to Arden, standing beside me. She was gazing out over the water as a soft smile played across her lips.

At the sight of her, I almost smiled, too. But then, I caught myself. *She was making me nuts.*

Her obsession with the house was contagious, like a bad rash or something worse.

In reply to her statement, all I said was, "Hey, you can never have too much."

She blinked, as if she'd lost track of our debate. *She wasn't the only one.* My own thoughts had travelled way too far for my liking, and it was time to rein them back in.

Arden said, "But that's not true." She turned to face me. "And this house – it means *nothing* to you, not in the big scheme of things."

She was wrong. *As usual.*

I said, "Hey if you're still pissed that I bought it—"

"I'm not."

I crossed my arms. "Is that so?"

"Yes." She hesitated. "And no."

"*Now* who's being evasive?"

She sighed. "It's just that *yes*, I'm glad someone bought it who's going to fix it up, but you *know* I'd be lying if I didn't admit that I'd love the chance to buy it myself."

This again?

I gave her a hard look. "With what?"

"Money. How else would I buy it?"

"And how much money do you have?"

Her cheeks, already flushed, grew a shade redder. "Well…none right now. But there's the bonus."

"Which I already told you, won't be enough."

"It might be for a down payment."

"You can say that all you want," I said. "It doesn't make it true."

Her mouth tightened. "Well, maybe I'm not the type to give up so easily. Did you ever think of that?"

I recalled how she'd been in high school. "Hell, I don't *think* it. I *know* it."

She smiled. "See?"

I didn't smile back. "That wasn't a compliment."

Her smile faded, which made me feel like a total dick. The truth was, I admired the way she went after the things she wanted – but not when the thing she wanted belonged to me.

She turned and looked toward the house – *and* then toward Roy, who was still filming us from afar. In a quieter voice, she said, "I think we've gone far enough."

Something in her tone suggested that she wasn't talking about distance. And hey, I wasn't about to argue. *She was right.* When it came to anything with me and Arden, less was always better.

But first I had to set her straight. "Listen, there's something I want you to know."

"What?"

"When I bought that house, I didn't know you had your eye on it."

She gave me a dubious look, but said nothing.

I held her gaze. "Believe me. Or don't. I just figured you'd want to know." And with that, I turned and began walking toward the house, trying like hell to ignore Roy and his camera, along with the sight of Arden, trudging along beside me like I'd just popped her favorite balloon.

As far as the camera, I felt its presence more than I should've. From the look on Arden's face, she felt it, too.

As we moved ever closer to the house, there was a part of me – the *dumb-ass* part of me – that wanted to shield her from the intrusion. But Arden wasn't mine to protect. And even if she were, she needed to realize – *and fast* – exactly what she'd signed on for.

And if she *didn't* realize it?

Hey, it wasn't *my* problem, and I'd be smart to keep it that way.

CHAPTER 30

Arden

On the phone, Cami asked, "So, do you believe him?"

"I don't know," I admitted. "But he didn't sound like he was lying."

It was nearly seven o'clock at night, and I was hunkered down in my bedroom, where I'd have no chance of being overheard.

The house was empty except for myself, but I was all too aware that either of my roommates could return at any moment.

I'd just finished a full day under the nonstop glare of Roy's video camera, and I was in no mood to be scrutinized by anyone. Even though my day hadn't been difficult by any stretch, all of those hours in the spotlight had left me feeling unsettled and stupidly exhausted.

Looking back, was it any wonder?

After that walk along the beach, Mitch, the sound technician, had fitted me with a wireless microphone. And then, he and Roy had taken me through the house, room-by-room, as I reacted to its horrible condition and shared stories of what the house had been like in years past, back when my grandparents had owned it.

As far as Brody, I'd seen him only in passing as he haunted the various rooms with a pencil in-hand, probably making notes on what needed to be fixed. Or who knows? Maybe he'd been writing a list of ways to torment me because, yes, he did seem the type.

Still, I had to admit, our walk along the beach hadn't been nearly as terrible as I'd expected. And, assuming it was true that he hadn't known about my family's connection to the place, maybe he wasn't quite as vindictive as I'd thought.

On the phone, Cami was saying, "Why don't you ask your cousin if Brody knew? *He'd* be able to tell you, right?"

At this, I couldn't help but scoff. "Yeah. Assuming I ever hear from him again." As Cami listened, I went on to tell her about last night's odd phone call with Jason and how he was apparently back to avoiding me.

Today, I'd called him several times, only to receive no response whatsoever. I couldn't even confront him in person because I had no idea where he lived. *And why?* It was because like a total idiot, I'd actually believed him when he'd told me that he was still living at our grandparent's place.

When I explained all of this to Cami, she said, "Did you try him at work?"

"Oh yeah." I gave a bitter laugh. "Get this. I call his office at the local college, and do you know what they tell me?"

"What?"

"They *tell* me that he's on leave, something about a family emergency."

"Really? What kind of emergency?"

"Oh, that's the best part," I said. "Apparently, his 'cousin' is having health problems."

"Which cousin?"

My voice hardened. "Guess."

"You don't mean you?"

"Well, I *am* his only cousin."

"That dip-wad!"

"Yeah," I muttered. "Tell me about it."

"But he can't avoid you forever."

I gave another scoff. "That won't stop him from trying though. I mean, he *must* know that I'll be expecting my money back."

"What money?"

"All the money I gave him for the house. You know, the payments, the repairs, everything." I made a sound of disgust. "God, I was such an idiot."

"You were not," she said. "Come on, if you can't trust family, who *can* you trust?"

This was *so* easy for Cami to say. Unlike me, she had the kind of family you could really count on – parents who loved her and a whole bunch of siblings, too.

But me? I had nobody. Sure, I had parents, but they were off doing their own thing. And even my mom, who *should* care about the house, hadn't cared one bit about keeping it in the family, even when I'd begged her for just a tiny bit of help.

Now, thinking about it, I almost wanted to cry. But I'd cried plenty already, especially three years ago, when my grandpa had passed away so suddenly.

At the memory of him – and my grandma, too – my eyes grew misty like they always did.

Desperate to focus on something else, I said to Cami, "Hey, do you want to hear something funny?"

"It can't be *too* funny," she said.

"Why not?"

"Because you sound like you're gonna cry."

"I am *not* going to cry," I said, wiping a stray tear from my eye. "I'm gonna throttle Brody."

"For what now?"

"Well, remember when I told you how the film crew was walking me through the house, making me talk about the damage and stuff?"

"Yeah?"

"Well, get this. We get to the upstairs hallway, and I see this hole that wasn't there before."

"What kind of hole?" she asked.

"Oh, that's the funniest part," I said. "It's like, well… a peep-hole."

"A peep-hole?" She hesitated. "Into what?"

"The bathroom." When she made no reply, I felt compelled to explain. "You know, the one where Brody barged in on me."

"Ohhhhhh, *that* bathroom. So, do you think he's a perv?"

"No. I think he's a jerk."

"You do realize, you can be a perv *and* a jerk at the same time, right? In fact, I'm pretty sure they go hand-in-hand."

"Not with Brody," I said.

And then, there was the thing I *didn't* say. Even if Brody *were* a perv, he would never get pervy with me.

In fact, other than our attic encounter – which had ended only with my humiliation – Brody had shown so little interest in me that I might've gotten some sort of complex if I happened to be interested in *him*, which I totally wasn't.

"So if he's not a perv," Cami said, "why the peephole?"

"I'll tell you why," I said. "He was thinking of shooting me."

She hesitated. "You mean with a gun?"

"Well, I'm not talking about his 'love gun', if that's your other guess." I sighed. "Anyway, the next time I see him, I'm gonna let him have it."

I meant it, too.

And just fifteen minutes later, I had my chance.

CHAPTER 31

Arden

Brody gave me a look. "Hell yeah, I made a peephole. What, you think I'm nuts?"

We were standing in the kitchen of the crew house, and I'd just confronted him about that hole in the wall.

If Brody were anyone else, he would've been mortified at my discovery, or at least a little embarrassed. But Brody was *neither* of these things, and his lack of shame was a real kick in the pants.

With growing indignation, I considered his question. *He was nuts, alright.* And he was making *me* nuts, too.

I glared up at him. "How am I supposed to answer that?"

"With an honest opinion," he said. "Pretend you're me. It's the middle of the night. And you hear someone in the bathroom — someone who doesn't belong. So tell me. Are you gonna look to see who it is? Or wait for them to come at you first?"

I rolled my eyes. "And do what? Shoot you through the door? That *is* what you implied earlier, wasn't it?"

Too late, I recalled where he'd said such a thing. It had been in the attic, where we'd had that unsettling encounter.

Then again, nearly all of my interactions with Brody were unsettling.

In fact, I was feeling a little unsettled *now*. His shirt was slightly damp, and his face and arms were glistening with perspiration. The muscles in his arms were gloriously defined, not just by the sheen of his skin, but also by the lingering after-effects of whatever he'd been doing.

He was majorly pumped.

And so was I – but in a totally different way.

As I watched, he lifted the hem of his T-shirt and used it to wipe the sweat off his face.

The movement shouldn't have been sexy. I mean, who liked sweat, right? And yet, I couldn't help but notice how his abs glistened, and how the tendrils of his damp hair curled on the very ends.

He looked so "donkable" that I felt myself swallow.

When he finished, I gave him an annoyed look. "What were you doing, anyway?"

"When?"

"Before you walked in," I said. "Like why are you all…" I made a vague fluttering motion with my hands. "…hot and stuff."

And just like that, my cheeks were flaming.

I cleared my throat. "And just so you know, I said hot *and* stuff. Not 'hot stuff.' That's totally different."

His lips twitched at the corners. "So you think I'm hot stuff, huh?"

Damn it. He was goading me again. "That's *not* what I said, as I *just* explained. And you never answered the question. What were you doing?"

"Working. What else?"

"Doing what?"

"I was ripping out some plaster."

Speaking of ripped, I could totally envision it, except in my visions, his shirt wasn't just damp. It was gone entirely, leaving him naked from the waist up. In my mind's eye, his muscles bulged, and his body glistened as he went to work on the house, hammering at something or other. I didn't even know what. I just knew he looked very good doing it.

As the image lingered in my brain, my tongue brushed my upper lip. *Oh, boy.* The vision was *very* thought-provoking.

Double damn it.

I shook my head and tried to focus on something that didn't involve my nemesis half-naked. "But wait," I said. "Does that mean you started working on the house already?"

"Some."

I felt my brow wrinkle in confusion. "But doesn't that ruin the 'before' footage?"

Broody shook his head. "They finished it today. Remember?"

"Oh." He was right. That was, after all, part of the reason they'd taken me through the house and filmed my reaction to the damage. It was to showcase how terrible the house looked now, *before* its upcoming restoration.

Still, there was something I didn't understand. "But don't you have crews to do the plaster ripping and stuff?"

"Sure," he said. "But I wanted to see what was under there."

"Under where?"

His eyes filled with amusement, although for the life of me I couldn't imagine why.

I asked, "What's so funny?"

"You said underwear."

I stared up at him as the urge to snicker warred with my better sensibilities. In the end, I decided to stick with the facts. "No. I said *under* and *where* – two different words."

He gave a slow nod. "Oh. Like hot stuff."

My gaze drifted to his pecs. *Oh boy. He was hot, alright, as he damn well knew.*

With renewed horror, I jerked my gaze upward. "No. Like hot *and* stuff, as I already explained." As I said it, I snuck a teeny glance at his mid-section. "And you're just trying to distract me."

"From what?"

Well, not from your amazing abs, that's for sure.

Oh, for God's sake.

Stiffly, I replied, "From that peep hole, that's what."

"If you want an apology," he said, "forget it."

I made a sound of protest. "But that was so intrusive!"

"No kidding," he said. "But hey, you can apologize any time."

"For what?"

"For breaking into my house."

"For the last time," I gritted out, "I didn't break in. I had a key."

"Not anymore," he said.

"What?"

"They're changing the locks tonight."

Crap. "Why tonight?"

"Because the real work starts tomorrow. So if I were you, I'd be ready."

Ready for what, I didn't know. And I never had the chance to ask, because just then, Waverly walked in through the side door and stopped short at the sight of Brody standing in the kitchen.

Her lips parted, and her eyes smoldered. She eyed him up and down like he was good enough to eat.

For some stupid reason, I didn't like it. Without thinking, I blurted out, "So, who wants dinner?"

Dinner? I hadn't been thinking of dinner. But hey, it *was* dinner time. And besides, if I flung Waverly a biscuit or something, maybe she wouldn't start munching on Brody's ass, because she totally looked like she wanted to.

Waverly smiled like I'd just suggested a Brody butt-munching marathon. "That sounds like an excellent idea," she said, looking to Brody. "Dinner for two? Maybe something on the river?" Her voice grew husky. "Like last night?"

Last night?

I tensed, although heaven knows why. Yesterday evening, they'd both disappeared for several hours, and they hadn't returned until midnight. It was beyond easy to guess that they'd gone out for dinner, and possibly something more.

And Brody *did* have a condo on the river. For all I knew, they'd gone to *his* place for a nightcap of the naked variety.

The thought bothered me more than it should've. But it also posed an odd question. I looked to Brody and said, "There's something I don't get. If you live right here in the city, why wouldn't you just stay at your own place?"

Brody looked at me for a long moment before saying, "Good question."

Hey, I thought so. And yet, he still wasn't answering. I waited, refusing to let him off the hook.

Finally, it was Waverly who broke the silence. "It's not *that* good of a question," she said. "His condo's thirty minutes away. So *of course* he'd want to stay closer to the site to keep an eye on things." Her gaze slid to Brody. "Me too. We run a *very* tight ship."

It was a decent story. *But I wasn't buying it.*

And judging from Brody's continued silence, the story wasn't quite as simple as Waverly had made it sound.

I was still trying to figure it out when Waverly turned back to Brody and practically purred, "So, should we shower before we go?"

We?

Did that mean what I thought it meant?

I mean, sure, if they wanted to hop into the shower together, it was none of my business. And yet, an odd empty feeling settled in the pit of my stomach. It wasn't even hunger. It was something worse.

Disappointment.

What on Earth was wrong with me, anyway?

I didn't even *like* Brody. And besides, I wasn't the type to get naked with someone just because they were pretty – not that Brody had ever offered.

In the end, I turned away with some off-handed comment about ordering pizza for myself, only to turn back at the sound of Brody's voice.

"Sounds good," he said. "Make sure there's pepperoni. My treat."

Next to him, Waverly sputtered, "Pizza? Seriously?"

He gave her a look. "You got something against pizza?"

"No. Definitely not," she stammered. "I *love* pizza. It's just that…"
She lowered her voice. "I was thinking of something more intimate."

He glanced in the general direction of the driveway. "You've got a
car," he said. "So get whatever. I won't stop you."

I looked to Waverly. "Wait, you have a car?"

"Of course I do," she said. "Don't you?"

"Not at the moment," I admitted. "But even *you* didn't have a car
yesterday."

"Well I do now," she said. "It was just delivered. So where's *your*
car?"

I bit my lip. "Actually, I'm sort of between cars at the moment."

With a sly smile, she asked, "So how'd you get here?"

"I, um, got a ride, actually."

"Yeah," she said with a laugh. "In a Greyhound bus." She looked
to Brody as if sharing a secret joke. "We saw the ticket, remember?"

Heat flooded my face. "When?"

Waverly was still laughing. "Last night, when you were hiding in
the bathroom."

"I wasn't hiding," I said. "I was talking to my cousin." I turned and
gave Brody an accusing look. "And you went through my stuff?"

He frowned. "That's what you think?"

Before I could answer, Waverly chimed in, "Oh, please. We didn't
go through anything. The ticket was just sitting out there for anyone to
see."

Damn it. She was right. I'd left that stupid bus ticket along with
some other receipts on the dresser. Tonight, I vowed, I'd rip the ticket
to shreds and burn the pieces.

But for now, I still felt violated – or maybe I was just embarrassed
by the fact that I was twenty-four and had no car of my own.

Again, I looked to Brody, and it struck me all over again how
different his life had turned out compared to mine. He probably had a
dozen cars and a dozen houses. But me, I had zero of both.

When our gazes met, he gave me a look that I couldn't quite decipher. Our gazes held, and the moment stretched out longer than it should've.

The moment – or whatever it was – might've lasted even longer, if not for Waverly practically jumping between us to announce, "On second thought, pizza sounds fabulous."

In the end, it *was* pretty fabulous. At Brody's suggestion, I ordered it from a local place, not a national chain. By the time it arrived, Brody had already showered – *alone*, by the way – and had dressed in dark running pants, along with yet another T-shirt.

He looked amazing as usual, even while he paid the driver and gave him a tip so generous, the guy smiled like it was Christmas morning.

Afterward, all three of us ate together in the living room. There wasn't a ton of conversation, but there was more than enough to hold my interest. I was especially interested to learn that Brody and Waverly had dined last night *not* at Brody's condo, but at a sandwich place on the opposite side of the river. And, if Waverly's demeanor was any indicator, she'd seen his condo *only* from the outside.

In passing, I also learned that the film crew was staying at a local hotel, and that a full team of construction workers would be on-site the very next morning.

Apparently, this included Brody's two brothers – Chase and Mason.

By the time I crawled into bed, I was actually looking forward to the next day's activities. It would be interesting. And I'd get a sense of how quickly the house might be restored to its former glory.

But then, when the morning actually arrived, the experience proved to be anything but glorious.

CHAPTER 32

Arden

A male voice from somewhere behind me said, "What are you doing here?"

At the sound, I almost flinched. He'd said it like an accusation, not a question.

Slowly, I turned to look. And there he was, Mason Blastoviak – Brody's oldest brother. He wore jeans, a denim work shirt, and a scowl so ominous, I felt myself swallow.

I'd never met the guy in person, but I'd seen him plenty of times on TV.

On screen – and in real life – he looked a lot like Brody, with the same square jaw and the same muscular build. But there were plenty of differences, too. His hair was shorter, his eyes were darker, and his mouth was compressed so tight, I took an involuntary step backward.

I was standing out in the front yard of what used to my grandparent's place. Around us, construction workers were busy lugging around tools and supplies while Roy and Jerry wandered through the commotion, filming as they went.

It wasn't quite eight o'clock in the morning, and I'd been trying to stay out of the way until I was called to do otherwise.

The weather was brisk and windy – so windy that even out here in the front yard, the sounds of waves crashing against the beach behind the house was so loud that I hadn't heard Mason approach.

Still, I tried to smile as I said, "Sorry, I didn't hear you come up."

Without smiling back, he repeated his original question, more slowly this time. "*What* are you doing here?"

My smile faltered. "You don't know?"

"If I knew, I wouldn't be asking."

Okay, I *definitely* wasn't smiling now. "I was hired as a consultant."

From the look on his face, this wasn't what he wanted to hear. In a tight voice, he asked, "To consult about what?"

It was a good question, and the answer was confusing even to myself. "Well, you see...." I blew out a nervous breath. "My family used to own the house, so they wanted someone to help with the historical stuff, I guess."

His expression only darkened. "Who?"

By now, I was seriously rattled. "Sorry, what?"

"*Who* hired you?"

His hostility was a force to be reckoned with, and yet I tried not to take it personally. This was, after all, Mason Blastoviak, the least likeable of the three brothers.

From watching the show, I already knew that he wasn't a happy-go-lucky kind of guy. In fact, he could be a real bastard sometimes – like now, for example.

But of course, I reminded myself, this might not be so random as it seemed. Although we'd never actually met, he'd surely heard my name years earlier, and not in a good way, after I'd torched Brody's pickup.

Was he putting my face with that name?

But of course he was. Nothing else could explain his overt hostility. I sighed. "Let me guess. You're angry about that thing from high school. I mean, when *I* was in high school. Not you, of course." At the memory, I almost cringed. "You know, that thing with Brody's truck?"

Without bothering to reply, he said it again. "*Who* hired you?"

I had to give the guy at least *some* credit. He could definitely focus. "Alright, fine," I said. "It was Landon Tarrington. There. Are you happy?"

His only answer was a low curse.

By now I felt like cursing, too. "Is that a problem?"

"What do *you* think?"

Why lie? "I think you're being awfully rude."

"And *I* think you don't belong here."

"Hey! I belong here you just as much as you do."

He crossed his arms. "Do you?"

Too late, I realized the ridiculousness of my statement. "Okay, maybe I don't belong *quite* as much as you do. But I *do* have a contract."

"Not anymore, you don't." He flicked his head toward the street. "So pack your stuff and go. You're fired."

My jaw dropped. "You can't fire me."

"Yeah? Why not?"

Just then, I heard another male voice – this one a lot more familiar – say, "Because I say so, that's why."

I turned to look just in time to see Brody stride up from somewhere behind me. He looked to his brother and said, "So drop it, alright?"

Mason's jaw tightened. "You're not serious."

With growing concern, I looked from brother to brother. I felt like I should say something, but I had no idea what.

Brody told Mason, "I'm plenty serious. And you're forgetting something."

Looking anything but forgetful, Mason replied, "And what's that?'

"This is *my* job. Remember?"

"Yeah. And *my* company."

"*Our* company," Brody corrected. "And it's my fucking house."

Looking more pissed off than ever, Mason replied, "Yeah? So?"

Brody stepped forward until they were standing chest to chest. "So, do I tell *you* how to run *your* shit?"

But Mason still wasn't backing down. "Not if you're smart, you don't."

"Exactly," Brody said. "So leave her alone, alright?"

Hearing this, a wave of gratitude washed over me. And yet, I couldn't help but feel incredibly awkward for causing such tension between the brothers.

I looked to Mason and said, "Look, you're obviously angry. And I totally get it. Really, I do –"

"You're wrong," he said.

I frowned up at him. "What?"

"You get nothing." He turned back to Brody and said, "You want this? Go ahead. But don't come bitching to me when she torches the place."

Oh, for crying out loud. "Hey! I'm not the torching type!"

My claim hung there like a cloud in our midst, because all three of us knew that yes, at least *some* torching had happened in the past – specifically to Brody's truck. And me? I'd been the one holding the lighter.

After a long, awkward moment, I muttered, "Okay fine. But that was a total accident."

And it was, *really.*

CHAPTER 33

Arden – Six Years Earlier

Un-freaking-believable.

It was my last week of high school, and everyone was in a glorious mood. *Everyone but me.*

It was early Wednesday afternoon, and I'd just walked out of school with an advance printout of my final grades. *They weren't good.* Or at least, they weren't good enough.

In spite of blowing up the chemistry lab and being suspended for two whole weeks, by some miracle – not to mention a whole bunch of extra credit – I'd still managed to pull my grades out of the gutter.

I'd even managed to pass chemistry, but just barely. But barely wasn't good enough, and my scholarship was officially torched, just like my eyebrows.

I looked like a goblin, and I felt like one, too.

But Brody? He looked as amazing as ever. I knew because I still saw him in class – well, whenever he showed up, that is.

We never spoke, not even to argue about what had happened.

After that senseless explosion, I'd called him every name in the book – not that he'd seemed to care, just like he hadn't cared that we'd both been suspended, or that I'd gotten half of the blame for *his* recklessness.

And why did I share in the blame? It was because although he'd held the lighter, *I'd* opened the door. The whole thing had been caught on camera, thanks to video surveillance in the hall, and there was no denying the fact that both of us had played a role in what had happened.

Still, it was all so incredibly unfair.

I hadn't done anything wrong. Not really.

But there was nothing I could do about it now. I'd argued and explained until I'd been blue in the face, but none of it had done any good, not even when my grandparents had argued on my behalf.

According to the school administrators, I was just lucky I hadn't been sued for damages or kicked out of school entirely.

Lucky? Not the way I saw it.

Goodbye scholarship. Hello...? Well, I didn't quite know yet.

But I'd have to think of something.

As I trudged along the lonely sidewalk, I reached into the pocket of my jeans and felt around for that godawful lighter. On that fateful day, I'd found it halfway down the hall just before ducking into the girls' restroom to wash my face and stare at my new reflection – the one with singed hair and missing eyebrows.

When I was done staring at the damage, I'd slipped the lighter into my pocket, intending to wave it in Brody's face, just like he'd done to me.

But I didn't – because by then, I was in more than enough trouble already.

And yet, for some inexplicable reason, I'd been carrying the lighter with me ever since. Why, I wasn't quite sure. Maybe I was superstitious. Or maybe I just figured that by holding onto it, I was keeping it away from Brody.

It was ridiculous, I know.

I mean, as if he couldn't buy another cheap lighter any time he wanted.

As I walked aimlessly down the street, I pulled out the lighter and gave it a tentative flick. The flame flickered to life for only a moment before a sudden breeze snuffed it out – much like my scholarship had been snuffed out by Brody's carelessness.

I gave the lighter another flick, and this time, the flame held.

In my other hand was the printout of my grades. I looked from the lighter to the printout and back again.

A bitter scoff escaped my lips. *Maybe I should torch the paper and be done with it.* After all, the report card wasn't a keeper, not even literally. All too soon, I'd be getting a final one in the mail.

Just as I'd decided that I wasn't the torching type, I happened to spot Brody's truck parked along the curb of the very next block.

I flicked off the lighter and kept on walking as I eyed the vehicle. It was definitely Brody's. I'd seen him driving it in the school parking lot so many times, I'd recognize it anywhere.

It was a big red, rusty thing with an extended cab and a long dent along the side. From bumper to bumper, the truck was old and ugly. But hey, I wasn't one to judge. At least Brody had a vehicle, which was more than I could say for myself.

Me? I was still taking the bus.

Not today though.

Today, I'd actually done the unthinkable. I'd skipped my final class to leave school early.

I didn't even know where I was going or how I'd be getting back to my grandparent's place. I just knew that I was about to pop – or burst out crying – and the last thing I wanted to do was cry in class.

That class was chemistry, where I'd be sitting in the same classroom as Brody. Or at least, we *would've* been sitting in the same classroom if only both of us hadn't apparently decided to be somewhere else.

By now, I'd reached the familiar red pickup but saw no sign of its owner. Still, he couldn't be too far away. The truck's windows were rolled all the way down, as if Brody might return any moment.

Or maybe he always left it open like this.

Either way, it only went to prove how careless he was, even with the little things.

I stopped walking and took a long, silent look around. By now, I'd traveled maybe a dozen blocks away from the school.

The area was pleasant and peaceful, with big, beautiful houses and nicely kept yards.

Was this where Brody lived?

The house nearest to his truck was a two-story bungalow with neatly trimmed hedges and a wide, welcoming porch, complete with an old-fashioned porch swing and pots of red flowers lining the front steps.

Weird.

For some reason, I'd always envisioned Brody living someplace a lot rougher. But hey, it just went to show, huh?

Never judge a book by its cover and all that.

As I stared at the house, a wave of bitterness washed over me. Somewhere nearby, a lawnmower was humming along, and the scent of freshly mowed grass lent a sweetness to the air that might've lightened my mood if only all of my plans hadn't just gone up in smoke – and I meant that literally.

As my thoughts swirled, and my anger burned, I looked once again to Brody's pickup. If I were a different kind of person, I'd light my report card on fire and toss it into his truck, maybe leave a nice burn mark where his ass met the upholstery.

To my surprise, I was actually considering it.

My hands were loose at my sides, and I was still holding the lighter and the printout. The lighter was off, and the printout was fluttering in the breeze.

Was it fate that had carried me here?

I stared long and hard at the truck before finally shaking my head. *No. It wasn't fate. It was stupidity.* And whatever else I might be, I wasn't stupid, even if I *was* stupidly angry at everything Brody had cost me.

I sighed. *Talk about pathetic.*

Even when it came to revenge, here I was, still playing by the rules, for all the good it did me.

I was such a sap.

But then, with sudden inspiration, I raised the lighter and the paper. With one hand, I wadded up the paper into a nice, tight ball and then flicked on the lighter.

I held the wadded paper to the flame and watched as the flame caught. With a bitter laugh, I tossed the flaming wad not into the cab of his truck, but into the bed of it, where it would do no damage whatsoever.

It was a pointless gesture, and yet, it *did* make me feel just a little less pathetic. Maybe the paper would burn to ashes. Or more likely, the flame would sputter out, leaving a semi-burnt blob for Brody to find the next time he ventured into his truck bed.

Either way, I was done with the whole sordid thing.

I turned and began walking once again down the peaceful street. I'd gotten maybe two full blocks before an odd burning smell made me stop and turn back to look.

My eyes widened. *Oh, my God.*

Brody's truck. The whole truck bed was in flames. *What the hell?*

At the sight, my stomach lurched, and my heart skipped a beat.

Had *I* done that?

I hadn't meant to.

Without pausing to think, I plunged toward the truck, intending to put out the fire somehow, maybe grab a garden hose or –

Or nothing.

I was still a full block away when his truck literally exploded, sending flames shooting not only from the truck bed, but from the passenger area, too.

A split second later, Brody emerged from somewhere behind the house. He rushed toward his truck, and then stopped short in the middle of the front yard, as if realizing that his truck was already beyond saving.

He looked around and spotted me almost immediately. As our gazes locked, something slipped from my hands.

The lighter.

With a muttered curse, I leaned down and scooped it up. By the time I stood with the lighter in-hand, Brody's expression had gone from shock to raw hatred. He was still glaring when I shoved the lighter back into my pocket.

Why I bothered, I had no idea.

I was so busted.

Already, neighbors were rushing out of their houses to gawk at the flaming pickup. Within just a few moments, a small crowd had gathered on either side of the formerly quiet street.

In spite of the surrounding commotion, Brody's gaze didn't waver. And neither did mine.

As our gazes held, I felt myself swallow. *Should I run away? Or walk toward him and face the music?*

It took me only a moment to realize that running was useless. I mean, I'd already been caught red-handed. And he knew who I was. *I might as well try to explain, or help, or something.*

I hurried toward him, for all the good it did. By the time I reached his side, he was already doing what I'd only thought of doing.

In the short time it had taken me to clear the final block, he'd strode to the nearby house, yanked a garden hose from among the shrubbery, and rained water down on his truck – or rather, what used to be his truck.

Now, it was mostly a burnt-out shell.

Bracing myself, I sidled next to him and said in a horrified whisper, "It was an accident, honest."

He was still hosing down his truck. His jaw clenched, and without so much as a glance in my direction, he said, "Right."

"You don't believe me?"

At this, he turned and faced me head-on, even as he continued to spray the smoking vehicle. In a tight voice, he said, "Does it matter?"

"Yes. It does, actually."

His expression darkened. "Why?"

"Well, because…" I bit my lip. "I guess I'm in big trouble, huh?"

The words had barely left my lips when a police car, quickly followed by a fire truck, screeched up to the smoking remnants of Brody's pickup.

With a sound of disgust, Brody told me, "Go."

I wasn't following. "What?"

"Go," he repeated.

"Why?" I scoffed. "So you can tell your side of the story and get me in even more trouble?"

With a cold smile, Brody said, "You think *that's* how I'm gonna deal with this?"

His smile made just a little bit nervous, and I gave the police car a worried glance. Already, two officers had gotten out of the car and were warning the small crowd to back away from the smoldering truck.

Into my silence, Brody said, "You're gonna get it, alright. But not from the police – so if I were you, I'd get the fuck out of here while you can."

It was so tempting. Still, I hesitated. *Was this a trap? Or maybe some sort of trick?*

If I left, would Brody send the police chasing after me, to be cuffed and stuffed like a common criminal?

My shoulders slumped. *Cripes, probably I deserved it.*

More to myself than to him, I said, "It really was an accident."

With that same cold smile, he replied, "Yeah? And when I get payback, we'll call *that* an accident, too."

"Payback? Like revenge?"

His only answer was a half shrug.

Again, I felt myself swallow. "What kind of revenge?"

"Trust me. You'll know it when you see it."

Fast forward six years, and here I was, enjoying the fruits of Brody's long-delayed revenge – except he'd already told me that he knew nothing of my connection to the house.

What did that mean? Revenge was still somewhere on the horizon? I shuddered to think.

As far as the truck, I still had no idea why it had exploded like that, or what he'd told the police. I just knew that I never got in trouble, not even a little.

And for some reason, that made me just a little bit nervous.

CHAPTER 34

Arden – Present Day

As the memories swirled, I looked from brother to brother. Neither one of them looked happy. But hey, *I* wasn't happy either.

I tried again. "That whole thing with the truck, it really *was* an accident."

With a low scoff, Mason turned away, not bothering to reply. As he strode toward the house, he called back to Brody, "Just remember what I said."

It took me a moment to recall the last thing he'd told Brody. But soon enough, Mason's exact words came flooding back. *"Don't come bitching to me when she torches the place."*

I looked to Brody and said, "I wasn't lying. I didn't mean to torch anything."

Brody crossed his arms. "So you said."

"What, you don't believe me?"

"I saw what I saw."

"Which was…?"

"The truck in flames and you with the lighter."

"Yeah, well…" I winced. "I know it looked bad, but just listen. I'm walking by, and I happen to see your truck—"

"So you torch it."

"No," I said. "I just lit something on fire."

"Yeah. My truck."

I sighed. "I didn't mean your truck. I meant *one* crumpled piece of paper. It wasn't even that big."

When Brody said nothing in reply, I continued. "And this paper, well, I um, tossed it into the truck bed. That's all."

His voice was flat. "That's all."

"I didn't know it would blow up like that." My brow wrinkled at the memory. "And speaking of which, why *did* it blow up?"

"What, you don't know?"

"How would I?" I said. "I don't even know why it caught on fire."

He gave me a dubious look. "Is that so?"

"Okay, yes, I realize that my flaming paper wad had something to do with it, but the last time I checked, paper – even flaming paper – doesn't burn metal."

"It does if there's gasoline in the back."

I frowned. "How much gasoline?"

"A five-gallon can."

"Oh." I paused to think. "But if the gas is *inside* the can, a little piece of paper wouldn't catch the can on fire. Would it?"

"It would if I'd just filled it up."

I still wasn't following. "But why?"

"Why do you think?"

Once again, I tried to envision it. Thinking out loud, I said, "Is it because there was gas spilled along the side or something?"

"Probably."

"But you don't know for sure?"

His gaze locked on mine. "Hard to check when your truck's on fire."

"Okay, fine," I said. "But even if all five gallons *did* catch on fire, it wouldn't make your whole truck blow up." I bit my lip. "Would it? I mean, that was a pretty big explosion."

"No kidding."

"But why would the whole truck explode?"

"Because I'd just filled up the tank."

"You mean the truck's fuel tank?"

"Yeah. Twenty gallons."

"Oh." Finally, I saw what he meant. His truck had been old and rusty, so it wasn't *that* inconceivable that flaming fuel in the truck bed would've sparked a larger explosion in the main gas tank.

Reluctantly, I said, "I guess that makes sense."

Brody eyed me with obvious contempt. "Good to know."

Ignoring his attitude, I said, "But wait, why would you be hauling around gas in the first place?"

"Because," he said, "I was mowing lawns on the side."

He was? I tried to envision the scene from six years ago. "But I didn't see a mower in the truck bed."

"Right. Because I was mowing out back."

"Oh." His explanation was surprisingly simple. And yet, it wasn't what I'd expected. "So *that's* why you were skipping class? To work?" I stared up at him. "Seriously?"

"What, you're surprised?"

"Well, yeah, actually. I mean, I always figured you were cutting class for the fun of it."

"Want to know what *I* always figured?"

"What?"

His gaze hardened. "That I was done with you."

His words stung, but for the life of me, I couldn't figure out why. The two of us had never been friends. And, as I'd learned the hard way in high school, just because we were working on a common project, that didn't mean we were working on the same side.

Still, I dreaded the idea of fighting with him for four long months while the house was being restored. It would be miserable for both of us – me in particular, since I was so much lower than him in the pecking order.

I gave him a pleading look. "Look, it's been what? Six years? Don't you think it's time we put the past behind us?" I forced a laugh. "I mean, you don't see me complaining about my eyebrows, do you?"

His gaze flicked to my brows. "Hey, they grew back."

Talk about callous.

And besides, he was missing the point. *As usual.*

I tried again. "Yeah, but my grades didn't. That stunt in chemistry? It destroyed my grade point average. You *do* realize that, don't you?"

With something like a sneer, he said, "What, your perfect piece of paper?"

"It wasn't just a piece of paper," I said. "There was a lot more to it than that."

"Yeah? And maybe there was more to my truck."

I didn't doubt it. Still, a truck was replaceable. My scholarship wasn't. But Brody would never understand, and in the interest of mending fences, I tried to focus on the positive.

"Look," I said, "I know the truck was important to you. I get that. And I tried to pay for it. Remember?"

It was true. Being the kind of sap who always played by the rules, I actually *did* offer to pay for the stupid thing, even though I had nearly no money of my own. Embarrassingly, the offer was only possible because the truck was so old and crappy, it was practically worthless – even if it *was* an extended cab.

Still, I *had* offered. And I hadn't wasted any time either. I'd made the offer in class the very next day, only to have Brody tell me – and not too nicely either – that he'd rather have revenge than money.

The jerk.

At the memory, I felt the familiar pang of bitterness and frustration. Maybe *he* should pay *me* for the lost scholarship. But I never asked, whether due to misguided pride or the realization that Brody Blastoviak had even less money than I had.

Well, at the time, anyway.

Funny how much things had changed.

And now, he still hadn't responded to my statement. I tried again. "You do remember me offering to pay for it, right?"

His jaw clenched. "I didn't want your money."

Right. Because he'd wanted revenge instead.

So much for mending fences.

I glared up at him. "Well, goodie for you. So I guess you're pretty happy now, huh?"

He frowned. "Do I look happy?"

No. He didn't.

And neither was I.

Still, I had to say it. "Well you should be happy. You could buy a million trucks now if that's what you want, so why are you still mad about that one?"

The more I talked, the more pissed off he looked. In a tight voice, he replied, "It was more than a truck."

"Yeah. And it was more than my eyebrows, too."

When his only reply was a stony look, I threw up my hands. "You know what? Forget it." And with that, I turned away, intending to stalk off toward the beach.

That didn't happen.

I'd taken barely two steps when I spotted Roy standing near the side of the house, almost directly in my path. He was holding that godawful video camera. And yes, it was pointed straight at me.

Terrific.

With a sigh, I turned in the opposite direction, looking to avoid Roy and his camera, at least while I regained my composure.

Maybe it was cheating. But at the moment, I couldn't bring myself to care.

Turns out, that was a mistake. In the process of changing course, I nearly collided with yet *another* brother.

Oh, for crying out loud.

I felt like a human pinball, bouncing from Blastoviak to Blastoviak. It was like they were crawling out of the woodwork or something. This latest one was the middle brother, Chase, who was dressed in jeans and a T-shirt.

Like Brody and Mason, he looked obnoxiously good, even in work clothes. And for some reason, I only found this more annoying.

It was like all three of them had been sprinkled with "lucky dust" or something. They were rich, famous, and so good-looking, they might as well be movie stars. But then, I remembered. They *were* stars – just of a smaller screen, that's all.

Well, goodie for them, too.

After the near-collision, I told Chase, "Excuse me," and made a move to go around him.

As I did, he said in a tone that was almost friendly, "So, you're the pyro, huh?"

My steps faltered. *Pyro? As in pyromaniac?*

Well, this was just delightful.

I stopped and turned to face him. "I'm *not* a pyro."

He grinned. "Hey, I meant it as a compliment."

It was vintage Chase. From watching the show, I'd seen enough of him to know that everything was a joke to him. *But didn't he get it?*

This was no joking matter.

With a stiff smile, I turned in the opposite direction, heading once again toward the beach, having decided that it was better to brave Roy's camera than to deal with *anyone* named Blastoviak.

Still, as I marched toward the back of the house, I felt like a giant toad for being so rude to this latest brother. After all, he'd been the only Blastoviak who hadn't acted like I was some sort of psychopath, even if he *had* called me a pyro, which admittedly wasn't much better.

As I walked, I gave Roy a nervous glance. Sure enough, he was filming my march of shame like it was the most interesting thing he'd seen all morning, even amidst all the other commotion.

Ignoring the camera as best I could, I picked up the pace and kept on going. Probably, I looked like a total idiot.

But this was exactly what I'd signed on for, wasn't it?

Still, my thoughts churned like the waves crashing against the shore. The construction project had just barely begun, and already I was asking myself a serious question.

What on Earth had I been thinking?

CHAPTER 35
Brody

Next to me, Chase said, "You never mentioned she was hot."

He'd just sidled up to me after nearly colliding with Arden. *On purpose? Maybe.*

Ignoring my brother's bullshit, I watched Arden as she stalked around the side of the house, heading toward the beach. She was wearing jeans and a plaid long-sleeve shirt – just like your average construction worker, except she didn't look average to me.

She looked like apple pie and homemade cookies – assuming the pie was poison, and the cookies were filled with sand.

She was trouble.

Even the way she moved was getting under my skin.

From the sidelines, Roy and his video camera captured her movements in one long, candid shot. When Arden gave the camera a worried glance, I had to stop myself from jumping between her and the guy wielding it.

Not my problem.

And yet, I was still looking.

I watched in silence as she turned and disappeared behind the house. When Roy turned away, seeking another target, my shoulders relaxed, and I let out a long, unsteady breath.

Chase said, "Nice ass, too."

I felt my fingers clench. *Arden's ass was none of my brother's business.* A dumber guy would've told him so. *But me? I knew better.*

I knew what Chase was doing. He was trying to get a rise out of me.

I wasn't biting. Without turning to face him, I replied, "If you want her, go ahead."

But even as the words left my mouth, I knew that if he put the moves on her, I wouldn't like it. *I wouldn't stand for it either.*

And I wasn't the only one.

If Chase hooked up with her, Mason would lose his shit long before I did. He wasn't a forgiving guy, and Arden had committed the ultimate sin. She'd messed with something important to him – and I didn't mean the truck.

Chase laughed. "Nice to have your permission."

He didn't need it. He didn't even *want* it. He was just stirring the pot, as usual.

I looked to him and said, "Don't you have a hammer to swing or something?"

"Sure," he said, glancing at his watch. "But not for ten minutes."

As part of the show, we'd already restored nearly forty houses now. We had a system, and it worked well enough, even on days like today, when my brothers were sticking their noses where they didn't belong.

On the upside, they'd be gone by noon.

I'd done the schedule myself. Mason and Chase would spend the morning ripping down drywall or taking a hammer to something or other.

And then, when the crews broke for lunch, my brothers would go back to their primary gigs – Mason running the company and Chase making sure that our products kept on selling.

And me? I'd be staying here to get the job done.

I wasn't complaining. The show made our company a shit-ton of money, and the job was important. I liked what I did, and wouldn't trade places with anyone. This included my two brothers.

Next to me, Chase said, "She's not as crazy as I hoped."

I stiffened. "Who?" *As if I didn't know.*

"Arden," he said. "I figured she'd be giving off that crazy vibe, like a freak in the sheets, you know?"

If he meant his own sheets, I didn't want to hear it.

But I still wasn't biting. "Trust me," I said. "She's crazy enough." I frowned. "But not *that* crazy. I mean, she's no freak, if you know what I mean."

"You never know," he said. "Sometimes, it's the quiet ones."

My jaw clenched. "She's not quiet."

"So…" His tone grew speculative. "You think she's a screamer, huh?" He gave a slow nod. "Nice."

He was my brother. And I loved him. *But man, he could be such a dick.*

I gave him a long, irritated look. "Just what the hell is your problem?"

He laughed. "I knew it."

"What?"

"You've got a thing for her."

"Oh, fuck off. I do not."

"Why?" he laughed. "Because you told me to give her a go? Get real. You didn't mean it."

He was right about that. But it didn't matter. If I had *my* way, nobody – including myself – would be putting the moves on Arden Weathers.

CHAPTER 36

Brody

Two weeks into the project, Roy pulled me aside to say, "Hey, there's something I want you to look at."

It was nine o'clock at night, and the others were long gone. This included Waverly and Arden, who'd both returned to the crew house across the street – Waverly at four o'clock, and Arden just an hour ago.

I asked Roy, "What is it?"

"Some footage," he said. "I was wondering if you'd give me an opinion."

Reviewing footage wasn't my thing, but hey, like a lot of stuff, it was part of the job. And the truth was, the longer it kept me here, the better.

I'd been spending far too much time with Arden, and the more I got to know her, the harder it was to hate her.

Like tonight, the reason she'd stayed so long was because two laborers had gone home sick, and she'd jumped in to finish what they couldn't. This included hauling debris out to the dumpster and sweeping the construction site from end to end.

It was a dirty job that needed doing. *Tonight, not tomorrow.*

Tomorrow morning, we'd be filming on the ground floor, and the last thing I wanted was someone tripping over shit that didn't belong there.

I hadn't asked Arden to do it. But according to Roy, she'd volunteered after hearing that I was looking for someone to pick up the slack.

It was nice.

And it was a problem.

It was hard to hate someone when they were doing you a favor, and even harder when they looked so cute doing it. By now, she had her own hard hat and her own safety glasses, too.

She should've looked ridiculous, but she looked adorable as hell, even when pushing a broom.

Oh yeah. It was definitely a problem.

As Roy set up a video monitor on a nearby work bench, I grabbed a bottle of water for each of us and waited for whatever he was going to show me.

It wasn't what I expected.

The footage was over two weeks old. It featured Arden walking through the house, reacting to its sorry condition.

Five minutes in, I looked to Roy and asked, "What's the question?"

His ruddy face was all innocence. "What do you mean?"

"You said you wanted an opinion. An opinion on what?"

"The footage," he said. "What do you think of it?"

It was an obvious setup. Roy had been nudging Arden into my path from the beginning. Whether he was hoping we'd fight or fuck, I had no idea and refused to speculate.

Still, I glanced at the monitor, where the footage was still running. *What did I think?* I thought Arden was easy on the eyes and more interesting than I cared to admit.

The current footage was taken in the kitchen, before we'd gutted it down to the studs. On the monitor, Arden gave a shaky laugh as she pointed to the oven. The thing was old, ugly, and the most putrid shade of green I'd ever seen.

It had to be at least forty years old – not vintage, just ugly as hell. It was one of the first things we'd ripped out during the demolition phase.

Now, I listened as Arden talked about using that oven to make oatmeal cookies with her grandmother. "Except," Arden added with a laugh, "*she* was the real brains of the operation. I just followed her instructions, you know, on account of her arthritis."

Arden's eyes grew misty as she added, "I still have her cookie sheets in storage. And her recipe box, too." Arden smiled through unshed tears. "As soon as I get a place of my own, I'm gonna make a big batch of them in her honor."

Watching, I got a funny feeling in my chest.

Shit.

The whole thing made for some great television. But that wasn't the appeal. *Not for me.*

I was more interested in the way Arden looked, the things she said, and the way she made me feel. I didn't know what it was, but it was warm and sweet, like a homemade cookie fresh out of the oven.

I'd never had one, but I could imagine it just fine. Hell, I could imagine a lot of things.

This wasn't good.

As I continued to watch, Arden talked about helping her grandpa haul in wood for the fireplace and using that fireplace to keep warm whenever the furnace couldn't keep up.

I'd seen the furnace. The thing was too small for a house this size, and even older than the oven. And this was Michigan, not Florida, which meant that a fireplace wouldn't do much good, unless you were hunkered down right in front of it.

I kept on watching as Arden talked about painting the living room in her grandma's favorite color, and reading by candlelight on windy nights, when the electricity flickered off and on.

She'd said nothing about her parents.

And now, for the first time, I asked myself, *"Where the hell were they?"*

In high school, she'd never talked about them. But at the time, it was no big deal. Hell, I never talked about *my* parents either, and with good reason.

But Arden had talked plenty about her grandparents, just like she was doing in the footage. And the longer she talked on the screen, the more it became obvious that she'd been living here at the house, not just visiting on Saturday afternoons.

What did that mean?

By the time the footage ended, I'd half-forgotten that I wasn't alone. As the screen went dark, I felt a pang of something I hadn't felt in a long while.

With my eyes trained on the screen, I asked, "Is that it?"

"From *that* segment," Roy said. "What, you wanna see more?"

It was obvious bait to lure me in. But already I'd seen more than enough to get me thinking. *And feeling.*

I didn't want to think *or* feel – not about her.

I told him, "Nah, I'm good."

He paused. "So, uh, what'd you think?"

I gave a tight shrug. "It'll make for some good TV." As I turned to look at him, I said, "So, what'd Waverly think of it?"

Roy grimaced. "Don't ask."

In theory, Waverly was the producer, which meant she had the final say in how the episodes were cut. I asked, "So, is she gonna air that footage or not?"

"Oh, it's gonna air," Roy said. "You can bank on *that*."

I believed him. Roy was bucking for a promotion. And I had no doubt he'd get it. As far as Waverly, with every day that passed, she was taking less of an interest in doing her actual job.

I wasn't surprised. Hell, I'd seen it coming.

I knew her type.

Probably she'd expected it to be all glamor and glitz, when in reality, it was hard work on both sides of the camera – and even harder when you couldn't keep your head on straight, as I was learning firsthand for myself.

CHAPTER 37

Arden

During the past couple of weeks, things had gradually improved.
Thank goodness.

Unlike that first awful day of construction, Brody's brothers were rarely on-site. Instead, they showed up for a few hours here and there to look gorgeous for the cameras, before scuttling back to wherever, leaving me in relative peace.

As far as my dealings with Brody, we'd settled into a shaky truce. We never discussed his flaming truck or that incident with the chemistry lab. In fact, we never discussed anything from back in high school.

It was a good thing too, because there was more than enough tension floating around already.

But this time, I didn't mean arguments.

I meant something else – something that was a lot harder to put my finger on. It might've been friendship. Or might've been something a whole lot scarier.

Regardless, it was growing by the day.

Brody and I were living together, working together, and sometimes even laughing together. I discovered that he was a surprisingly fun roommate, and that he loved a lot of the same things I did.

We both liked toast with crunchy peanut butter, funny action movies, and classic architecture. We both hated McMansions and developers who didn't respect the character of historic neighborhoods.

And we both loved the house.

We spent at least some portion of every night pouring over restoration plans, much to the annoyance of Waverly, who kept angling to get Brody alone.

But for whatever reason, he wasn't biting.

As far as the house, tonight I'd left the job site later than usual. A couple of laborers had left early with some sort of stomach bug, and I'd volunteered to finish their work so the project wouldn't fall behind.

I hadn't done it for Brody's benefit. I'd done it for the house – or least that's what I kept telling myself.

And besides, I was making a terrific amount of money for very little work, so it seemed only fair to balance the scales wherever I could.

As for Waverly, she was looking anything but balanced. Standing in the kitchen, she looked twitchy and unsettled, like a junkie in need of a fix.

That fix had a name. *Brody Blastoviak.*

She wanted him, bad. Even now, this was glaringly obvious by the way she kept glancing at the side door, as if preparing to pounce on him the moment he walked in.

With an irritated sigh, she said, "It's ten o'clock."

I'd only ventured out of my bedroom to grab a bottle of water from the fridge. "Yeah? So?"

"So why is he still working?"

The answer should've been obvious. Brody was juggling a ton of details. Over the past couple of weeks, I'd gained a new appreciation for how much work went into fixing up such a massive old house.

Add in a film crew, a prickly producer, and two older brothers who were no help at all, and it was surprising that Brody had any free time whatsoever. Plus, I knew for a fact that he was laying the groundwork for two other restoration jobs in two different states.

The guy had his hands full and then some.

When Waverly made some snide comment about him needing a course in time-management, I couldn't stop myself from saying, "Oh come on. He's got a lot going on."

"So do I," she said. "And you don't see *me* skipping dinner."

I bit my lip. Actually, Brody *hadn't* skipped dinner. Sometime around seven, we'd had pizza delivered to the job site. By then, nearly everyone had already left for the day – everyone except for me, Brody, and Roy.

When Roy took his pizza to the SUV to make some phone calls, that left me and Brody to dine alone.

It had been nice, actually.

Even though we'd taken only fifteen minutes to eat, we'd sat near the beach, talking about color schemes for the home's exterior.

Waverly would've hated it.

But *I* didn't. To my surprise, I was loving the whole project, and not only because it was my grandparent's place. There was something magical about taking something neglected and making it beautiful again.

Of course, the house was far from beautiful now. In fact, it looked worse than when we'd begun. But that was only a temporary phase – the dark before the dawn, the demolition before the restoration, and the mess before the cleanup.

I felt a wistful smile tug at my lips. If only my grandparents could've seen the progression, they would've totally loved it.

But here at the crew house, Waverly was still griping. "And Roy's been acting all funny. I think he wants my job."

I almost scoffed in her face. *Didn't she see?* Roy was *doing* her job, along with his own. And, as much as his camera irritated me sometimes, I still liked and respected the guy.

How messed up was that?

To Waverly, I suggested, "Well, maybe you should spend more time at the job site."

Her lips pursed in obvious annoyance. "I was there all day."

"You were not," I said. "You didn't even show up 'til noon."

"So?"

"And you left at four."

"Hey, I'm in management!" she said. "I shouldn't have to *live* there."

I held up my hands in mock surrender. "Fine. Never mind. It was just a thought."

"Well, next time I'll thank you to keep your thoughts to yourself."

I smiled. "You're welcome."

"What?" she sputtered. "I wasn't thanking you for real."

"Good," I said. "Because I wasn't 'you're-welcoming' you for real."

"Oh, shut up," she said. "That's not even a thing." She sighed yet again. "This whole job's a total pain."

Now, I did scoff. "Which is why they call it a job." Even as I said it, it suddenly struck me that it wasn't feeling like a job to *me*. In some ways, it felt more like a vacation, probably because I hadn't had one in years.

Waverly said, "I don't care what they call it. This *isn't* what I signed on for."

Just then, the side door opened, and Brody walked in, looking surprisingly pensive.

At the sound of his footsteps, Waverly whirled to face him. "Finally," she said.

He stopped just inside the doorway. "Finally what?"

"Finally you're home." She gave him a winning smile. "So, what's for dinner?"

"Nothing," he said. "We already ate."

Her smile faded, and she gave me a long sideways glance. "Who's 'we'?"

Brody replied, "Everyone at the job site."

"And who was that?" she asked.

"If you wanna know," he said, "show up sometime."

She drew back. "What?"

"And you should know," Brody added, "Roy's been working his ass off."

"Yeah," she said. "Because that twat-waffle is bucking for my job."

Brody gave her a look. "You mean he's doing your job."

Waverly made a sound of annoyance. "What is it with you two? " She gave me an irritated look before continuing. "First I've got to hear it from *her*. And now from you, too?"

When Brody's glanced in my direction, I looked heavenward in shared commiseration.

Waverly said, "I saw that!"

I tried not to smile. "Saw what?"

"That eye-roll." She looked back to Brody. "You saw it, right?"

Without bothering to reply, he said, "We done?"

"We can't be done," she said. "We haven't even started."

I asked, "Started what?"

She looked to me and said, "I wasn't talking to *you*."

"Good," I said, "because I wasn't listening."

"You were, too!"

Now, I did smile. "Sorry, what'd you say?"

"I *said*..." But then, her eyes narrowed. "Wait a minute. I see what you did there." She looked back to Brody. "You see how she's ganging up on me?"

I almost laughed. "I can't be ganging up anyone. I'm only one person."

"Yeah, and I'm Little Miss Lollypop," she said. "What of it?"

Little Miss Lollypop? I couldn't help it. I snickered. And when I looked to Brody, he looked dangerously close to snickering, too.

But Waverly looked ready to pop. "Stop laughing!"

When I tried – and failed – to wipe the smile from my face, Waverly said, "You know what? Forget it. You're both fucking nuts. It's always 'the house this' and 'the house that.' Well you know what?" Her voice rose. "I fucking hate that house!"

And with that, she turned and stalked toward her bedroom. When the door slammed behind her, I swear, it shook the whole place.

This left me and Brody alone in the kitchen. With an awkward smile, I said, "So, honey, how was *your* day?"

As the question echoed out between us, I almost winced. *Honey?* I hadn't meant to say that. I forced a laugh. "Never mind. Bad joke." As I said it, I turned away, intending to slink back into my bedroom before I made an even bigger fool of myself.

From behind me, Brody said, "Wait."

I stopped and turned to face him. "For what?"

With no trace of humor, he said, "I've got a question."

"About what?"

"The house across the street," he said. "What happened with it?"

I wasn't quite sure what he was getting at. "What do you mean?"

He gave me a serious look. "I mean, why don't you own it?"

CHAPTER 38

Arden

I stared up at him. "Is that a serious question?"

Brody frowned. "Do I look like I'm joking?"

No. He didn't. In fact, he looked more serious than he had in a while. Still, I didn't get it. "Well, you must be joking," I said, "because you *know* the reason I don't own it."

"Which is...?"

"Because *you* own it."

"But I didn't always."

As if I needed the reminder. "Yeah, because you bought it from my cousin." I sighed. "And me. Sort of."

"You?" His eyebrows furrowed. "But you never owned it."

"Well, not *officially*," I said.

"What does that mean?"

It was such a long, convoluted story, I hardly knew where to begin. "Well, you already know that my grandparents owned the place, right?"

"Right."

"Well, my grandma – she died about six years ago, right after I graduated from high school." At the memory, my heart clenched like it always did. Still, I went on. "And then, three years after that, my grandpa passed away." As the memories swirled, my voice grew quiet. "It was *really* sudden, too."

Brody took a single step closer, and then stopped. His gaze met mine as he said, "I'm sorry."

He actually looked it, too. I tried to smile. "Yeah, well, he was almost eighty, so I guess I should've expected it, huh? But you know how it is with grandparents."

He shook his head. "No. I don't."

"What do you mean?" I asked.

"I never knew my mine."

I could hardly imagine. "Not on either side?"

"No."

"Why not?" I asked.

"Ask me later," he said. "We're talking about the house."

Right. The house. "Well...the point is," I continued, "my grandpa wanted the house to stay in the family like it always had, so he willed it to my mom." I paused for emphasis. "*And* to my cousin Jason."

"Why Jason?"

"Because my grandparents had two kids – my mom and her brother. But my mom's brother – my Uncle Chet – he died like five years ago."

"And?"

"And Jason – being Chet's only kid – ended up with Chet's half."

"What about you?" Brody said. "What'd you end up with?"

"Nothing." I hesitated. "Actually, that's not quite true. After my grandma passed away, my grandpa gave me all of her baking supplies, even her mixer, which was a *really* big deal. The thing cost a fortune." Realizing who I was talking to, I added, "Well, in relative terms, anyway. It wouldn't have seemed like that much money to *you*, for example."

I shook my head. "But forget the mixer. The cost wasn't important. It was just that she loved it so much, so I loved it, too." I smiled at the memory. "And then, there were the cookie sheets, and the cookie cutters, and her favorite mixing bowls. They're all in storage now, but when I get settled someplace, I'm going to put them in my own kitchen, and carry on the traditions, you know?"

Was I rambling?

I felt like I was rambling.

And now, in the quiet kitchen, there was something in Brody's gaze that was making me feel nearly naked – and not in a sexual way. In a low voice, he said, "Go on."

"Anyway, back to the house. My mom didn't love it the way I did. And neither did Jason, which is probably part of the reason he sold it."

To you.

But I didn't say that last part, because the subject of Brody's ownership had been beaten to death already.

No need to give it a few more whacks, right?

Brody studied my face. "But a minute ago, you said that *you* owned part of it."

"Not just *part* of it," I said. "Half. It's sort of complicated."

"Hey, I've got all night."

Oddly enough, I believed him. During the past couple of weeks, there'd been plenty of nights we'd stayed up late talking, sometimes well past midnight. On *those* nights, we'd talked not only about the house, but about other things, too.

Even so, we'd discussed nothing quite this serious.

As far as the house, I wasn't quite sure how to explain how I'd come to lose it. The story was so stupidly embarrassing, because I'd been such an idiot, and the thought of confessing my mistakes – to Brody of all people – was *not* my idea of a good time.

But he looked so sincere that I continued, anyway. "Alright. The thing is, when my mom inherited *her* half, she didn't want it."

"What do you mean?" he asked.

"All she wanted was the money. And Jason? He didn't want the house either."

"But *you* did."

With an embarrassed laugh, I said, "Gee, how could you tell?"

At this, he looked almost ready to smile. "Call it a hunch."

"Anyway, my grandparents weren't what you'd call wealthy. But they were *really* good with money, and the house was completely paid off, which meant that when they died, there was no mortgage or anything. This meant there were no payments except for the taxes and the upkeep. So after the reading of my grandpa's will, I beg my mom – and no, not on my knees, in case you're wondering—"

"I wasn't."

Heat flooded my face. "Sorry. Bad joke."

"You weren't joking." Brody's voice softened. "We both know that. But that's alright. I get it."

Did he? I wasn't sure. Still, I continued. "The point is, I literally *beg* her to hang on to her half of the house, so I can buy it from her – and Jason's half, too, after I graduate from college."

Recalling my initial optimism, I explained, "You see, by this time, I've got only a couple of years left until college graduation, so it's not that awful long. But when I ask my mom for the favor, do you know what she tells me?"

"What?"

"She tells me that I should let it go." A bitter scoff escaped my lips. "As if the place means nothing. And besides, she tells me, she wants *her* money now, *not* in a couple of years. And *then*, when I push the issue, she claims she's doing me a favor by selling it."

"To Jason, you mean?"

If only.

I shook my head. "Actually, she and Jason were *both* going to sell it. They had a realtor lined up and everything."

"So what happened?" Brody asked.

"So by then, I already know that my mom won't listen. But Jason, he's a little more reasonable."

"He can't be too reasonable," Brody said, "if he sold the place out from under you."

Well, there was that.

Still, I kept on going. "So I beg Jason to buy out my mom's half. I explain to him that it won't even be that hard, because he *already* owns half of the house on his own. So he'd just need a mortgage for the other half, and not even a big one, payment wise, because he's got plenty of equity, and..." My words trailed off as I remembered where this was going.

My story *didn't* have a happy ending.

Brody's gaze locked on mine. "And...?"

Oh, screw it. "And besides, it won't be *Jason* making the payments."

CHAPTER 39

Brody

What the hell?

I knew what she was getting at. But the question had to be asked. "So who *would* be making the payments?"

She winced. "You can't guess?"

Shit. "You?"

She nodded. "Right. And it's not just the payments either. There was the money for taxes and repairs—"

"Repairs?" I said. "You're joking, right?"

"Well, yeah," she said. "I mean, no. I'm not joking. And yes, I *do* realize that Jason didn't actually make them." Under her breath, she added, "*Now*, anyway."

"And you never checked?"

"At the time?" With obvious reluctance, she replied, "No, actually."

I didn't get it. Arden was no slacker. And she sure as hell wasn't stupid. I asked, "Why not?"

"Because I was always so busy, and it's not like I had any family in the area – well, not anymore. I mean, yeah, there was Jason, but he's pretty anti-social. And whenever I talked about visiting, he got all funny."

I didn't like where this was going. Cousin or not, she should've known the guy was up to no good. Working hard to keep my cool, I said, "Oh yeah?"

She nodded. "Yeah. It was like he thought I was just trying to check on the house or something."

No shit. "Yeah, because you should've."

Her mouth tightened. "Thank you, Captain Obvious."

"Hey, I'm just saying."

"Well, don't." She sighed. "I mean…you don't need to, okay? I *know* I should've checked. In fact, that's why I was at the house when you caught me in the shower. I was checking on my so-called investment."

I gave her a look. "And how'd *that* go?"

"You *know* how it went," she said. *"Terrible."*

I wouldn't have called it terrible. But yeah, it hadn't gone terrific – unless I counted the sight of Arden with no clothes on. *That* hadn't been so terrible.

In my mind, I could still see her bare silhouette. She'd looked good. *Too good.* Through the shower's frosted glass, I hadn't seen much, but what I *had* seen had been more than enough to get me thinking.

I was *still* thinking.

But now, the thought of Arden naked was a distraction I didn't need. Already, my body was responding, which only served to piss me off. As I shifted my stance, I told her, "Hey, I was there. Remember?"

"I *know* you were there," she said. "But you just asked how it went. What, you didn't want an answer?"

"That's not what I'm saying."

"Then what *are* you saying?"

I was still putting the pieces together. "I'm saying, tell me something I *don't* know."

"Like what?" she asked.

"Like what happened before I got there."

"Nothing happened," she said. "Jason's supposed to be living there, right? But when I show up, the house is empty, and Jason's nowhere in sight, which makes no sense whatsoever, because I called him beforehand to let him know I was coming. He even promised to meet me." Her shoulders slumped. "But he never showed."

What an asshole.

On that same night, I hadn't shown up until well past midnight, which meant that Arden had been alone in a vacant house for longer than was safe.

When I considered what might've happened to her, I felt my jaw clench. "And then?"

"And then I start texting him. *And* calling him. And emailing him, too."

Her story jived with what I'd seen on her phone – lots of messages going out and none coming back in.

The way it looked, she'd been had.

I wasn't sure what pissed me off more – that she'd fallen for an obvious scam, or that I'd ended up with swindled property. As far as the house itself, although I hadn't handled the transaction personally, I'd paid a fair price – hell, more than fair, considering its sorry condition.

And now, like a dumb-ass, I was angry on Arden's behalf.

I wanted to find that cousin of hers and beat the money out of him. It wasn't about the cash. Hell, if I wanted, I could give Arden that on my own.

It was the principle.

The guy had cheated his own cousin. *And then there was Arden's mom.* She sounded like a real piece of work – not as bad as mine, but bad enough.

"So about your cousin," I said, "did he ever get back to you?"

"Yeah, once." Arden rolled her eyes. "After I leave him like a hundred messages. We talked for barely ten minutes. And the whole time, he's acting all funny, like he's scared or something – which of course, he *should* be, considering that I'll be wanting my money back."

"You mean for the payments."

"Right. And the taxes." She blew out a long, trembling breath. "And the so-called repairs, including some that he *supposedly* made just last month."

What the fuck?

I shook my head. "So let me get this straight. You kept on writing him checks?"

"Well, yeah," she said. "I didn't want to lose the house – *or* see it fall apart. The way Jason talked, it was in terrible shape, a lot worse than I ever realized."

No kidding. Another few months, and the house would've been beyond repair. Forget the plumbing and the electricity. It was the roof that was the real issue. Once you have water pouring into any structure, it's only a matter of time before everything goes to pot.

My blood was boiling now as I considered all the ways she'd been cheated.

I told Arden, "But he didn't fix a damn thing."

"Well…we don't know that for sure." She bit her lip. "I mean, he might've made *some* repairs."

"Trust me. He didn't. And you should've checked."

She frowned. "Yeah. I know. And you don't need to keep telling me that, alright?"

I'd say it a dozen more times if that's what it took. "You sure about that?"

"Of course I'm sure. And besides, what if I *couldn't* check?"

It was no excuse. I had dozens of properties all over the country, and I kept a close eye on all of them. I replied, "Then you should've had someone else do it."

"Oh yeah?" she scoffed. "Like who?"

"Hell if I know."

"Exactly!" she said. "And hell if I knew either. And let's say I *did* know someone who was willing to do it, *and* who knew at least a little something about construction, what was I supposed to do? Have them show up on Jason's doorstep and demand to see the repairs?"

"Sure, why not?"

"Because he's my cousin. Don't you think that would've been kind of rude?"

"Compared to what?" I said. "Taking your money and doing fuck-all with it?"

Now she looked ready to cry, and I felt like a prick for pushing the issue. But this was Arden Weathers. And her story was filled with holes.

She wasn't stupid. *So why all the dumb decisions?*

What the hell was this? Some sort of ploy to get *my* house into *her* name?

I mean, yeah, I was angry on her behalf, but that didn't mean I was blind to what she was going for. If she'd been willing to beg me on her knees to fix up the place, she might do just about anything to get what she wanted.

Did that include dishing up a sob story?

Maybe.

I'd been around the block a time or two. And I'd seen far worse from people I knew better.

I wasn't a trusting guy.

Arden glared up at me. "You're acting like I'm some sort of moron for believing him."

She was no moron. I knew this for a fact. But I *also* knew that when she wanted something, she wasn't one to give up.

And then, there was her story – the sad tale of a girl who'd been wronged. The more I thought about it, the more it made no sense. Either it was missing a few chapters or it was mostly fiction.

"I know you're not stupid," I told her. "And that's the problem."

She blinked. "What? Why?"

"Because your story's a crock."

She drew back. "What?"

"You own half a house for what? Three years? And you don't check on it? You just keep writing checks? That's not the Arden *I* know."

"Oh yeah?" Her voice rose. "Then maybe you don't know me at all. You ever think of that?"

I *had* been thinking that, but not in the way she meant now. And this wasn't the time to get into it.

When my only reply was a tight shrug, she said, "And *this* is why I didn't want to tell you."

"Yeah, I can see why."

"You know what?" she said. "Forget it. I'm sorry I told you anything."

"And *I'm* sorry I asked."

"Oh, boo hoo," she said. And with that, she turned and stalked back toward her bedroom.

As I watched her go, I might've smiled if I weren't so pissed off. *Boo hoo?*

Like an idiot, I almost went after her, because there was part of me – a very stupid part of me – that wanted to yank her into my arms and tell her that I'd make everything alright.

It would be easy. *Too easy.*

As far as giving her back the house, hey that would be easy, too. I had plenty of money, and the deed free and clear. One quick phone call, along with a few signatures, and the house could be hers for good.

But who would be the sucker then?

Me.

And I was no sucker.

I held my ground, even as she disappeared into her bedroom and slammed the door so hard, I felt it in my bones.

Shit.

As I stood alone in the silent kitchen, I stared toward her bedroom, fighting like hell to keep myself from striding down the hallway and knocking on her door – or busting through it, if that's what it took.

I wanted answers. And yeah, I wanted *her.* She was like an itch that I couldn't scratch, and it was making me fucking crazy.

But I wasn't so crazy that I'd act on any of those impulses. So instead, I played it smart and headed in the opposite direction, leaving through the same door I'd come in.

CHAPTER 40

Arden

He was *such* a jerk.

I stewed for almost two hours in my bedroom before I decided that Brody deserved a piece of my mind – and not a nice piece either.

But when I left my bedroom to find him, he was nowhere in sight. Neither was Waverly. Both of their bedroom doors were shut, and the rest of the house was eerily silent even if the lights were still on.

By now, it was past midnight. *Were they asleep?*

Probably.

After only a moment's hesitation, I marched up to Brody's bedroom door and pounded on it anyway.

Nothing happened.

When I pounded again, the only door that opened was Waverly's. She emerged from her room wearing black silky pajamas and matching slippers. At the sight of me standing at Brody's door, she gave a loud sigh. "What do you want?"

"I wasn't knocking on *your* door," I said. "I was knocking on his."

"Oh, give it up," she said. "It's a waste of time, and you know it."

I *so* wasn't in the mood for this. "What exactly do you mean?"

"I *mean* he's not interested."

Oh, for God's sake. "In what?" I said. "Sex? Is that what you're getting at?"

"Obviously." She smirked. "You *do* have it, don't you?"

In theory, yes. In reality, it had been a while. In college, I'd had a few steady boyfriends, but none that had lasted, mostly because I'd been far too busy for any kind of relationship.

Plus, I wasn't a quickie kind of gal, which made Waverly's comment all the more irritating. "For your information," I told her, "I'm not knocking for sex. I'm knocking because there's something I need to tell him."

"Oh yeah?" She was still smirking. "What?"

Where to begin? For starters, I was going to tell him that he was the biggest jerk on the planet for asking me about the house and then acting like such an ass after I'd given him an honest answer.

And then, I was going to tell him to shove his condescending attitude where the sun didn't shine. *And after that?* Well, I wasn't quite sure, but I had plenty of material. All I needed was an audience. *And Waverly wasn't it.*

I coldly informed her, "That's between me and Brody."

"Just admit it," she said. "You're knocking because you want to hate-fuck him."

Huh? Was that really a thing? I shook my head. "What?"

"Oh, stop acting all innocent," she said. "I see the way you look at him."

"Oh really?" I scoffed. "Is it the same way *you* look at him?"

Her smirked disappeared. "I have no idea what you mean."

"Sure you do," I said. "You've been drooling over him since the beginning."

"I have not!"

"You have, too," I said. "Maybe *you* should hate-fuck him."

Her chin lifted. "Maybe I will."

"Good." But even as I said it, I knew that the idea of them together didn't make me any happier than I was now. And *that* was saying something.

After a few more barbs back and forth, Waverly huffed back into her bedroom and slammed the door behind her.

In the now-silent hallway, I shoved a hand through my hair and tried to think.

By now, I was so tired of everything – Brody's attitude, Waverly's sniping, and most of all, my own thoughts. The sad truth was, I *had* been thinking of Brody in ways that weren't *totally* innocent.

In fact, some of my thoughts were guilty as heck, especially in the dead of night when my imagination wandered and my fingers roamed. During the last week in particular, he'd been starring in all of my hidden fantasies.

How pathetic was that?

It made no sense. I really *did* hate him, most of the time anyway. Sure, we'd been getting along better lately, but so what?

Obviously, he hated me just as much as I hated him. Otherwise, why would he act like such a jerk?

Now I felt doubly unsatisfied.

I hadn't been able to give him a piece of my mind *and* I'd expended a sad amount of energy in trying to deny that yes, I might be attracted to him just a little.

Okay, more than a little.

Damn it.

With a sigh, I wandered to the living room, intending to sulk on the sofa.

I never made it.

And why?

It was because when I happened to glance out the front window, I saw Brody's truck in the driveway across the street.

So he was still around?

I flicked off the living room lights and edged closer to the window. Across the street, the lights were on, in spite of the late hour.

What on Earth was Brody doing?

Working?

It wasn't completely impossible.

In spite of my anger, I had to admit, Brody worked incredibly hard – and long hours too. But that didn't change anything. *He was still a jerk.*

And damn it, I wanted to tell him so.

Almost before I knew what I was doing, I'd already thrown on my sneakers and was heading straight across the street.

He was *so* going to get it.

And boy did he ever.

CHAPTER 41

Arden

Dumbfounded, I stood staring at the bathroom door. *Brody wasn't working.*

He was *showering.*

But why here?

It made no sense. Back at the crew house, we had two perfectly good showers. Okay, *one* of those showers was in my bedroom, but that was beside the point.

The whole thing struck me as just a little bit strange.

I was standing in the same upstairs hallway where I'd begged Brody on my knees to save the house. And *he* was in the same shower where he'd surprised me on that very same night.

At the memory, I crossed my arms and glared daggers at the bathroom door.

It was shut, and probably locked too. It's not like I'd tried the knob or anything, even if I *was* tempted.

It wasn't for lust, or even curiosity.

It was for justice.

What Brody needed was a taste of his own medicine.

I should barge in there and see how *he* liked it.

Unlike so many walls throughout the house, the walls surrounding the bathroom remained intact. Soon – probably tomorrow – the plaster would be stripped away, and new drywall would take its place.

No doubt, the old plaster would've been gone already, if not for the fact that it would render the bathroom unusable to anyone not wanting to put on a show while conducting their personal business.

Privacy – we all needed it, right?

But Brody hadn't cared about *my* privacy. *No. Not him.* What *he'd* done was make a hole in the wall to spy on me. And then, he'd busted through the door like some sort of axe-wielding psycho.

Axe or no axe, he'd scared me half to death.

And had he ever apologized?

Not hardly.

The longer I thought about it, the more irritated I became.

Inside the bathroom, the shower was still running. I could hear it, even if I couldn't see it. Still, I could imagine what it looked like in there – or rather, what *he* looked like in there.

If I were a betting person, I'd bet my last penny on the odds of him looking very fine. *He'd be naked. And wet. And probably all sudsy, too.*

At the mental image, I felt my body start to respond in ways that were more than a little unsettling.

Damn it. I hadn't come here satisfy my ill-advised lust. I'd come here to chew his ass out.

And yet, the thought of Brody's ass – with or without bite marks – made me swallow in the quiet hallway.

I glanced toward the peephole – the one he'd made on that very first night. Someone – heaven knows who – had stuffed a wadded paper napkin into the hole, which meant that unless I was willing to yank it out, peeping on Brody was completely out of the question.

It didn't matter. I'd never do such a thing. It felt sneaky and weird. Plus, I'd look totally pathetic if I were caught in mid-peep.

Knowing Brody, he'd read it completely the wrong way. He wouldn't see it as me getting some justifiable revenge. *No. Not Brody.* As arrogant as he was, he'd probably assume that I was ogling his naked body, giving myself a good eyeful of the sudsy water sliding down his muscular torso before heading southward.

In my mind's eye, I could already see it, all those slippery suds, easing down his six-pack and heading toward the package below.

I recalled all of those rumors from back in high school. Apparently, he had a very nice package. And, he was extra good at delivering, if you know what I mean.

At the mere thought, I blew out a shaky breath. *Oh, boy.*

I was doing it again.

And for some reason, this was the final straw.

Forget peeping. Perving out would be pathetic *and* useless. The shower door was made of frosted glass. Even if I did peep, I'd only see his silhouette.

It would be a nice silhouette, for sure. But it was hardly worth the risk. And besides, I reminded myself, that's not what I'd come here for.

No. I'd come to give him a taste of his own medicine.

With sudden inspiration, I decided to do the same thing to *him* that he'd done to me. *I was going to bust through that freaking door and scare the crap out of him.*

Take that, jerk-face.

With mad determination, I glanced around, looking for some sort of assistance – a stray battering ram and maybe a small army to wield it.

Of course, I found neither of these things. *No surprise there.*

But I did have my own legs and a scary amount of determination – so I strode forward and gave the door a good hard kick, swat-team style.

At the impact, I stifled a yelp. *Son-of-a-bitch.*

The door held firm, and the bottom of my foot hurt like heck.

But hey, I reminded myself, Brody hadn't succeeded on his first try either. I mean, this wasn't like in the movies, that's for sure.

By now, I was breathing fast and hard – whether from raw nerves or the adrenaline pumping through my veins.

With a sound of defiance, I hauled back and kicked the door again, and again, until it finally flew inward. It hit the neighboring wall and bounced back, nearly whacking me in the face. I gave the door a final, irritated push – not hard enough to bounce it back, but firm enough to keep it out of my way.

And then, feeling like a total badass, I strode right in.

The bathroom was steam-free, and surprisingly cold. Inside the shower, the water was still running. My chest rose and fell as I eyed the silhouette inside.

Oh, yeah. It was definitely Brody.

I'd know his fine form anywhere. And even if I couldn't tell by *looking*, his voice was all too familiar – and annoyingly calm – as he said, "Yeah?"

I shook my head. *Yeah?*

Well, that was disappointing.

I made a sound of annoyance. "Yeah, what?"

"What do you want?"

Well, for starters some sort of reaction would be nice. It's not like I'd expected him to scream in terror or anything. This *was* Brody Blastoviak, after all.

Still, I'd expected *something*. Anger. Surprise. Maybe even embarrassment.

But I got nothing, and his calm demeanor was a real kick in the pants.

Even his question was irritating. *What did I want?*

As I eyed his naked silhouette, I could think of multiple answers, but none that I'd ever act on.

The bathroom's towel rack was long gone, which meant that Brody's pelvis – unlike mine a couple of weeks ago – *wasn't* obscured from view.

Even through the frosted glass, I saw way more than I'd ever anticipated. His body wasn't sudsy, but it was definitely wet.

My gaze drifted to his pelvis, and my breath caught. The cold temperature hadn't impacted him at all, if you know what I mean.

At the sight of his glorious form, I felt heat rise to my face and then, even worse, drift downward to settle somewhere in the middle – and I *didn't* mean my stomach.

As far as his question, I knew exactly what I wanted, and it was the dumbest thing in the world.

I wanted *him*.

But I *wasn't* dumb. Or at least, I tried not to be.

Shaking off the distraction, I boldly announced, "I came for revenge, that's what."

At this, he laughed. It wasn't a big laugh, but it *was* annoying.

Damn it. I was supposed to be throwing *him* off *his* game, not the other way around.

I demanded, "And how'd you know it was me?"

"Aside from seeing you through the glass?"

Not too long ago, I'd been in Brody's position – naked in the shower after someone had barged in. During that whole embarrassing fiasco, I hadn't recognized him at all. Then again, my shower had been a lot steamier, and Brody hadn't been on my radar in the least.

And that wasn't the only difference between the two scenarios. From what I could gather, Brody hadn't panicked one single bit, even as I'd been kicking like a madwoman at the door.

This could only mean one thing. "Wait a minute. You knew it was me *before* I busted in."

Sounding annoyingly amused, he asked, "What makes you say that?"

"Because you stayed in the shower."

"No kidding," he said. "I wasn't done."

Well, goodie for him.

"So, tell me," I persisted. "How'd you know it was me?"

"Easy," he said. "You're the only one crazy enough to do that."

I felt my jaw clench. So *I* was crazy? *Not him?*

Talk about nerve.

"Hey!" I said. "You did it to me first."

"So?"

"So maybe you deserved a taste of your own medicine."

"Yeah? How's that workin' out?"

For me? Actually, the whole thing was horribly unsatisfying. I hadn't gotten the reaction I'd wanted, and I was hugely – pun intended – distracted by his naked silhouette.

If I didn't know any better, I'd say that his body was happy to see me – and not just a little.

Again, pun intended.

Even worse, *his* body wasn't the only happy thing in the room. Logically and emotionally, I felt like throttling him. But my own body? Well, let's say it had other ideas.

The traitorous hussy.

Obviously, both of our bodies were idiots – unless he *always* walked around with a massive erection. *And I do mean massive.*

And yet, here he was, carrying on a normal conversation like nothing was out of the ordinary.

As for myself, I felt beyond foolish. I might've skulked away then and there if only I hadn't recalled just in time what had driven me here in the first place. It was that conversation back at the crew house. *He'd been completely awful.*

If that jerk thought I was letting him off the hook, he was even crazier than I was.

I told him, "You know you were a jerk, right?"

He was silent for a long moment before saying, "No."

I bristled. "Oh yeah? Well—"

"I wasn't a jerk. I was an asshole." He paused. "And I'm sorry."

"Oh." And now I didn't know what to say. "Seriously?"

"Hell yeah."

"Oh." Yes, I was repeating myself, but none of this was going remotely how I'd planned. The whole thing was like opposite day.

Judging from the steam – or lack thereof – his shower wasn't hot. It was cold.

He wasn't embarrassed. But *I* was.

And of course, he didn't seem the least bit afraid. But me? I was stupidly terrified.

And why? It was because now that I was here, I didn't want to leave. I wanted to move closer – a lot closer.

How messed up was that?

I asked, "What happened? Did you run out of hot water?"

"No."

I tried to think. "So…you always take cold showers?"

"I do, now," he said.

"Since when?"

"Maybe a week ago."

"Why?"

"Because my roommate's crazy."

I stiffened. I wasn't even sure who he meant. Yes, I realized that he probably meant me. But Waverly was twice as crazy as I was. And she was also his roommate, right?

I told him, "I hope you mean Waverly."

"Sorry, guess again."

Great. So he *did* mean me? *I should've known.* "Gee, thanks," I said. "And what does that have to do with showering, anyway?"

"I'll tell you what," he said. "Crazy or not, I can't stop thinking about her."

At this, I swallowed so hard, it felt more like a gulp.

Woah.

I hadn't seen *that* coming.

CHAPTER 42

Brody

I hadn't planned to tell her that. But I didn't regret it either.

My crazy roommate – and yes, I did mean Arden – had been on my mind too much over the last week. Yeah, we talked a lot about the house. And yeah, we had our share of disagreements. But it wasn't the house that warmed my blood and sent my thoughts into overdrive.

As far as the shower, it was cold for a reason. And that reason was standing just inside the bathroom doorway.

Through the frosted glass, I couldn't make out her face, but I could tell plenty by the set of her shoulders and the tilt of her chin.

She was thinking again.

I liked that about her.

And she had a way of surprising me, too. I couldn't imagine any other girl busting through the door to – in Arden's own words – give me a taste of my own medicine.

My blood was pulsing harder now. *I wanted a taste alright, but not of anything medicinal.*

From outside the shower, she gave a shaky laugh. "Do you want to hear something *really* crazy?"

"What?"

"Before I came over here, Waverly told me…" Arden cleared her throat. "…that I should, um, in her words – not mine – 'hate-fuck' you."

Hate fuck?

I knew what it meant, but it wasn't my thing. And yet, the thought of driving into Arden Weathers was enough to make me nearly groan out loud.

I'd been wanting her for days, maybe longer.

Did I hate her?

At one time, I did.

But now? I didn't know what I felt, but it wasn't hate.

I replied, "That's *one* idea."

With another laugh, she said, "I know. Crazy, right? I mean, it's not like we'd ever do it."

"Got that right."

Something in her posture changed, and not for the better.

Before she could even *think* of turning away, I said, "I'm not into the hate thing."

Her shoulders relaxed. "Oh. Uh, yeah. Me neither." She paused. "So, what *are* you into?"

I felt my lips curve into a knowing smile. "If you wanna come in, I'll show you."

"You mean in the shower?" She hesitated. "How cold is it?"

I gave it some thought. It wasn't too cold. But it *was* cold enough to make her nipples harden into nice little knobs. At the mental image, my pulse jumped, and my erection throbbed. *Her nipples wouldn't be cold for long.* I'd warm them nice and slow with my tongue, and then with my mouth.

She'd be shivering, alright, but not from the cold water.

It was a nice thought. But it wasn't the way I wanted to start. I wanted her warm and willing, so I reached for the shower handle and turned it up a few notches. "It's not cold anymore," I said.

This was only half-true. It would take maybe thirty seconds for the water to fully warm. But the point remained the same.

When she spoke again, her voice was filled with breathless speculation. "I dunno…I mean, the shower's pretty narrow."

I smiled. "I know." But that was part of the appeal. *We could be nice and close.* And, I could think of all sorts of ways to make the tight space work in our favor.

Through the frosted glass, I gave Arden's silhouette a good, long look. I still couldn't make out her face, but I knew in my gut that if I opened the shower door for a better look, she'd be chewing on her bottom lip.

She did that when she was thinking.

She had nice lips – full and sweet. For a while now, I'd been wondering what they'd look like wrapped around my cock. Or maybe I'd focus on her *other* lips. I was good at that sort of thing. I could part them just enough for me to lick and suckle her secret places until she lost all control.

Now *that* would be something.

Or hell, forget the oral stuff. Maybe I'd just take her the old-fashioned way until she climaxed so hard, she forgot the whole "hate" part of the equation.

I didn't want her to *hate* me.

I wanted her to *want* me.

Because I wanted *her.*

I wanted her more than I'd wanted anyone in a long time.

Sure, I had plenty of other options, including one right across the street. But there was only girl I wanted, and she was standing on the other side of the shower door.

I said, "Or if you want, I'll come out."

"No." She hesitated. "I mean, actually, joining you wouldn't be *so* bad."

She had no idea.

It wouldn't be bad at all. I'd make damn sure of it.

I waited, giving her time to think. *And anticipate.* And imagine all of the nice things I was gonna to do to her. Knowing Arden, she was thinking about it right now. And me – I wasn't gonna rush it.

When she edged closer, I smiled.

"Well…" she said. "If nothing else, it would be good to get it out of our system, right?"

Wrong.

The way she talked, she was looking at a one-time deal. I saw what she meant, but it wasn't what I had in mind.

But hey, I knew – because yes, I *was* an arrogant bastard – that a single time wouldn't be enough. She'd be coming back for more. I'd make damn sure of *that*, too.

I pushed open the shower door, not caring that water splashed onto the outdated bathroom tile. I held out my hand and teased, "You know you want to."

"Yeah, but…" Her words trailed off as she studied my outstretched hand.

With the shower door open, I could see her face clearly now. Her eyes were bright, and her lips were parted. Her hair was long and loose, and she was wearing jeans and some sort of flannel overshirt. The shirt was open to reveal a thin gray tank top underneath.

No bra? That was *my* guess. But hey, I'd be finding out soon enough.

Silently, I waited, letting my outstretched hand do all the talking.

With a breathless laugh, she finally said, "Okay. Yes. I mean, hang on. I'll get undressed."

I shook my head. "I've got a better idea."

"Really? What's that?"

I grabbed her hand and gave it a gentle tug. "Get in with your clothes on."

Her breath hitched. "But they'll get all wet."

I grinned. "I know."

She laughed. "But *you're* not wearing any clothes. It doesn't seem fair."

"I know," I repeated. "But fair's for pussies. And trust me." I lowered my voice. "When I get done with you, you *won't* be complaining."

CHAPTER 43

Arden

Oh, boy.

Was I really going to do this?

He was wet and naked.

I was dry and clothed. *No.* That wasn't quite true. I was wearing clothes alright, but deep inside, I was soaking wet. Even now, I could feel the proof of my arousal dampening my panties to the point of embarrassment.

Or at least, I *should've* been embarrassed.

This wasn't me.

I didn't even like him. He was impossible. Cocky. Stubborn. He'd been my arch-enemy for years, ever since high school.

But he was also the sexiest thing I'd ever seen. And, from the looks of him now, I wasn't the only one caught up in the madness. By some fluke, he wanted *me* just as much as I wanted *him*.

If his hand on my wrist wasn't proof enough, his massive erection told me everything I needed to know.

I glanced down – not to his pelvis, but to my own hand, where his fingers encircled my wrist. In spite of his obvious interest, he'd made only that initial tug.

I knew what this meant. It was up to me if I *really* wanted to join him.

I bit my lip. *Did I?*

Oh, please. Who was I kidding?

There was no way on Earth I'd say "no" now. And the reason for this was achingly simple. *I didn't want to.*

My pulse jumped, and my breath caught. Slowly, I looked up to study his face. His hair was soaking wet, curling in dark tendrils over his forehead. His eyes were warm, and his lips were curved into a knowing smile.

He knew exactly what I was going to do.

The cocky bastard.

My breath hitched as I gave a single nod. "Okay."

Talk about a massive understatement.

With a wicked grin, he yanked me closer. My feet barely hit the tile floor as he practically dragged me into the shower and pulled the door shut behind us.

The space was narrow, and my clothes were already getting soaked. The shower was *not* meant for two people, even if I could totally see the appeal. With a breathless laugh, I asked, "Are you sure this is safe?"

His arms closed tightly around me, and he lowered his head to nuzzle my neck. Against my skin, he said, "Oh yeah."

His lips were warm and soft as his hands slid up my back, tugging at my flannel overshirt. Taking the hint, I let my arms fall loose, giving him the chance to remove the shirt all the way.

Without skipping a beat, he yanked the shirt free of my arms and let it fall onto the wet shower floor. One of his hands returned to my back, while the other went straight for the button of my already-damp jeans.

By now, I was practically panting. And yet I still felt compelled to ask, "Are you sure?"

With a smile in his voice, he said it again. "Oh yeah."

I laughed. "I meant about the shower. Like, it's not gonna break or anything is it?"

"It doesn't matter," he said, giving me the sweetest nibble on my earlobe. "We're replacing it next week."

Already, I could hardly think. But at least *one* of us had to keep our wits about us, right? I gasped, "But what about the floor? I mean, we don't want to fall through or anything."

With a low laugh, he said, "Trust me. We're fine."

I *felt* fine, that's for sure.

Already, he'd unzipped my jeans and was now tugging them down past my hips. As he did, I used my own feet to frantically work at my wet sneakers, trying to nudge them off without stooping to use my hands.

I actually managed to do it, too, stepping out of my shoes just as Brody used first his hand, and then one of his bare feet to shove my jeans first past my knees and then all the way down to the shower floor.

On raw instinct, I stepped out of the damp mess, leaving my socks lost somewhere in the denim fabric.

I was now wearing only my panties and a gray cotton tank top – no bra, because the tank top was tight enough to serve as an undershirt *and* as support for the girls, if you know what I mean.

And speaking of support, I recalled all too well that the house *still* had its share of issues. I just had to say, "You *do* know what you're doing, right?"

With that same smile in his voice, he replied, "What do *you* think?" As he said it, he reached between us and took one of my hard, wet nipples between his fingers. Through the thin cotton of my tank top, he rolled and teased the nub, making me groan in pure bliss.

And still, I somehow managed to say, "I meant about the floor. Like what if there's water damage underneath us or something?"

At this, his tone grew teasing. "Underneath us, huh?" His words weren't the only thing teasing me. He had a way of using his fingers – tugging, pinching, caressing, all the while alternating everything just enough to keep me on the edge of going crazy with desire.

Through the fog of my lust, I almost whimpered as I said, "I just mean, like what if the floor doesn't hold?"

With a low chuckle, he said, "Trust me. It'll hold." As he continued to toy with my nipple, he said in a voice filled with sin, "Underneath us, we've got structural two-by-fours."

Something in the way he said it sent a new rush of heat straight to my core. "Really?"

"Really," he said, worrying my wet nipple between his warm fingers. "And not the flimsy new stuff either."

On a sigh of pure bliss, I murmured, "Oh."

"I'm talking historical hardwood," he said. "The real deal."

Hard wood.

I *really* liked the sound of that. On a whimper, I said, "I love it when you talk construction to me." As the words left my lips, I almost groaned out loud.

I hadn't meant to say that.

With a trembling laugh, I said, "That's really weird, isn't it?"

Sounding amused as hell, he replied, "Ask me in a minute."

"Why in a minute?"

"Because," he said, "I'm gonna yank down your panties, and press you up against that load-bearing wall, and show you just how much pressure it can take."

I whimpered, "Oh, God."

Sometime within the last minute or so, my hands had slid down to his naked ass. I gripped it tight, and savored the perfect shape of it. If I'd thought it *looked* good, the feel of it was even better.

Now, I couldn't help but wonder how the muscles in his ass would feel against my palms as he pounded against me – not like a hammer to a nail, but flesh to flesh.

His hardness. My softness.

Together at last.

Beyond eager now, I slid my right hand between us and reached for his massive erection. When my hands closed around the base of it, Brody gave a muffled moan against my neck. "You're nothing but trouble. You know that, right?"

"Me?" I laughed. "You're ten times the trouble I am."

"We'll see."

And with that, he released my nipple and trailed his fingers lower, easing them past my navel and then lower still. When his fingers reached the intersection of my thighs, I parted them as much as I could in the narrow space and gave a soft moan when his fingers grazed that special spot.

When he rubbed the hardened, aching knob through the thin fabric of my panties, I gave another whimper. He knew exactly where to go, and what to do – almost like he knew my body even better than I did.

If I'd thought he'd played my nipple perfectly, it was nothing compared to what he did with my clit.

Into my ear, he said, "And that wall behind you?"

Breathlessly, I said, "Yeah?"

"Like I said, it's a full load-bearing wall, which means..." His teeth grazed my earlobe as he whispered, "it'll hold no matter what I do to you."

And just like that, I was whimpering again. "Oh, wow."

"No kidding," he said, giving me the most delicious stroke against my panties before shoving aside the lacy fabric and slipping one and then two fingers into my slick opening.

Sounding just as excited as I felt, he murmured against my skin, "You're so fucking wet."

"I know."

Slowly, he pulled back and gave me a long, lingering look, raking me from head to toe. From the warmth in his eyes, he liked what he saw.

I liked what I saw, too. The warm water was cascading down his perfect body, making it glisten and shine even in the relatively low light. His muscles were taut, and his chest was chiseled. His abs glistened in all their glory, defined not only by his fine physique, but by the water sliding down all those wonderful dips and ridges.

I was still gripping his length, stroking and squeezing, loving the way it pulsed against my fingers. And he was still stroking me to distraction. Suddenly, it was almost too much—the look of him, the feel of him, the sensation of him, and even the gleam in his eye as he confessed, "I've been thinking of this for days."

I swallowed. "Really?"

With a slow nod, he said, "Oh, yeah."

Now, it *was* too much. My stomach clenched, and the walls of my wetness convulsed around his fingers. On a ragged whimper, I somehow managed to say, "Maybe we should find a bed or something."

With a knowing smile, he said, "Forget that. I'm taking you right here. *Right now.*"

Oh, boy. I loved the way that sounded.

The truth was, I loved all of this. And I especially loved it when he reached around and grabbed my ass, lifting me tight against the shower wall.

As he did, my legs wrapped around his waist, almost like they had a mind of their own. With one hand, I reached around his back, looking to steady myself as I used my other hand to guide his hardness toward my opening.

His hips surged forward, slowly at first, and then with one decisive push. He was huge and hard, and filled me nearly to the breaking point. But I was slick and hot and welcomed every wonderful inch.

Just like he'd promised, he took me right then and there, giving me exactly what I'd been craving for days, or maybe even longer.

And almost before I knew what was happening, I was climaxing yet again. I shuddered against him just as the water began to lose some of its heat.

But Brody – he was warm enough for the both of us. When he reached his own climax, driving into me harder and faster, I felt like I'd died and gone straight to heaven, even as the water turned cold in earnest.

But now, the cool water felt surprisingly good. I was hot and sated, and very, *very* relaxed. He was still holding me tight against him, and I let my head drop onto his shoulder. On a long, happy breath, I murmured, "Wow."

CHAPTER 44
Brody

Wow was right.

Maybe it should've been a one-time thing. But just like I'd predicted – and made damn sure of, too – Arden couldn't get enough.

And the real kicker was, *neither could I.*

It wasn't just sex.

With most girls, they loved the trappings – the money, the fame, and yeah, me too while they were at it – but none of them had ever loved the nitty-gritty of what made me tick.

But with Arden, it was different. She was smart and fun, and not afraid of chipping a nail or getting her hands dirty to make something happen.

It was sexy as hell, and so was she.

Whatever we had between us, it was our guilty secret. And both of us wanted to keep it that way – me because there'd be a shit-storm with my brothers, and Arden because she thought it was a temporary deal.

It wasn't.

She might not know it, but an easy fling wasn't what I had in mind. *Not anymore.*

As far as my brothers, I'd deal with them later, when the house was finished and Arden was free of cameras and contracts.

For her sake, I'd handle it in private. No video footage. No drama. Just me and my brothers, hammering it out – *without* an audience.

Until then, I was keeping Arden to myself. *And trust me, she wasn't complaining.*

As the days turned to weeks, her interest in the house extended beyond the original project, and I found myself wanting her opinions on other projects, too – which houses to restore, which ones to pass up, and what to do with the properties that were next in the show's lineup.

Together, we pulled up plans and looked at pictures. It wasn't just about color schemes and window dressings. It was the layout of the houses, where we'd put in an extra bathroom, or what we'd do with an old kitchen or back patio.

Technically "we" wouldn't be doing anything, because Arden wasn't scheduled to be involved. But I loved her ideas. And her energy. And the way her eyes lit up whenever we brainstormed ways to modernize something while keeping its original structure intact.

Much of this – the house-planning, the brainstorming, the debating back and forth – we did in front of Waverly.

And it was driving her batshit crazy.

Judging from her sorry attitude, she felt ignored and neglected, even more so when I suggested – and none too nicely either – that if she didn't like the way things were going, she could find somewhere else to stay.

Too bad she didn't.

Instead, she stuck around, giving us more scrutiny than we wanted. Every few days, I debated kicking her out – or hell, just taking Arden back to my condo, where it would be just the two of us on our own.

But I didn't. It would only arouse more suspicion *and* a corresponding amount of camera time. Plus, Chase was my neighbor, and he was suspicious enough already.

I didn't want the extra attention. And neither did Arden. So we played it cool when the others were around. On the job, at the house, wherever – we worked like hell to act like there was nothing going on.

Were people buying it?

Hard to say. But we did our best. And we had a riot sneaking around.

Every night, I'd crawl out my bedroom window like a sex-crazed teenager, slink around the side of the house, and crawl in through the window beside Arden's bed.

And she'd be waiting.

Oh, boy, would she be waiting.

It was a good thing she had her own bathroom, because without it, we'd be showing up for breakfast reeking of sin and sex instead of soap and shampoo.

It also helped that we showed up alone.

Just before dawn, I'd use those same two windows to sneak back into my own room and come out looking reasonably innocent – or at least that was the general idea.

As far as the house we were fixing up, Arden and I no longer argued about who owned it. It was a good thing too, because I already had a plan to make it right.

When the thing was done, I was going to surprise the hell out of her in more ways than one. Until then, I was saying as little as possible.

And so was she.

Maybe she knew I was up to something. Or maybe – and this was my favorite theory – I kept her so satisfied between the sheets, she was finding it hard to complain.

And me? I was asking some serious questions, the kind that should've scared the hell out of me.

Except they didn't.

CHAPTER 45

Arden

"My dream life?" I said in reply to Brody's question. "Well, I guess I'm living it, huh?"

It was long after midnight, and the two of us had snuck out for a quiet walk along the beach. Back in high school, I'd done the same thing plenty of times while living with my grandparents.

But never this late. And never after having had the best sex of my life. Again.

In spite of the cool breeze, I felt warm and wonderful, walking beside Brody as the moonlight shimmered across the quiet, endless water.

He'd just asked me to describe my dream life, and the strangest thing was, I couldn't envision anything better than what I was doing right now.

He gave my hand a playful squeeze. "It's a serious question."

"I know," I laughed. "But that was my serious answer, honest. I really *am* having a wonderful time."

With a smile in his voice, he said, "So you *like* ripping down drywall, huh?"

I had, actually. One of the new pipes had sprung a leak in the kitchen, and part of the wall had gotten seriously damaged. The soggy drywall had to be ripped out so new drywall could take its place.

At the time, I'd just seen Waverly throw herself at Brody for what felt like the millionth time, and I'd been eager to burn off some steam. So when Brody had mentioned in passing that he was going to get someone to take a crowbar to the wall, I figured the activity would be just the ticket for releasing some of my endless frustration with Waverly's antics.

In my mind, the wall had been Waverly's face, and the crowbar had been, well, a crowbar actually. I never would've committed such violence in real life, but the whole thing had been surprisingly fun, just like last week when I'd taken the same crowbar to an upstairs closet.

To Brody, I said, "The funny thing is, I like all of it."

"All of it?" he said. "Even Roy's camera?"

I knew what he meant. For whatever reason, Roy seemed to take a particular interest in whatever I was doing, especially if I was doing it near Brody. I knew it was part of the job, but there were times when it *was* a little unsettling.

With a laugh, I admitted, "Well, maybe I could use a *little* less camera time."

"You want me to talk to him?"

The offer caught me off guard. "What would you say?"

"I'd tell him to knock it off, find someone else to focus on."

I felt my brow wrinkle in confusion. "But even *you* said he's just doing his job."

"It doesn't matter," Brody said. "Say the word, and I'll make it stop."

Judging from his tone, I almost believed him. "You wouldn't, really?"

"I would," he said.

He sounded absolutely sincere, and I was embarrassingly touched by the offer. Still, it seemed wrong to take Brody up on it. After all, I'd signed a contract, and I wasn't the type to not live up to my end of the bargain.

"Nah," I said. "But thanks. Seriously."

"You sure?"

"I'm sure." I perked up. "And besides, it will be fun to see the finished product."

"You mean the house?"

"The house *and* the show." Still, at the thought of things actually ending, I felt an all-too familiar pang in my heart. As we walked along, I added, "If you want the truth, I'll be a little sorry to see it done. I mean, I'll be glad to see the house restored and all, but it'll be strange when it's over. You know?"

His voice grew quiet. "I do."

We were silent for another long moment, and I couldn't help but wonder if Brody was thinking the same thing I was thinking.

What would happen when the house was done?

Would we go our separate ways?

I hated the thought more than I cared to admit. And judging from Brody's lingering silence, maybe *he* wasn't too thrilled with the idea either.

Or maybe that was just wishful thinking on my part. *I hadn't been lying.* The last couple of months had been some of the happiest of my whole life.

I adored what I was doing – and who I was doing it with.

Brody.

He was nothing like I'd expected.

And now, I couldn't help but recall how much I'd hated him back in high school. As we continued along the moonlit beach, I said, "Hey, can I ask you something?"

"Sure."

"Remember that English assignment? The fiction-writing thing?" With an embarrassed laugh, I said, "You know, the one with the candy store?"

"I remember."

"Why did you hate it so much? I mean, I could see where you wouldn't love it. But it seemed like it almost made you mad or something."

He was quiet for several long moments. "You want the truth?" he finally said. "I wasn't mad. I was jealous."

I stopped walking. "Jealous? Why?"

"Maybe it was all the candy." His tone grew teasing. "And wasn't there ice cream, too?"

There *had* been ice cream, not at the candy store itself. But in my fictional world, the parents had been stupidly fond of taking the family out for ice cream.

In hindsight, I guess it *was* pretty ridiculous. Still, I teased, "What do you have against ice cream?"

"Nothing," he said. "Maybe I was hungry. And you had it all."

"Oh stop it," I laughed. "You *know* it wasn't real, don't you? I mean, look at *your* paper. Yours had an alien eating the world. I knew *that* wasn't real, so you had to know that mine wasn't real, too. Right?"

He gave my hand a tender squeeze. "I know *now*."

And something in his voice made me wonder if there was more to what he was saying. But I didn't ask – just like I didn't ask a lot of things as the house moved ever closer to completion.

CHAPTER 46

Arden

"So," Cami said, "is he going to let you buy it?"

She meant the house, of course.

The question was a dark cloud over my otherwise happy mood. "I don't know," I said. "We never talk about it."

It was almost seven o'clock at night, and I was hunkered down in my bedroom talking to Cami on my cell phone while Brody was away, meeting with his brothers on some company business.

Cami said, "But why wouldn't you talk about it?"

"It just seems wrong. That's all."

"Why?" she laughed. "Because you're donking him?"

I didn't see the humor. "Yeah. I guess."

"So?" she said.

I sighed. "So I don't want him to think that I'm 'donking' him for all the wrong reasons, like to get him to sell me the house or something."

"Oh, please," she said. "He'd never think that."

"But how can you be sure?" I asked.

"Because no one would. You're not the type."

I frowned. "And what type is that?"

"Oh, you know," she said. "The type to ho yourself out for a beach house, or cripes, even rent money."

She was right.

I wasn't the type. And yet, her words served as yet another reminder that in spite of everything, I *still* wanted the house. And Brody still wasn't giving it up – at least not that I knew of.

Maybe it was time to give it another try.

By now, I'd had a steady paycheck for nearly three months. It was true that I'd spent some of that money on student loan payments, along with some basic necessities here and there. But I'd saved almost all of the rest. And I still had the bonus coming at the end of my consulting gig.

If I played my cards right, I'd have at least thirty thousand dollars after taxes. *Was it enough for a down payment on the house?*

I tried to think. *No. Not according to Brody.* He'd told me so himself way back in the beginning, and I had no reason to doubt him.

To Cami, I said, "Honestly, I don't think I could afford it."

"But why not?" she asked.

"Aside from the fact it's waterfront property?"

"Yeah. Aside from that."

"Well, for starters," I said, "you should see what Brody's doing to the place."

"Really?" She hesitated. "Good or bad?"

"Good. *Really* good." Now I couldn't help but smile. "You should see it, Cami. It's amazing. Granite countertops, marble sinks, a brand-new kitchen. I mean, it's not finished yet, but I've seen almost all of the plans."

I'd had a hand in creating those plans, too.

As I told Cami all about it, I heard the excitement in my own voice as I detailed the many improvements Brody would be making – or in some cases, had made already.

I loved every single thing on his list. And, later this year, when the next season of "Blast Brothers" would begin airing on the Home Network, the rest of the world would love it, too.

I just knew it.

Inside and out, Brody was working some serious magic. *And me?* I had the happy luck of seeing the magic unfold in every area of the house, well, except for the attic, which was still off-limits for safety reasons.

On the phone, I finished by saying, "And when he's completely done, it's going to look brand new, but even better because he didn't ruin the original character." I gave a happy sigh. "It really *is* amazing." And it wasn't just the house that was amazing. *It was Brody, too.* Even if we *hadn't* been romantically involved, I still would've admired not only his work ethic, but his skill in bringing out the home's natural beauty.

On the phone, Cami said, "Well that stinks."

My smile faded. "Why?"

"Because," she said, "if he were taking a more modest approach, you might be able to afford it, the house, I mean."

Well, there was that.

When I said nothing in reply, she added, "And granite countertops? Seriously?"

Her words stung. "What's wrong with granite countertops?"

"Nothing," she said. "They're beautiful if you can afford them. But *you* can't."

She was right. And yet, I couldn't really complain. After all, I'd had a hand in selecting those countertops. In fact, I'd helped select a lot of things – flooring, kitchen cabinets, appliances, and more.

At first, I'd gravitated mostly to the cheap stuff, but Brody had insisted on going high-end with everything. And, I had to admit, he definitely knew what he was doing.

Plus, I had to face facts. It was *his* house, not mine.

There was a time, not too long ago, when I might've blamed Brody for buying it out from under me. But over the last few weeks, I'd come to realize something. *It wasn't Brody's fault.*

For whatever reason, my cousin had decided to sell. And Brody had decided to buy. He'd probably paid cash, too.

Sure, it was a crazy coincidence that Brody of all people had been the buyer, but at least the house was in good hands – *very* good hands.

And besides, I reminded myself, even if my cousin *hadn't* screwed me over, I still would've been screwed in the end when the house caved in around me. Repairs were expensive, especially for a house that big and in that bad of shape.

Forget the granite countertops. The roof alone would've busted my budget. Just last week, I'd seen the roofing bill with my own two eyes. *It was a doozie.*

To Cami I said, "Look, I get what you're saying, but going high-end was the right decision."

Sounding less than convinced, she said, "Oh yeah? Why's that?"

"Because it's a huge, waterfront home." I recalled what Brody had told me when I'd tried to go cheap on the countertops. He'd explained that a house in such a prime location should have the interior to match. *He'd been right.*

Still, Cami did have a point. If Brody had stuck with basic repairs and nothing else, maybe I could've afforded the house on my own eventually.

I was still mulling all of this over when Cami said, "And really, you wouldn't even need a bank."

I wasn't following. "Sorry, what?"

"I'm just saying, Brody owns the house on his own, right? Like, he doesn't have partners or a mortgage, does he?"

"I don't think so."

"And he's got plenty of money." Sounding more excited now, Cami said, "Maybe he could give you a loan."

I stiffened. *No. Absolutely not.* I was horrified by the mere idea. "I'm not gonna ask him for money."

"You wouldn't be asking him for money," she said. "You'd be asking him to do what a bank does."

"Except he's not a bank."

"But so what?" she said. "Bank or not, he could still charge you interest. And *you'd* get the house. See? It's a total win-win."

She made it sound oh-so simple. But I knew it wasn't. "Honestly, I don't think Brody would see it that way."

"Hey, you never know," she said. "It's called a land contract. I looked into it." Sounding even more enthused, she explained, "It's where a private person finances a property they already own. *They* sell the house, and you pay them directly."

I'd heard of such things, but I still didn't see it working out. "So he'd be what?" I tried to laugh. "My landlord?"

"No. Because you'd be buying it, not renting it. And as long as you made the payments, the house would be yours in the end, just like if you got a mortgage from a bank."

I had to admit, it *did* sound like an interesting idea. Still, I had to say it. "I can't ask Brody to do that."

"Why not?" she said. "You know you'd do it for him if *you* had the money."

She was right. The truth was, I was coming dangerously close to falling for him. *Or maybe I already had.*

He was fast becoming one of the best friends I'd ever had. Plus, he was an amazing lover. *And* an amazing colleague. Yes, I knew that on the show's totem pole, he was at the very top while I was just a lowly stump at the bottom. But he never treated me like that.

He actually asked for my ideas, and took a ton of my suggestions. On every front, we made a great team. Or at least *I* liked to think so.

And yet, a little voice in my head whispered that we never talked about the future *or* went out in public. I'd never even seen his condo. *And forget his family.*

The only family he had were his brothers, and although I'd met them in person many times by now, my relationship with them wasn't exactly friendly.

Mason, in particular, seemed to truly despise me, while Chase seemed content with just giving me a hard time.

As far as I could tell, neither Mason nor Chase knew that Brody and I were more than colleagues.

As I tried to explain all of this to Cami, I started to feel just a little bit silly for falling so hard and fast. To Brody, our relationship – or whatever it was – might be just a passing thing.

But for me? Maybe it had started out that way, but I was fast becoming hooked. *Really* hooked.

Was that a good thing? Or a bad thing?

I wasn't sure.

And by the time I got off the phone, I wasn't nearly as happy as I'd been when the conversation had begun.

Just maybe, I decided, it was time to broach the subject of the house again, if only to gauge Brody's response. It would tell me a lot – and not *only* about the house.

CHAPTER 47

Arden

"Ask me later," Brody said.

His words sounded vaguely familiar. And then I remembered why. He'd said the same thing a few months ago when I'd asked him why he'd never known his grandparents.

Since then, I'd approached the subject of his family several times, with little success. Obviously, it was a sore subject, so I tried not to push it.

But tonight, I hadn't been asking about his family. I'd been asking about the house.

It was long past midnight, and we were lying naked in each other's arms. In the quiet darkness of my bedroom, I asked, "Why later?"

"Because it's not the time."

"When *would* it be the time?"

With a smile in his voice, he replied, "Later."

I pulled away, putting some distance between us. "Look, if you want to say no, just say it."

"Alright. No."

My heart sank. "Just like that?"

In a teasing tone, he said, "Hey, you wanted an answer."

I had. But his flippant attitude still grated. My question had been simple and straight-forward. *Was there any chance at all that he'd ever consider selling me the house?*

Apparently, his answer was still *no.*

It was a quick, dismissive *no,* too, leaving me little hope that he'd ever change his mind.

Maybe it shouldn't have surprised me. But for some stupid reason, it did.

And now, I was almost sorry that I'd brought it up.

There was only one upside. At least I hadn't mentioned Cami's crazy idea of asking Brody to finance the venture. Now *that* would've been embarrassing.

As far as the house itself, I decided to take a different approach. "You know, I've got a job interview next Tuesday."

"Oh yeah? Where?"

"A shipping center near Midland. We're doing a phone interview."

I still hadn't purchased a car, mostly because I didn't need one at the moment. Brody had a food service that stocked our groceries, and we ordered takeout all the time. Brody always treated, even though I offered time and time again to chip in.

But he always refused, which made me feel just a bit guilty. Still, it wasn't *all* bad, considering that I was saving nearly every penny, just in case he ever changed his mind about selling the house.

And now in the bedroom, I waited to hear what he'd say about my interview. Midland was only forty minutes away, definitely within commuting distance.

To me, this was good news. And yet, Brody said nothing.

I waited for a long, tense moment, thinking that he'd eventually say *something*. But he never did.

Was he even listening?

I tried again. "And the pay is pretty good, too."

With an obvious lack of enthusiasm, he said, "Good to know."

Was it?

I thought so. But Brody's reaction wasn't what I'd been hoping for. I asked, "Aren't you excited?"

With a wry laugh, he said, "Not at the moment."

I frowned in the darkness. "Why not?"

"Because I know what you're gonna say next."

"You do not."

"Sure I do," he said. "You're gonna make another play for the house."

Another play? With a sound of annoyance, I said, "What, like it's some sort of game?"

"Listen," he said. "Just let it go, alright?"

I didn't want to let it go. But I also realized that when it came to the house, Brody held all the cards. This had been true right from the beginning, and maybe I'd been naïve to think that anything had changed.

Still, I felt like hurling my pillow across the room. The whole thing was beyond frustrating, especially now, when I'd come up with an exciting new idea for paying the monthly mortgage – assuming that I ever got to that point.

My idea – and I still thought it was a good one – was to get a couple of roommates to share expenses. It was a decent plan, one I probably I should've come up with sooner.

The house was huge and located right on the beach. Soon, the place would have double the bathrooms, a brand-new kitchen, and loads of extra closet space.

With all of the new features, I'd have no trouble at all finding a couple of gals to move in and split expenses.

They could pay me a set monthly amount for rent, and I could use that rent to pay for a big chunk of the mortgage. The rest of it, I could cover on my own.

It wouldn't even be that hard.

But I was getting ahead of myself, wasn't I?

Until I had an actual job – as opposed to merely an interview – I'd never qualify for a mortgage in the first place, even if Brody *did* agree to sell.

Reluctantly, I decided to table the house discussion for another time, *after* I had a job offer in-hand. Until that point, Brody and I would only be arguing for nothing.

But there was something I *could* get answers on. "So about your grandparents," I said, "you never did tell me. Why didn't you ever get to know them?"

With no trace of a smile, he said, "Trust me. You don't want to know."

Judging from the tone of his voice, he wasn't any happier with *this* subject than the last one. Or maybe he was still irritated about the house.

Buy hey, I was getting irritated, too. And my question was perfectly reasonable. Brody and I had been together for months now. Maybe it wasn't a huge amount of time, but it was certainly long enough to justify asking basic questions about his family.

I said, "But I *do* want to know. I wouldn't have asked otherwise."

"Alright," he said, not sounding too happy about it. "You wanna know why? It's because my parents were fuck-ups."

"Oh." Now, I hardly knew what to say. From watching the TV show, I already knew that both of his parents had died in separate accidents sometime within the last few years – his dad in a car crash and his mom in a house fire.

At the time, both of them had been living in different states – away from their children *and* from each other.

Brody never wanted to talk about it, and I could totally see why. But until just now, I hadn't realized that Brody harbored such hard feelings for them.

After a long moment, I said, "How so?"

"Let's just say, family wasn't important to them."

"But what about your grandparents?"

"Dead."

I winced. "All of them?"

His voice was quiet. "Yup."

"Gosh, I'm really sorry."

"Don't be. Like I said, I never knew them, so…" His words trailed off into silence – the kind that didn't welcome further discussion.

Still, I persisted, "So you're saying you never met them at all?"

"Never," he confirmed. "So hey, they could be fuck-ups, too, for all I know."

The more he talked, the less I liked what I was hearing. *Did he seriously just call his dead grandparents fuck-ups?*

And earlier, his parents, too?

I felt my eyebrows furrow. It was true that I had plenty of issues with my own parents, but I still loved them, even in spite of their flaws.

And, as far as Brody's grandparents, his pronouncement seemed terribly unfair.

Hoping to get him thinking, I said, "But about your grandparents, if you've never met them, how can you truly know anything?"

"I don't." His voice hardened. "And that's the point."

"I know," I said. "But I'm just saying, maybe they were wonderful people."

With a low scoff, he said, "And you think that's better?"

"I don't know," I admitted. "Maybe."

"Well it's not," he said.

"Why?"

With a new edge in his voice, he replied, "Because the way *I* see it, I'm better off if they weren't worth knowing."

I still didn't get it. "But why?"

"Because then I wasn't missing anything."

Finally, I saw what he meant. Still, the whole thing made me feel strange and sad – and even sadder when Brody announced, "I'm gonna head out, alright?"

I felt my brow wrinkle in confusion. "Head out? What do you mean?"

"I'm gonna head back to my own room, maybe get some sleep."

Maybe get some sleep? I hesitated. "Oh. Okay."

He'd never done such a thing before. Normally, he stayed until just before sunrise, and left with obvious regret.

With no sign of regret now, he said, "And about the house. I meant what I said. Drop it, alright?"

Drop it?

Like it was *so* easy.

I refused to lie. "I can't promise you that."

"Yeah, well that makes two of us."

I wasn't even sure what he meant. But judging from his tone, it wasn't anything good.

Before I could even think of something to say, he was already out of bed and pulling on his clothes. In the shadows, I could see only his silhouette, but that didn't make it any less painful to watch as he prepared to leave.

And me? I didn't try to stop him.

I mean, hey, if he wanted to go, I wasn't going to beg him to stay – even if there was a pathetic part of me that was sorely tempted.

But all too soon, he was heading out. He didn't even leave through the window, but rather through the bedroom door, slipping out into the hall and shutting my door firmly behind him.

Alone in the quiet bedroom, I closed my eyes and tried to block out whatever had just happened.

My bed wasn't terribly huge, just a basic double. Still, it felt too big and empty after his sudden departure.

The whole thing was incredibly strange – and even stranger the next morning when I learned something that I *should've* heard directly from him.

But I hadn't. *And I didn't like it.*

CHAPTER 48

Arden

I stared at Waverly. "What do you mean he's gone?"

With a smirk, she replied, "I mean exactly what I said. He's gone. G.O.N.E, gone."

I gave her an annoyed look. *Thanks ever so much for the spelling lesson.* We were standing in the crew house kitchen, and she was talking about Brody.

I asked, "Gone where?"

"To California, of course."

I shook my head. "California? But why?"

"Because, he was *supposed* to be there weeks ago."

He was? If so, this was the first I'd heard of it.

It was just past seven o'clock in the morning, and my day was off to a bitter start. After Brody's sudden departure from my bedroom last night, I'd slept fitfully at best and woke way too early feeling disgruntled and upset.

Still, I tried not to let our argument – or whatever it was – get me down. During my morning shower, I'd comforted myself with the fact that I'd be seeing Brody over breakfast, which would give us the chance to try to figure things out.

Instead, I'd emerged from my bedroom to see Waverly smirking in the kitchen like she knew something I didn't.

Turns out, this was true.

Looking obscenely delighted, she'd greeted me not with a "good morning," but with the news that Brody had left for the airport long before sunrise.

And now, she was saying, "We *are* restoring other houses, you know."

Oh, I knew alright. There was that long-neglected estate in California wine country along with that three-bedroom bungalow in Nashville, plus a farm house in Iowa.

Even though I'd never seen the houses personally, I'd seen plenty of pictures and video footage, too. Over the past couple of months, I'd helped Brody with some of the advance planning – brainstorming bathroom and kitchen layouts, along with countless other details.

I'd loved every minute of it, even when we disagreed, which wasn't as often as you'd think. But now, his sudden departure made me wonder what exactly I'd been missing.

Yes, I *had* realized that Brody would eventually need to travel to the new sites. But I'd always figured that I'd have some advance warning when that actually happened.

And yes, there was a part of me that had hoped to be included, not with the actual show, but as Brody's, well, I didn't know what.

Girlfriend?

Lover?

Friend?

Colleague?

I was still trying to figure it out when Waverly announced, "And *I'm* leaving for California tonight."

I stiffened. "What?"

"Well, I *am* the show's producer," she said.

It was funny. These days, I never thought of her as the producer, mostly because she didn't do much producing. Instead, she spent most of her time talking on her cell phone, shopping on-line, or complaining that no one ever listened to her ideas.

I stood in stunned disbelief as she went on to imply that Brody might be gone for a while.

With growing concern, I asked, "Do you know when he'll be back?"

With another smirk, she replied, "Sure."

"Well?"

"Well what?"

"Aren't you going to tell me?"

She paused, as if thinking. "Why should I?" she finally said. "You never tell *me* anything."

By now, I felt like screaming. "I have no idea what you mean."

"Sure you do," she said. "You're fucking him, aren't you?"

I tensed. *Crap.*

My face grew uncomfortably warm, even as I coldly informed her, "That's none of your business."

"I'll take that as a yes," she said, looking decidedly displeased. "I knew I shouldn't have told you that."

"Told me what?"

"To hate-fuck him."

Good grief. That was months ago. But apparently, she hadn't forgotten.

I replied, "Not that it's any of your business, but I *didn't* 'hate fuck' him."

This was technically true.

Even though I'd started out hating Brody, our encounters had *not* been hate-filled, not even in the beginning.

Her lips pursed. "Oh, please. I *saw* him come out of your bedroom last night."

At this, I almost groaned out loud. *Damn it.*

Now I didn't know what to say.

Into my silence, Waverly said, "That's why he suddenly left town, wasn't it?" With a brittle laugh, she said, "What'd you do? Get all clingy? Guys *really* hate that, you know."

By now, my head was swimming so hard, I could hardly keep up with my own thoughts. I didn't *think* I was clingy. It was true that Brody and I had been spending a lot of time together. But it hadn't felt like I'd been chasing him, much less crowding him.

And besides, I reminded myself, Brody had been sneaking into *my* bedroom, not the other way around.

Still, a little voice in my head whispered that he'd left awful quickly when I'd broached the subject of his family.

It was a bad sign, for sure. After all, true intimacy didn't come from sex so much as sharing secrets and what-not.

Maybe he *did* think I was clingy.

Throughout the day, I texted him several times – and even called him, too – but I never *did* get ahold of him, or receive any response whatsoever.

And, as if this weren't bad enough, I had a surprise visitor late that very same night.

Probably I should've been happy to see him. But I wasn't, not after I heard what he'd come to tell me.

CHAPTER 49

Arden

Waverly – along with all of her luggage – had left for the airport nearly four hours ago, and I was sitting alone in the crew house living room.

Apparently, I'd be staying here on my own. But for how long, I had no idea.

After Waverly's departure, I'd poked my head into Brody's bedroom in search of some clue on how long he might be gone, or if he planned to return at all.

What I saw gave me at least *some* hope. The way it looked, some of his stuff was still there, which suggested that he'd return eventually.

But until I actually talked to him, I had too many questions and no answers whatsoever.

As the hours passed, one question loomed larger than the rest.

Were we broken up?

But maybe that didn't even apply. Maybe we'd never truly been together. After all, our relationship had been a total secret, except to Cami, who now wanted to kill him, thanks to me crying on her virtual shoulder just an hour ago.

As for my calls to Brody, they remained unanswered. With every passing minute, I grew more and more angry. Already in my head, I'd told him off at least a dozen times.

While I stewed on the couch, I was working on yet another way to tell him exactly what I thought of his recent behavior when a knock sounded at the front door.

Startled by the sudden noise, I gave the door a perplexed look. It was nearly ten o'clock at night, late for visitors, especially when I wasn't expecting anyone.

Across the street, the film and construction crews had stopped working hours ago, leaving me utterly alone for the first time in months.

Reluctantly, I stood and made my way toward the door.

Before answering it, I peered out through the front window blinds, trying to get some sense of who might be visiting at such an odd hour.

I saw no vehicle in the driveway – here *or* across the street. But there *was* someone standing on the front porch.

It was someone I instantly recognized, someone who'd been avoiding me for way too long.

But it wasn't Brody.

It was my cousin Jason.

Finally.

When I flung open the door, he greeted me with a sheepish grin. "So, how's it going?"

I stared, dumbfounded. "Is that a serious question?"

Jason was tall and thin with wavy brown hair. Tonight, he was wearing gray slacks and a white button-down dress-shirt. He looked slightly rumpled and sleepy-eyed.

Ignoring my attitude, he said, "So, can I come in?"

With a sound of annoyance, I opened the door wider and stepped out of his way, figuring it was better to kill him in the living room rather than outside on the front porch, where there might be witnesses.

As he shuffled inside, I said, "And just where have you been, anyway?"

Without meeting my gaze, he mumbled, "Around."

I shut the door and got straight to the point. "So what happened with the house?"

"Uh...." He shifted from foot to foot. "Which house?"

Oh, for God's sake. "You know which one." Still, I jerked a thumb vaguely toward the house across the street. "*That* one. Remember?" I made air quotes. "The ol' family homestead?"

He frowned. "I don't suppose you've got any snacks?"

Already I felt like throttling him. "Snacks? Seriously?"

"Sorry, but I'm starving," he said. "I've been sitting in the car for hours."

I didn't get it. "What car?"

He jerked his head toward the left side of the house. "I parked down the street."

"Why?" I asked.

"So I wouldn't get caught."

"By who?"

"Anyone," he said. "Do you know I've been driving by here for weeks now?"

"Here? You mean this place?"

He nodded. "Oh yeah. Sometimes I'd even park down the street and wait. One night, I fell asleep in my car." With a grimace, he reached up and rubbed at his shoulder. "Woke up with one hell of crick in my neck. The thing's *still* sore."

Maybe I should've felt bad for him. But I didn't. I couldn't, not after that stunt with the house.

I gave him an annoyed look. "If you want me to feel sorry for you, forget it. You totally screwed me over. You know that, right?"

At this, he had the nerve to look insulted. "I did not."

"You did, too," I said. "You took my money and then sold the house out from under me. How is that *not* screwing me over?"

"Hey, I told you I'd make it right."

During our phone conversation months ago, he *had* said such a thing. And I might've been inclined to believe him, if only he hadn't been avoiding me ever since.

I crossed my arms. "Oh yeah? How?"

He stood just a little bit straighter. "I brought you something."

When my only reply was a stony look, he reached into the front pocket of his shirt and pulled out a folded check. With a little flourish, he held it out between us. "Here."

Silently, I snatched the check and lifted it for a closer look. It was a personal check made out from Jason to me. The total was for forty-one thousand, two-hundred dollars, and twenty-two cents.

As I tried to process what I was seeing, Jason announced, "It's all of your money. I'm paying you back." Sounding annoyingly smug, he added, "With a nice bonus, too."

I was still staring at the check. A couple of weeks ago, in a fit of pique, I'd actually added up all the money that I'd sent Jason during the past three years. The total came to forty-one thousand, one hundred dollars and twenty-two cents, exactly.

I compared *that* amount to what I saw on the check. The so-called bonus was for one hundred measly dollars. Okay, a hundred dollars was nothing to sneeze at, but in the big scheme of things, it was hardly worth the grief I'd suffered while working my ass off to keep up with all of the payments and repairs.

Cripes, I'd paid more than a hundred dollars just on credit card interest alone for the groceries I'd had to finance with plastic after sending Jason most of my money.

Not bothering to hide my contempt, I said, "Wow, a hundred bucks, huh? How *very* generous."

He grinned. "I know, right?"

I sighed. "I was being sarcastic."

His grin faded. "Hey, legally, I didn't have to give you anything."

"That's not true," I told him. "What, you thought I'd just let it go?"

"Well…" He paused. "You wouldn't sue me or anything. I mean, we're family, right?"

It was such a pretty thought. But for all I knew, the check wasn't even good. And Jason hadn't been acting like family at all.

Undaunted, Jason continued. "So it seems to me you'd be at least a little grateful."

"Grateful?" I practically sputtered. "After you lied to me about the house?"

His mouth tightened. "I didn't lie."

"Sure you did."

"About what?"

"Well, for one thing, about the repairs. Just admit it. You didn't repair a darn thing."

He glanced away. "Well...I did *some* repairs."

"Oh, please," I said. "You did not."

"I did, too."

"Really?" I gave him a no-nonsense look. "Like what?"

"Lots of things," he said. "I even did some of them myself."

Jason and I weren't terribly close, but I'd seen enough of him to know that he barely knew which end of the hammer met the nail. Plus, according to Brody, absolutely nothing in the house had been fixed.

I believed him, too. When it came to construction, Brody definitely knew what he was doing.

But even without Brody's expert opinion, I knew what I'd seen with my own two eyes. Unless I was terribly mistaken, Jason hadn't done a single thing to keep the house from falling down around him, even while hitting me up for all kinds of money.

With a scoff, I said, "Oh yeah? Which repairs?"

"Well, like the shrubs," he said. "I repaired those last year."

Oh, for God's sake. "You don't 'repair' shrubs. You trim them." I didn't bother pointing out that even if he *had* trimmed them, he'd done a pretty sorry job, considering that they'd been way overgrown by the time *I* ever got to them.

When Jason's only response was a sullen look, I asked, "And what about the roof?"

"What about it?"

"Did you know it was shot?"

He drew back. "Like, with a gun?"

Was he joking? "No," I said. "I mean, 'shot', as in used up, in need of repair, leaking, whatever."

"Oh." He visibly relaxed. "Then why didn't you say so?"

"I did. Just now."

"No. You told me it was shot."

"Alright, forget the roof," I said. "The house – why'd you sell it?"

"Because I had to."

Now, *this* I had to hear. "Oh yeah? Why?"

He glanced toward the kitchen. "Didn't you mention snacks or something?"

Oh, I'd give him a snack, alright. Through gritted teeth, I said, "No, *you* mentioned snacks."

"Well, I really *am* hungry," he practically whined. "I've been sitting in the car for hours, you know."

"Fine," I sighed. "I'll find you something. But I'm warning you, you'd better tell me everything."

And to Jason's credit, he actually did.

By the time he finished, I wanted to kill him. And this time, I didn't mean my cousin.

I meant Brody.

CHAPTER 50

Brody

Arden answered my phone call with a sleepy, "Hello?"

I smiled at the sound of her voice. "Hey, it's me."

She paused. "What do you want?"

Now I paused, too. "I wanted to talk."

"Oh, really?" she said, sounding half asleep. "Then maybe you should've called sooner."

I was sitting in a rental car outside a strip mall, where I'd just purchased a basic burner phone. "I would've," I said, "but my phone's missing."

"So?"

"So I had to get a new one."

"Gee, it must be nice," she said.

I didn't get it. "Nice how?"

"I'm just saying, it must be nice to buy a brand-new phone without even thinking."

It hadn't been nice. It had been a pain in the ass. I wasn't an entourage type of guy, so I'd hit the store on my own. I didn't mind the effort, but when it came to the attention, I wasn't in the mood.

I glanced toward the cell phone store and frowned. At least a dozen people were standing at the front window, staring out at my car. The car was a basic rental, just like I'd asked for. But the gawkers weren't staring at the vehicle. They were staring at *me*, just like they'd done inside.

So much for keeping a low profile.

I fired up the engine and backed out of the spot.

As far as the new phone, it was a temporary thing. I still figured the old one – the one with all of my contacts – would show up eventually.

To Arden, I joked, "Hey, if you want it, it's yours."

She sighed. "What?"

"My new phone." As I spoke, I pulled into traffic and turned toward the hotel. "If you want it, you can have it."

"Forget it. I don't want your hand-me-downs."

Shit.

Sleepy or not, she sounded ticked. *But it wasn't about the phone.* I knew that.

I'd left this morning with no advance warning and no kiss goodbye. *And* I'd been out of touch all day.

Here in California, it was just past nine o'clock at night, which meant that it was after midnight in Michigan.

I asked, "Did I wake you?"

Sounding sleepier than ever, she said, "Would you care if you did?"

What the hell?

"Yeah, I'd care." *And I would.* I almost hadn't called for that reason. But I'd wanted to clear things up between us, and I'd been dying to hear her voice.

On the phone, she replied, "Well, if you cared so much, maybe you would've called sooner."

"Except I didn't have a phone. *Or* your number."

With a sleepy scoff, she said, "Right."

Okay, I felt bad for messing up, but something wasn't right. I asked, "Is there a problem?"

"Well, I *guess* I'm just wondering which story you're going with. Did you not have your phone? Or did you not have my number?"

Arden was smart. But her question wasn't. Still, I didn't want to be a dick about it, so I explained, "Your number's in my phone, so to answer your question, I didn't have both – my cell *or* your number."

In the end, I'd gotten her phone number from the production company after finding *their* number on the rental car paperwork. The trip itself wasn't for fun, and the missing phone wasn't helping.

And now, Arden was saying, "Then maybe you should've learned it by heart."

"Is that so?" I asked, "Do you know *my* number by heart?"

She paused. "What?"

"My cell number," I said. "What is it?" When I heard fumbling on the other end, I added, "And don't look in your contacts. That's cheating."

"Cheating, huh?" With a sleepy laugh, she said, "Well, that's rich."

"Meaning?"

"Forget it."

I didn't like where this was going. "What, you think I'm cheating on you?"

"Oh, please," she scoffed. "You can't 'cheat' if we're just screwing around, right?"

I gripped the phone tighter. "What?"

"Sorry," she said. "What I *meant* to say is, we *were* screwing around, as in past tense."

Fuck.

Okay, I realized that I had some explaining to do, but the more she talked, the more aggravated *I* was getting, too. "Listen—"

"No. *You* listen," she said. "Whatever you're up to, I don't care. I just want to buy the house and be done with it, okay?"

What the hell?

Again, with the house?

I asked, "What are you getting at?"

"Just what I said. I want to buy it."

"With what?"

"Money," she said. "What else?"

"I already told you, you can't afford it."

"That's what *you* think."

"Wrong," I told her. "It's what I *know*."

"No. *You're* wrong," she said. "After I get my bonus—"

"Forget the bonus," I said. "You'd need double that for just the down payment."

"Excellent," she said. "Because I have it. There, it's settled."

Settled, my ass. There was no way on Earth that Arden had come up with that kind of money in less than a day. *She was bluffing.*

She had to be.

But hey, I'd play along if it would take the edge off. I asked, "So, where'd you get the money?"

"That's none of your business," she said. "But trust me, I've got it."

It didn't sound like a bluff. And now I took a moment to think. *Had she come into a decent chunk of money?* It seemed unlikely, but hey, stranger things had happened. When I returned home, I'd get to the bottom of it. Until then, we were just spinning our wheels.

I said, "We'll talk when I get back, alright?"

"And when will that be?"

"A week, maybe sooner."

"Terrific." She sighed. "And when you get here, where *exactly* will you be staying?"

"At the crew house. Where else?"

"But don't you have your own condo?"

"Yeah, so?"

"So why don't you stay there instead?"

If I wanted to be a dick about it – which I didn't – I might've told her that I *owned* the crew house, which meant that I could stay there any time I wanted.

But this was Arden, and she meant something to me. And hey, if the situation were reversed – if *she'd* taken off with no warning – I'd be pissed, too.

With an effort, I softened my tone. "Because *you're* not at the condo."

"That's right," she said. "And I never was. Why is that?"

"What do you mean?"

"I mean," she said, "why is it that I never – not even once – saw the place that you call home?"

It was a good question, one I should've been asking myself. The truth was, the condo didn't *feel* like home. *It never had.*

But the crew house, it felt different, almost like a real home, even if I'd been living out of a duffle.

Giving it some thought, I suddenly realized *why* it felt different. *It was because of Arden.* She made the crew house – as unimpressive as it was – feel like something I'd never had.

Come to think of it, it was the same way with the house we were fixing up. And *that* place wasn't even livable.

Holy shit.

Home was where *she* was.

It was the only thing that made sense.

The realization was a kick to the gut, and I wasn't ready for it.

I got another nice kick when Arden informed me that if I was planning to return to the crew house, she'd be finding a different place to stay.

This wasn't what I wanted to hear.

Still, I tried to keep my cool. "Listen, I don't want you to go."

With a humorless laugh, she said, "Oh, I just bet."

The more she talked, the less I liked what she was saying. But *I* was the one who'd messed up, and I didn't want to make it worse.

What I *wanted* to do was hop on a plane and fix this, whatever it was. But I'd flown out to California for a reason, and the reason hadn't changed.

The house in wine country was next on our list, and it was dangerously behind schedule – even more so after an electrical fire had gutted its kitchen less than twenty-four hours ago.

I'd gotten the emergency call maybe an hour after leaving Arden's bedroom late last night.

Into the phone, I said, "So, you wanna hear why I left?"

"Where?" Now, she sounded ready to cry. "My bedroom? Or the state?"

Like a dumb-ass, I realized far too late that she hadn't been asleep. *She'd been crying.*

The realization cut me to the core. In a softer voice, I said, "Both."

"How about neither?" she said with a choked sob. "Because I'm just saying, I don't care."

"Baby—"

But already, she'd hung up.

Shit.

If she didn't care, she wouldn't be crying. And *I* wouldn't feel like a dick for hurting her.

I hadn't meant to. But I saw why she was upset. *Last night, I'd been an ass.* And then I'd left with no warning.

On top of that, she'd had a whole day of radio silence, giving her plenty of time to assume the worst.

I wanted to make it up to her.

Maybe what she needed was a nice surprise – something to make her smile until I returned to fix things.

A few phone calls later, it was a done-deal.

The surprise – she was going to love it.

CHAPTER 51

Arden

In the crew house living room, I woke to the sounds of knocking. It was a Saturday afternoon, and I'd fallen asleep on the living room sofa – mostly because I'd slept so badly after last night's tense conversation with Brody.

On the phone, I'd been awful to him, but I refused to regret it. After what I'd learned from my cousin, I *should've* called Brody every name in the book.

But I hadn't.

I was saving *that* for the next time I saw him – whenever that would be.

As I rubbed the sleep from my aching eyes, I got up and trudged to the front door. Without much enthusiasm, I opened it up, only to come face-to-face with someone I never expected to see today.

It was Cami.

Her auburn hair was tied in a loose ponytail, and she was wearing jeans, a T-shirt, and white sneakers. With a happy smile, she squealed, "Surprise!"

Huh? For a long moment, I was so disoriented I forgot to smile back. With sleep-addled confusion, I took everything in – the sleek town car idling in the driveway, Cami standing out on the front porch, and the battered suitcase resting by Cami's feet.

I was still trying to make sense of everything when Cami lunged forward and gathered me up in a hug so tight, it took my breath away.

For the first time in what felt like forever, I felt myself smile. And then, I laughed.

Into her hair, I asked, "How'd you get here?"

It was a valid question. Since college graduation, Cami had been staying with her parents, who lived nearly three hours away in Petoskey. She had a car, but it wasn't what you'd call reliable. And forget hopping on a plane. Between security checks and the lack of nearby airports, flying would've taken twice as long.

Of course, it would've been better than taking a bus, which I knew all too well from my own pathetic experience.

In reply to my question of how she'd gotten here, Cami pulled back and pointed to the town car, still idling in the driveway. "I took that."

I shook my head. "A town car? Seriously?" Okay, yes, I realized that the unfamiliar vehicle had obviously brought her here. *But from where?*

The airport?

Or the bus station?

On the porch, Cami glanced toward the vehicle. "Is *that* what you call it?"

"Actually," I admitted, "I'm not really sure."

The vehicle was long, dark, and expensive-looking. It wasn't quite a limo, but it wasn't a regular car either.

Whatever it was, it *wasn't* leaving. In a hushed voice, I asked, "Do we need to pay him or something?"

Cami shook her head. "Nope. It's already paid for."

"But what about the tip?"

She grinned. "That's paid for, too. And it must've been bigger than what he normally gets, because the driver was so happy, he smiled the whole way here."

None of this was making any sense. I felt my brow wrinkle in confusion. *So, Cami had tipped him ahead of time?*

I felt like I was missing something, but I had no idea what. Absently, I murmured, "Really?"

Cami nodded. "Oh yeah. Like every time I caught his reflection in the rear-view mirror, he'd be grinning like he just won the lotto."

I didn't even play the lotto. But sleepy or not, I was suddenly grinning, too.

Cami was the closest thing I had to a sister, and I'd been dying to see her.

Still, I never would've expected her to travel all this way, especially knowing that her car tended to break down at the worst possible times.

And then, there was the matter of money. Much like myself, Cami was drowning in student debt. And although we'd both recently graduated from college, she wasn't yet employed, even if she *did* have something lined up for the fall.

This begged a serious question. *How on Earth had she come up with travel money?*

I planned to ask, but now wasn't the time.

She'd obviously gone to a lot of trouble to surprise me, and there was no way on Earth I'd ever ruin it by dwelling on our financial troubles.

So, with a smile, I said, "And you *are* staying here at the house, right?"

Whether she realized it or not, her visit had been perfectly timed. Waverly was gone, possibly forever. And Brody was away, too.

This meant that I didn't need to feel guilty or awkward for having a surprise houseguest stay at a place that wasn't truly my own.

But already, Cami was shaking her head. "I'm not staying *here.*"

I glanced down at her suitcase. "Oh?"

"Because," Cami said with a laugh, "I'm whisking you away."

I wasn't quite following. "To where?"

Her eyes brightened. "To a hotel on the river. We've got a suite and spa treatments, and—"

"But wait." I couldn't help but wince. "Who's paying for all of this?"

I really hated to ask, but I'd rather be a kill-joy than put a friend
further in debt.

With a smile, Cami replied, "*He* is."

He? I still wasn't following. "Who?"

"Brody."

CHAPTER 52

Arden

That single word – the name of the guy who'd given me so much grief – hung between us in the open doorway.

Cami was still smiling. "I'm *so* glad the two of you made up."

I shook my head. "But we didn't." At the mere thought of him, my eyes stung with unshed tears. "And we won't. It's over." I swallowed a lump so big, it literally hurt. "*Really* over."

Cami's smile faded to nothing. "Are you sure?"

"Of course I'm sure," I said. "I mean, I *would* know, right?"

The truth was, I'd talked to Brody only one time since his sudden departure. It was the conversation we'd had late last night. I'd hung up on him, and with good reason, too.

On the front porch, Cami murmured, "Oh, crap." She bit her lip. "Gosh, I'm *so* sorry." Slowly, she turned and gave the town car a long, worried look. "What should I do?"

By now, I was so confused, I could hardly think. "For starters, you could tell me what's going on."

And so she did, right there on the front porch while the town car lingered in the driveway.

Apparently, some sort of courier had shown up at her parent's house early this morning and had asked for Cami by name.

When she came to the door, the messenger – an older guy in a business suit – had informed her that she was the recipient of an all-expense paid vacation here in Bayside. And then, he'd given her a packet of pre-paid reservations, along with a phone number to call for more information.

The number, as she'd learned after calling it, was to Brody's new cell phone. On the phone, he'd explained that he'd messed up in some sort of way and wanted to make it up to me with a nice surprise.

The surprise, apparently, was a local spa vacation with my best friend.

As part of that surprise, Brody had even sent a car and driver to transport Cami from her parent's place to where I was staying at the crew house.

In theory, after I packed a suitcase of my own, the same town car would carry both of us to the hotel.

According to the schedule provided by the courier, the car and driver would be returning to Bayside next Saturday to drive Cami back to her parent's place.

As I listened to all of this, tears pricked at my eyes. The whole thing was so incredibly thoughtful – or at least it *would've* been thoughtful if only I didn't know the ugly truth.

Brody was a snake, through and through. Even worse, he was a dangerous snake, considering that he'd been fooling me from the beginning – lying straight to my face, over and over, even as I'd been falling hard for the guy I *thought* I knew.

I'd been such an idiot.

And now my troubles were impacting Cami, too. After a brief discussion, she and I sent the town car on its way and retreated into the crew house. As I carried in her suitcase, I said, "Hey, can I ask you a question?"

"Sure."

I set down her suitcase and shut the door behind us. "If you didn't think we were staying here, why'd you bring your suitcase to the front door?"

"Oh, that?" She gave a weak laugh. "It was for dramatic effect. You know, to put you in the vacationy mood."

Funny, it actually had, but not because of any hotel or spa plans. It was because I'd been so thrilled to see her.

I was *still* thrilled. But now I felt slightly ashamed about how she'd gotten here in the first place.

I didn't want to be ungrateful to anyone, not even to Brody.

Did that make me a sap?

Probably.

And yet, if things had been even slightly different, his gesture would've melted my heart.

But not now.

Now, all I felt was despair. And I hated that Cami had been caught up in the middle. I gave her a concerned look. "Are you disappointed?"

She sank down onto the living room sofa. "About what?"

I claimed the sofa's opposite end. "Oh, come on. You know. That we're just staying *here*."

Together, Cami and I had agreed on this revised plan because neither one of us had felt right about taking something so extravagant from Brody when my relationship with him was decidedly over.

But for Cami's sake, I still felt guilty for the bait-and-switch. I glanced around. "I mean, this is no luxury hotel."

"Forget the hotel," she said. "You were the main attraction."

"Are you sure?" I asked. "Because you really *do* look disappointed."

"Of course I'm disappointed," she said. "But not because of the spa or whatever."

"Oh. Then what is it?"

She sighed. "I'm disappointed because I actually believed him. He sounded *so* sincere. And I was so happy for you – for both of you, actually."

I knew the feeling. There was a time, and it wasn't too awful long ago, that I'd been happy, too.

With a wistful smile, Cami continued. "It was all so thoughtful. Or at least, I *thought* it was. And in the car, all the way down here, I kept thinking how lucky you were to find that special someone, you know?"

I did know. Until a couple of days ago, I'd been feeling pretty lucky myself. Whatever Brody and I had, it had seemed so achingly real.

But now I knew better. The whole thing was built on a foundation of lies.

It really *was* depressing.

On the couch, Cami gave me a hopeful look. "Are you *sure* you're not over-reacting, at least a little?"

I stiffened. "What?"

"I just mean, I know he bolted without telling you and all, but —"

"That's not it."

She hesitated. "What do you mean?"

The last time I'd talked to Cami, I'd been angry about Brody leaving so suddenly with no warning, and *also* for avoiding my phone calls after the fact.

But all of this was nothing compared to what I'd learned from my cousin. I'd been planning to call Cami later on tonight to give her the full story. I would've called her even sooner except I'd been too busy crying.

Now, I saw no reason to put it off.

But where to begin? Finally, I settled on, "See, the thing is, Brody's been lying to me all along."

CHAPTER 53

Arden

When I finished talking, Cami stared in obvious disbelief. "He didn't."

With a bitter laugh, I replied, "Oh, but he did."

In spite of everything I'd been led to believe, Brody had purchased the house under less than honorable circumstances. And, as if that weren't bad enough, he'd known all along about my connection to the place.

He'd known. And he hadn't cared.

Or worse, he'd cared only enough to buy the house out from under me as some sort of twisted revenge for what had happened back in high school.

Either way, he'd been lying to me from the start. And he was *still* lying to me now.

Cami frowned. "But are you sure?"

"Of course I'm sure."

This should've been obvious. After all, I'd just spent the last hour telling her everything I'd learned from Jason when he'd stopped by just last night.

Turns out, selling the house hadn't been Jason's idea at all. Instead, he'd been forced to sell when a prospective buyer had started making trouble with the city.

On the couch, Cami was saying, "But you can't be *totally* sure. I mean, Jason has lied to you before, right?"

I knew what she was getting at. "You mean about the repairs? Yeah, I know. But this time it's different."

On the couch, Cami still looked unconvinced. "How so?"

"Because this time, there's paperwork to prove it."

"Paperwork?" She leaned forward. "Did you see it with your own eyes? Because I'm just saying, maybe Jason's lying about *that*, too."

I had to give Cami credit. She was working awfully hard to come up with a happy ending to this story – an ending that *didn't* involve Brody being a total lying ass-hat.

Sadly, I could actually relate.

I'd gone through the same process last night when Jason had started weaving his tale of woe. I'd flat-out refused to believe him – until he'd gone out to his car and returned with proof. *And plenty of it.*

"Wait here," I told Cami as I got to my feet.

I returned a minute later with a big stack of papers. With a sound of disgust, I tossed them onto the sofa, where I'd been sitting.

As I sank down onto the nearby armchair, I gestured toward the scattered paperwork. "Go ahead. Pick one. See for yourself."

With obvious concern, Cami picked up a random sheet of paper and asked, "So, what are these, anyway?"

"Letters from the city," I said. "*And* from Brody's lawyer. And a few fines. And notices. And all kinds of stuff. None of it's good."

And that was putting it mildly. Together, all of those documents told the full story of what I'd already explained to Cami.

When it came to the house, Jason had been backed into a corner. If he didn't get the property up to code within sixty days, the house would be condemned, which meant that it would surely be torn down – probably sooner rather than later.

The whole thing sounded like a total nightmare.

Cami studied the sheet of paper in her hand. "Three thousand dollars?"

I nodded. "And that's just *one* of the fines. There's a whole bunch of them."

She looked up. "So your cousin had to pay *all* of these?"

"Sure," I said. "Unless he made the repairs – *or* sold it to someone who would."

"So what are you saying?" she asked. "He sold it to avoid the fines?"

I nodded again. "He felt like he had to. Whether it was fines or repairs, there's no way he could've paid *all* of them." I paused. "Or should I say there's no way *I* could've paid all of them."

And yet, it would've been nice to have the chance to try.

I was still miffed at Jason for not telling me what had been going on. He'd *claimed* that he hadn't wanted to worry me during my final semester of college. But even now, I was finding this hard to believe.

Probably, Jason had been too afraid to admit that he'd let the place fall to pieces around him. And then, he'd been afraid of Brody.

That was a story in and of itself.

Cami's eyebrows furrowed. "So basically, your cousin was *forced* to sell?"

"Right." I'd explained all of this to Cami already in painful detail. But from the look on her face, it had taken the paperwork to truly drive the point home.

It had been the same way with me.

But there was one particular document that really broke my heart. I stood from the chair and reached toward the pile of papers. I began rummaging through it until I found the thing I was looking for.

It didn't take long for me to locate it, probably because in a fit of anger last night, I'd actually wadded it up and hurled it against the wall.

Oh sure, I'd tried to straighten it out afterward, because the document wasn't officially mine. But I'd done a sorry job of it, which meant that it stuck out like a sore thumb.

I handed it to Cami and waited in silence for her to read it.

The document was a personal letter from Jason to Brody, where Jason had practically begged Brody to buy only *half* of the house, meaning Jason's half, which would've left *my* half intact.

In the letter, Jason had confessed that his younger cousin – meaning me, of course – secretly owned half of the property and was, in Jason's owns words, "emotionally attached to the place."

In that same letter, Jason had gone into an awkward amount of detail on how I'd been working two jobs to keep up with the payments and how I'd lived there with my grandparents back in high school.

And on and on.

The letter was five pages long and pretty darn embarrassing, even if it *was* all true.

Embarrassing or not, I had to give Jason at least some credit for trying. Of course, his idea was totally impractical. I mean, why would Brody – or any other investor – be willing to buy only half of a house?

It didn't help that the secret owner – again, meaning me – appeared nowhere on the deed or in any other legal document related to the property.

And it *especially* didn't help that buyer – meaning Brody – totally hated me at the time of the transaction.

This was beyond obvious by the way Brody had responded to Jason's letter. He'd returned it with only a handwritten note, scrawled across the bottom of the letter's first page.

The note said, and I quote, *"Not my problem."*

When Cami finished reading the letter, she flipped back to the beginning and gave it a long, perplexed look. Finally, she looked up. "Not my problem? What does that mean?"

"It means he's a jerk, that's what."

"Yeah, but that was months ago, before you two were together." With a hopeful smile, she added, "I'm sure he would've responded differently now."

It was such a nice thought. But I couldn't quite agree. And that wasn't even the point. I told Cami, "This isn't about the house."

She gave me a dubious look. "Are you sure?"

r"Of course I'm sure," I said. "Look, yes, I would still love to buy
it. In fact, I told Brody so on the phone." Under my breath, I added,
"Except I wasn't so nice about it, I guess."

Cami asked, "So what *is* it about?"

"It's about him lying to me." I blinked away sudden tears. "Look, I
get that he didn't want to share ownership, especially when I had
nothing to offer. But what I *don't* get is why he never told me the truth,
not even after we got so close."

Cami paused as if thinking. "Well…Maybe he was embarrassed."
She gave the letter another quick glance. "I mean, he *does* come across
as a cold S.O.B."

"Yeah, but he *still* could've told me. Given our history, I would've
understood."

"But maybe he didn't know that."

"Well, he should've," I said. "And even if he didn't, why make a
point to keep lying to me?"

"Well…" Cami bit her lip. "Maybe he didn't want to lose you."

I made a sound of frustration. "Why are you sticking up for him?"

"I don't mean to," she said. "I'm just saying, maybe he never got
up the nerve to tell you the truth."

At this, I had to laugh. It wasn't a happy sound. "Trust me," I said.
"If there's one thing Brody has it's nerve. And plenty of it."

"Yeah, but he's also crazy about you."

"Oh, please," I said. "He can't be."

"Sure he can." Her tone grew wistful. "And love makes you do
funny things."

"Love?" With a choked sob, I said, "He doesn't love me. Cripes,
he probably doesn't even like me."

"Oh come on," she said. "That's not true. If it were, I wouldn't be
sitting here right now."

I saw what she meant. And if things were just a little bit different, I
might've seen it that way, too. But obviously, Cami still wasn't getting
it.

Desperately, I tried to explain. "Do you have any idea how many times he lied to me? And that's not all either."

She gave me a wary look. "There's more?"

"Oh yeah," I said. "Get this. Jason is banned from the house."

Cami shook her head. "Banned? What do you mean?"

"I mean," I said, "if he comes anywhere near it, or even talks about it, it'll cost him, bigtime." I pointed to the scattered paperwork. "Do you know, he took a huge risk in showing me those?"

Cami glanced down at the documents. "Sorry, I'm not following."

"It was part of the deal," I said. "Apparently, he signed some sort of non-disclosure agreement, where he can't talk about the place, not even to me."

Cami frowned. "Is that even legal?"

"I don't know," I said. "But it's legal enough to make Jason act all funny about it. Do you know, I practically had to wrestle those documents away from him last night?"

"Really?"

"Oh yeah," I said. "I had to beg over and over for the chance to go through them on my own. And he only agreed to that *after* I assured him that Brody was on the other side of the country."

I gave the paperwork another glance. "Jason's picking them up later on tonight. And get this. I had to swear up and down that I wouldn't make a copy of anything either."

Cami's brow wrinkled. "Well, that's weird."

"I know," I said. "But it's not Jason's fault. You should see him. He's terrified. He was even afraid to stop by, or call me or anything. In fact, he only *did* stop by in the end, because I was the only one around."

On the couch, Cami was looking more concerned with every passing moment.

I waited, wondering what she'd say next. And when she said nothing, I asked, "So...what are you thinking?"

She winced. "I'm almost afraid to tell you."

"Why?"

"Because you're not gonna like it."

I sighed. "Is this where you tell me that I was stupid for trusting Brody in the first place?"

Cami shook her head. "No, I'd never say that. But I *will* say this. I think you should call him."

My jaw dropped. "What? Why?"

"To give him the chance to explain."

"You're kidding, right?"

"Just hear me out," she said. "He obviously cares for you. And I *know* you care for him—"

"I do not." I hesitated. "Or at least, I shouldn't." And yet, I did, *so very much.*

How pathetic was that?

Cami reached out and gave my hand an encouraging squeeze. "Look, I know you're mad, but for your sake, just do it, alright? And if he doesn't come clean, you can say, 'I told you so.'" She smiled. "Deal?"

After a long, tense moment, I felt myself nod. "Okay. Deal."

CHAPTER 54

Brody

I was standing in the charred remains of the California kitchen when my new cell phone rang. I picked it up and glanced at the display. It was Arden.

Knowing what the call was about, I answered with a smile. "Hey."

After a long pause, her voice – sounding cold and distant – replied, "Hey."

My smile faded. "Is something wrong?"

"No. Well, maybe." She sighed. "First, I *guess* I should thank you, huh?"

I frowned. I hadn't expected her to kiss my ass, but I *had* thought she'd be happier than she was now.

Had something gone wrong with my surprise?

I said, "So, Cami got there alright?"

"Yeah, she got here. And I *guess* that was really nice of you."

Again with the "guess."

She continued, "So, um, thanks. I guess."

What the hell? In a tight voice, I replied, "You're welcome."

"So, um…have you thought any more about the house?"

I felt my jaw clench. "No."

She sighed, but said nothing in reply.

With growing anger, I asked, "Is there a problem?"

"Well…I guess I'm just wondering if there's anything you want to tell me."

"About what?"

"I don't know. Maybe…" Again, she paused. "About the house?"

By now, there were plenty of things I wanted to tell her, and none of them were nice. Working hard to keep my cool, I tossed the ball back into her court. "If you've got something to say, just say it."

"See, the thing is…maybe *I'm* not the one with something to say. Maybe *you* have something to say." She paused. "Maybe something you meant to tell me sooner?"

I had no clue what she meant. "About what?"

"The house."

My grip tightened on the phone. "If you're asking if I've changed my mind, I already gave you my answer."

And the answer was no. *I wasn't going to sell her the house.* The truth was, I'd been planning something better. But now, I was thinking that I'd dodged a bullet by waiting.

Something had gone off the rails. Or maybe, I'd been reading things wrong from the beginning.

Either way, this wasn't the Arden I knew. And now, I had to wonder, which one was the real deal? *The girl I'd fallen for? Or the girl on the phone?*

Because they weren't the same girl.

And now, she'd grown silent.

I said, "You still there?"

"Uh, yeah," she said. "Okay, how about this? If you won't sell me the *whole* house, maybe you'd think about selling me half?"

She was kidding, right? "What?"

"Or *maybe*," she continued, "you *did* think about selling me half, maybe even before I showed up. And *maybe* that's something you want to talk about now."

Or maybe I'd heard enough. "Half a house? You serious?"

"Of course I'm serious."

The more I heard, the shittier I felt. There was a time – hell just a few days ago – when sharing a house with Arden would've been nice to think about.

But not now. Not with whatever was going on.

On the phone, she was still talking. "I'm just saying, like in the beginning, maybe you didn't think everything through, like when you were buying it."

"Trust me. I thought plenty."

"Trust you?" she scoffed. "You're kidding, right?"

I wasn't kidding. I was insulted, and with good reason. "You done?"

"With what?"

"You tell me," I said. "Because you're acting like I screwed you over. And we both know that's not true."

Her tone grew sarcastic. "Oh, do we now?"

"*I* do," I said. "Don't you?"

"Oh, I know *something.*"

"Uh-huh. What's that?"

"You're not the person you pretend to be."

"Yeah?" I said. "And neither are you."

"What do you mean by that?"

"Hell if I know," I said. "You called me to say what? That I screwed you over?"

Her voice grew quiet. "So...*did* you?"

By now, I was seriously pissed. "What do *you* think?"

"Well, I think you screwed me," she said with a choked sob. "I just don't know which way." And with that, she ended the call.

I looked at my phone for a long moment before hurling it across the kitchen. It hit the side wall, and the case popped off. As for rest of the phone, whether it was damaged or not, I didn't know, and I didn't care.

Whatever was going on, I'd had more than enough. And the way it sounded, so had she.

Good.

I didn't mean it. But it felt better to think that way, at least until the sun fell and the night closed in around me. And then, I had to ask myself, "*What the hell was going on?*"

CHAPTER 55

Arden

The next few days passed in a long, depressing blur, which really sucked – for me *and* for Cami, because no matter how hard I tried, I just *knew* that I was pathetic company.

Oh sure, I tried to be upbeat and not obsess too much over Brody, but the unhappy truth was, I couldn't help but feel sad and confused about the way things had turned out.

Adding to my confusion, I learned from Roy on Monday morning that Brody had made arrangements for me to have the whole week off – and with pay, too – so I could spend more time with my friend.

It was so thoughtful and so baffling at the same time. *How could someone so dishonest do something so wonderful?*

None of it made any sense. And now the unexpected time off was giving me way too many hours to dwell on how idiotic I'd been to get attached to Brody in the first place.

I should've known it was too good to be true.

Or rather, I should've known that *he* was too good to be true.

But now *nothing* felt good, especially as the days passed without any interaction between us – no calls, no texts, no nothing.

Meanwhile, festering in the back of my brain was the knowledge that Waverly was in California with him. She'd been chasing after him for months. *Had she finally caught him?*

I tried not to think about it.

Meanwhile, across the street, I saw construction crews coming and going – sometimes working late into the night.

I wanted to be part of it. *And* I wanted to crawl into a hole and hide. With every passing day, I found myself caring less about the house and more about whatever was going on with Brody.

I missed him like crazy, especially at night, when I was alone in the living room. I'd been sleeping on the couch, having insisted on giving Cami my bedroom, which had the only private bathroom in the house.

As for my own sleeping arrangements, I'd opted for the sofa because Waverly's bedroom was probably off-limits, and the thought of sleeping in Brody's empty bed was too depressing to consider.

One night, while gazing up at the living room ceiling, I came to the embarrassing conclusion that if I had to choose between Brody and the house, I'd pick Brody a million times over, if only he'd come clean about what he'd done.

And hey, an apology might be nice, too.

Oh yeah. I was definitely pathetic. And I was making Cami feel pathetic, too. She never complained, but on Thursday, even *her* usually chipper mood took a sudden turn for the worse.

By the time we said our goodnights, she seemed just as depressed as *I* felt.

It was all my fault, and I decided I had to do better.

When the sun rose on Friday morning, I vowed that no matter what, I'd show Cami a good time. Even if it killed me, I'd be cheerful and upbeat. I wouldn't talk about Brody. I wouldn't even *think* about Brody. I'd simply pretend that he never existed.

For starters, I got up and began making pancakes and bacon, intending to surprise Cami with her favorite breakfast.

I was just mixing up the pancake batter when I heard a quiet knocking sound. I paused in the mixing and glanced toward the front door. The knock had been *so* quiet, I wasn't sure that I'd heard it at all.

But soon, I heard it again.

I set down the mixing bowl and made my way to the living room. I cracked open the front window blinds and peered outside, only to frown in new confusion.

Standing on the front porch was a little girl, maybe seven or eight years old.

She was utterly alone.

What the heck?

I hustled to the door and answered before she could run off. Summoning up a smile, I said, "Hi."

She grinned up at me, revealing one missing front tooth. "Hi."

My pint-sized visitor had long brown hair, big brown eyes, and a smattering of freckles across her nose. She wore dark jeans, a pink T-shirt, pink sneakers, and a little black jean jacket.

I had no idea who she was, or what she was doing here. "So...are you looking for someone?"

"Sort of." She leaned forward. "But I'm not supposed to."

I hesitated. "Oh yeah? Why not?"

She glanced around before whispering, "Because I snuck out."

She was so adorable, I didn't know whether to laugh or call the police. "Really? From where?"

"Home, that's where." She frowned. "Veronica was asleep. Last night, she was up super late talking to her boyfriend. And she's *not* a morning person. That's what she told me on her first day." Her little eyebrows furrowed. "And on her second day, too. She says it a lot."

I nodded in encouragement. She'd just given me a lot of information, even if very little of it was actually useful. Still, I made a point to smile. "So, who's Veronica?"

"She's my nanny. She doesn't want to be. But she still is."

I felt my brow wrinkle in new confusion. "Oh yeah?" In my whole life, I'd never met anyone with an actual nanny, even here on this street, where the waterfront homes tended to be a lot pricier than average.

I was no expert on nannies, but even *I* knew that Veronica had to be a pretty bad one if she'd lost track of her charge. *And what was the deal about her not wanting to be this girl's nanny?*

Had Veronica actually said that to her?

Even though I'd never met this Veronica person, I disliked her already.

Still, I smiled down at the little girl. "And what's *your* name?"

"Willow."

"Willow what?"

"Willow Taylor."

Taylor. Taylor…

I tried to think. *Wasn't there a Taylor family a few doors down? No.* They were the *Tylers.*

I said, "By any chance, you don't mean Tyler, do you?"

Willow frowned up at me. "I know my own name, Silly."

"Oh. Of course you do. Sorry."

And just like that, she was smiling again. "That's okay. Veronica gets my name wrong, too."

I felt my jaw clench. *Worst. Nanny. Ever.*

Right then and there, I decided that when I tracked down this Veronica person, I'd tell her exactly what I thought of her nannyship. Or nannyhood. Or whatever it was called.

I asked Willow, "So, where do you live?"

Willow extended her arm and pointed somewhere off to the left.

I looked to where she pointed, but couldn't be sure which house she meant. I pointed in the same direction. "So, that big blue house on the water?"

Willow shook her head. "Nope. Not that one."

I kept my smile plastered in place. "The yellow one next to it?"

Again, she shook her head. "Nope."

I hesitated. "But, um…I'm pretty sure that's where you pointed." Or at least, it was *one* of the two houses.

Willow gave a snort of laughter. "Yeah, but I live *way* past that."

"Oh." The longer this went on, the more concerned I was getting. It was barely seven o'clock in the morning, and she was out here on her own.

Surely *someone* would be looking for her. With a smile, I said, "How about I'll grab my shoes and walk you home?"

Willow peered around me and gave a long, drawn-out sniff. Her eyes brightened. "Is that bacon?"

I knew I liked this kid.

But then I froze. *Oh, crap. The bacon.*

I held up a finger. "Don't go anywhere, okay?"

And with that, I left the front door open and practically sprinted to the stove, where the bacon wasn't quite yet burnt. Frantically, I shut off the burner and moved the pan aside. And then, I sprinted down the hallway and knocked on the bedroom door where Cami was sleeping.

She had a whole bunch of siblings and a degree in primary education. *If anyone could handle this, it was Cami.*

CHAPTER 56

Brody

"I'll tell you why," Chase said. "She's playing you."

This wasn't what I wanted to hear, especially at seven o'clock on a Friday morning.

I'd just flown back from California, and I felt like shit.

It wasn't because of jet leg. It was because of Arden.

I'd been pissed off all week, and I was having a hard time shaking it. Rather than returning to the crew house, I'd gone instead to my condo for a change of clothes and some time to figure out what the hell I'd be doing next.

But instead of finding peace and quiet, I'd found Chase in my kitchen, drinking the last of my orange juice straight from the carton.

In the kitchen doorway, I'd stopped short at the sight of him. "What are you doing?"

"Drinking juice," he'd said, like it should be obvious. "What are you doing?"

"I just got back from California." Eyeing the carton in his hand, I'd asked, "And don't you have juice of your own?"

"Sure," he'd said, "but I've also got a guest, and she won't stop talking." With his free hand, he'd made yapping motions in the air. "Shit," he'd said with a laugh, "I thought she'd never shut up." But then, he'd frowned. "What's wrong with you?"

And like a dumb-ass, I'd actually told him. Even dumber, I'd asked for his opinion on why Arden had gone off the deep end.

And this is when he'd informed me that Arden was – in his words – playing me.

Fast forward to now. I told Chase, "You don't know that."

"Sure I do," he said. "You said she's nuts about the house, right?"

Oh, yeah. She was nuts, and not just about the house.

I'd been thinking *that* for years, until she'd shown me a different side, a side that I couldn't get enough of, a side that, even now, I missed more than I should.

With a shrug, I replied, "Yeah, so?"

"So hey, you've got to give her credit for trying."

I frowned. "Trying what?"

"To get you thinking with your dick, and not the brain upstairs."

Shit.

All week, I'd been toying with the same theory – not liking it, but not willing to let it go either.

But I should've seen the signs.

After all, Arden wasn't the first girl to try such a stunt. For years, I'd been dealing with chicks pretending to be this or that. A few of them had worked it pretty hard, too, trying to convince me that they were "the one."

They weren't.

And the way it looked, neither was Arden, even if I'd been thinking just the opposite.

But I had to face facts. Chase was right, even if it wasn't what I wanted to hear.

With a scoff, I considered how Arden had been acting until just recently. And I *did* mean acting.

Nuts or not, she'd put on one hell of a show. When I considered all of the hours she'd spent looking at floor plans, paint samples, kitchen layouts, and shit-knows-what-else, I wanted to kick myself for not seeing through the act.

Good thing she couldn't keep it up.

If she'd been just a little more patient, I would've given her more than the house – and counted myself a lucky guy.

I wasn't feeling so lucky *now*.

In the kitchen, Chase said, "Aw come on. Girls are like busses, right?"

I was only half listening. "What?"

"Another one will roll up any minute." He glanced toward my condo's main door. "Hey, you want the rest of mine?"

I wasn't following. "Your what?"

"My date."

I gave him a look. "No."

"You sure?" He grinned. "She's hot and ready."

Chase and I never shared. I saw his twisted offer for what it was, an attempt to distract me from my own sorry mood.

I loved him for it, but that didn't mean it was working. The way I felt now, it would take more than a crude joke to make me laugh.

When my only reply was a tight smile, he added, "If you act now, I'll throw in a muzzle."

I didn't get it. "A muzzle?"

"Or ear-plugs," he said. "Like I said, she's a real yapper."

It was typical Chase.

He was full of shit, and we both knew it. I replied, "I'll pass, thanks."

"Eh, smart move," he said. "Get this. I'm supposed to be picking up breakfast."

I glanced toward the kitchen cupboard behind him. "I think there's cereal on the top shelf."

"Not anymore," he said. "I ate that on Wednesday."

I didn't get it. Chase had a shopping service, a maid, and plenty of women dying to cook for him. *But what was he doing?* Eating my cereal and drinking my juice.

But hey, to each his own.

It's not like I missed whatever he was taking. I had plenty of money and a shopping service of my own. I'd only been stopping by the condo a few times a week anyway – mostly to swap out clothes and pick up the mail.

And besides, it wasn't juice I wanted now. It was something with a lot more kick.

I was still mulling that over when Chase's phone chirped in his pocket. He pulled it out and glanced at the display. As he did, the blood drained from his face. "Shit."

"What?"

He looked seriously rattled. "I've gotta go."

Chase had a thing for crazy chicks. From the look on his face, his so-called date had just threatened to light the bed on the fire. *Hey, it wouldn't be the first time.*

I said, "So your date wants you back, huh?"

Chase shook his head. "It wasn't her. It was Veronica."

I froze. "Willow's nanny? Why would *she* be texting you?"

"Because," Chase said, "she lost track of Willow, and she wants my help."

CHAPTER 57

Arden

Walking along the sidewalk, Cami pointed to the latest white two-story house. "Is *that* it?"

Willow shook her head. "Nope."

Cami and I were walking side-by-side with Willow between us. Already, we'd traveled nearly half a mile and had passed at least ten houses matching that description.

Over Willow's head, Cami and I exchanged a look.

No doubt, she was thinking the same thing I was thinking. *Maybe we should've called the police.*

But for Willow's sake, we hadn't. Instead, we'd decided to escort her safely home and take it from there.

There was only one problem. We couldn't seem to *find* Willow's home.

It didn't help that she didn't know her own address *or* a family phone number. But she *had* given us a description of where she lived.

According to Willow, she lived in big white house that had an upstairs *and* a downstairs. And she lived on the water.

It sounded simple enough. And yet, she hadn't recognized any of the houses we'd passed.

And by now, we'd passed plenty.

With a strained smile, Cami looked to Willow and asked, "Are we getting close?"

Willow was skipping along between us. Without missing a beat, she replied, "Nope."

The funny thing was, she seemed to be having a terrific time. I could see why, too.

Until just a couple of minutes ago, Cami had been entertaining both of us with a whole series of knock-knock jokes. But now, after twenty minutes of fruitless searching, even Cami had grown mostly silent.

Me too, and with good reason.

Someone was missing a kid. And if we didn't find out who, we'd need to do more than simply walk her home. *And what if Willow was in some sort of trouble?*

Between us, Willow said with a laugh, "Hey, I know. Knock knock."

Cami said, "Who's there?"

"Orange."

"Orange who?"

Willow giggled. "*Orange* you glad that wasn't my house?"

I wasn't glad. I was worried. And obviously so was Cami. With a strained smile, she asked, "Are *you* glad?"

Willow nodded. "Oh yeah. You're more *way* more fun than Veronica." Willow looked to me and added with a grin. "You are, too."

For her sake, I smiled back. "Thanks. You're pretty fun yourself."

"I know." And with that, she continued skipping along, oblivious to the growing tension that Cami and I were both trying to hide.

This wasn't going well.

By now, I wasn't even sure who to blame – Veronica for losing track of a seven-year-old, me for not calling the police right away, or Cami for suggesting that we simply walk Willow home.

Probably we were *all* idiots, because by now, it was painfully obvious that Willow was a lot more lost than we'd first realized.

Either that, or she was stalling for some other reason.

Regardless, I was coming to the sad realization that we'd probably end up calling the police anyway. After all, a kid that young who'd wandered half a mile on her own was no laughing matter.

I was just bracing myself to make the call when Cami said, "Hang on a minute, okay?" When we all stopped, Cami crouched down to

Willow's level and said, "Are you *sure* you don't know your phone number?'

Willow snickered. "I don't have a phone, Silly."

With an encouraging smile, Cami said, "But what about your mom? *She* has a phone, right?"

Willow's laughter faded. "I don't have a mom."

Ouch.

Cami's eyes filled with sympathy. "Oh, I'm sorry, sweet pea." She tried for yet another smile. "How about your dad?"

Looking almost disgruntled now, Willow said, "He's busy."

I felt my jaw clench. *He wasn't just busy. He was neglectful.* That much was obvious by the fact that his daughter was roaming around unprotected while he was off doing who-knows-what.

Following Cami's lead, I crouched down toward Willow and said, "Do you know *his* phone number?"

With a shrug, Willow replied, "Nope."

I studied her face. I was no expert on seven-year-olds, but I had the distinct impression she wasn't being completely honest.

I tried another approach. "But surely, you know his name, right?" "Maybe."

"So…what is it?" I already had a last name, Taylor. But when I'd looked on the Web before setting out, I'd found no Taylors living nearby.

Still, if I had a first name, I could do another internet search on my phone, maybe see if we were heading in the right direction.

Willow grinned. "Guess."

"Guess what?" I asked.

"His name."

I didn't feel like guessing. But hey, at least I knew part of his name already. Trying to be crafty, I said, "If I guess his last name, will you tell me his first name?"

Willow gave it some thought. "I guess so."

"Alright. Is his last name…" I pretended to think. "Taylor?"

She laughed. "No. That's *my* name."

Crap.

But of course, I should've realized there was no guarantee that she and her dad would have the same last name. Still, my sense of unease was growing.

Working hard to keep calm, I said, "Alright, I give up. Why don't you just tell us?"

Willow was frowning again. "But you only guessed once."

When I looked to Cami, she said to Willow, "If you tell me *your* dad's name, I'll tell you *my* dad's name. And it's a funny one, too."

Willow perked up. "Really?"

"Oh yeah," Cami said. "But you tell us first. What's *your* dad's name?"

Willow replied, "Mason."

I froze. *Oh, no.* It couldn't be *that* Mason. *Could it?* Cami and I exchanged another long, worried look. Finally, it was Cami who asked the question I'd been dreading. "And what's his last name?"

And that's when Willow said it. "Blastoviak."

Shit.

I felt the blood drain from my face – and not only because I knew that name all too well. It was because just then, a big black sedan screeched to stop on the street beside us.

I recognized that sedan, just like I recognized the driver, who'd already bolted from the car. He slammed the driver's side door behind him and moved toward us with long, angry strides.

From the look on his face, he was about to accuse us of stealing his kid, which posed an unsettling question.

Had we?

CHAPTER 58

Arden

In stunned silence, Cami and I watched from the sidewalk as Mason – with a surprising degree of gentleness – escorted Willow straight to his car and got her settled in the back seat.

And then, after shutting the car door behind her, he strode back to where we stood. With murder in his eye, he demanded in a low voice, "What the hell were you doing?"

I resisted the urge to cringe in the face of his quiet wrath. "We were walking her home." My chin lifted as I considered who was truly at fault here. "And as long as we're all asking, what the hell were *you* doing?"

He glared down at me. "So you're gonna walk ten fucking miles? With a seven-year-old? *That's* what you want me to believe?"

I blinked. "Ten miles? Really?"

Well, that explained why we'd never found the house.

"Cut the crap," he said. "What do you want?"

Wasn't it obvious? "I *wanted* to take her home."

"Oh yeah?" he said. "And where the hell is that?"

Oh, for God's sake. "In case it wasn't clear," I said, "I meant *her* home, not mine." This should've been obvious. I mean for one thing, I didn't even *have* a home.

But apparently, Mason was too angry to think straight. With a low scoff, he said, "Is that so?"

I made a sound of frustration. "And I didn't *know* it was ten miles, okay?"

He gave me a hard look. "So what's your angle?"

"I don't have an angle," I said. "I already told you, I was trying to get her home."

"Nice story," he said. "So tell me. How the hell did you get her?"

Get her?

Okay, that made no sense whatsoever. I shook my head. "What?"

Speaking very clearly now, he repeated the gist of his question. "How did you get her?"

"I didn't 'get' her," I said. "She got me."

His jaw clenched. "Was Brody in on it?"

I felt my brow wrinkle in confusion. "In on what?"

"You tell me."

"I can't tell you," I said, "because I have no idea what you mean."

We were still arguing back and forth when Cami – facing Mason, not me – nudged her way between us. With a strained smile in her voice, she told him, "You need to stop, okay?"

Mason was tall – a lot taller than me and Cami, which meant that I could see his face all too clearly when he replied, "And who are you?"

With that same smile in her voice, she said, "I'm the one who's going slap you silly if you don't calm down."

From the look on his face, her words *felt* like a slap, even if she hadn't actually done it. In a tight voice, he replied, "What?"

Cami craned her neck to stare at him. "The question isn't *what*," she said. "It's *why*. As in why you need to calm down." In a near whisper, she continued. "And the answer to *that* is, 'Because you're scaring your daughter.'"

Slowly, Mason turned to look.

So did I.

Sure enough, inside the car, Willow's face was pressed tight against the glass of the side window. She was staring at all of us with obvious concern.

I dug deep and summoned up what I hoped was a smile. I gave her a friendly wave, as if to say, *"Everything's fine, really."*

From the look on her face, she wasn't buying it.

Smart kid.

Still, I kept the smile plastered in place until finally, she waved back, looking sick to her stomach.

By now, I wasn't the only one waving. Mason gave her a single stiff wave while Cami put a lot more effort into it, giving Willow a big, friendly wave *and* a thumbs-up.

Cami was still waving at Willow when Mason turned back to face me. In a dangerously low voice, he said, "I'll deal with *you* later."

Yikes.

If that wasn't a threat, I didn't know what was.

But soon, he was gone, leaving me wondering, *What on Earth had just happened?*

CHAPTER 59

Brody

Chase and I made a deal. I'd tell Mason while he dealt with the nanny. Bracing myself, I called Mason's cell phone.

Sounding more pissed off than usual, he answered with a terse, "What?"

He was obviously in a shitty mood. But hey, what else was new?

Whether he realized it or not, his mood was about to take a serious turn, and not for the better.

I got straight to the point. "Listen, I've got some bad news."

"I bet."

I didn't know what he meant, but I'd called for a reason, and I wasn't about to be sidetracked. "Before I tell you," I continued, "I want you to know, we're already working on it, alright?"

With a humorless laugh, he said, "Funny. Me, too."

I wasn't following. "What?"

"And here's *my* news," he said. "Your girlfriend – she's gotta go."

I frowned. "Who do you mean?"

"Cut the crap," he said. "I know you're fucking her. And before you ask, yeah, I mean Arden Weathers."

I didn't like the way he said that *or* the realization that I hadn't been as discreet as I'd thought. And if we weren't facing a family emergency, I might've taken the time to inform him that Arden and I weren't a thing. *Not anymore.*

But I didn't *have* that kind of time, so I ignored the now-familiar ache in my gut and said, "Forget that. Listen, Willow's missing."

With a scoff, he replied, "Nice try, asshole."

What the hell? "I'm not kidding."

"I don't know what you're playing at," he said, "but that chick's messing with your head."

I felt my eyebrows furrow. "What?"

"So I'll say it again." His voice hardened. "She's got to go. Not tomorrow. Not next week. *Today.*"

"Hey, *asshole*," I said. "Aren't you fucking listening? I just told you, Willow's missing."

"Are you at the office?"

"No. I'm at your place."

"Good," he said. "I'll be there in ten minutes." He paused. "*With* Willow."

"Wait, what?"

"I've got her." And with that, he ended the call.

Confused as hell, I shoved my new cell phone back into my pocket and looked to Chase. "He's on his way."

Next to Chase, Veronica was still crying. Through choked sobs, she said, "She must've been kidnapped. That's the only thing that makes sense."

I gave Veronica a long, irritated look. She was a leggy brunette with a hard mouth and roaming eyes. *I didn't like her.* Or maybe I was pissed off because she'd failed at the one thing she'd been hired to do – and it *wasn't* to look pretty.

Alright, so Willow was safe. *She was with Mason, not missing.*

That didn't the change the fact that Veronica had fallen down on the job.

She was still crying. Or pretending to cry. *Hell if I knew.*

Either way, the question was the same. *How could she not know where Willow was?*

It was seven-thirty in the morning, for Christ's sake.

I shoved a hand through my hair and tried to think. *Maybe Mason had taken Willow out for breakfast while Veronica was still asleep?* Was *that* why Veronica thought she was missing?

No. Mason might be a dick, but he ran a smooth household – too smooth in my opinion.

But he had a real soft spot for Willow. He'd been a decent dad, too. And I knew damn well he'd never take Willow anywhere and forget to tell the damn nanny.

He was too buttoned-up for that.

A few feet away, Chase was saying to Veronica, "Tell us again. When's the last time you saw her?"

Already, we had dozens of employees walking the neighborhood, looking for a lost little girl. *Turns out, she wasn't lost.*

But *something* was going on. And I didn't want to discuss it, not in front of Veronica. *She wasn't family.* And for all I knew, she'd put Willow at risk. Or hell, maybe she'd staged a fake kidnapping, looking to cash in on the family fortune.

A crazy theory?

Maybe. But with the kind of money we had these days, anything was possible.

Veronica was still blubbering when I pulled Chase aside and told him in a low voice. "Mason's got her."

His surprise was obvious. "No shit?"

I shrugged. "That's what he said."

"Huh." Chase frowned. "Weird."

In unison, we both looked to Veronica. She was standing on the opposite side of the room, sobbing alone by the side window.

Maybe I should've felt bad.

But I didn't.

And neither did Mason when he arrived ten minutes later – *with* Willow, just like he'd said.

Thank God.

I gave Willow a quick once-over. She looked fine, happy even. But not Mason. *He looked royally ticked.*

At the sight of Willow, Veronica squealed, "Oh, my God. There you are!" She threw open her arms wide and called out, "Oh, sweetie! Come here."

Willow didn't budge.

Neither did anyone else.

Mason looked down to Willow and said, "Go up to your room. You're still going to summer school."

Willow frowned. "But I'll be late."

With a tight smile, Mason replied, "Then you'd better hurry." After Willow left, Mason turned his attention to Veronica. He wasn't smiling anymore. "Pack your shit," he said. "You're fuckin' fired."

Veronica shook her head. "But why?"

I spoke up. "Because, *dumb-ass,* you lost the kid."

Veronica turned pleading eyes on Chase. "Don't you have something to say?"

Oh, for fuck's sake. I could guess what this meant. *Chase was screwing the damn nanny.*

Again.

In reply to her question, Chase told her, "Yeah. Pack your shit, like Mason said."

Her mouth fell open. "My shit?" she sputtered. "I'll have you know, I have nice stuff." She turned accusing eyes on Mason. "That's why you hired me, wasn't it? To be a good role model?"

I knew what she was getting at. Veronica might be hard as nails, but she looked all prim and proper in her form-fitting skirt and nice, white blouse. She'd been on the job for only three months, and she wouldn't be missed.

Mason gave her a cold look. "Role model, my ass."

"But—"

"You were hired to look after Willow. You failed." He glanced at his watch. "A driver's on the way."

"A driver?" she said. "What kind of driver?"

"The kind that'll take your ass out of here."

"To where?"

"Don't know, don't care," Mason said. "And if you want a severance, you'll be out by nine o'clock."

She perked up. "A severance?"

"That's what I said." Again, Mason glanced at his watch. "You've got eighty minutes. And just so we're clear, if it takes you eight-one, you get nothing."

"But–"

"So if I were you," Mason said, "I'd get your ass in gear."

He didn't need to tell her twice. Even in high heels, she was sprinting for the stairs.

When she disappeared from sight, Mason turned away, heading toward his study.

And me – I strode after him. Because this conversation *wasn't* over.

CHAPTER 60

Arden

As Cami and I walked back to the crew house, I felt lower than I had in a long time. And considering how low I'd been feeling lately, that was truly saying something.

I gave Cami a sideways glance. Normally, she was the most upbeat person I'd ever met. But now, she trudged along beside me looking nearly as depressed as I felt.

With an apologetic smile, I said, "I bet I know what you're thinking."

"Oh yeah? What's that?"

I forced a laugh. "Worst vacation, ever."

She shook her head. "Nah. It wasn't so bad."

"Oh come on, Cam. We both know that's not true. Listen, I know I've said it already, but I really *am* sorry."

"Oh, stop it," she said with a weak laugh. "I meant what I said. I actually had a pretty good time."

Funny, she sounded like she actually meant it. And yet, I was finding her words a little hard to believe. "But you couldn't have," I protested. "Not really."

"Why not?" she said. "You and I got to hang out. And I finally got to see the house. I've been wanting to see it forever, you know."

She *had* said as much. And, with the help of my own key, I'd been thrilled to give her the grand tour – minus the attic, of course.

I'd gotten the key from Brody not too long after he'd changed the locks. *Would he be wanting the key back, now that we weren't together? Probably.*

Like everything else today, the thought *wasn't* a cheery one.

Next to me, Cami was saying, "And we went to the beach nearly every day. That sounds like a vacation to *me*."

She was being way too generous. It was true that we'd spent lots of time at the beach. But mostly this involved walking along the shoreline while I whined about Brody.

But today, the topic of Brody was firmly off-limits. I'd made that promise – if only to myself – and I fully intended to keep it.

I said, "Well, it was no spa vacation, that's for sure."

"Forget the spa," she said. "I already told you, that's not why I came."

I believed her. Really, I did. And yet, I couldn't shake the feeling that something was truly bothering her.

Hesitantly, I said, "Is anything else on your mind?"

"Eh, nothing big."

I stopped walking. "Wait. So something *is* wrong? What is it?"

She stopped walking, too. "Don't worry. It's nothing important."

I studied her face. *Oh yeah. She was definitely hiding something.* "Then tell me," I urged. "What's wrong?"

"Alright. The thing is…" Her shoulders slumped. "I sort of lost my job."

My stomach sank. "What?" In the back of my mind, I had visions of Cami getting fired for taking the week off to spend time listening to me complain. "Oh, my God. I didn't realize you *had* a job."

"I don't," she said. "I mean, yeah, I've been doing some tutoring on the side. But I meant the job I'm supposed to be starting in the fall."

My heart went out to her. "Oh, no. Not your teaching job?" In September, Cami was supposed to begin teaching second grade at a wonderful little school not too far from Michigan State.

Cami blew out a long, shaky breath. "Yup. That's the one."

"What happened?"

"She decided not to retire."

"Who? The teacher you were replacing?"

Cami nodded. "That's the one."

"Oh, gosh. I'm really sorry. When did you find out?"

"Just yesterday."

I winced. "And you never said anything?"

Cami shook her head. "Nah, it was too depressing to mention."

I knew why, too. We'd been so focused on *my* problems that she hadn't wanted to add hers to the mix.

Now I felt *really* terrible. *And guilty. And stupidly helpless.*

I said, "Do you have any other offers?"

"Not yet." She tried to smile. "But I'm sure something will come up."

I wasn't so sure. Yes, Cami was truly amazing, but now she was getting a late start compared to everyone else. *Probably, all the good jobs had been filled already.*

At something in my expression, Cami said, "Oh, stop it. It'll be fine." With a smile, she said, "And if I don't get anything, I'll just go back to school, maybe work on my master's degree 'til next year."

The idea made sense. And yet I knew all too well how eager she'd been to get a full-time teaching job, along with the full-time paycheck to match.

By the time we started walking again, my mind was already churning, trying to think of some way to help.

For starters, I decided, I could try to be better company.

So that's what I did, all the way back, working like crazy to make up for how glum I'd been all week. And who knows, I might've been able to keep it up, too – if not for what I saw when we neared the crew house.

It was Brody's truck in the driveway.

CHAPTER 61

Arden

I found Brody in his bedroom, gathering up his stuff.

From the open doorway, I watched in agitated silence as he shoved wadded clothing into his duffle bag.

He was working hard and fast, as if the house were on fire or poisoned with toxic waste. He *had* to know that I was standing here. And yet, he kept on going, like I was utterly invisible.

Finally, I spoke up. "So you're leaving?"

He was wearing the same thing he usually wore – jeans and a T-shirt. His posture was stiff, and the muscles in his arms bulged as he turned to face me. In a tight voice, he said, "It's either me or you."

I bit my lip. His words stung even if they weren't exactly surprising.

When I said nothing in reply, he added, "I'll be gone in five."

"Five what?" I swallowed. "Minutes?"

"That's what I said."

"Actually, you *didn't* say. I mean, you *could* have meant five hours. Or five days." *Or a lifetime.*

Shit.

He said, "You knew what I meant."

"I know. I'm just saying…" My words trailed off into silence.

Crap. What was I saying? Okay, I fully realized that we couldn't be together, not with him refusing to own up to what he'd done. And yet, my heart ached just the same.

Did his?

From the look in his eyes, I couldn't be sure either way.

Stupidly, I finished by asking, "Do you care at all?"

His gaze darkened. "What do you think?"

"I think you're angry."

His tone grew sarcastic. "You think?"

"That's what I just said, isn't it?"

In my peripheral vision, I saw Cami watching from the far end of the hallway. When I gave her a worried glance, she pointed toward the front door and mouthed, *"I'm going for a walk."*

Oh, great. Now, on top of everything else, I'd forced her out on yet another fruitless walk. *Poor Cami.* Somehow, I'd need to make it up to her.

But I had just a few minutes with Brody, and I couldn't afford to waste them. Plus, there was something I had to tell him before he heard it from someone else. "I ran into Mason today."

"Yeah. I heard."

"You did?" I shook my head. "When?" It couldn't have been too long ago, considering that barely an hour had passed since Mason had sped off, taking Willow with him.

Apparently, news traveled fast.

When Brody's only reply was a tight shrug, I reluctantly asked, "Did Mason say anything?"

"He might've." Brody's voice grew several degrees colder as he said, "But you're not fired, if that's what you're asking."

"I wasn't."

Stupid or not, I hadn't expected to be fired. But I had expected *something*, like for Mason to throw me off the roof or run me down with his car. *And I wasn't even sure I was joking.*

I asked, "Is Willow okay?"

"She's fine." And with that, Brody returned once again to his clothes. In less than a minute, he was done packing. When he zipped up his duffle bag, I felt a surge of raw, inexplicable panic.

This was happening way too fast.

And Brody still hadn't answered my question. I tried again. "So, do you?"

"Do I what?"

"Care." Again, I felt myself swallow. "About us, I mean?"

He hoisted the bag over his shoulder and turned to fully face me. "You think I don't?"

"Honestly, I don't know what to think." My stomach clenched. "I mean, you're obviously leaving." It was a useless thing to say. Not only could I *see* that he was leaving. He'd just told me so during the last few minutes.

Plus, days ago, on the phone, I'd practically demanded that we separate. *Wasn't this exactly what I'd wanted?*

Yes.

And no.

The thought of us separating for good was nearly impossible to bear. "Well?" I said. "Do you?"

Brody dropped his duffle bag onto the floor and strode toward me. He stopped so close, I could've fallen into his arms.

I wanted to. *Oh, boy did I want to.*

But I didn't. *I couldn't.* Because he still wasn't being honest.

In a low voice, he said, "What, you think I don't care? Even now?"

"I don't know." I craned my neck to stare up at him. "*Do* you?"

"You *know* I do." His jaw clenched. "But I'm done."

My eyes filled with unshed tears. The whole thing was so totally unfair. If anyone should be angry, it was me.

Why should Brody get to leave in a huff when I was the one who'd been wronged?

With a choked sob, I said, "Oh, for God' sake, why don't you just admit it already?"

By now, he looked on the verge of losing it. "Admit what?"

"The thing with the house." I gave him another pleading look. "I mean, come on. You *know* what I mean. Just tell me. *Please?*"

I held my breath and waited.

With a hard scoff, he said, "What? You want me to tell you I'm sorry? For what? 'Stealing' it?" He shook his head. "Well, I'm not. So deal with it. Or don't. Your choice."

I wanted to scream in frustration. *He still wasn't getting it.* Or maybe he just didn't want to.

Desperately, I tried again. "I don't think you stole it, not technically."

"Then what *do* you think?"

"I think you cheated." I bit my lip. "And *maybe* you lied, at least a little." There was no "maybe" about it, and the lie *hadn't* been small. But heaven help me, I still wanted to hear it from him.

With another scoff, he said, "Right."

"Oh come on, Brody. You seriously don't think you did?"

"You wanna know what I think?"

"What?"

"I think you're nuts." He shook his head. "Hell, I *knew* you were nuts. But I fell for you anyway." His mouth twisted as he said, "My mistake."

My breath caught. "You fell for me? Seriously?"

"It doesn't matter now, does it?"

"It would if you'd just be honest."

"Yeah? Well honesty's a two-way street."

I was openly crying now. I didn't want to, but I couldn't seem to help it. "Alright, you want me to be honest?" I said. "I think you knew the house was mine all along, and you wanted to take it from me, because you hated me." I sucked in a ragged breath. "And maybe part of you still does."

My voice rose as I continued. "And here's the best part. If only you would've come clean, I was so stupid, I would've forgiven you almost anything. So who's the dumb-ass now?"

He looked at me for a long moment. As he did, I saw the unfiltered emotions flicker in his eyes – first pain and then so much anger, I fought a sudden urge to step back.

But I didn't.

Instead, I waited stubbornly for his response.

When his reply finally came, it was just a single word, spoken so softly, it might've been a whisper. "Me."

I shook my head. "What?"

"Me," he repeated. "*I'm* the dumb-ass, because I bought that act of yours."

"What act?"

Ignoring my question, he said, "But hey, it was a good one, right?"

I shook my head. "It was no act."

"And about the house," he continued. "Fuck yeah, I'm glad I bought it. The place was going to shit. Another year of neglect, and even *I* wouldn't have been able to save it."

He pointed to the floor. "So maybe you should get down on your knees and thank me if the place means so much to you."

By now, I was literally sobbing. I hated myself for doing it, but I couldn't seem make myself to stop, not even when I reminded myself that he wasn't worth it, not if he couldn't be honest after everything we'd shared.

But apparently, we were done talking.

Without another word, Brody squeezed past me and left the bedroom entirely, leaving his duffle bag where he'd dropped it.

And me? Like a total idiot, I called out after him, "Wait, you forgot your stuff!"

He kept on going, pausing only long enough to turn back and say. "Wrong. I've got everything I need. And baby, that's not you."

With that, he turned toward the front door. He'd barely left my sight when I heard the front door open and then slam quickly shut.

A moment later, I heard the sound of a vehicle – his truck, obviously – squealing out of the driveway.

And that's when I totally lost it.

It was over, truly over.

No second chances. No nothing.

I don't know how long I cried, but it was long enough to know that I was the worst hostess ever.

Instead of being upbeat for Cami, I spent most of the day – and then half of the night – crying on her shoulder.

This was the last night of our so-called vacation, and I wasn't sure who I hated more – Brody for everything he'd done or myself for crying over him when he wasn't worth it.

At noon the next day, the town car arrived right on schedule to drive Cami back to Petoskey.

For all kinds of reasons, I hated to see her go, especially in a car provided by Brody.

If only I'd taken some time to think, I might've planned another method of getting her back home. But with everything else going on, I hadn't.

Now I felt awkward and embarrassed about the whole arrangement – especially later that afternoon when Waverly returned with all of her suitcases, along with a new smugness that was hard to ignore.

She had news.

And, like everything else today, it wasn't good.

CHAPTER 62

Arden

When Waverly made her little announcement, I couldn't help but stare. "You're kidding, right?"

She smiled. "Nope. Sorry." And yet, she didn't look sorry. She looked like she was loving every minute of this.

Just a few minutes ago, she'd started out by telling me how much fun she'd had in California. She hadn't mentioned Brody by name, but the implication had been obvious.

According to Waverly, "Everyone had a lovely time." *I didn't believe it.* From what I'd seen of Brody, his trip had been anything but lovely.

Still, Waverly's claims were making a bad situation even worse, especially when she dropped her latest bombshell – one related to the show.

With obvious delight, she'd just informed me that the show was bringing back Miss LaRue to consult on the house across the street.

I felt my brow wrinkle in confusion. "But the house already has a consultant."

"You?" Waverly laughed. "But you're hardly a professional."

She was right. I wasn't. But I hadn't been hired for my professional design skills. I'd been hired for my connection to the place.

Miss LaRue *had* no connection, as she so aptly proved during the very next week by suggesting so many odd changes, they kept me in a constant state of panic.

Thankfully, very few of her ideas were actually implemented, whether because Brody kept overruling her, or because her ideas would've thrown everything off schedule.

For starters, she'd wanted to tear down the front porch and replace it with something called a "welcoming deck" – whatever *that* was.

It didn't matter.

After much debate – and not all of it friendly – the idea was vetoed by Brody personally.

Thank God.

Still, her presence was throwing everything off-kilter. She and I constantly disagreed – sometimes quite loudly – which made Roy positively orgasmic whenever he happened to catch us in mid-argument.

This happened at least once a day. By the second week, I felt ready to pop.

But it wasn't Miss LaRue – or even Roy with his camera – that was making it hard for me to get up in the morning or to fall asleep at night.

It was Brody.

Supposedly, he and I were still working together. But in reality, we avoided each other whenever we could. We never talked, unless we absolutely had to. And even those conversations were short and tense under the constant glare of Roy's video camera.

And yet, there were times when I'd happen to round a corner and nearly collide with Brody face-to-face. Or even worse, I'd sometimes find myself alone with him in the same empty room.

It was in *those* times that everything still felt unfinished.

And I didn't mean with the house.

Judging from Brody's dark demeanor, he wasn't any happier than I was.

As for the source of his unhappiness, it was impossible to say. Maybe he was just unhappy that I hadn't quit already.

I'd actually considered it.

But whether it was because I needed the money, or because I was determined to finish what I'd started, I kept on going, even when I didn't feel like it, which was almost all of the time.

I was explaining all of this to Cami on the phone when she said, "Just admit it. You're staying because of him."

"I am not," I said. "I'm staying because I can't afford to quit." I frowned. "And because if I leave, Miss LaRue will probably have the house painted puce or something."

"Puce?"

"It's this purple-brownish color." I gave a little shudder. "Get this. She wanted to use it on the kitchen ceiling."

"A brown ceiling? You're kidding, right?"

"I wish." I forced a laugh. "But forget that. We're not supposed to be talking about *me*. We're supposed to be talking about *you.*"

It was the reason I'd called. I'd been praying for good news about Cami's search for a new job. But just now, when I'd asked her about it, she'd replied by turning the conversation back to me.

It was a bad sign. Still, I had to ask, "So…has anything come up?"

"Not yet. But I'm sure it will." She paused. "Maybe."

That didn't sound good.

Still, I refused to add to Cami's worry. "Yeah. Totally. I mean, any school would be lucky to get you." I meant it, too. *Cami was amazing with kids.* Still, in the back of my mind, I couldn't help but fear that time wasn't on her side.

September was fast approaching. If she didn't have something by then, her odds would drop to nearly zero.

And now she was saying, "So how about you? How's *your* job search coming?"

As she listened, I told her that I'd had a second interview with that distribution center, but so far, I'd heard nothing more.

When I finished, she asked, "And what about Brody?"

At the sound of his name, my heart clenched like it always did. "What about him?"

"Are you still avoiding him?"

"As much as I can," I said. "But mostly, I think he's avoiding me."
I tried to laugh. "You might call it mutual avoidance."

"So how much time is left?"

"'Til the house is finished?" I said. "Barely three weeks."

Would I make it to the end? I wasn't so sure, especially on the very
next day when Miss LaRue suggested her dumbest idea yet – and in
front of Brody, too.

CHAPTER 63

Arden

The new kitchen cupboards had been installed just this week, which made Miss LaRue's suggestion all the more idiotic – even if she *did* look very French while making it.

Her lipstick was dark red, and her hair was jet-black, cut in a classic French bob. She wore a flared black miniskirt, a black turtleneck sweater, and – not even kidding – a little black beret set at a jaunty angle on her head.

None of this changed the fact that her suggestion was totally insane.

I gave her a perplexed look. "But we already have cupboards." I pointed to the nearest row of kitchen cabinets. "See? They're installed and everything."

On the opposite side of the kitchen, Roy was holding his video camera trained in our direction. A few feet away, standing in the kitchen doorway, Brody watched in grim silence, looking even more ticked off than usual.

But hey, I was ticked off too.

At the moment, it had nothing to do with Brody. It had to do with the fact that he and I had *already* selected the kitchen cabinets. And they were wonderful in every way.

I hesitated. Okay, I guess this *did* have a *little* something to do with Brody, but not directly. After all, *he* wasn't the one suggesting that we change everything last-minute.

Still, I felt a pang in my heart when I recalled how much fun we'd had that day, going to the cabinet maker's workshop and picking out the perfect Maplewood for the cabinets, along with the perfect honey-colored stain to bring out the natural patterns in the woodwork.

Just yesterday, the woodworkers had finished installing the gorgeous granite countertops, which Brody and I had also picked out together.

By now, the kitchen was nearly completed, which made Miss LaRue's suggestion all the more ridiculous.

Her lips pursed as she eyed the cabinets. "But they're completely wrong."

No. *She* was completely wrong. As for the cabinets, they were completely right.

I crossed my arms. "Oh yeah? How so?"

With a condescending smile, she said, "The *current* trend is counter-less cupboards."

I shook my head. "What?"

"Counter-less cupboards," she repeated. And then, as if to drive the point home, she marched to the nearest upper cabinet and pulled open its door. With a delicate scoff, she said, "See? This will never do."

I looked, but saw only perfection. The cabinets looked wonderful. They even *smelled* wonderful – all woodsy and clean, like the rest of the house, under Brody's expertise.

Hey, I could give credit where credit was due.

Grudgingly.

To Miss LaRue, I said, "I have no idea what you mean."

She pointed to the countertop just below the open cupboard. "The newest trend," she announced, "is to have the cabinet doors *skim* the countertop when they open." Her chin lifted. "Counter-*less*. See?"

I frowned. "So wait a minute. What you're telling me, is that you want to replace *these* with cabinets that will make the countertops impossible to actually use?"

She bristled. "No. That's not what I mean at all."

"Are you sure?" And then, as if speaking to a two-year-old, I said, "Because the way you describe it, any time you open a cabinet door, whatever's on the counter will be knocked off."

She gave a curt nod. "Right. It's the newest trend."

I was finding this a little hard to believe. "Even if it is," I said, "it's totally stupid."

Her mouth tightened. "And why is that?"

"Because," I said, "what are you gonna do with your toaster? Or your coffee maker?"

"I presume you'll make toast. Or coffee." She gave a delicate scoff. "And your point is....?"

Obviously, she still wasn't getting it.

I marched to the same cupboard that she'd opened just a moment ago. I closed it and glanced around, searching for something to help make my point. On a nearby work bench, I finally spotted a big, crumpled fast food bag, obviously destined for the trash.

I set the bag on the granite countertop underneath the cabinet door that I'd just shut. With a smile, I pulled the door open again. As expected, the bag stayed put. "See?" I said.

Miss LaRue gave me an annoyed look. "Yes. I see. It's a bag. What of it?"

I shut the cabinet door. "Just bear with me." I glanced around and spotted some discarded cardboard. Using stray electrical tape, I taped the flat cardboard to the bottom of the cabinet door, extending the door so low, it would skim the countertop, just like she'd described.

Again, I opened the cabinet door. This time, the bottom of it – meaning the cardboard extension – knocked the bag onto the floor.

I looked to Miss LaRue. "See?" I said again.

She spared the bag half a glance. "It's still a bag."

"Right. But it could've been a toaster."

"Except it's not."

"But it *could've* been," I insisted. "I'm just saying, the way you describe it, you won't be able to put anything on the countertops."

"Yes. Well maybe *some* people prefer a clean look."

"Yeah? Well maybe *other* people like to make toast in the morning." As I said it, I thought of Brody. *He loved toast.* In the mornings, he slathered it with butter, peanut butter, *and* jelly.

The way he did it, it really *was* a masterpiece.

Miss LaRue said, "Maybe the toaster doesn't belong on the countertop."

"Oh yeah?" I said. "Then where *does* it belong?"

"Inside the cupboard."

I almost laughed in her face. "You can't make toast that way."

"You can if you pull it out and plug it in."

"Yeah, but if you do, you'll knock it off the moment you open the cabinet."

Through gritted teeth, she said, "Then I suggest you *don't* open the cabinet while you're making toast."

"But what if you need peanut butter?" I gave Brody a sideways glance. "*Crunchy* peanut butter, because it *really* is the best."

On Brody's face, I swear I saw the hint of a smile. And something about it – even as small as it was – went straight to my heart, making me long to throw myself into his arms.

How stupid was that?

And now I was all distracted.

As for Miss LaRue, she was focused enough for all of us. With a sound of annoyance, she lunged for the cabinet door and tore off my cardboard extension. She hurled it onto the kitchen floor and eyed me like I'd just crapped on the countertop.

I stared down at the cardboard. "Why'd you do that?"

"Because," she said, "your point's ridiculous."

"*My* point's ridiculous?" I scoffed. "Well, *your* point – no, your *idea* – is *completely* ridiculous."

She crossed her arms. "Is it now?"

"Of course it is," I said. "This is a house, not a showcase – which means that someone will actually be living here. And they'll be making toast. And coffee, too."

"I'll have you know," Miss LaRue said, "that Felicity St. James has counter-less cupboards in *her* new kitchen, and she absolutely adores them."

"Felicity St. James?" I laughed. "The actress?"

With a smug smile, Miss LaRue said, "The very same."

I gave a snort of derision. "I'm sure she *does* 'adore' them. And you wanna know why?"

"I'm sure you're about to tell me."

Oh yeah. I'd be telling her, alright. "It's because," I said, "she probably has her own private chef."

"Of course she does. So?"

"So she doesn't make her own toast. *Or* her own coffee."

"Of course she doesn't," Miss LaRue said. "She's a *very* important person."

"Yeah, well so is Brody." As I said it, I realized how very true it was. He was beyond rich and famous. If he wanted, he could have a private chef of his own.

But he wasn't like that.

In fact, there'd been plenty of mornings when he'd made toast for the both of us. And bacon, too. As for myself, I'd specialized in pancakes, slightly crispy on the outside and fluffy in the middle, just the way Brody liked them.

In fact, we loved them the same exact way.

As the memories hit, I felt a pang of longing so deep, I almost wanted to cry. Or maybe I was just tired of all the drama.

Unable to stop myself, I turned to look at the guy who'd been haunting my thoughts nonstop. He looked so amazingly good, standing there in the open doorway like he used to, back when we were friends. *And lovers.* And partners, in a roundabout way.

As our gazes locked, his smile, faint as it was, slowly morphed into a frown.

I didn't like it. I didn't like any of this. And yet, I couldn't bring myself to look away.

I was still lost in the memories when Brody yanked his gaze from mine and looked to Miss LaRue. "Fine," he said. "Tear them out. Hell if I care." And with that, he turned to go.

And me? Like an idiot, I scurried after him.

CHAPTER 64

Brody

Screw the cupboards. And the toaster, too.

I'd been off toast for a while now, ever since moving out of the crew house. *I'd been off just about everything. Even bacon.*

That's how I knew it was bad.

My plan now – assuming I had one – was to get into my truck and get the hell out of here before I said something I'd regret.

I was halfway out the front door when Arden called out, "Brody, wait!"

Shit.

I turned around and gave her a long, silent look.

She rushed toward me. "You can't be serious."

"About what?"

"You *know* what," she said. "Counter-less cupboards? Seriously?"

"Yeah, so?"

She bit her lip. "But how will you make your toast?"

"Screw the toast."

I was standing just outside the front door. She was still inside. But even from here, I could smell the scent of her shampoo and see the flecks of gold in her troubled brown eyes.

Quietly, she said, "What, you don't like it anymore?"

These days, I wasn't liking much of anything. Everywhere I looked, I saw the Arden I *thought* I knew.

And now, even the maple cabinets pissed me off.

We'd picked them out together. The granite countertops, too.

And we'd had a good time doing it. Back then, Arden had made everything better – more interesting, more fun, more like home. *A real home.*

As far as the kitchen, I recalled my promise to lift her sweet ass onto the finished countertop and screw her silly, just the way she liked. But of course, I hadn't counted on us being broken up by the time the kitchen was actually done.

Now, just looking at Arden made me feel sick inside. She looked so sweet, with her big brown eyes and long, brown hair. She was wearing dark jeans that hugged her hips and a pale pink T-shirt that made me recall the pink of her nipples and the taste of her lips.

Like a dumb-ass, I still missed her. Not just her body. The whole package, inside and out.

What a cluster.

As our gazes locked, she moved closer and said in a near whisper, "If it makes you feel any better, I hate toast, too."

She hadn't always.

But I got what she meant.

Misery loves company, huh?

But hey, this was *her* doing, not mine. And for all *I* knew, this latest scene was just another ploy to get what she wanted – the *only* thing she wanted.

The house.

I told her, "It's not your house, remember?"

She blinked. "I never said that it was."

"Yeah? Then how come you're acting like it?"

She took a small step backward. "I'm not." She frowned. "I just don't want you to have a terrible kitchen, that's all."

With a laugh, I said, "Get real, will ya? It's not about me. It's about you."

She shook her head. "It is not."

"Right." And with that, I turned away.

"Wait!"

Once again, I turned back. "Why?"

Her face was flushed, and her eyes were accusing as she said, "Because I want to know why you're being like this."

"Yeah? And I wanna know things, too. But hey, that's life. Deal with it."

"Deal with it?" She made a scoffing sound. "That's soooo easy for you to say. Everything works out for *you*."

"Is that so?"

"Definitely," she said. "Even that thing in high school, *you* were the one who started it – the thing that made us hate each other in the first place."

Where the hell had that come from? "What?"

"The lab," she said. "It was *your* fault it blew up."

"No kidding." With a tight smile, I leaned toward her and said in a low voice, "Boom."

She flinched. "That's not funny."

"Maybe not to you."

"No. It's not funny, period." She glared out at me. "Although I can see why *you'd* think so. *You* came out just fine."

"We were *both* suspended," I reminded her. "Not just you."

"Yeah, but I didn't do anything to deserve it. And you? You didn't even care about being suspended. But *I* did."

"So?"

"So it cost you nothing. And it cost me everything." In a quieter voice, she added, "At least as far as school."

"Yeah, well." I shrugged. "That was a long time ago. So like I said, get over it."

"Get over it?" she repeated. "Do you even remember how awful you were that day?"

I didn't want to talk about. I didn't want to *think* about it either. But hey, if she was gonna toss it in my face, maybe I'd do some tossing of my own.

"Yeah?" I said. "I was awful. And you wanna know why?"

"Why?"

"Because my mom had just told us – in a fucking letter, no less – that she wasn't coming back."

Arden froze. "What?"

"That's right," I said. "She told us she found someone she liked better."

"Better than who?" She hesitated. "Your dad?"

I laughed. It wasn't a happy sound, but fuck it. "No. Dad was long gone by then."

Her eyes filled with sympathy. "You mean dead? *That* long ago?"

"No. I mean, he ran off."

"But—"

"He died after. No big loss, the way *I* see it."

From the look on Arden's face, she didn't agree. And hey, maybe I didn't agree either. But it was better to hate both of them than to mourn the parents they'd never been.

"So…" Arden hesitated. "When your mom said she found someone better, she meant…?"

"Better than us kids."

Arden sucked in a breath. "No."

With a bitter smile, I replied, "Yeah."

Arden moved closer. "But if that's the case, who were you living with? Back in high school, I mean."

"Nobody. It was just us."

"You mean…" She shook her head. "You and your brothers?"

"And Willow."

"Oh, right. But about your mom – not coming back, I mean – you found out *before* you met me at the lab that day?"

"That's what I said."

"But…" Again, she paused. "If that's the case, I'm kind of surprised you showed up at all. So, why did you?"

"Because I told you I would."

"But—"

"So I did. End of story." I forced another laugh. "Bad for you, huh?"

"No. I mean, yes. Wait…"

I didn't stick around to hear what she was going to say next. *I was done talking.* And the truth was, I hadn't meant to tell her any of this.

During the months we'd been together, she'd asked plenty about my family. It was a sore subject, and maybe I'd done a sorry job of explaining why it still pissed me off – *and* why I didn't want to sully a good thing by dwelling on something so bad.

Still, I should've done better. If nothing else, I should've mentioned Willow. But that was a sore subject of its own.

And hey, what's done was done, right?

When I backed my truck out of the driveway, Arden was still standing in the open doorway, looking too stunned to move.

And me – I sped off, and didn't look back.

CHAPTER 65

Arden

At the crew house, Waverly was saying, "Why do *you* care? It won't be *your* kitchen."

She was right. It wouldn't be.

But I wasn't obsessing over the kitchen. I was obsessing over Brody.

I couldn't stop thinking about what he'd told me yesterday – that basically both of his parents had abandoned him – cripes, abandoned *all* of them – while Brody had still been a minor.

The whole thing was incredibly sad. And now, in hindsight, I couldn't help but wonder about so many other things I'd assumed, even back in high school.

Back then, Brody had missed a ton of classes. I'd always figured he was just a classic cut-up. And then, after accidentally torching his truck, I'd figured he was out mowing lawns during school hours because he valued cash over his education.

But now, come to find out, he'd been dealing with problems a lot worse than *I'd* ever faced.

In the crew house, Waverly was still talking. "So it just seems to me, you're getting all worked up for nothing."

She had no idea.

Today was Saturday, which meant I had the whole day off. I'd spent most of the morning in my bedroom, and had only emerged at noon because I'd thought the house was empty.

No such luck.

I'd found Waverly at the kitchen table, drinking coffee and – judging from her computer screen – shopping for new luggage.

As if she didn't have enough already.

I'd been hoping she'd simply ignore me. But she hadn't. Instead, she'd surprised the heck out of me by asking why I looked so depressed.

Like a total sap, I'd felt compelled to give her at least *some* answer. So I'd briefly mentioned my concerns about Brody's kitchen, specifically Miss LaRue's plans to replace the current cabinets with something totally unworkable.

In reply to her latest statement, I said, "Yeah, but doesn't Brody deserve a kitchen he can actually use?"

"Oh, chill out," she said. "If it's unworkable, he'll rip it out and start over. The guy's totally loaded. He can do whatever he wants."

She was right, of course. Brody had the money *and* the expertise.

He was smart, too, which made his recent decision about the cabinets all the more confusing.

But it wasn't thoughts of the cabinets that had kept me up late last night, tossing and turning in my cold, empty bed.

It was thoughts of Brody. I couldn't stop thinking about his childhood. I felt awful for him. And now, a *new* question was haunting my thoughts. *Why hadn't he told me any of this when we'd been together?*

Was it because he didn't trust me?

Or because he'd seen me only as a fling?

Or maybe he was just allergic to sharing *any* truth between us.

At the thought, I felt my mood sink even lower.

To Waverly, I murmured, "Yeah, I guess you're right."

Already, I'd grabbed a bottled water and was just about to return to my bedroom when she said, "And if you ask me, you're just lucky he lets you stick around."

I stiffened. As much as I hated to admit it, she was probably right about this, too. Yes, I fully realized that Brody wasn't the one who'd hired me and that he technically wasn't my boss.

But I also realized that if he wanted me gone – *truly* wanted me gone – he'd have plenty of power to make that happen.

So why didn't he?

To Waverly, I said, "Yeah, well, maybe he'll fire me tomorrow."

"He can't fire you tomorrow," she said. "It's Sunday."

"Fine. Monday then."

"If you ask me, he *should* fire you," she said. "The way *I* hear it, you could've killed his sister."

"What?" I shook my head. "He doesn't even have a sister."

With a mean little laugh, she said, "If you say so."

"I *do* say so." I didn't bother pointing out that I'd known Brody since high school. And more recently, I'd known him intimately. *Very intimately.*

During those few blissful months, we'd talked for hours, and not only about the house. I might not know *everything* about him. But I *did* know this. *He had zero sisters.*

At the table, Waverly actually snickered.

I asked, "What's so funny?"

"You." In a snotty voice, she mimicked what I'd said a moment ago. "He doesn't have a sister."

"He doesn't," I insisted.

"Sure he does," she said. "And *you* could've killed her."

I summoned up a stiff smile. "Yes. And the Easter bunny *could've* stolen my shoes." I froze. *What did that even mean?*

I had no idea.

But in my own defense, Waverly wasn't making much sense either.

With a smirk, she said, "They all hate you, you know."

Her words felt like a slap, but I refused to flinch. "Who? The brothers?" I tried to laugh. "Yeah. Tell me something I don't know."

"I already did," she said. "And you didn't believe me."

"Oh, please," I scoffed. "I think I'd know if I could've killed a sister who didn't exist."

"Oh, she exists," Waverly said. "And from what *I* hear, Mason was absolutely livid."

Mason? I paused. "Wait a minute. You're not talking about Willow, are you?"

Waverly smiled. "I don't know. Am I?"

I frowned. "But Mason's her dad, not her brother."

Waverly's smile grew sly. "Oh, really? Are you sure?"

No. I wasn't.

Not a hundred percent.

And for some reason, this shook me to the core.

I *should* be sure. Brody and I had been close, *really* close.

Hadn't we?

But then, I recalled the situation with his parents. He hadn't shared *those* details either – not until yesterday at the tail end of our argument.

Plus, for months, he'd been lying to me about how he'd acquired the house.

All things considered, was it really *that* far-fetched that he'd neglect to mention a sister, too?

No.

It wasn't.

Talk about depressing.

At the table, Waverly said, "See? You *know* I'm telling the truth."

I tried to think. "But even if Willow *is* his sister, I only met her the one time. And all I did was try to walk her home."

Even as I said it, I recalled Mason's reaction when he'd found us. He'd been angry, *really* angry, like he'd caught me trying to kidnap her or something.

More to myself than to Waverly, I murmured, "They seriously think I would've harmed her?"

The accusation hurt more than it should've. It wasn't like I'd driven up in a van and offered Willow candy. *No.* She'd literally knocked on my door.

Whether she'd said so or not, she'd needed help getting home. And I'd tried to help. In hindsight, maybe I should've done things differently, but at no time whatsoever had Willow been in any danger – not while she'd been with me, anyway.

I'd been looking out for her.

Not the nanny. Not Mason. Not Brody either.

But me, along with Cami.

Even now, I still had no idea how Willow had ended up on my doorstep in the first place.

If I had to guess, I'd say it had something to do with the house across the street, like maybe she'd hitched a ride with one of her brothers and had been forgotten in some sort of confusion.

Brothers?

Oh, God. Brody was her brother.

And me? I hadn't known.

At the table, Waverly said, "That's all I know. But you didn't hear it from me."

By now, I was practically quivering with agitation. I still felt sorry for Brody's childhood, but that didn't change the fact that apparently, I'd never known him at all.

And forget his brothers. They were totally awful. *Mason in particular.*

I felt like throttling him.

I felt like throttling *all* of them.

This wasn't good, especially a couple of hours later when I happened to glance out the front window and see who else, but Mason Blastoviak, standing in the driveway across the street.

The way it looked, he was just about to get into his car – the same one he'd been driving on the day I'd tried to walk Willow home.

At the sight of him, I felt my jaw clench. He might not know it, but he *wasn't* leaving – not without hearing a little something from me first.

CHAPTER 66

Arden

Without bothering to put on my shoes, I bolted barefoot out the front door of the crew house.

Already, Mason had opened his car door as if preparing to leave.

Not so fast, Buddy.

I called out, "Hey!"

He turned to look. At the sight of me stalking toward him, he frowned.

Without breaking my stride, I yelled, "Don't you dare leave!"

He was wearing dark slacks, a dress shirt, and a tie. No jacket. Still, he looked exactly like the person he was – a rich, ruthless bastard who cared for no one beyond his own family.

And yet, he waited, looking only mildly impatient, as I crossed the street and joined him in the driveway.

Without wasting any time, I said, "So how's Willow?"

"Fine."

"Really?" I said. "Even after her 'near-death' experience?"

His eyebrows furrowed. "What?"

"The way I hear it," I said, "I almost killed her." My tone grew sarcastic. "That must've been pretty traumatic for all of you."

His mouth tightened. "Yes. It was."

I almost rolled my eyes. "I was being sarcastic, as you darn well know."

"It's no joke," he said.

"Well it's not funny. I'll grant you that. But you must be joking if you think I would've done anything to harm her. Do you realize, she showed up on my doorstep with no adult in sight?"

I gave him a hard look. "And where were *you* when all of this happened?" Before he could even think of responding, I added, "And just so you know, your nanny sucks. Do you realize, she actually told Willow that she doesn't like being a nanny? Can you imagine how that makes Willow feel?"

I made a sound of disgust. "And then, the nanny freaking loses track of her. What's up with that? And what's up with you? Where were *you* when your kid's wandering around on her own?"

Now that I was going, I couldn't seem to make myself stop. "Oh, and here's another thing," I continued. "Is she your daughter? Or your little sister? Because it seems to me, that detail's pretty darn important in the big scheme of things."

Thinking of Brody, I swallowed an unexpected lump in my throat. "I mean, I should've known. Maybe not from you, but I'm just saying…"

I sighed. "I don't know what I'm saying. Not about that. But about the rest of it, I don't appreciate being made the villain here. Willow, she's a great kid. And super smart, too. And I never would've harmed her regardless of what *you* might think."

By now, I was nearly breathless, whether from talking nonstop or from all of the conflicting emotions swirling around in my head. I was so angry, I could hardly think. And yet, through all of that anger, I still felt the dull ache of loss – the loss of Brody of all people, although for the life of me, I couldn't imagine why.

As for Mason, he looked way too composed as he stared down at me. After a long moment of silence, he asked, "You done?"

"I guess." I shrugged. "For now."

I half expected him to simply get into his car and drive off without telling me squat. But to my surprise, he didn't. Instead, he said, "You're right about the nanny."

I blinked. *I knew I was right.* Still, it felt obscenely good to hear him admit it. "Really?'

"And she's gone," he said. "So don't worry about it."

"So she quit?"

"No. Fired and replaced."

"Oh. Well, that's good." I hesitated. "Is the new one any better?"

"Ask me in a month," he said, not looking too hopeful.

"So…" I bit my lip. "Willow…is she your daughter? Or…?"

"I'm her dad," he said. "And that's all you need to know."

"But that's not true," I protested. "I *do* need to know."

"Oh yeah? Why's that?"

It was a good question. But the answer was too complicated for me to put into words, so all I said was, "I just do. It's important."

He studied my face for several beats before saying, "I'm both."

"Sorry, what?"

"I'm her dad. And her brother."

Eauw. "Really?"

He gave me a look. "I'm not talking biology."

"Oh. Of course not." I winced. "Sorry. And, uh, you were saying?"

"She's my sister. But yeah, I'm the only 'dad' she's ever known."

"So…Does she know that you're *really* her brother?"

"She knows."

"But she calls you her dad?"

His expression darkened. "Yeah. Because she wanted one. And a mom, too."

Now *that* made me pause. "But about a mom, she told me—"

"That she doesn't have one. I know. But hey, it is what it is."

"Oh, well yeah. I mean…" I gave an awkward laugh. "Those aren't so easy to get, huh?"

Good lord. What on Earth was I saying?

By now, I had no idea. The truth was, Mason had already told me a lot more than I'd ever expected. And even though I'd never call him friendly, he was acting surprisingly civil, all things considered.

And now, I just had to ask, "So, how'd Willow end up on my doorstep? Do you know?"

"I do. And it won't happen again."

"But what happened?" I persisted. "Did she stow away in your car or something?"

"You might say that." Mason flicked his head toward my grandparent's place. "I drove out here looking for Brody, and didn't realize that Willow was hiding in the back seat."

"So you didn't see her when you got into your car?"

"I didn't look," he said. "*And* she was hiding under a blanket."

As I listened, Mason went on to briefly explain that according to Willow, she'd snuck into his car while it had been parked in the garage at home. And then, she'd snuck *out* of the car when Mason had gone inside my grandparent's place to look for Brody.

Apparently, Willow had planned to take a quick look at the beach and then return to her hiding spot before Mason emerged from the house.

Unfortunately, thanks to bad timing, she'd returned to the driveway only to discover that Mason's car was already gone, leaving her stranded.

When Mason finished talking, I said, "But I don't get it. Why didn't she just tell me all of this herself? I mean, I *did* ask."

"My guess?" Mason said. "She figured that if you walked her home, I'd be none the wiser."

"But you said it was ten whole miles."

He gave a curt nod. "Which to Willow is a fifteen-minute drive."

I saw what he meant. She was, after all, only seven years old. "But speaking of driving," I said, "how'd you happen to drive past us that day? Were you out looking for Willow?"

"No, because I didn't know she was missing." He grimaced. "So you can imagine what I thought when I saw her walking down the street with a couple of strangers."

I bristled. "Hey, I'm no stranger."

"You were to *her*."

"But not to *you*," I pointed out.

"Trust me," he said. "That's no mark in your favor."

So much for civility. I couldn't stop myself from saying, "Just why do you hate me so much, anyway?"

"You've gotta ask?"

"So you're admitting you hate me?" This shouldn't have been a surprise. And yet, it bothered me more than I liked. "Is this about Brody's truck?" I said. "Because it really *was* an accident."

"So he says."

Now *that* got my attention. "You mean *Brody* says? When?"

In what felt like a change of topic, Mason said, "Do you know why you weren't fired?"

"Fired from what? My consulting job?"

"What, you got another one?"

"Not yet," I admitted. "But even with this one, I was never almost fired."

"You sure about that?"

"Reasonably sure," I said. "I mean, I think I'd know, right?"

"Wrong," Mason said. "That day I saw you with Willow, I told Brody you had to go." He gave me a serious look. "*And* that if *he* didn't fire you, *I* would."

Unbelievable. "But you can't fire me," I protested. "I don't even work for you. And technically, I don't work for Brody either."

"Trust me," Mason said, "if we wanted you gone, you'd be gone."

I started to argue, but stopped myself just in time. His claim was truer than I cared to admit. In fact, I'd concluded the very same thing on my own not too long ago.

Mason continued. "And you wanna know what Brody told me?"

"What?"

"That if you were forced out, he'd leave, too."

My jaw dropped. "What? He didn't."

"He did."

"But when?" I asked. "And why?"

"The 'when' is easy," Mason said. "It was after I brought Willow back home. By then, I'd gotten the full story on what had happened, and…" He gave a tight shrug. "I figured I *might* owe you an apology."

Holy Hell.

So he was admitting it?

I gave him a tight smile. "Oh, you might, huh?" With an expectant look, I added, "Just so you know, you can start any time."

"Later," he said. "*And*, as to your second question, the 'why,' – Brody said it wasn't right for you to pay for *my* screw-up."

"Wait. *Your* screw-up?"

"Willow's my responsibility. Not yours. And not Brody's. It was *my* fault she went missing."

"And the nanny's," I said.

"Nanny or not," Mason said. "Brody was right – even if he *was* lying his ass off."

"Wait, what?"

"His reason was bullshit, and I told him so."

I wasn't following. "But you just said you agreed with it."

"No. I said I agreed with his analysis – that it was my fault, not yours. But that's not why he threatened to walk." With a rueful laugh, Mason added, "Or kick my ass."

"Wait, he did?" I was so stupidly touched, I felt my eyes grow misty. "Seriously? He did that for me?"

"He did it for *someone*," Mason said. "And it sure as hell wasn't me."

I stared up at him. "But why are you telling me this?"

"Because I owe you," Mason said. "And I always pay up. For good *or* bad."

That last part sent a shiver down my spine, and I suddenly recalled how much he hated me, even now. Choosing to focus on the positive, I asked, "But why would you owe me?"

"For your help with Willow. And for doing it low-key." He shook his head. "We've worked hard to keep her out of the spotlight. And if you'd played it differently, well..." He paused. "Let's just say I don't want to see her name or picture on the internet."

I saw what he meant. Still, I had to say it. "I don't want to be rude or anything, but if all of this is true, why did you wait so long to tell me?"

"Good question."

"So...?" I prompted. "What's the answer?"

"Maybe that's how long it took."

"For what?" I asked.

With something that was *almost* a smile, he said, "For me to pull my head out of my ass."

I was so shocked, I could hardly speak.

Mason said, "So consider this your apology."

I almost laughed. "So, are you gonna actually say it?"

"I'm sorry," he said. "There, you happy?"

As far as apologies, it was seriously lacking. And yet, I *was* surprisingly happy. But it wasn't because of the apology. It was because of the rest of it. I was insanely touched that Brody had fought – almost literally – to keep me from getting fired.

But all too soon, my happiness faded as I recalled everything else that had come between us, the lies in particular.

To Mason, I said, "Well, thanks. Not just for the apology, but for letting me know that Brody stuck up for me."

"You're welcome." And with that, Mason turned once toward his car.

Apparently, I was being dismissed.

But then he paused and turned back. "There's something else you should know."

"Really? What?"

He flicked his head toward my grandparent's place. "That house? It's all Brody's. But *I* handled the transaction. Not him."

CHAPTER 67

Arden

Cami said, "Oh, my God. Is that true?"

As usual, I was hunkered down in my bedroom trying to talk on my cell phone without Waverly overhearing. I'd just finished repeating to Cami everything I'd learned from Mason, and she sounded just as shocked as I felt.

I replied, "That's what he said."

"Wow," Cami breathed. "Talk about a snork-show."

This wasn't the word I would've used, assuming it *was* a word at all. But I knew exactly what Cami meant. Mason had driven away from my grandparent's place nearly an hour ago, and I was still reeling from everything he'd told me.

Into the phone, I murmured, "Yeah, tell me about it."

"So, what are you gonna do?" Cami asked.

"I don't know," I groaned. "God, I've been such an idiot."

"Oh, you have not," Cami said. "I mean, how were you supposed to know that Mason was the *real* lunk-blaster in all of this?"

Lunk-blaster was right. As I'd just learned first-hand, it was Mason who'd done everything I'd been blaming on Brody.

It was Mason who'd strong-armed my cousin into selling the house. It was Mason who'd handled all of the paperwork. It was even Mason who'd written that callous note on the bottom of Jason's heartfelt letter.

In my mind, I could still see those three irritating words scrawled on the bottom of the first page. *"Not my problem."*

Boy, he was right about *that.*

Now it was *my* problem, because I'd been so awful to Brody.

To Cami, I said, "Well, I could've asked Brody what was going on. But did I? *No.* Instead, I just hinted around, hoping he'd tell me on his own." With a bitter laugh, I said, "But now, come to find out, there was nothing to tell."

"But *you* didn't know that," she said.

"Right. Because I never asked." I sighed. "No wonder he's so angry."

"But I don't get it," Cami said. "Why'd Mason tell you any of this at all? I mean, if he hates you so much, he surely would've preferred for you and Brody to stay mad at each other."

"Well, that's the funny thing," I said. "At first, Mason tells me that he's doing it to repay me for helping out with Willow. But then, just before he leaves, he says the strangest thing."

"Oh yeah? What's that?"

"He tells me that he loves his brother more than he ever hated *me.*"

At this, Cami's tone grew thoughtful. "Huh. Well that's something."

"So, any theories?" I asked.

"My guess?" she said. "He feels bad for Brody."

"But why?"

"Isn't it obvious?" she said. "He's broken-hearted over losing you, just like *you're* broken-hearted over him."

I didn't bother denying this last part. I *had* been pretty miserable, as Cami had seen firsthand during that so-called vacation.

Oh, God. The vacation.

Brody had gone to a lot of trouble to deliver Cami straight to my doorstep. And what had I done? I'd spent the whole week making both of them miserable.

Thinking of it, I felt like crawling under a blanket and hiding until I *didn't* feel like the worst person in the universe.

Plus, who was I kidding? I was broken-hearted for a reason. I'd totally fallen for him. Call it love. Call it stupidity. Call it craziness. But even in spite of our history, I did love him, even now.

Cripes, I probably loved him more *now* when I considered just how much trouble he'd gone to on my behalf, even in spite of my rotten attitude.

I perked up. But that's right. He'd defended me, even *after* I'd been so awful. *What did that mean?*

My breath caught. *Maybe there was still hope.*

Cami and I were still talking when my cell phone buzzed with an incoming call.

When I glanced at the display, my heart nearly leapt out of my chest.

It was Brody. He was calling from his old cell phone number, not the new one. In a rush, I told Cami, "Sorry, but I've gotta go, okay?"

"Wait, why?"

"Brody's calling."

"Right now?"

"Yeah. Right now. I'll call you back later, alright?"

"You'd better," she warned.

I was literally trembling when I answered the new call. "Hello?"

But it wasn't Brody who replied. It wasn't even a guy.

It was a vaguely familiar female voice, who wasted no time in demanding, "Who's this?"

Disappointment coursed through me, even as I said, "It's Arden. Who's this?"

"No one." And with that, the caller disconnected.

I stared at my phone for a long moment before I realized with a start why the voice sounded so familiar.

It was Waverly.

I was almost sure of it.

I dropped my phone and bolted from my bedroom, determined to find out what the heck was going on.

CHAPTER 68

Arden

Waverly glowered up at me. "I have no idea what you mean."

I'd found her in the living room, perched on the sofa scrolling through her cell phone. Not wanting to waste any time, I'd asked her flat-out if she'd just called me from Brody's old number.

And of course, she'd denied it. *Repeatedly.*

I didn't believe her.

And it wasn't only because I'd recognized her voice. It was the sly look in her eye, even now, as she feigned innocence.

I told her, "You're lying. I can tell."

"Oh, so that's how it is?" Her voice rose. "You're calling me a liar?"

I crossed my arms. "Yup."

"Well, I don't appreciate it."

"Good," I said, "because I don't appreciate it either. And why were you calling me, anyway?"

"Because I *wasn't* calling you," she said, "as I've already made clear."

I didn't bother hiding my disbelief. "And where's Brody's phone?"

"I don't know," she said. "You'll have to ask Brody."

At the mere thought of asking him anything, something squeezed at my heart. *If only it were so easy.*

Sure, I had his new cell phone number, but I could only imagine how delighted he'd be to hear from me *now.*

Somehow, I vowed, I'd make things right between us. Even if I'd ruined any chances of us being together, at least I could tell him that I was sorry for thinking the worst of him.

But first things first. I looked to Waverly and said, "So tell me. How'd you get the phone? Did you steal it or something?"

She made a sound of annoyance. "Oh, so first I'm a liar, and now I'm a thief? You really *are* crazy. You know that?"

Maybe I was. But I wasn't *so* crazy that I'd take Waverly at her word. With sudden inspiration, I said, "Maybe I should check your luggage." And with that, I turned toward the bedrooms.

She was off the couch in an instant. "You wouldn't!"

She was right. I wouldn't. And now, I didn't need to, because resting on the sofa behind where Waverly had been sitting, was Brody's old cell phone, contained in its familiar rugged black case.

"I knew it!" I lunged for the phone just as Waverly turned back to look.

"Hey!" she said. "That's mine."

"Nice try," I said, snatching the phone off the couch. I gripped it tight and jostled my way past her, heading toward my bedroom.

She hollered out after me, "I was gonna give it back!"

Without breaking stride, I called over my shoulder, "Sure you were!"

"And the battery was dead!" she called. "I had to charge it myself."

"Oh, boo hoo!" I called back.

Just as I reached my bedroom door, Waverly yelled, "And I found it in the coat closet. How was *I* supposed to know whose it was?"

She knew. Of this, I was certain – just as I was certain that it would take a lot more than the return of Brody's cell phone to make things right between us.

But hey, it was a start, right?

CHAPTER 69

Arden

Brody eyed the plate of oatmeal cookies that I held out between us. With a frown, he asked, "What are those?"

"Cookies." I summoned up a smile. "*Oatmeal* cookies. My grandmother's. I mean, they're not *her* cookies exactly, because I made them on my own. But they're her recipe. And I remember you saying a few weeks ago that you'd never had the homemade kind, so…" I let my words trail off as I nudged the plate closer. "Try one. I made them just last night."

It was early Monday morning, barely past six-thirty. I'd been standing out on the front porch of my grandparent's place since sunrise, waiting for Brody to show up.

As expected, he'd been the very first person to arrive, which was a huge relief, considering that the last thing I wanted now was an audience.

With a dismissive shrug, he said, "I already ate."

"Oh." I hesitated. "Well, if you don't want one now, maybe you could put them in your truck for later."

Without making any move to take them, he said, "What's this about?"

"Alright. The truth is, I owe you an apology." I lifted the cookies higher. "And hey, how about a peace offering, too?"

His eyes were dark, and his lips were compressed into a thin, angry line. He looked like he'd rather grind my cookies into dust than trust me not to poison him with baked goods. In a tight voice, he said, "An apology for what?"

I glanced toward the front door. "Do you want to talk inside?"

"No."

"Then maybe in your truck?" I forced another smile. "I mean, the last thing we want is for Roy to show up and film us, right?"

With no trace of warmth, Brody said, "Roy's just doing his job. I suggest you do the same." He glanced down at his watch. "And you don't start for ninety minutes."

Ouch.

It wasn't just a hint. *It was a dismissal.*

It reminded me of how things used to be, way back in the beginning, when both of us hated each other. It seemed like a long time ago. And yet, here we were, back to the beginning. Except I didn't hate him.

Not anymore.

At his cold dismissal, my smile faltered. "Right. At eight o'clock. I know. But this isn't about work. And don't you want to know what prompted this?"

"I *already* know," he said.

"You do?"

"Yeah. I heard about your talk with Mason."

I should've known. "So he told you?" I said. "When?"

"Saturday."

It was the same day Mason had confessed to me what he'd done. This meant that Brody had learned two days ago about the misunderstanding and hadn't made any effort to get in touch.

But then again, why would he? This was *my* fault, not his.

Cautiously, I asked, "So, what exactly did he tell you?"

"Does it matter?"

At his tone, I almost flinched. "Well, yeah. It does, actually." I stared up into Brody's eyes, willing him to understand. "Did he tell you everything he did with the house? I mean, how he practically forced Jason to sell?"

"Yeah, so?"

Now I was frowning. "So, you *seriously* don't think there's anything wrong with that?"

At this, Brody's expression only darkened. "If you think I've changed my mind about selling, forget it."

"But that's not what this is about," I protested. "Did Mason *also* tell you that I thought it was you who did all those things?"

"Yeah. He told me."

"So you see why I was angry, right?"

"Why?" Brody scoffed. "Because you thought *I'd* do things differently?"

I hesitated. "Well, *wouldn't* you?"

"I guess you'll never know."

Obviously, Brody still wasn't getting it. "But just listen," I said. "I thought you were lying, telling me that you didn't know anything about my connection to the place when you really did."

"So?" he said again.

"So don't you think that's kind of a big deal? Lying, I mean?"

"Except I didn't."

Well, there was that. Still, I felt compelled to try again. "But can't you see why I was upset? The way it looked, I thought you'd purchased the house for some sort of revenge – and then, lied to me about it, even *after* we'd gotten so close. That's all."

That's all?

Wasn't that enough?

And yet Brody remained silent.

Desperate to keep the conversation going, I switched gears. "So…do you think that's why *Mason* bought it? Because he wanted to get back at me for torching your truck?"

Brody's jaw clenched. "He didn't buy it. *I* did. So if you want to be pissed at somebody, you're looking at him."

Yes. I *was* looking at him. He looked as amazing as ever – maybe a little leaner than he'd been a few weeks ago, but amazing none the less.

If only he weren't eyeing me with such coldness, I might've melted into his arms right then and there. And maybe, if he weren't so angry, he might've gathered me close like he used to.

And maybe together, we'd look at making a fresh start.

With that in mind, I tried again. "Yeah, but you're still not getting it. This isn't about the house. It's about us. And honesty. And integrity. And all that other stuff."

The amazing sex.

The fun we'd had, even while working.

The look he used to give me whenever we crossed paths, before all of the misunderstandings had torn us apart.

I was still holding up the cookies, and the longer this went on without Brody actually taking them, the more stupid I felt about such a small, useless gesture.

As if cookies would make any difference at all.

Recalling my *other* peace offering, I adjusted the plate of cookies in my grip so I was holding it with only my left hand. With my right hand, I reached into my pocket and pulled out Brody's old cell phone.

I held it up between us. "Oh, and I brought you this, too."

He spared the phone half a glance. "Keep it."

I did a double-take. "I can't. I mean, it's not mine. It's yours. It's the one you lost." I nudged it closer. "See?"

"So toss it," he said.

I shook my head. "But it's still got service."

Brody still made no move to take it. "It's just a phone."

No. It wasn't just a phone. Not to me. After I'd snagged it from Waverly, I'd finally figured out why she'd called me from that phone in the first place. Not only was I the very first contact in Brody's list of favorites, I was listed under some initials that I didn't recognize.

And now, I couldn't stop myself from saying to Brody, "And speaking of your phone, why was I listed under 'L.O.L.'?" I tried for another smile. "Was it because we liked to joke with each other or something?"

He stiffened. "You went through my phone?"

If I weren't trying so hard to be civil, I might've pointed out that he'd just offered me this very same phone, which made his reaction now just a little bit ridiculous.

Still, I saw what he meant, so all I said was, "No. *I* didn't. Waverly did. And *she* was the one who pointed it out."

It was true. Just before I'd slammed my bedroom door in Waverly's face, she'd demanded to know what exactly I'd done to deserve the top spot in Brody's contact list. And then, she'd made some snide comment about Brody listing me as "L.O.L." because I must've been one big joke to him all along.

This posed a distressing question. *Was I?*

But then I remembered something. With renewed hope, I looked to Brody and said, "When Mason and I were talking, he also mentioned how you stuck up for me."

Looking almost bored now, Brody said, "How so?"

"*You* know. How you told him that if he fired me, you'd walk off the show." I searched Brody's face for any sign of warmth. "Is that true?"

Sounding colder than ever, he replied, "It is."

Something in my shoulders eased. "Thanks. I mean, that was really nice– "

"It wasn't."

"Sure it was."

"Forget it," he said. "I wasn't doing it for *you.*"

"Oh." Again, I hesitated. "So, if you weren't doing it for me, who *were* you doing it for?"

"I was doing it for myself."

Was that good? Or bad? With my heart in my throat, I said, "Really? Why?"

"Because it's *my* responsibility, not Mason's."

I blinked. "Sorry, what?"

"The show," Brody said. "It's not *his* job. It's mine – which means he doesn't fire *anyone* without my say-so."

"But…" I bit my lip. "You stuck up for me."

"Wrong. I stuck up for myself. Big difference."

As the distinction hit home, heat flooded my face. *Yes.* It *was* a big difference. *Huge, actually.*

And now I felt so ridiculous, I could hardly stand it.

Of course, I understood what Brody meant. From what I'd seen of Mason, he'd be all too willing to steamroll over anyone to get what he wanted, so it only made sense that Brody would need to push back just as hard.

Even so, this latest news was a serious blow to my hopes – and to my pride, too, if I were being totally honest.

And now I couldn't help but dwell on the other thing I'd learned on Saturday – first from Waverly and then from Mason.

It was a biggie.

Willow was Brody's sister.

But I was still hoping – and maybe praying, too – that there was some reasonable explanation for Brody not telling me about Willow himself.

In my best-case scenario, Brody and I made up, and I got the chance to ask him nicely why he'd neglected to tell me something so important.

But now, judging Brody's demeanor, the opportunity for niceness was fading fast.

With growing humiliation, I realized that my left hand was actually starting to tremble from holding up the plate of cookies for so long in the same position.

Reluctantly, I looked down at my pathetic peace offering. *Cookies, what a joke.* Still, I really *had* made them with the best of intentions.

It hadn't been a simple job either.

All of my baking stuff was still in storage near Michigan State – my grandmother's mixer, the mixing bowls, the cookie sheets, everything to make perfectly wonderful cookies.

The stuff was too far away to retrieve in a day, especially with no vehicle. So yesterday afternoon, I'd taken a ride-share to the nearest shopping center, where I'd purchased everything to make homemade cookies at a house that wasn't my own.

I'd even called my mom to get my grandmother's cookie recipe, since I didn't know it by heart. In hindsight, it was shocking that she'd had it at all. The whole time I'd been growing up, she'd *never* made cookies, not even once.

It wasn't a big deal. I mean, I didn't expect her to stay home and bake or anything, especially when she'd preferred to save her calories for booze and bar snacks.

Great.

Now I felt foolish *and* depressed.

Oh, screw it. I lowered the cookies to hip level and said to Brody, "Hey, can I ask you something? Why didn't you tell me you had a sister?" I searched his face for clues. "In fact, why didn't you tell me anything about your family?"

With a tight shrug, he replied, "Maybe it's a sore subject."

"You mean because of everything that happened with your parents?"

"That – and what happened with *you.*"

With me? "But wait, I don't get it."

"Yeah. You don't. So let's make a deal. You want the bonus, right?"

It took me a moment to realize what he meant. "You mean for finishing the show?"

"Right." He reached into the front pocket of his jeans. "I'm gonna pay up. Right here, right now." As he spoke, he pulled a check from his pocket.

He set the check directly on the plate of cookies.

I asked, "What are you doing?"

"You want the money?" he said. "There. I'm paying you to leave." His jaw clenched. "And not come back."

My heart sank, and I felt the first sting of tears.

It was in this godawful moment that the familiar white SUV pulled into the driveway. As I turned for a better look, Roy emerged from the driver's side – *with* his camera.

Oh, my God.

He pointed the camera straight in my direction, even as I felt the color drain from my face.

I could only imagine how I looked, standing there like a total idiot, holding the plate of cookies in one hand and Brody's cell phone in the other. As I stood frozen in place, a runaway tear slid down my cheek, making me feel doubly pathetic.

With both of my hands full, I couldn't even wipe at my eyes, not without drawing further attention to my lack of composure.

Desperately, I looked down. As I did, my gaze landed on the personal check, lying face up on the plate of cookies. The check was already filled out, with my name right there in blue ink. *The amount was for thirty thousand dollars.*

If I felt capable of doing math, I might've pondered the fact that the amount included the full twenty-thousand-dollar bonus plus another ten thousand on top. It was more than I'd earn if I simply stayed on the project as planned.

As I zoomed in on the date of the check, something in my heart twisted. *The check was dated ten full days ago.*

Just how long had Brody been planning this?

And why, oh why, had he let me stand here and make a fool of myself?

I had no time to contemplate, because by the time I looked up again, Roy was already striding up the walkway, keeping his camera trained exactly where I didn't want it.

On me.

I knew I wasn't supposed to look at him – or the camera. I was supposed to pretend the camera wasn't there. But at the moment, I simply couldn't.

I stared stupidly at the camera, even as Roy strode forward, letting his instrument of torture lead the way.

I was still staring when suddenly my view of the camera was blocked by Brody's back. He lunged toward Roy, saying, "Get that fucking thing out of her face."

Roy had no chance to respond before Brody ripped the camera from Roy's grip and hurled it onto the walkway, where it broke into several pieces.

I couldn't see Roy's face, but I *could* see the veins in Brody's arms as he stood blocking me from Roy's path.

On a choked sob, I asked, "Why'd you do that?"

Brody turned to face me. "Because," he said, "you don't work here anymore."

CHAPTER 70

Arden

"So," Cami said, "are you gonna cash it or not?"

It had been five days since my ill-fated apology.

After the camera's destruction, Brody had hustled me back to the crew house and silently watched as I'd gathered up my things.

Unsurprisingly, I had much more than when I'd arrived – more work clothes, cute little work boots courtesy of Brody, my red hard hat, and safety glasses, too.

By the time I'd finished shoving everything that would fit into my duffle bag, and then crammed the rest of it into a white garbage bag of all things, a town car had already arrived to take me wherever I wanted to go.

"Wherever" turned out to be Cami's parent's house, where I was sharing Cami's old childhood bedroom.

I knew I couldn't stay here forever, but Cami swore up and down that she was glad for the company, and Cami's parents were being surprisingly nice about the whole thing.

I was still waiting on a decent job offer, but so far, none had materialized.

In the meantime, I was trying to repay the hospitality of Cami's parents by repainting their front porch – *and* fixing the loose boards on the back deck.

I wasn't quite a pro, but I'd learned a lot while helping to fix up my grandparent's place.

No. Not *their* place.

Brody's place.

It was his house, fair and square, and I needed to accept that.

As far as the check from Brody, I'd left it, along with the cookies, in my bedroom closet at the crew house while Brody had slipped briefly away, presumably to order the town car.

Or who knows, maybe he'd scheduled the car in advance, knowing that he was about to give me the old heave-ho.

Either way, it wasn't the last I'd seen of the check. It had arrived by overnight mail shortly after noon today. The envelope had contained nothing else. *No note. No letter. No crushed cookies, either.*

To Cami's question about whether I planned to cash the check, I replied, "I don't think so."

"But why not?" she said. "It's thirty thousand dollars. That's a fortune."

Not to Brody, it wasn't. But I saw what she meant. "I know. But when you think about it, I didn't *really* make it to the end."

"Of the show?" she said. "But that's Brody's fault, not yours."

"I dunno. Maybe it's both of our faults."

"So cash *half* of the check," she said. "Or how about this? Cash the whole thing, and send *him* a check for fifteen thousand."

I tried to laugh. "Oh sure. Then he can refuse to cash his, and we'll be starting the cycle all over again."

Cami frowned. "So he didn't say *anything* to you while you packed?"

She'd asked me same question several times already. I realized why. It really *was* hard to believe that not a single word had passed between us during the whole time I'd gathered up my things.

But that's the way it happened.

At the time, I'd been too heart-broken to talk, even as I tried not to show it. And Brody? He'd been stone-cold silent, showing no emotion whatsoever.

Who knows? Maybe there was none to show.

We never *did* say goodbye.

Was I crying over him now?

Oh yeah. But I tried to do it quietly, and only in the middle of the night, so Cami wouldn't have to suffer along with me.

And I *was* suffering – not only because I missed him like crazy, but also because I realized that much of my misery was of my own making.

I should've asked him directly for the truth.

But I hadn't.

So here I was.

Where *he* was, I couldn't be certain. And maybe that was for the best – or at least, that's what I kept telling myself – over and over.

For all the good it did.

CHAPTER 71

Brody

I stopped short at the sight of Chase standing in my kitchen. "What the hell are you doing?"

"Eating cookies," he said from behind the counter. "What does it look like?"

Fucker. He wasn't eating cookies. He was eating *the* cookies – the ones Arden had baked for me.

The cookies – still on their original plate – were sitting on the main counter where I'd left them three days ago after finding them, along with the check, in Arden's old closet at the crew house.

I hadn't eaten any. But I hadn't thrown them out either.

Now in my kitchen, I looked down at the plate. From what I could tell, Chase had eaten three, maybe four cookies, leaving a dozen or so left.

I grabbed the plate and shoved it aside, far out of his reach. "Those aren't for you," I told him.

In his hand was a half-eaten cookie. "What?" he laughed. "You want this one, too?"

I did. But hell if I'd admit it.

When my only reply was a long, pissed-off look, Chase popped the remainder of the cookie into his mouth and grinned. "I don't know why you're pissed," he said. "They're stale as fuck."

I felt my jaw clench. "Then why are you eating them?"

With a mouthful of cookie, he said, "Because they're damned good."

Good, stale, or both – I didn't want them. And yet, I hadn't thrown them out either. Instead, I'd brought them all the way to my condo, where they'd been sitting there, taunting me from the same countertop for three days now.

Chase said, "Hey, you wanna hear something funny?"

I didn't.

I didn't feel like laughing. I hadn't smiled for weeks now, not since Arden and I had called it quits.

But there was no stopping Chase when he had something to say, so I answered with a resigned shrug.

He leaned sideways against the counter and said, "You remember Kenny Smits?"

I'd known Kenny in high school. The guy was a major douche-bag. "Yeah. What about him?"

"Yesterday, I see him at the gym, and we get to talking – nothing big, just, 'How've you been?' and stuff like that. But then, as we're heading out, he says to me, 'Hey, tell your brother I owe him.'"

"Oh yeah? Which brother?"

"You," Chase laughed. "You're the one he graduated with."

In high school, Kenny and I had run in opposite crowds. I didn't like the guy, but I didn't hate him either.

One thing I knew for damn sure. *I hadn't done him any favors.*

To Chase, I said, "Thanks for what?"

"You wanna guess?"

"No."

"You want a hint?"

Oh, for fuck's sake. "Just spit it out."

"Well, ol' Kenny got himself a full ride to Michigan State – room *and* board. Plus a stipend. Did you know?"

I shook my head. "Didn't know, didn't care. What does that have to do with me?"

"Well, get this," Chase said. "His scholarship – it was a last-minute thing, because it was supposed to go to someone else until that someone messed up."

By now, I was only half listening. It had been this way for a while now. I felt like I was going through life in a dark, empty fog.

I knew why, too.

I looked to the cookies and felt myself swallow. It wasn't from hunger. It was from something else, something I'd been trying to ignore for weeks.

I was doing a sorry job of it, too. Everywhere I looked, I saw her face. I saw her standing in the house on the beach, with that look she got when she was thinking. I saw her smiling up at me the way she did sometimes when the two of us shared a secret joke. I saw her at the crew house, nibbling at the edges of peanut butter toast, savoring it like it was the priciest pastry from the fanciest shop.

And at night, well, let's just say I wasn't sleeping so good, and it showed. I'd been snapping at everyone for weeks, except for the times I kept to myself, which was far too often considering all the work crews who needed more direction than I'd been giving.

God, I missed her.

Chase said, "Don't you wanna know who?"

I was still eying the cookies. *Why couldn't I just throw the damn things out already?*

To Chase, I managed to say, "Who what?"

"Who had the scholarship first."

I didn't care. With my eyes trained on the cookies, I said, "Alright, who?"

Chase laughed. "Arden Weathers."

At the sound of her name, my head jerked upward. "What?"

"Arden Weathers," he repeated.

"I heard you the first time," I said. "But what are you saying?"

"The scholarship," Chase said. "It was Arden's until she lost it."

I stared across the kitchen counter. "Lost it how?"

"The usual way," Chase said. "Grades didn't measure up."

I shook my head. *No way.* Arden's grades were perfect, until—
Oh, fuck.

Instantly, all of the things she'd said during the past few months came flooding back to me.

"It cost you nothing."

"It cost me everything."

And what had I told her in reply? *"Get over it."*

I considered the house on the beach. If it weren't for me, she wouldn't have been saddled with student loans. She wouldn't have been working too many hours while getting her degree. She would've had a lot more fun – and a hell of a lot more money.

And the house – it would've been hers.

I knew it in my gut. If it weren't for that stunt I'd pulled with the lighter, she could've bought the house on her own. Yeah, it would've been hard. But one thing about Arden, she gave it her all when something mattered to her.

Again, I looked to the cookies. At the crew house, I'd found a brand-new mixer, along with new mixing bowls and cookie sheets.

Arden hadn't only made me cookies. She'd bought all the supplies to make them, too.

This was no small thing.

She didn't even have a car.

And why *was* that?

I recalled something she'd said in passing. She'd sold the car to pay for home repairs – repairs that were never made, for a house she'd never own.

Thanks to me.

Shit.

In the kitchen, Chase was laughing again. "I know. It's a riot, right?"

I wasn't laughing.

And the fact that was Chase was – well, I didn't like it. Through clenched teeth, I said, "You think that's funny?"

"It's not as funny as the look on your face," he said. "But yeah, I think it's pretty damn funny."

I *still* wasn't laughing.

And now I had a question. I knew the answer. But the question still had to be asked. "And Kenny was thanking me, why?"

"Because," Chase said, "if it weren't for you blowing up the lab, that scholarship would've been Arden's."

CHAPTER 72

Arden

From the front walkway, Cami called out, "Guess who called me on my way to work."

While she'd been gone, I'd been painting the spindles of her family's front porch. "Who?" I asked.

It was two in the afternoon, and Cami had just returned from her part-time summer job of tutoring grade schoolers at the local learning center. When she reached the front steps, she stopped and gave me a significant look. "Mason Blastoviak."

At the sound of that name – the *last* name in particular – the paintbrush slipped from my fingers and tumbled off the porch into the nearby shrubbery. "Crap!"

"No kidding," Cami said.

Already, my stomach was in knots. "What did he want?"

"*Two* things," Cami said. "First, he wanted to know the name of my dad."

I frowned. Cami's dad was away at work, much like the rest of the family, who were either working or at school.

Her dad's name was Engelbart, but I had no idea why this concerned Mason Blastoviak. "Why would he ask such a thing?"

"Do you remember when you and I were walking Willow home, and we were trying to figure out where she lived?"

At the memory, I almost cringed. "How could I forget?"

"Well, the thing is," Cami continued, "I promised to tell her *my* dad's name if she told me hers."

"Ohhhhhh. That's right." In all the commotion, that little detail had totally slipped my mind. "So he called because Willow still wanted to know?"

"Yup. Crazy, huh?"

Crazy was right. I didn't like Mason, even now. His hostility had been a huge source of friction between me and Brody. And then there was the matter of everything he'd done to cost me the only home I'd ever truly wanted.

Still, I had to give him credit where credit was due. In spite of his many other flaws, he truly did seem to care about Willow.

But he didn't care about *me* – not that he should, I guess. Bracing myself, I asked, "What was the second thing he wanted?"

"Well, *that's* where it gets interesting."

"Why?"

"Because it was about you."

I feared as much. Whatever Mason wanted, it couldn't be good. "Oh yeah?"

Cami nodded. "He wanted to know if you were still here."

In my stomach, the sick feeling only grew. "Did you ask why?"

"Sure," she said. "But all he said was, 'You'll see.'"

It sounded like a threat. Probably it was. Mason had a reputation, and it wasn't great.

Or at least, it wasn't great if you were on the receiving end of his wrath – as I knew all too well, considering how ruthless he'd been in acquiring the house.

If I were smart, I decided, I'd brace myself for a nasty surprise.

It didn't take long for it to arrive either – less than five minutes, actually – except it wasn't nasty. And didn't involve Mason at all.

CHAPTER 73

Brody

As I pulled into the unfamiliar driveway, I scanned the house, searching for any sign that Arden was still there.

She should be. Mason had called Cami just this morning. And assuming that Cami had been telling the truth, Arden was still staying at the neat two-story home that I was looking at now.

The home was probably a hundred years old, with a classic front porch, mature trees, and tall, dense shrubbery all along the front.

But I didn't care about the house. I cared about the girl inside, assuming she was still there.

Please, God.

The drive from Bayside to Petoskey had taken me two and a half hours, which had given me more time to think than I'd needed.

I didn't need time. *I needed the girl I loved.*

Yeah, I loved her. And only a dumb-ass wouldn't have realized it long before now.

But I'd wised up plenty during the past three days, ever since Chase had told me something I should've figured out on my own.

Turns out, I'd cost Arden not only her family home, but a scholarship that would've changed everything for her.

I owed her an apology – and more.

And hey, while I was at it, I owed myself the chance to reclaim what I'd lost.

Arden.

I was halfway up the front walkway when a sudden motion in the bushes made me stop to look. As I did, Arden's head popped up over the shrubbery. She stood and took a quick look around.

At the sight of me standing there, she froze.

I froze, too.

She was holding a narrow paint-brush, caked with dirt and white paint. She wore a thin, paint-splattered T-shirt, and her hair was tied in a messy ponytail, with loose tendrils curling around her face.

It was the face of the girl I loved.

The girl I'd lost.

Her eyes were wide, and her lips were full. There was a purple paint smudge along the side of her cheek and a streak of white just above her collarbone.

She was so beautiful, I could hardly breathe.

Paint or no paint, I wanted to take her in my arms and pull her close like I used to, back when she'd been mine.

But I didn't deserve it. *Not yet.* I moved forward and stopped on the opposite side of the shrubbery. "Hey."

Her voice, soft and breathless, said the same to me. "Hey." She took another quick look around. "So, um, what are you doing here?"

"You can't guess?"

Silently, she shook her head.

"Good," I said, "because you deserve a surprise."

"A good surprise?" She hesitated. "Or the other kind?"

She was so cute, I had to smile. "If I'm lucky, it's good. But hey, you might see it differently."

"Really?"

"Really." I moved forward until only the shrubs were between us. "But first, tell me something. That check I sent – why didn't you cash it?"

"Because I didn't make it to the end."

"So come back."

She bit her lip. "You mean back to the show?"

"Forget the show. That's not what I meant." I searched her face. "Arden?"

"Yeah?"

"Come back to *me*."

She sucked in a breath. "What?"

"I love you. I've loved you for a long time, except I was too dumb to see it. But I do love you. And I'm hoping – praying – that you'll give me another chance – a chance to make things right."

She blinked. "Wait, what'd you say?"

With a sheepish grin, I asked, "Which part?"

"The part about you being in love." She swallowed. "With me."

I couldn't wait another moment. I moved forward, wading through the shrubbery until I was standing close enough to touch. In a low voice, I said, "I love you, Arden Weathers."

Her eyes filled with tears. "Oh, wow."

"And you love me, too," I said. "Admit it." I held up a hand. "No, wait. *Don't* admit it."

"Wait, why not?"

"Because I don't deserve to hear it. Not yet. But tell me. Will you come back? Please?"

CHAPTER 74

Arden

Call me a sap, but it didn't take much convincing, especially after Brody sheepishly confessed that not only had he rescued the cookies from his brother, but also that he realized he'd been a total ass in refusing my peace offering in the first place.

According to Brody, the cookies were now hidden away in his freezer, where he'd cherish them until the end of time – or share them with me, if only I'd return.

And then, he'd threatened to make cookies of his own if I *didn't* come back – playfully warning me that he didn't know a mixer from a monkey wrench, and that any cookies he made would be no treat for anyone, especially me.

Still, with love in his eyes, he vowed to keep on baking until I agreed to return.

By the end of his petition, I was laughing in spite of myself.

And Brody? Well, let's just say his words were a balm to my battered soul. And the look he gave me when I finally said "yes" was something I wouldn't soon forget, along with the feel of his lips brushing my ear as he leaned close to whisper, "You won't regret it."

When we pulled out of Cami's driveway an hour later, I was wearing fresh clothes – casual shorts and little black T-shirt – along with a smile of wonder.

He loved me. In my mind, I could still hear him telling me those three magical words.

"I love you."

I wanted to say them back.

But Brody had been insistent, telling me that he wanted to make things right between us before I gave him anything he didn't deserve.

I didn't even know what he meant. And I had no opportunity to ask him in private until we were already on the highway, heading back to Bayside, with my belongings in the back of his luxurious black SUV – one I'd never seen him driving until today.

My head was reeling, and I hardly knew what to think. Looking to say *something*, I asked, "Is this a new vehicle?"

"Yeah," he said. "Do you like it?"

"I love it," I said. "But I loved your truck, too."

"Good," he said. "Because I've still got it."

"Oh, really?" I teased. "How many vehicles do you have, anyway?"

"Counting this one? Two." He paused. "But hey, I'm open to more. You want a motorcycle or maybe a Winnebago?"

I snickered. "Not really."

"Good," he said. "Because I'm more into houses."

"And how many of *those* do you have?"

He gave me a sideways glance. "One less than I had two days ago."

"What does *that* mean?"

"You'll see," he said.

As I gazed over at him, I felt my heart go all warm and gooey. He was wearing dark slacks and a short-sleeve polo shirt that showed off his muscular arms as he drove with one hand draped casually over the steering wheel.

He looked content.

I *felt* content.

It was crazy to think of how much had changed in the span of just an hour or two.

As my gaze lingered, I heard myself say, "So, what happened?"

"What do you mean?" he asked.

With a trembling laugh, I said, "Well, the last time I saw you, I was pretty sure you hated me."

Brody shook his head. "Nah. I hated myself, and you wanna know why?"

"Why?"

He gave me a warm glance. "Because I couldn't get over you, no matter how hard I tried."

I loved the way that sounded. Still, I had to tease him at least a little. "You had a funny way of showing it."

"No kidding." As we drove along the empty highway, he stared straight ahead as he added, "There was baggage – stuff I should've let go a long time ago. And that goes double for my brothers."

"What do you mean?" I asked. "Like stuff with your parents?"

"No. Stuff with Willow." He paused. "And you."

I wasn't quite sure what he was getting at. "You mean because of that day I tried to walk her home?"

"No. Because of the day you torched my truck."

"Wait, what does that have to do with Willow?"

Brody's expression turned serious as he eyed the road ahead. "The thing is, she was supposed to be in it."

I tensed. "What?"

"On the day it happened," he said, "I was there picking her up from the lady who watched her when we couldn't." With a glance in my direction, he added, "That's where my truck was parked – in front of that lady's house."

I shook my head. "But wait, I thought you were parked there to mow the lawn."

"I was," Brody said. "I was mowing for the lady who watched her. The lawncare – it was how we paid for the service."

"So, you exchanged lawn care for babysitting?"

"Lawncare *and* handy work," he said. "I did the lawn. My brothers did the rest. But as far as mowing, I'd pull up, cut the grass, and then load up Willow. But on *that* day, I was running maybe five, ten minutes late."

I tried to picture it. "Oh?"

"Yeah," he said. "And around the time you torched the truck, I was *supposed* to be loading Willow into the car seat." He shook his head. "*Or* running back into the house because I forgot her favorite stuffed animal or something."

As his words hit home, I felt the color drain from my face. "So she could've been inside the truck?" I sucked in a breath. "Alone?"

As I said it, Waverly's accusation came flooding back. *"You almost killed his sister."*

I turned sideways to stare at Brody. "But on the day it happened, why didn't you tell me? Why didn't you tell *anyone?*"

"Because it wasn't as bad as it *could've* been." He frowned. "*And,* because we didn't want her taken away."

I was still reeling. "What do you mean?"

"After my parents took off – first my dad, and then my mom – we were trying hard to fly under the radar, pretending that mom was still around so Willow wouldn't get put into foster care."

As I listened, my heart went out to him. It went out to *all* of them – Brody, Chase, Willow, and even Mason. I murmured, "So *that's* why they hate me."

Brody nodded. "*And* why we never said anything – not to you or to the police."

Thinking out loud, I said, "So you figured that if it looked like a freak accident, they'd just let it go?"

"Yeah. Which they did. A good thing, too, because I sure as hell didn't want them coming to our house, asking for mom or whoever."

"But what about Mason?" I asked. "He was an adult, right?"

"Oh yeah," Brody said with a rueful laugh. "He was an adult at ten."

In my mind, I could totally see it, and it nearly broke my heart.

"The thing is," Brody continued, "by that time, Mason had been the dad for a while."

"You mean to Willow?"

"Her *and* to the rest of us," he said, "whenever we'd let him, which in *my* case, was pretty much never."

I'd never liked Mason. Even on the show, he'd struck me as a total hard-ass who hated anyone not named Blastoviak. But I'd be lying if I didn't admit that it would be nice – really nice – to have a sibling with that kind of loyalty.

And now, I didn't know whether to pity them, or be totally jealous. *The Blastoviaks really did stick together.*

This reminded me of something I'd meant to ask earlier. "Willow's last name," I said, "why is it Taylor, and not Blastoviak?"

"Because it isn't," Brody said. "Taylor's her *middle* name."

"Ohhhhh." I turned forward once again. "I guess I should've realized that."

"No." Brody said. "What you should've gotten was an apology."

I didn't get it. "For what?"

"For all the bullshit we put you through."

I wasn't quite sure I agreed. Still, I tried to smile. "Well Mason *sort of* apologized." Thinking of Willow, I couldn't help but add, "And from what I know now, I'm not even sure I deserved it."

"Oh, you deserved it," Brody said. "And more. A lot more."

"*A lot* more?" I teased.

"You know it," he said. "And hey, the day's not over yet."

CHAPTER 75

Arden

I was so thunderstruck, I could hardly speak. Brody and I were standing alone in the kitchen of what used to be my grandparent's place.

The kitchen was completely done – and not in "counter-less" cupboards either. *No.* The cabinets were the same ones that Brody and I had picked out together all those months ago.

But that wasn't even the biggest surprise. It was the fact that the whole house appeared to be totally finished – with fresh paint, new carpet, and refinished wooden floors. The place smelled brand new and looked it, too.

All it needed now was furniture to make it anyone's dream home.

We'd just returned from Petoskey, and Brody had given me the grand tour, minus the attic as usual. Everything was just as I'd envisioned, only better.

The place had new light fixtures, new bathtubs, new sinks, new everything – except for the things worth keeping, like the wonderful woodwork and vintage chandeliers.

It was truly amazing.

I was still reeling – not only over the state of the house, but over the fact that I was here at all, after everything that had happened.

I looked to Brody and asked, "How'd you get it done so fast?"

"Easy," he said. "I bribed them."

"Who?"

"Anyone who needed bribing," he said. "We've had crews working around the clock for the last three days."

"Why three days?" I asked.

"Because," he said with a sheepish grin, "that's when I realized what a dumb-ass I'd been."

"Oh, stop it," I laughed. "We were both dumb-asses in our own way. I mean, *I* didn't do everything perfectly either."

His smile faded. "You did in high school."

I felt my brow wrinkle in confusion. "But what does high school have to do with it?"

Brody reached out and took my hand. "Your scholarship," he said. "The one you lost. Why didn't you say something?"

I stared up at him. "Wait, how'd you hear about that?"

"Chase ran into the guy who got it in your place," he said. "But forget *them*. Why didn't you tell me?"

"You mean when it happened?" I blew out a nervous breath. "I dunno. Maybe I felt bad about the truck and figured that I couldn't really complain after costing *you* something, too."

As the memories came flooding back, I tried to sort it out for myself. "Like right after it happened, when the police showed up, you didn't even try to get me in trouble. And I know you could've."

"But what about later?" he said. "Why didn't you tell me when we were together?"

"I tried," I said. "But it was such a sore subject, and we both had things to be sorry for. I mean, *I* didn't like you bringing up what happened with the truck, so…" With a loose shrug, I finished by saying, "It just seemed better to let it go. Or at least, I *tried* to let it go."

His gaze softened as he said, "But the lab explosion – it didn't just cost you the scholarship. It cost you the house, too."

I saw what he meant. And there was a time not too long ago when I would've agreed. But I had to be fair. "It wasn't just you," I said. "I'm sure there are things I could've done better, too. And besides, I never could've fixed up the house like you did." Now, I did smile. "And you know what?"

"What?"

"I'm glad you own it." I searched deep in my heart and realized that I truly meant it. I looked around, taking in how beautiful the place looked now. *My grandparents would've loved it.*

And I loved it, too.

But more than that, I loved the guy who'd made it happen. As I stared into his eyes, I couldn't stop myself from saying, "I love you, Brody Blast."

His eyes warmed, and he smiled in a way that tugged at my heart. He was still smiling when he pulled me close and wrapped me in his arms just the way I liked.

Into my hair, he teased, "You were supposed to wait."

I laughed against his chest. "I didn't want to wait." As I spoke, I burrowed tighter against him. *I never wanted to let go.* The feel of him, the scent of him, the sound of him – all of it was like coming home to a place I'd been searching for my whole life.

And this had nothing to do with real estate.

Thinking of the camera crews, I asked, "Where *is* everyone, anyway?"

"Gone," he said.

"For how long?"

"Forever."

That word, *forever* – it sounded *so* good on his lips. I smiled against him. "Are you sure? Like no one's gonna come back to reclaim an extension cord or something?"

"They can try," Brody said. "But they'll need permission first. The place is firmly off-limits. And you wanna know why?"

"Why?" I asked.

"Because the owner deserves some privacy."

I laughed. "Yes, you do."

"I don't mean me."

I pulled back to look at him. "What?"

"I mean you."

I blinked. "What are you saying? You're willing to sell it?"

He shook his head. "I was never willing to sell. But I *am* going to make things right."

I smiled up at him. "They're *already* right."

"Not yet," he said. "But almost." He flicked his head toward a nearby kitchen drawer. "In there, there's something I want you to see."

"What is it?" I asked.

With a smile, he replied, "You won't know 'til you look."

Slowly, I turned and opened the drawer where he'd indicated. Inside, I spotted a neat stack of papers. When I read the big, bold letters on the top sheet, my heart leapt into my throat. "It's the deed."

"You mean *your* deed."

Holy crap.

He was right. There was my name, right there in black and white. From what I could tell, he'd actually *gifted* me the house.

I whirled to face him. "You don't mean it?"

"The hell I don't," he said. "I told you, I was going to make it right."

"But I didn't pay you."

"You payed me plenty."

"But that's not true," I said. "I can't accept it."

"You can. And you will." He smiled. "You belong here. You know it's true."

"Yeah, but I wanted to *buy* it, not force you to give it to me."

"Force me, huh?" He laughed. "Good luck with *that*."

I couldn't help but smile. Brody was one of the most stubborn people I'd ever met. *And* the most wonderful. But I'd meant what I told him. *I couldn't accept it.*

And I told him so repeatedly until he finally said, "Alright. How about this? I'll ask you again in a month."

"Why a month?"

He grinned. "Why not?"

Well, I couldn't argue with *that* – so I didn't.

Instead, I melted into his arms and said, "Do you remember that day we picked out the cabinets?"

His chest was hard, and his embrace was steady. "Uh-huh."

"Do you remember what we talked about?"

With a smile in his voice, he replied, "Oh yeah."

"So, um…What do you think?"

CHAPTER 76

Arden

Brody pulled back and gazed deep into my eyes. "I think you're mine."

I almost giggled. "You *think* I'm yours. What, you don't know?"

"Oh, I know," he said. "Do you?"

For all kinds of reasons, I couldn't stop smiling. "I do now."

"You bet your ass, you do." Slowly, he lowered his head and pressed his lips to mine. He kissed me like he meant it, and I leaned into him, savoring the feel of his lips and the taste of his tongue.

I'd missed him so very much – the sound of his voice, the feel of his body, the smell of his soap. In every possible way, he filled my senses, making me ache deep in my core.

I wanted him.

I'd wanted him almost from the start, even back when we'd supposedly hated each other. *But that was then. This was now.*

Now, he was mine. And I loved him so very much.

And he loved *me.*

Talk about a crazy wonderful world.

When his hands slid up the back of my shirt, I felt the familiar tingle of anticipation. His hands were big and warm – not smooth, but strong and steady.

Beyond eager, I reached under *his* shirt, too – yanking and pulling at the fabric until with a laugh, he pulled back and let me practically rip the polo shirt over his head, leaving him naked from the waist up.

His waist was lean, and his chest was picture-perfect, just like I remembered. But it wasn't his body, or even his handsome face, that made my breath hitch and my heart skip a beat.

It was the look in his eye when he said, "You're amazing. You know that?"

"No. *You're* amazing."

And he was, from head to toe.

As he stood shirtless in the kitchen – whose kitchen, I didn't even know – I felt like this was the fresh beginning I'd been longing for, a way to reconcile the past with the present and whatever future came our way.

And speaking of longing, already I could feel my body responding, growing slick and warm in anticipation.

With a grin, Brody said, "You know what I'm gonna do next, don't you?"

Already, I was breathless and giddy. I couldn't help it. I snickered. With mock innocence, I said, "I have no idea."

"Yes, you do." He glanced down at my shorts. "But first, these have gotta go." With that, he reached for my waist and unfastened the button. One zip and few yanks later, I was standing in my panties, with the small of my back pressed against the nearest granite countertop.

Slowly and gently, Brody lifted my shirt over my head, and then tossed it aside. My bra – pink and lacy – was the kind that fastened in front. With love in his eyes, Brody unfastened the clasp with one hand and lowered his head to my neck. As his lips brushed my skin, he murmured, "I missed you."

My breath caught. "I missed you, too."

He pulled back to look at me. "You're so beautiful."

I *felt* beautiful. And happy — happier than I'd felt in, well, forever, actually. As I searched for the words to tell him so, he took one of my hardened nipples between his fingers and toyed with it just the way I liked.

With a soft moan, I went straight for his pants, fumbling first for the button and then for the zipper. When I pushed down his slacks and saw the massive bulge in his briefs, the warmth inside me only grew.

He was so immensely hard, and I was so slick and willing. We'd kicked off our shoes somewhere in all the fumbling, and I was pretty sure I knew what came next.

But I was wrong. Instead of hoisting me up onto the counter, he reached down to the floor beside us and picked up his discarded shirt.

I laughed. "If you put that on, I swear, I'm gonna lose it."

With a wicked grin, he informed me, "You're gonna lose it anyway, I promise you that." He lifted the shirt higher. "But the shirt's not for me. It's for you."

He reached around me and placed the shirt on the countertop directly behind where I stood.

"Ohhhh," I laughed. "Padding."

"You know it." And then, Brody reached for my panties and gave them a hard yank. As he did, I fumbled for his briefs, pushing them down toward the floor, first with my hands, and then with my foot.

Soon, we were both naked, right there in the brand-new kitchen.

Finally, he reached for my hips and lifted me effortlessly onto the shirt-covered countertop, kissing me as he did.

When his finger grazed my clit, I moaned into his mouth. With one hand, I reached between us, stroking his massive erection. I wanted him inside me, and I didn't want to wait.

I pulled back and breathed, "If you wait one more second, I think I'm gonna die."

"Oh yeah?" He smiled like this was a good thing. "We'll see." And with that, he slid a finger deliberately inside me, making me whimper with desperate need.

My eyelids fluttered as I breathed, "See?"

With honey in his voice, he asked, "Wanna know what *I* see?"

"What?"

"The girl I love." As he spoke, he circled my clit with his thumb, making me squirm with lust while his finger – and then *two* fingers – stroked my insides in a way that made my hips surge and my breathing grow ragged.

Everything he did, he did right. And this was no exception. By the time he finally entered me, I was already a quivering, trembling mess.

I swear to heaven, I climaxed on like his third thrust, shuddering against him as he drove into me harder and faster while I wrapped my legs around his waist and held on for dear life.

And what a ride it was.

I could feel the muscles in his back moving in time with every thrust, driving me to distraction as he gave me exactly what I wanted, what I needed, too.

By the time he climaxed against me, I felt like I was floating away to the most wonderful place – a dreamland, where anything was possible – where enemies became lovers, and lovers became something more.

As our breathing subsided, I leaned my head on his muscular shoulder and murmured, "Oh, boy. A girl could get used to this, you know?"

With that familiar smile in his voice, he said, "As long as the girl is you, count me in."

CHAPTER 77

Arden

We spent the next month traveling back and forth from Michigan to California. We were officially a couple – in private *and* in public.

And boy, did Waverly love that. She especially loved it when I was offered another consulting contract, this one for the house in California, which was undergoing a serious renovation.

Speaking of California, I learned from Brody that Waverly's trip to that state hadn't involved him at all. Rather, Waverly had gone to visit her uncle at the production company, where she'd demanded that I be fired. *Or else.*

Instead, she'd been demoted to general gopher, and Roy had been given the producer job in her place. The new assignments were set to begin with the very next house – a house that I would have a hand in restoring.

I expected grief from Brody's brothers, but for whatever reason – whether because Brody had run interference, or because anyone could see that we were crazy about each other – things went a lot smoother than I might've expected.

During this whole time, Brody and I still debated – sometimes in jest, and sometimes in earnest – who should really own the house on the beach.

Legally, it was mine already. But in my heart, I still felt funny about taking it for nothing. But Brody, stubborn as ever, still absolutely refused to let me buy it.

In the meantime, the house remained vacant – not because we didn't want to move in, but because until we agreed on whose house it actually was, it seemed terribly premature to start filling it with our things.

And besides, somewhere in the back of my mind, I was hoping that a choice wouldn't have to be made at all – that the house could be *ours* in the most permanent of ways.

Regardless, I was having the time of my life. After my return to Bayside, Brody made another confession. During the past few months, he'd been avoiding travel so we could spend more time together.

I was insanely flattered, but horrified to learn that this had caused a delay with the other houses, including the place in California. In happier news, we were catching up just fine, and this time, we were doing it together.

For now, Brody and I were living like vagabonds, splitting our time between California and Michigan whenever we could.

While in Michigan, we stayed wherever the mood took us – sometimes at his condo, and sometimes at the crew house – minus Waverly, who'd quit the show in a huff when someone suggested that she actually "gopher" coffee early one Monday morning.

She wasn't missed.

Whenever we could, Brody and I spent an obscene number of hours at the beach house, wandering through its empty rooms and pondering what we'd do with all of the space.

It was during one such brainstorming session when Brody turned to me and said, "Hey, you wanna see the attic?"

The offer caught me off guard. Based on little things he'd said over the past few weeks, I'd assumed the attic was packed with junk and spare building materials.

Still, I gave a happy nod and let him lead me to the private stairway that led up to the long-forbidden space. When we reached the top step, I felt my eyed widen in surprise.

It wasn't packed.

It was a dream.

The whole room was painted in pink and white candy stripes. On the largest wall, in fanciful lettering was an old-fashioned sign. With a laugh, I read it out loud. "Clara's Candies." At this, I actually giggled. "Oh, my God."

With a self-satisfied smile, Brody said, "Take a closer look."

In a happy trance, I wandered toward the sign, and then burst out laughing all over again. On the lower corner, in red scripty letters was a grade. I read *this* out loud too. "An A, huh?"

"Not just an A," Brody said. "An A-plus."

I *still* couldn't stop laughing. "Who did this? I mean, I know you planned it and all, but did you design it yourself?"

"Hell no," he said. "I hired a pro."

"Who?" I asked.

"Miss LaRue."

"You're not serious?"

"The hell I'm not," he said. "This job? It was perfect for her skill set."

Yes. It was. And for some reason, it made the whole thing all the more ridiculous and wonderful.

I took another long look around. The sloped ceiling was not only fully repaired, but painted in a crisp white that showed off all the interesting lines and angles of the roofline.

And then, there was the new balcony. Where there used to be a big, old window overlooking the water, I saw a pair of classic patio doors that led out to a cozy perch for gazing out over the water.

Once again, I looked to Brody. "But wait, how did I *not* know this was going on?"

He grinned. "You were in California."

"Not all the time," I said. "And the balcony, I would've spotted *that* from the outside."

"I know," he said. "That's why the balcony was the last thing they put in. I had a hell of a time keeping it secret."

And yet, he had. With a wistful smile, I confessed, "It's like a dream."

"Just so you know," Brody said, "you don't have to keep it this way."

"Oh, it's staying," I told him, "regardless of who owns the house." I reached for his hand. "I love it. And I love you most of all."

"That reminds me," Brody said. "I never did tell you what L.O.L. stood for."

On his phone? Funny, I'd totally forgotten about that. But now I was beyond curious. "So, what *did* it stand for?"

When he answered, his voice was nearly a caress. "Love of my life."

As he said it, something squeezed at my heart. "You're kidding."

"Nope."

"But at the time, you didn't even *know* you loved me."

"I knew," he said. "I just wasn't ready to face it. That's all."

I smiled up at him. "You're the love of *my* life, too, you know."

He grinned. "I know. And *now*, we're gonna settle who owns the house." With that, he reached into his pocket and pulled out a small velvet box.

My breath caught. "Oh?'

With a smile, he got down on one knee and said, "Arden?"

My eyes were already misty. "Yeah?"

"I love you. You fill my life with everything I never knew was missing. I want to build a home, a life, a family. I want everything that you and I never had, *and* I want it with each other."

By now, I was openly crying, with happy tears sliding down my face.

And then, he opened the box, revealing the most beautiful diamond ring I'd ever seen. With love in his eyes, he said, "Will you marry me?"

I didn't even have to think about it. It was the thing I'd been hoping for, and I told him so, not just then, but many times over the next few weeks as we made happy plans for the future.

Turns out, that future included a more permanent presence on the Blast Brothers show, where I became a regular part of the cast, not just for the house in California, but for all of them.

It really *was* crazy, especially knowing that in a few short months, we – along with millions of other people – would be watching not just the transformation of the beach house, but also our journey from hatred to love.

Maybe I should've been embarrassed. But I was so happy with how everything turned out, all I felt was giddy anticipation.

And why?

It was because it was a journey I wouldn't have traded for anything, especially knowing how it ended.

Happily Ever After.

THE END

Other Books by Sabrina Stark
(Listed by Couple)

Lawton & Chloe
Unbelonging (Unbelonging, Book 1)
Rebelonging (Unbelonging, Book 2)
Lawton (Lawton Rastor, Book 1)
Rastor (Lawton Rastor, Book 2)

Bishop & Selena
Illegal Fortunes

Jake & Luna
Jaked (Jaked Book 1)
Jake Me (Jaked, Book 2)
Jake Forever (Jaked, Book 3)

Joel & Melody
Something Tattered (Joel Bishop, Book 1)
Something True (Joel Bishop, Book 2)

Zane & Jane
Positively Pricked

Jax & Cassidy
One Good Crash

Jaden & Allie
One Bad Idea

Flynn & Anna
Flipping His Script

Jack & Becka
Wordless

ABOUT THE AUTHOR

Sabrina Stark writes edgy romances featuring plucky girls and the bad boys who capture their hearts.

She's worked as a fortune-teller, barista, and media writer in the aerospace industry. She has a journalism degree from Central Michigan University and is married with one son and a pack of obnoxiously spoiled kittens. She currently makes her home in Northern Alabama.

ON THE WEB

Learn About New Releases & Exclusive Offers
www.SabrinaStark.com

Printed in Great Britain
by Amazon